GALAXY ON FIRE

PART 3: BOOKS 5-6

CRAIG ROBERTSON

ISBN: 978-1-7341363-3-3 (eBook)
978-1-7341363-4-0 (paperback)
979-8-3866993-6-9 (hardcover)

Cover design by Alexandre
http://www.designbookcover.pt/en/

Formatting services by Drew Avera
Available at drewavera@gmail.com

Edited by: Michael R. Blanche
Forest Olivier
Charles Pitts

First Edition 2019
Second Edition 2021

PART 1

DRAGON FIRE

BOOK FIVE OF THE
GALAXY ON FIRE SERIES

by Craig Robertson

Never Stop Believing in Magic!

Imagine-It Publishing
El Dorado Hills, CA

ASHES, Book 6

GALAXY ON FIRE BOXSET, Part 1, Books 1 & 2
GALAXY ON FIRE BOXSET, Part 2, Books 3 & 4
GALAXY ON FIRE BOXSET, Part 3, Books 5 & 6

RISE OF ANCIENT GODS SERIES (2018):

RETURN OF THE ANCIENT GODS, Book 1
RAGE OF THE ANCIENT GODS, Book 2
TORMENT OF THE ANCIENT GODS, Book 3
WRATH OF THE ANCIENT GODS, Book 4
FURY OF THE ANCIENT GODS, Book 5
FALL OF THE ANCIENT GODS, Book 6

TIME WARS LAST FOREVER SERIES (2019)

RYAN TIME, Book 1
LOST TIME, Book 2
FRAGMENTED TIME, Book 3
SHATTERED TIME, Book 4
FINDING TIME, Book 5
HEALING TIME, Book 6

THE TIMELESS VOID (2021)

RYAN'S GAMBIT, Book 1
RYAN'S PHANTOMS, Book 2
RYAN'S ENIGMA, Book 3
RYAN'S UNDOING, Book 4
RYAN'S REBOOT, Book 5
RYAN'S RESOLUTION, Book 6

THE WHALES OF TIME (2023)

Ryan In UnWonderland, Book 1
How Ryan Saves Time, Book 2
Saving Alice Ryan, Book 3

NON-RYANVERSE BOOKS:

A Teenager's Guide to Saving The Earth (2025)
An Apocalypse and Then Some, Book 1
How to Survive Surviving the Apocalypse, Book 2
Is This Apocalypse Over Yet?, Book 3

TIME DIVING (2024)

Letters From Hell, Book 1
Purgatory's Best Shot, Book 2
Heaven Says Wait, Book 3
Into the Nexus, Book 4

ROAD TRIPS IN SPACE SERIES (2019):

THE GALAXY ACCORDING TO GIDEON, Book 1
THE EARTH ACCORDING TO GIDEON, Book 2

OLDER, STANDALONE WORKS:

THE CORPORATE VIRUS (2016)
THE INNERgLOW EFFECT (2010)
WRITE NOW! THE PRISONER OF NaNoWRiMo (2009)
ANON TIME (2009)

For more information about Craig, his books, various series, or to see images and videos for some of his wild alien characters, please visit his

website. You'll be glad you did: https://
craigarobertson.com/

To sign up for Craig's newsletter to get
announcements, updates, and his
recommendations for other great Sci-Fi reads go
to: https://preview.mailerlite.io/forms/2369493/
188634426375144501/share

This book is dedicated to the innocent mass-shooting victims, especially the children, as well as their families, and their communities. We face such horrors much too often. They all deserve better.

ONE

"I say we may safely ignore both you *and* your report." Harsher words had never been spoken in the chamber of the Secure Council. But High Wedge Lesset was a person of passion and excessive pride. Plus, he wielded the ultimate power both on the council and in the empire. His word became dogma.

Transit High Wedge Varsor was aware of the position he'd just been placed in. He never liked the council Prime, but he'd never openly tangled with him, either. Most who had were soon dead. The few who survived did so in anonymity, serving in some far-flung backwash of the empire. Still, his intelligence report was both accurate and alarming. To the best of his knowledge, nothing like this had ever confronted the mighty armies of the Adamant. He only hoped that doing the right thing didn't get him and his family deleted.

"I will overlook the tone of your remarks," said Varsor evenly, "in the interest of the security of the Empire. I cannot, however, turn a blind eye to your flippant disregard of a potentially critical development."

The other ten members of the council either sat stone-like or looked away. The certainty of a cataclysmic collision was not something any of them wanted to witness. It wasn't that any of them were kindly, empathetic, or actually interested. It was that the impending bloodshed would only cause confusion and delay in the business of the council. Nothing useful would come of it. By tradition, the combatant who survived would choose the loser's successor. For the other ten, there wasn't even the prospect of juicy political infighting when the confrontation was complete.

"Do you have so many mites in your ears that you failed to comprehend? As council Prime it is my duty to the emperor to keep these proceedings focused and moving along at a productive pace. The airing of inconsequential, irrelevant, and imbecilic issues runs contrary to those efforts. Please defer for the remainder of your designated-speaking time, or I will be forced to remove it by fiat."

"I will *not* defer my time when I have a report that needs to be addressed. My spies have constructed a cohesive picture of alien planets actively working together ahead of our invasion of their sector. This is unheard of and must factor into our planning."

Leaning forward, Lesset angrily knuckled the table. "I will address your precious concerns, fool. If every world in the sector lashed their planets together like a gigantic raft and swung their pitiful paddles at our forces, it would alter *nothing*. We always sweep away resistance in one fell swoop. If these primitives fight separately, together, or not at all, they will die as civilizations just as swiftly and completely. The only possible difference it will make is how harshly we deal with them when the fighting stops. Are you as happy as a pup sucking on his mate's *teat* now, Varsor? May we proceed?"

"I would like to query the other council members to

see if they feel this new and unprecedented cooperation should be factored into our assault plans," Varsor said defiantly.

Lesset glowered at the toad he was facing. Then he spoke loudly with a melodramatic tone. "Fine. I call for a vote. All in favor of listening to the squeals of this frightened lunatic, signal so by raising his paw. I see no paws raised," he said without even pausing to take a breath, "so the motion fails just like its author. High Wing Oltimure, I believe the floor is now yours for the next ten minutes."

"What of my remaining time?" howled Varsor as he leaped to his feet.

"By fiat, I declare you are out of time," replied Lesset coolly. He drew his sidearm and blew away most of Varsor's throat.

Varsor seized his throat and tried to keep his head from toppling. Blood geysered through his digits. He took a step toward Lesset.

"No, not in this direction," screamed Lesset. "You'll ... ah, there you've done it. You have ruined my *favorite* jacket. I have half a mind to call a medic to resuscitate you, just so I may kill you again for that affront."

Well before Lesset finished, Varsor was dead on the floor.

"Everything that fellow did was annoying. Look at the mess he's made," remarked Lesset casually. "Well, there's nothing for it, we'll have to continue the meeting covered in a traitor's blood. No time to clean up and remain on schedule." He pointed to Oltimure. "Sorry, you're down to six minutes now. Please begin."

"I defer my allotted time, Prime." Oltimure wished to remain as invisible as possible while Lesset's blood lust ran so high. He was a wise and prudent High Wing. He was a survivor.

TWO

"Jon, swim over to me. I see a turtle under the pontoon," Jenna yelled to me joyously.

She was always full of joy, come to think of it. She exuded the stuff. She was my best friend, even though I only saw her for two weeks once a year. That's when both our families vacationed together in the log-cabin campground near town. For us, it was Tom Sawyer and Nancy Drew all rolled into one nonstop adventure. She was ten; I was about to turn nine.

The specific problem I faced was that I didn't want to swim over to where she was on the floating platform. It hadn't been a full hour since I had that ice cream cone. I didn't want to risk drowning because of a stomach cramp. My parents swore it was a certainty and made me promise years before never to attempt it. My dad said it was because we were such a poor family that if I died, they couldn't afford to bury me. Mom slugged him good for that crack, but he just laughed. Dad was always funny, a regular cutup.

"I'll be there in a few minutes," I shouted back as I checked my Timex.

"No, he'll be gone by then." She pouted. From two hundred yards I could see it plain as day.

I decided if I swam real slow, maybe my stomach wouldn't know I was cheating the clock, and I wouldn't go under in pain. I always told everybody I wanted to be an astronaut. Heck fire, they took all kinds of risks. I had to stop being a sissy and get used to it. I walked out in the lake as far as I could and then dog-paddled slower than any dog ever did all the way to the float. I looked back at the shore. I was not, in fact, dead. Maybe my parents were wrong. Maybe there were exceptions to the rule. Or maybe the rules didn't apply to me. That thought made me kind of happy.

"Over here, Jonny. He's nearly gone."

I walked over to where Jenna had her torso craned down to view the underside of the platform.

"How do you know it's a boy?" I asked as I bent over to join her.

"It's leaving before I'm done looking at it. Only a boy would be so rude."

"Oh, ya mean like this?" I ripped a juicy fart.

"Oh, you're so gross. Now look," she pointed, "you can just see him over there."

Sure enough, there was a snapper turtle pulling at some plants growing on a pontoon.

"You know why he's diving down?" I asked very seriously.

"No. Did we scare him?"

"Naw. He saw us, sure. But he's going under to be able to bite off one of our toes when we get back in the water."

"He's not that smart, Jonny. You're just trying to scare me."

"No, it's true. It's all instinct with them. He knows we have to try to make it back to shore sooner or later. Even if we wait for it to get dark, he'll be happier because he'll be more invisible. Why, last year over at Lake Dakota, a kid got—"

I was about to cook up some bull about his bones being picked clean like a piranha ate him, but Jenna was up and running. She dived into the water so fast she was a blur.

She surfaced, threw her hair off her face, and challenged me, "Come on, scaredy pants. See if you can beat me to the shore." With that, she spun and started swimming like a pro.

I flew into the water and swam for all I was worth. Just when I was about to catch her, maybe ten yards from the beach, a thought hit me. I started treading water. She scurried up onto the muddy sand and turned to me with her hands triumphantly planted on her hips.

"Hey, Mr. Slow Boat to China, I knew you—"

Jenna stopped talking when I lifted my feet off the bottom and screamed in terror. I disappeared under the water for as long as I could hold my breath, then jumped up real high. Reaching for my feet, I screamed, "He's got me." Then I went under briefly. The next time I was at the surface, I yelled, "Find a gun and shoot him!" Then I vanished under the water.

By the time I was forced to come up for air, Jenna was by my side. She kicked and splashed with her arms like a girl possessed. Then she put her arm across my neck, the way we were taught when saving a drowning person. She began to walk/swim, dragging me to safety.

I wasn't sure what to do, but when we got to shore, and she saw I wasn't bleeding, she gave me a stern look. Then she began to laugh. We plopped onto a beach towel and both had a good laugh. Jenna was the best.

"Jon, when you die, would you rather be alone or with somebody?" she asked me after we calmed down.

14

"What a weirdo question," I replied. "How should I know? I mean, it's not like they always give you a choice, you know?"

She pulled her knees up tightly to her chest. "I died alone, and I didn't like it one bit. I was scared *and* lonely. You should die with people you love all around you." She sounded quiet, authoritative on the topic.

"One prob, goofball. You're talking to me, so you're not *dead*. That means you never died, because if you did, you'd be dead."

"Can't you be serious for one minute of your life, Jon Ryan?"

"What?" I reached over and pinched her hard.

She jumped. "Ouch. Why'd you do that?"

"To prove you're alive. I rest my case."

"Well, Perry Mason, you miss my point. I died alone." She pointed at the pontoon. "I was swimming to that very float, and I bumped my head on it and drowned. I was all alone. You didn't come up here in time, or you'd have been with me and I wouldn't have died." She reached over and punched me. "It was all *your* fault." Then she threw herself belly down on the blanket. "But I forgive you because I love you."

What? Did a girl just say she *loved* me? Did I need to marry her now? Gross.

"How can what never happened be my fault when I wasn't here?"

"Exactly. Now remember, you should die in the company of loved ones. Okay?"

"Sure. I promise. Hey, maybe you can be there when I croak. That way I'll have all the company I need."

She sat and balled up, clutching her legs tightly again. "No, Jonathan, I can't be there. You won't die for several billion years. By then, I'll probably be too busy

15

somewhere else. Who knows, maybe I'll have kids of my own and can't leave them because they'll need me."

"What, you gonna have a family after you're dead and gone?"

She looked at me like my fourth grade teacher Mrs. Blum. I was so scared of that witch. "I may be dead, but who says I'll be gone?"

"Can we like talk about something less creepy?"

"Sure. How about a snack?"

"I'm always up for that."

"My mom packed us some sandwiches," she pointed, "over there. Grab the basket."

I retrieved it and she studied the contents.

"Jon, I will miss you so terribly much, you know, after I die and you won't, for almost ever."

What a screwy conversation. "I'll miss you, too." I said more as a question.

"No, you won't. You'll have long forgotten me. Plus, you'll be busy saving everybody and trying not to get yourself killed. No, by the time you die, no one will remember me at all. I'll be just some silly girl who bumped her head."

"Please stop saying that. You're scaring me."

She rested an ice-cold hand on my forearm. "I know you're scared, Jonny. But don't be. You're not going to die now, not today." She angled her head. "Who knows, maybe you never will. Or maybe it'll be tomorrow. But you will not die at your own hand today."

"Please, Jenna, you're freaking me out. What? Are you saying I'll commit suicide? Jenna, please help me."

"Jonathan, I am." She leaned over and kissed me gently on the forehead. Her lips were as cold as deep space. "Now you go show that mean robot who's boss."

"Where will you be? What mean robot?"

She extended her arms. "Right here at our lake. I'll

always be here. Now go, before I start missing you even more."

I'd looked toward the lake when she gestured to it. When I looked back, Jenna was gone. *Poof*. She'd simply disappeared. It was like she was never there but like she was always there, at our lake. I started to cry but forgot to. I was distracted by something. Something painful. Something bad. Something slapping my face in rage and hate.

My eyes popped open. I gasped. I tried to sit up. I was lashed down and couldn't move an inch. Someone slapped my cheek again, very hard.

"Wake up you piece of rat *shit*," wailed EJ as he drew his arm above his head to repeat the action. "I don't have time to waste getting a useless machine out of his trance." He pounded my face again.

"Stop!" screamed a female voice from somewhere. "He's coming to. Stop hitting him." It took a second, but I figured it out. It was Sapale, my Sapale, not the little girl I'd saved.

EJ lowered his arm and peered at me from directly above. "Why, so he is." Then he slapped me twice more. "Now I'm done; for now, that is."

"Leave him be, you monster!" Sapale yelled.

He turned to her. There she was, cowering in the corner of the large room. "STFU, bitch. Remember my warning. If you so much as help him take a *piss*, I'll kill your entire family, kids first."

Wow, he was crazy mad. And I hadn't urinated since the day I became an android. What kind of stupid threat was that?

Sapale shrank farther into the corner. It was pitiful to watch.

"Now, as for you, Sleeping Beauty, here's the deal. I need Risrav and I need it *now*."

"Huh?" was all I could muster. Some of my components were still not back online yet.

"Risrav! You know, lunkhead, the stone that negates mine, stops me from using my magic on you?" He slapped me again.

"I'm awake now, if you hadn't noticed," I snarked.

"I know but beating the crap out of you is better than sex."

"Now I know we're not identical. You're an *idiot*."

Yeah, he slapped me a few more times, but it was worth it.

"Now, I need that rock. I went over you good, but I can't find it. I have two options. One, you can tell me where it is, then I kill you quickly and painlessly."

"Don't even tell me choice two. That one sounds delectable."

"Smart ass. Option two is I rip you apart piece by tiny piece."

"I said don't tell me number two. Now I can't decide which is better."

"But if I do that I risk damaging Risrav. *That* I can't afford to do. So, cupcake of shit, which will it be? Oh, and just as an added incentive, if you just tell me where it is, I promise not to kill Sapale before your weeping eyes. If you force me to grind you up, she gets the same treatment."

I ran some quick systems checks. Everything was on and functional. My entire body was strapped to a metal table with redundancy. I couldn't see my hands, but they were balled into fists and covered with a hard shell, maybe a cast. EJ was taking no chances. Well, he was taking too great a risk by waking me up at all. I was going to get out of this and spring my plan on him with extreme prejudice, the sorry son of a bitch. By the way, I'd hidden Risrav in my scrotum. Yeah, clever of me, eh? I knew that if this exact scenario ever transpired, EJ would never check there.

"I'll make you a deal," I said coolly. "Let the both of us go, and I'll give you the rune."

He rolled his eyes and shook his head. "Let me think about it. No. That would be the dumbest thing for me to do. No, pal, the only way you're leaving this room is as scrap."

"I'll sweeten the deal. Seriously, listen hard. If you let us go, I won't do to you what I was planning to."

"It might help if you told me what I'm being *spared*, lame brain."

"*Spoiler* alert. You'll just have to trust me."

"Let me repeat that last line back to you. *You'll just have to trust me.* Do you think in your tiny processors that there is the remotest chance in hell I'd trust you to do *anything*? You must have skipped your last hundred upgrades, moron."

"Oh well, don't say I didn't warn you."

He folded his arms. "You know what, Jon? I'm sick as shit of hearing this brave-gonna-get-out-of-this crap. Hell, I've said the same things myself, back in the day. But, seriously, you're not going to manage a last-minute miracle. You're not going to save the damsel in distress," he pointed to Sapale. "Most poignantly, you're not going to see tomorrow, so spare me the macho speech."

"J ... Jenna told me I wasn't going to die today. Maybe tomorrow, she said, but definitely not today."

"Who the hell's *Jenna*. I need to find her and let her know her prediction was the opposite of correct."

"She's at the lake, our lake."

"Oh great, I must have fried your brain. You're delusional. Crap, now I can't be certain you'll appreciate the fact that I'm killing you when I do." He turned and paced away. The dude was seriously pissed.

19

My, how I'd changed. I was criminally insane *and* a whack job.

"Jon, I'm so sorry," said Sapale, taking advantage of EJ's silence. "At least we'll be together again in death."

God, I loved that woman. "Let's not get ahead of ourselves here. We're getting out of this." I nodded my head at EJ. "He's the one who should be worried."

"I said no stupid bravado," he snarled, and he slapped me again. "You're making me nauseous."

"Well, chalk one up for Good Jon," I replied with a stupid grin.

He leaned over and came nose to nose with me. "Oh, so you're the *good* me, and I'm the *evil* me. That how you see it, chump?"

"To be fair, many people agree with me, EJ."

"You're such a fool, such a Pollyanna. You still think it's about good versus evil, right versus wrong." He harrumphed. "What a piece of work."

"So, Master Yoda, what is it about if it isn't what it's always been about?"

He thumbed his chest angrily. "It's all about me. Whatever *I* want, whatever *I* need, and whatever *I* fancy. Period. End of story. Do Not Pass Go, and Do *Not* Collect Two Hundred Dollars."

"I'm so glad I'm not you. You're more pathetic than I ever imagined. Seriously, EJ, do yourself a favor and blow your head off. If you're too chicken, I volunteer to help."

"Enough with the wasting of my endless time. Back to the issue at hand. What'll it be? The easy way or the hard way? You've got thirty seconds."

Captain, are you there? Sir, we'd lost you, but I detect your signal. Captain, what is your status? Al popped into my head. Oh yeah, I'd been gone a while, hadn't I? Wait, he had to know about the electrical discharge and my seeing EJ. Until my systems went down, he had access to everything I saw.

I'm here. My status is debatable. My body is functioning well. EJ, however, has me tied up and is about to begin removing parts. Oh, Sapale's here and says hi.

We regret to learn about your situation, sir. May we help in any way, General Ryan?

What was with all the formality?

I don't think so. Wish you could.

I guess that softens the blow of our update, sir. There are approximately ten thousand Adamant troops swarming up the hill to your location. As we speak, the skies are filling with warships. We estimate they will overrun your position in the next four to five minutes.

It was then I noted the very odd look on EJ's face, sort of puzzled mixed with baffled. He could hear Al, too. Of course, he could. He's done it all the time on our shared voyage with Al on *Ark 1*. Al had to know that fact. Wait, wait. That's why he was speaking so formally. He knew I'd be suspicious, but EJ almost certainly wouldn't. Hell, it'd been two *billion* years since they last spoke.

Then either way I'm a goner, Al. Tell Blessing *I love her and that I'll miss you both dearly.* I was stretching things out. Calling *Stingray* by her real name would let Al know I read him clearly. If EJ bought the ruse, he'd want to eavesdrop a while, but he also had to split soon if he wanted to avoid capture. It'd take him a couple minutes to get me off this table, so the likelihood of him taking me with him was dropping to no way.

Remember the Zeno-One Protocol, Al? After I'm dead, you must execute it at once. Do you copy?

Not the dreaded Zeno-One Protocol, Captain. I do not know if I will be able to perform it, it being so dreaded.

Al, listen carefully. I'm no good at being noble, but it doesn't take much to see that the problems of three little artificial life-forms don't amount to a hill of beans in this crazy world. Someday you'll understand that. You must execute the protocol. The part where you must mix the hyperdrive fuel with the neutron stream will be tricky, pal, but I know you can do it. I know you're stronger than you know.

God that sounded awful. Way too corny, but I was ad-libbing to beat the band. It must've been working, because EJ was still angling his head and staring at the floor. Now, if he didn't kill me gratuitously, I might not die today. I had to guess he'd leave me alive, so he could someday recover Risrav. If he killed me here and now, the Adamant would gain possession of my remains, and he'd never get the rune. Then again, he was insane, so it was hard to count on anything.

General Jonathan Ryan, it has been an honor and a privilege to serve alongside you. I will faithfully initiate the Zeno-One Protocol upon confirmation of your demise. God speed, my captain.

"Okay, I'll bite. What the hell is the Zeno-One Protocol?" demanded EJ.

I did my best to look shocked. "How did you kn ... Wait, you can still *hear* Al, can't you, you *scoundrel?*"

"Get over your damn self, pissant. I have to get the hell out of here, but I want to know." He pulled a blaster out of his belt and pointed it at Sapale. "I don't think I have to tell you I'll do it, Ryan."

Holy *crap!* Now I had to come up with some version of the bullshit protocol I invented to stall for more time. If I failed to convince him, he might realize the entire Al call was a con.

"It ... it's nothing that involves you—"

EJ started a countdown. "Three ... tw—"

"Okay, stop. I'll tell you everything. The Zeno-One Protocol is a suicide procedure designed to incapacitate and possibly destroy the vortex. I can't allow it to fall into enemy hands. There, that's it."

"All that drama about self-destructing one damn ship. Man, I wish I had time to kill you, squirt. I'd be doing you and the universe a big favor. But, I'll have to save that until next time, sucker." He mock saluted me and tipped his imaginary hat to Sapale. Then he ran from the room. His ship had to be close by.

"Thank Davdiad, he left you alive," said Sapale rushing to my side.

"It won't—"

I started to say it wouldn't take him long to discover our lies, but Sapale had her lips pressed to mine so hard I couldn't say a word. I started talking with my mouth shut. That got her to open her eyes and look at me kind of funny. She pulled back a few inches.

"That was great, honey, but Al made all that up. EJ'll be back in a few seconds. Release me as fast as you can."

Fortunately, she must have seen EJ strap me in, because she moved nimbly to free me. It took a full minute. I knew EJ was overdue, even madder than he was to begin with.

"To the vortex," I said heading for the door.

"But your hands," she shouted.

That's when I got a good look at them. They were steel-jacketed. EJ had actually molded steel mittens on me to secure my weapons.

"No time. I left it open. I'll think of something by the ..."

Time was up. A plasma bolt struck the wall between us. EJ was back.

Sapale whipped a pistol from the back of her waist and returned fire. She just missed him, and he jerked back out of sight.

"Come with me," she said. "My family is in the next room. I can't leave them. He'll butcher them."

I couldn't disagree with her, but we were out of time. I nodded, and we ran.

EJ figured out where we were going. He must have sprinted the back-way, because he blasted the door frame just after we shot through it. The three adults and two kids jumped to their feet.

"We need to fight our way to his ship," she said to the frightened group. "Pick up a child and stay behind us."

Sapale shoulder rolled out the door and opened fire in EJ's direction. He tried to get off a round, but she had him pinned back.

"*Go*," she shouted.

I led the family out the door and to the right. Sapale kept up a blistering line of fire on the corner EJ hid behind.

When we were all around the turn, I yelled, "We're clear. Retreat."

She backed away but never stopped blasting. The two walls that made the corner were chewed to bits. She ducked in next to me. She held up a hand signal for *stop*. Then she used the one for *I'm going to look*. Sapale needed to see if EJ was following or had taken another path. Her head wasn't a millimeter past the edge when a blast struck the wall. EJ was a coming. She stuck her gun around the corner and fired blindly while she signaled with her left hand for us to go.

"Two lefts and a right," I said in her ear, indicating where the ship was. Then I led the group away as fast as we could move.

We made it to *Stingray* in no time. I could hear the fierce firefight down the hall coming closer.

"Al," I held up my hands, "We gotta get these off. Otherwise we're sitting ducks."

"Place them on the utility bench," he replied. After I had, he said, "This will take time. I can cut through safely, but if I go too fast, the heat will melt your hands. They're no good to us if they don't work."

"Do your best."

A tiny laser beam started cutting the steel. Sparks flew, and I felt the temperature rise inside the covering.

"Estimated time to completion?" I asked.

"Ten to fifteen minutes, maybe longer."

"Crap, that's too long. Try and hustle."

The hull sounded off with a plasma bolt. They were here.

Sapale vaulted through the door and pressed up against the hatch frame. She fired blindly down the corridor.

"Al says ten minutes for my hand. Can you hold him off that long?"

She shrugged and smiled. Okay, odd thing to do in a tense situation.

"I could try if you'd like. I'd rather do this." She pointed her left hand at the floor and command prerogatives sprung to the deck. The wall instantly sealed. "Vortex manipulator, take us to the remnants of planet Earth," she called out.

I was stunned.

She walked over to me and looked down at the cutting process. "Do you ever get used to that nausea?" she asked casually.

"You feel it, too?" Then I furrowed up my brow. "Of course, you do. Hey, Als, any sign of pursuit?"

"None so far, Form One."

"What the hell's the one for?" I asked with mild irritation.

"It is customary to address the senior Form as *One*

25

and other ones numerically down the line. Sapale is Form *Two* in this case," responded *Stingray*.

"Oh," I mumbled. "Makes sense, I guess."

"We're so pleased you condone SOP, Pilot," responded Al.

"Can it and keep cutting, Al." To Sapale, I remarked, "So Toño gave you the Deavoriath tools, too." I bobbed my head. "Seems reasonable."

"Even though I didn't have a vortex, he figured they were useful anyway. Remember, he was putting them in a lot of people for a while there."

Yeah, during the fight with the Last Nightmare, he equipped all the Project Ark astronauts and a lot of human pilots with command prerogatives. That way we could field as many vortices as possible for the fight.

"I, for one, am glad he did," I said with a wink. "Why don't you check on your family. I'm good here." I nodded to my hand.

She went to them and everyone joined in a big old group hug. Sweet.

THREE

Sapale sat around the mess table with big mugs of hot coffee. She tucked her family in with a bite to eat and a place to lay down. They were shaken, but they were tough. They'd be okay. Sapale said she wasn't sure where to take them. Kaljax was spiraling down the toilet. I told her about Vorpace and how the humans there would be glad to provide them sanctuary. She said she'd consider it.

"So, the kiss thing," I began while studying the tabletop, "I guess it means we're a thing again?"

"By the Sacred Veils you're just as dense as the day I died. Are you really honing that skill, or is it just instinctive?"

I threw my palms up. "What?"

"No, Jon, we're not back together. I told you I *loved* you and the first thing I did when EJ was gone was to plant a wet one on your lips. That's the new way of saying *get lost* in Hirn." She turned a shoulder to me.

Okay, I think that meant *yes*, but it could sort of be interpreted as a *no*. Why didn't she just say what she was feeling? Oh, yeah, she was a woman. Nearly forgot. I would make a command decision and go with the

27

assumption—no, the *certainty* that she loved me and that we were back together again. Yes. That's how I'd play it. No, that's how I would *proceed*.

"I, for one, never stopped loving you," I said honestly. "If I'd known Toño had downloaded you to an android when it happened, I'd have woken myself up from death to find you." That came out well. I swelled internally.

"When you came to me on Kaljax just after you turned back on, I was in a dark and lonely place. I hated EJ so much I couldn't separate you from him. Before you tell me that's a silly notion, please try to understand how horrible life was with him. Two billion years of his increasing cruelty, loss of humanity, and growing insanity was bleak. I was his prisoner, and that gave him great satisfaction. When you turned up at the door, I hated you. Hell, I hated all males." She bundled herself up in her arms.

"But after you left, I worked through it." She turned back to face me. "I remembered how kind and gentle you were. I remembered that you were a *good* man. I remembered how much I loved you."

"Always will. Nothing anybody can do about that."

"And we'll be together forever," she said, smiling.

Oh boy. Better tell her about the Ralph Clause.

"Now here's the funny thing," I began.

She most definitely frowned. "Why don't I like the sound of that? Wait, are you remarried already?"

"No, of course I'm not married." I shrugged. "Haven't been for billions of years. No, it's that there's this marker that comes due in a little over six months."

She scowled. "What kind of marker?"

"The kind where I'm bound to suffer eternally under the close supervision of a terribly evil spirit."

Her shoulders dropped. "What kind of idiot makes a deal with a devil?"

"A desperate kind of fool. I saw a chance to turn the tide on the Adamant advance, and I made the deal."

"I wish I were noble enough to say I'd join you in your suffering. I'm not," she replied firmly.

"I wouldn't let you, if you asked."

"Oh, so you're in charge of me? You forbid me to accompany you into damnation?"

"You just said you weren't joining me." I was paddling, but my oars were out of the water.

"That was *my* decision."

"Okay, Sapale, please come with me to the bad place."

"No. I have work to do on this side of the veil. Thanks for the offer."

"Anytime," I said in defeat.

She thought a moment. "Is there any way out of this contract?"

"Yes and no. I have a notion, but I don't have a clue as to whether it'll work."

"What's the harebrained scheme?"

"I'll let you know when it's clearer to me."

"Oh great. A Jon-plan."

"Yeah, sort of."

"Well at least I have you for six months. That's better than nothing."

"I swell with pride knowing I'm better than nothing. Just how much better, I hesitate to ask."

She stood. "You talk a lot nowadays. You have a room or a cot on this rust bucket? Really, any room with a door that closes will work." She smiled in the way only my brood's-mate could. God, I loved that woman.

Later that afternoon, much later actually, we went to check on her family. The kids were out like the proverbial light bulb. Their mother, father, and crusty old Caryp were resting on bunks in the same room, keeping an eye on the children.

29

"How are you all doing," Sapale asked.

"Fine now," replied Caryp.

"How so," Sapale asked with concern.

"Maybe we can get some sleep now that the moaning, pounding, and giggling is complete."

Sapale covered her mouth and turned away.

"Who said it's over?" I responded. I raised a finger in the air and gestured between Sapale and myself. "Androids here."

"Oh, that's disgusting," shot back the old bat.

"Hey, don't kid yourself. You would if you could," I said with a wink.

"I did, and I might yet still. But I'd be a lot more *discrete*. I can tell you that."

"*TMI*, Opalf," replied Sapale.

"I have no idea what that means. If you're asking me to join you two in debauchery, you can forget about that right now."

I put my fingers in my ears. "TMI *and* distressingly gross."

The crone waved the back of her hand in our direction. "Rookies. You disgust me. Leave us alone to rest."

"I'll be at the system controls if you need me," replied Sapale, pointing over her shoulder.

Caryp narrowed all four eyes. "That what they're calling it these days?"

I grabbed Sapale by the back of her pants and pulled her toward the door. "Let's get out of here before she starts undressing."

Sapale wrapped her arm around my waist as we walked to the control station. We didn't need to talk. I sat behind the main panel, and Sapale sat next to me.

"So, was that the first time you ever flew a vortex?" I asked.

"Yeah."

"You did it like a pro. I may have to get you your own."

"I'm fine in this one. Hey, in six months I'll probably inherit it anyway."

"Oh, you do like to rub it in, don't you, you naughty girl?"

"Toño offered to let me test one way back when, but I said no. Didn't think it would ever be needed."

"But I bet he programed a ton of sims into you."

"Gigabit of the darn things."

"Whatever happened to Toño?" I asked. I'd never heard any news about him.

"No one seems to know. We didn't. After he set me up in this android, we saw less and less of him. After a few thousand years, we lost track of him altogether."

"Into different things?"

"To say the least. He continued to work tirelessly for the betterment of humankind. He pioneered new technologies, established top-level education for scientists, and continued to work with the political hacks."

"Some things never change, do they?"

"Not politicians, flakes, frauds, or felons. And so it goes," she mused.

"Amen." I toasted with my mug. She returned the salutation. "I wonder what happened to him, though."

"You don't think he might still be alive, do you?"

I shrugged. "We three are. If anyone could do it, he could. He'd not just replace parts, he'd design new ones and upgrade continually."

Sapale thought about that a minute. "Yes, he would, wouldn't he? By now, he could be so far advanced, we'd look like horse-drawn buggies next to him." Her eyes wandered.

"Dude could be a demigod by now, couldn't he?"

Her eyes returned to me. "No, not Toño. He's much too humble. He'd never go there."

"EJ sure changed a lot. Anything's possible."

"Amen, I say unto you."

"Do you have a theory as to why he fell so far off the rails?"

She shook her head slowly. "I sure thought about it a lot." She got a distant look in her eyes. "Those first twenty-five thousand years he spent alone before he went back in time and gave you the membrane technology were tough on him. As you know, *you* don't like to talk about stuff like that, so *he* didn't. I was able to piece together a dour picture of his past. For a long time, he only had the *Ark 1* ship, so his travels were painfully slow and lonely. When he finally managed to steal a fast ship, he was already pretty far down the path leading to a criminal life."

"Did he have a malfunction? A corruption or something?"

She looked very concerned. She knew I wanted *that* to be the reason he degenerated into such a hateful pariah. I didn't want to think it was something that lurked deep inside me, too.

"Maybe. But he positively would never talk about it. And he had his personal diagnostics encrypted, so I was never going to see them."

We sat quietly for a while. We both had a lot of thinking to do. That's when the now-rested kids burst into the room, the older one naturally chasing the younger one. Pretty quickly, little Sapale vaulted onto my Sapale's lap for protection from her older brother, Irtopal. The senior Sapale snatched him up into a restraining hug. She warned them that if they didn't calm down, she'd start kissing them. Irtopal squirmed just a little, and her assault was on. She kissed them on their heads, necks, and arms.

The kids put forth a lousy defense and giggled like crazy. It was a joy to witness. This, I missed.

Their mom came to try and establish control over her wild ones. Eaptetta was her name. Dad, who remained in the bedroom with Caryp, was named Qivrov. They seemed like wonderful people and appropriately doting parents. I collapsed back in my seat. It suddenly hit me how many perfect little families the Adamant had slaughtered in the name of empire. I almost lost it then and there. Those horrible sonsabitches had wiped out civilization after civilization. And it wasn't the grand political institutions or the cultures that made me the sickest. No, it was the annihilation of the love so many families created and shared.

My anger level rose to infinity. I began to shake. My vision went fuzzy. If I was still human, I'd have hoped and prayed I was having a stroke. But it was, for me, just another punishment of immortality. I was coming apart psychologically, damn it, not mechanically.

"...sweet love, you're scaring me. Jon, are you all right?"

I scanned the space before my face without recognition. Then I saw her, my vision, my lighthouse, my rock. My Sapale.

"There you are. What's happened, wensilack?" That was a Hirn term of goopy affection, like our honey pie.

"Nothing. Nothing at all."

She made a show of checking the chronometer on the display panel. "Nine hours. It took you all of nine hours to lie to me." She smiled and rested her head on my shoulder. "I've seen that look before. It's the angry-Jon-Ryan look."

"Those kids nearly died. If I wasn't there, maybe they would have. Hell knows why the Adamant returned to the basement. Angel, those cruel monsters are extinguishing everything good and worthy in my universe. I hate them more than I've ever hated any person, place, or thing before."

"We all do. And the kids are fine. You *saved* them." She tapped the tip of my nose. "That's what you do. But don't let hate control you. EJ did, and now look at him. Now, I'm not saying I'm worried about you, not yet. But understand this, man of my heart. There is just as much good in the universe as there is bad. Actually, I think there is more good." She held her palms up on either side of her torso. "It's all a matter of balance." She moved her arms up and down like a scale. "The Adamant are in their ascendancy. Goodness and light are ebbing. But there will be a reckoning. The balance will shift, and the Adamant will have to settle the very large tab they'll have run up. Trust me, you won't want to be them when the hammer falls."

"Wow, you've become a Gypsy psychic since we parted. Can you make an okay living at it?"

"You know a lot of women would be irritated by your remark. But not me. I missed you, Jon Ryan. You're as cute as a bean on a bun."

"You talk about the Adamant's downfall like it's a done deal. Wishful thinking, says I."

"No, it is fact. Jon, I've known you a long time. I have faith in you. Maybe more than you do yourself. If I were the Adamant, I'd sue for peace yesterday and make the one term of their surrender being that we keep you away from them." She shook her head. "Now, they're not nearly that smart, so it'll take an ass-kicking to knock them off their pedestal. But topple they will."

"When I start leading the charge?"

"No, sweet, you *are* the charge."

FOUR

"This is the stupidest plan I have ever heard of, and trust me, I've heard a lot of doozies in my day." Garustfulous was fuming.

"Given the constraints I'm working with, I rather like it," replied Harhoff quietly. He was having trouble not cracking a smile.

"But damn it, I'm *Adamant*. I'll not step out into public disguised as a slave."

"We've been through this a thousand times. You cannot be Adamant. You'd be subject to transfer away from my service and to bioscans whenever you enter a secure facility. I can't protect you then. That leaves only three options: Warrior. Possible, but you'd still be visible to those who might recognize you, and they do bioscan the Warrior class occasionally. Kilip. Let's just leave teacher of the young alone. Not going to happen. Descore. Perfect for your safety and cover. I've never heard of a Descore being interrogated, let alone bioscanned. A minimal amount of plastic surgery on your white mark, and you're Descore—*my* Descore."

"This is beneath my dignity. It is insulting, verging on the unholy."

"Ah ah, Garustfulous, we already established you have no dignity. Pride, yes. Honor, no. I plan on keeping you alive and using you as a covert agent. The match is too perfect to pass up. And there's only upsides for me. If you're uncovered, I won't be implicated in your ruse. I will have forged no documents nor deleted any computer files in your support. I have plausible deniability that you presented yourself to me as a Descore. No one will expect me to run a background check for one from your modest caste."

"Can I return to being what I am—an Adamant— someday? At least throw me that bone."

Harhoff pointed to a flask on the table. "Pour me some tea."

Garustfulous started to protest but realized this was a test. Huh. Not even an *if you please*. Oh well, courtesy would seem out of place directed at a Descore. He filled his master's cup. A noticeable amount either missed the lip or sloshed over it.

"Do practice in private, Jangir," chided Harhoff. That was his new Descore name.

"I haven't had the surgery yet, you hound. Don't *call* me that."

"The physician will be here in an hour. I have incriminating evidence of improper beliefs against him. We might as well get you into character." Harhoff glared at Jangir.

It finally hit Garustfulous. He bowed. "Yes, Master. Will there be anything else?"

"No. Have a seat over there and keep quiet. I wish to take a nap. Wake me when the doctor arrives." Harhoff curled up on his mat and was out in a flash.

Garustfulous sat staring at him. His jealousy was as overwhelming as his fatigue. But he knew Descore were only allowed to relax in their joint quarters. For the time being, he'd just have to pine for sleep as he seethed.

FIVE

"Opalf," Sapale said to Caryp, "you have a tough decision ahead of you."

"I know. It is not one I planned on facing, but there it is."

"I asked Qivrov the same question, and he said his family would follow whatever you decided as clan leader."

She shook her head wearily. "That part never gets easier, child. Deciding what path to choose is hard enough when it's just for oneself. Making critical decisions for others' lives is worse." Then she smiled faintly. "Here I complain because I was granted a choice *other* than death at the hands of the Adamant."

"If you're not ready, there's no hurry ..."

"No." She cut off Sapale. "There's only one course of action." She turned to me and set her steely eyes to mine. "You will take us to the planet farthest from the Adamant advance that will sustain us. Then, even if you two fail to stop these pigs, we will be afforded as much time as possible to regroup. Do you know which site will be best, or is there exploration that you must," she waved her bony hands in the air, "conduct?"

"I have some good ideas," I said softly. "With a little more—"

"There is no more time for my people. This is what you will do." She reached into her cloak and produced an ornate golden escutcheon. "You will deposit us immediately on a safe, distant world. Then you will take our clan medallion and return to Kaljax. In whatever time remains, you will round up as many Kaljaxians as possible. You will use whatever means are required. Showing this clan icon will convince all that you speak for me. Jon Ryan, we are in the final hours of my civilization. If we are to remain a viable race, you must spirit as many as possible to this safe, distant planet."

"I can help, Opalf," said Sapale.

"No. You will stay behind. When this craft returns, I expect it will be packed wall to wall such that people can barely breathe. You going means one less soul saved." She looked at me like I was an idiot.

"What?"

"Why are you standing there gawking at me, as pretty as I am? Are we on this new home yet?"

I jumped to. "No, ma'am, but we'll be there in two shakes of a lamb's tail."

"Why does he insist on speaking in riddles?" she asked Sapale.

"No one knows," was her reply. Hey, I might resent that.

I set us down on Kalvarg less than fifteen seconds later. Though technically still part of the Milky Way galaxy, the solar system it belonged to was a few kiloparsecs past the outer rim. At some point in the distant past, the entire system had been ejected from the galaxy by some perverse gravitational horseplay. Now it was an island of light in an immense sea of nothingness, heading farther into the void. Of course, if one was on any of the planets in the system one couldn't tell anything was unusual, except for the near absence of stars in the night sky. Instead of bright pinpoints of light in the night sky, they would see the confluent stars of their home galaxy only in one direction.

I'd never been there. The planet caught my attention on the Adamant maps only because it was so unusual. It was not just far away, it had several planets with independent sentient species. They ranged from primitive humanoids to advanced hexapeds to a far-advanced aquatic species. Kalvarg was the planet with the advanced water-based civilization. My hope was that they would not have a major problem with a sentient alien race occupying a small portion of dry land. I knew it was a big assumption. But I was also thinking of the annotation tagged to the system on the Adamant maps. *Unclear when, if ever, this system will need to be assimilated into the Empire.* That meant it was slated for destruction either a long time from now, or never. That was win-win in my book for the Kaljaxians.

In orbit, I became immediately impressed and encouraged. There were many artificial satellites. Most were communications and weather units. Some were orbiting space stations. That meant the civilization was a curious and advanced one. Also, the land masses were expansive and almost completely void of construction. Near coastlines and at scattered points elsewhere, small outposts or villages were present. But their sizes were always modest and isolated. They might have been scientific stations, sort of the reverse image of how it was on Earth. Humans had heavily populated continents with a few underwater scientific labs. The bottom line was that the dry land was open for the Kaljaxians to live on and cultivate.

Normally I'd have contacted the local government and would have asked permission to land. But I didn't have time. Typically, I'd alert them of my intent to resettle numerous aliens, too. Again, no time. If I was lucky, I had a few days left to me. The Adamant had overrun most of Kaljax at that point. There were a few unoccupied areas where I could collect Kaljaxians rapidly. After that, I was going to have to bob and weave into enemy territory to locate anybody left alive and not yet captured. If I took the time to play nice with the Kalvargians, it would cost lives. If they dragged their heels or put up resistance, many more would die. So, like it or not, I had to pull the classic hostile-alien-invasion card.

"Als," I said, "put us down near fresh running water where there is adequate cover. A temperate climate would be ideal, but beggars can't be choosers."

"We anticipated your request and have made a selection. Shall we proceed?"

"Is it near any coasts?"

"No," replied Al. "Why would that matter?"

"In case the LIPS stage an armed attempt to repulse our refugees, I want them to have to trek across as much terrain as possible."

"Ah, in that case, we've chosen an alternate that is nearly as good."

"Put us there ASAP."

The wall opened to a hatch before my nausea settled.

"Okay, Sapale, you're in charge. Grab anything you might need. There's a tent and rations in the back. Take all but one gun. Hopefully I'll be back within half an hour with reinforcements."

"Will do." She walked over to me, rose on her tiptoes, and planted a kiss on my cheek. "It's nice to be back in action with you." Then she led her family through the opening.

"*Stingray*, take us to the most populated area that is not currently engaged in active fighting."

"Of Kaljax, right?" she responded.

"Yes, of Kaljax." Silly computer.

We landed in the middle of an open, grassy area in the center of a large city.

"Als, I want to make a general announcement. Broadcast this on all local channels and put it on the public-address speakers, too. *I am Jon Ryan. I speak for Caryp of Clan Jarush-tah.*" I held up the medallion for the viewers on holo. "*She has sent me to rescue as many Kaljaxians as possible. Come to this location for transport to a safe planet. Come quickly, and come with only weapons, food, and tents. There is a limit to how many I can transport. Space will be given on a first-come, first-served basis.*"

I hit the off switch.

"Als, repeat that on a loop until we depart."

"Aye," replied Al.

Within five minutes, a sea of figures was surging toward *Stingray*. I anticipated this getting messy, but I think even my estimates were conservative. This was going to be bloody mayhem.

"Als, deploy a partial membrane with a single portal. I'll grab some flares and a rifle. Hopefully I can get people to line up without shooting anyone."

"Good luck, Jon," replied Al. "This is looking kind of ugly."

Before the first wave hit, I had flares lined up in an expanding cone to serve as a chute. That way, I only had to try and control the front of the line, as opposed to being rushed from all directions at once. As soon as the crowd was in ear shot, I began shouting as loud as I could. "Walk. Do not run. If anyone pushes, I *will* shoot."

Most on-rushers slowed, some didn't. I fired several shots into the air. That got everybody's attention.

"Single file. No pushing. I can only take one hundred at a time. I prefer to bring families but can't guarantee it." I kept repeating that.

Once an agitated but stationary line formed at the membrane opening, I started letting people past in twos and threes. "Go all the way to the back of the ship. This will be a very short flight. Do *not* worry about comfort." I said that periodically. The vortex filled up quickly and without problems.

I raised my rifle. "Stop. I'm full. Leave my landing spot clear, and I'll be back in ten minutes."

Because people are people, that's when the shit hit the fan, naturally. A fat, middle-aged male started pushing his way forward, knocking anyone in his way to the ground. "Wait, you *must* take me," he shouted frantically. "I'm a *council* member. I'm an important person."

I planted a blast at his feet. That stopped him. "*First*-come, *first*-served or I'll shoot higher, pal."

"You don't understand, you must take me *immediately*. I'm someone around here." He started to advance again.

"You are about to be someone with a gaping hole in his worthiness."

He stopped.

"I'll take you on the third flight."

"This is an *outrage*. I demand to know why I will not be on the *second* flight."

"Because you're an ass, and I don't like you. Now

you're on the fourth flight. One more word, and you're on the flight *after* my last trip."

He sure wanted to say something. Lucky for him, he refrained.

I stepped to the ship's hatch. "Everybody, take a deep breath in and move backward."

That created room for a few more. Then I backed in and sealed the wall. "*Stingray*, take us to the landing site on Kalvarg."

In an instant we were there. I had the passengers rush out as quickly as possible. Sapale had organized a temporary staging area and made sure everyone moved there without stopping. *Stingray* was empty in two minutes.

"You okay here?" I yelled to Sapale.

She gave me two thumbs up. I closed the opening and returned to Kaljax. By the time I arrived, the local police had begun organizing the ever-growing crowd. Bless their hearts. That really helped. They were getting relatives together and triaging the line in terms of societal value. Hey, it was going to be their new world. They could have me transport whomever they wanted. All I was concerned with was numbers, the bigger the better.

As people filed in, I called over to a police officer. "I want four officers on this trip. We need to maintain order on the other end, too."

She waved that she understood and buttonholed four cops. She pointed toward me as she gave them their orders. One seemed to protest. She shoved him away angrily and accompanied the other three policemen to the opening.

"What was that all about?" I asked her as she passed.

"Damn fool said he didn't want to leave without his family. Makes me sick to think any officer would put family ahead of duty during war."

I had to agree with her. "Welcome aboard," I said, gently pushing her in.

Over the next two days, I made nonstop shuttles between the two planets. I only stopped when the Adamant gunfire was so close the crowd had to disperse for its own safety. I did good. All in all, I rescued over five thousand people. Toward the end, when it was clear there wouldn't be many more trips, the police had the passengers arranged in tight groups. They'd selected mostly women and children but mixed in individuals who would be needed in the new world. Doctors, soldiers, educators, those type of people. Funny, because I asked specifically after we were finished; they did not send a single lawyer. Go figure.

Then the harder phase of my recovery efforts began. Sapale joined me for that part. Caryp demanded to come, too, but she realized pretty soon she wasn't up to the physical demands of the task. But it was nice to have her for her instant credibility. As a compromise, she recorded a short holo for us to show any stragglers we found to help convince them we were legit. We landed in relatively quiet zones and sought out survivors. It was slow going. It was also remarkably dangerous.

The damn Adamant figured out what we were doing quickly and made efforts to foil our recovery operations. They had troops spread out thinly, so there was less room for us to sneak around. We couldn't broadcast where we'd be, because the enemy would be there in greater number if we did. Over almost a month, we collected another two thousand random Kaljaxians. That was it. Granted, they would be forging a new society with more individuals than we had in the case of Azsuram, but still, less than ten thousand souls to start a brave new world with was dicey. But there were no other options. Plus, these were tough cookies. They'd be fine.

45

It hadn't taken the Kalvargians long to notice their uninvited guests. Fortunately, though it turned out they were not pleased, at least they didn't say hello with nuclear weapons. I was in for a rare break, which was fine by me. Since I wasn't one of the unannounced settlers, I wasn't involved in the negotiation process. I say negotiations because I honestly don't know another word for the interactions. They were not fun and giggles, that's for sure.

The region I pulled most of the Kaljaxians from was from a different clan than Caryp's. Their leader was a male even more ancient and withered than her. His name was Mesdorre. Together, they spoke for the mixed clans. Kaljaxians from other clans just had to accept that their leaders weren't present and that those two were the de facto spokespersons. Eventually, the clanless would pledge themselves to Mesdorre, since there were so few Kaljaxians left. A typical clan back on the home world numbered in the hundreds of thousands.

Once I was finished shuttling survivors, I got my first look at a Kalvarg local. I had a lot of experience with an aquatic species years ago, the Listhelons. They were vaguely humanoid. Not these guys. They were bullet shaped, like dolphins and whales. That made sense for an oceanic apex species. It meant, however, that they were particularly ungainly on land. Kalvargians had fins, and nothing like legs. Consequently, they moved across dry land on platforms with treads. They did have adaptive breathing devices, reverse-SCUBA, so to speak, as opposed to rolling around in bulky tanks. But if you took away their rides, they were—I just had to say it—like fish out of water. It was clear why they had ventured so little onto the surface of their planet. That did not, however, stop them from taking offense that someone migrated there without their permission—permission they most likely would have denied.

My only involvement in the interspecies lovefest was when I considered demonstrating my superior war technology. That would imply that the immigrants also possessed such weapons. Such an act might sway the proceedings, but I decided against it, at least to start with. Hopefully the negotiations were the first act in a play that would go on indefinitely. I wanted both parties to work matters out between themselves and to do so free of coercion. If need be, I could blow a big crater in the ground as a show of force. I loved doing that; the boom-boom stuff, not the show of force. Producing a massive smoking hole where there was once but flat boring dirt was always most cool.

When the locals first rolled up to the encampment, the mood was tense. Every able-bodied Kaljaxian picked up a weapon and formed a straight line on either side of the two leaders. It was clear the Kalvargian carts were well armed, too. Each had several turrets of varying sizes. There were over fifty vehicles. Fortunately, neither side was trigger-happy. They both also understood the need to translate the other's language. Mathematical symbols and formulae were exchanged to accomplish the preliminaries. Within thirty minutes, they were speaking effortlessly.

———

"I am Urpto. I am the Assistant Subtender for this region of Epsallor. State your identity and intention."

"I am Mesdorre." He rested a palm on his chest. Touching Caryp's shoulder, he said, "This is Caryp. We speak for the Kaljaxians present."

"You mean as opposed to those who are now dead?"

"No, I mean those whom you see before you. Those present here, now. Our intentions are to survive as a species."

"It is the same with all species. It is the same with us. Your words to not disclose why your invasion party has appeared."

"We are not invading your world. Our own world has been conquered and assimilated into the Adamant Empire. Are you familiar with them?"

"No. But we are not prepared to accept the representation you offer. We do not welcome you to Epsallor."

"Might I ask, is Epsallor this planet or simply this part of it?"

"This desert is part of the Kingdom of Epsallor. This planet is Morvip. You are not welcome in Epsallor. I doubt you are welcome anywhere on Morvip, but I do not speak for all the kingdoms."

What he referred to as a desert was a lush forested grassland. A desert to him, perhaps, being a merman.

"I will explain. First, however, may we find a comfortable place to talk? My bones ache from age."

"Why would ... ah, the effects of gravity. I am comfortable. If you wish to be also, that is permissible."

Hey, their first compromise. Where was my Polaroid?

"Now," began Caryp, "I will tell you that a ruthless hoard has taken our planet and killed most of our race. Those you see here are the last of our species. We choose to come to Morvip not to control it but because it is one of the rare safe planets that remains free. We appeal to your sense of morality to allow us to stay." The cagy old bat waited a few seconds before adding, "We do not wish to take Morvip from you by force. But we must have a place to live. Surely you can see how small our numbers are and how large the available land is."

"We have no interest whatsoever in living in or on the water. The resources there will remain yours alone," added Mesdorre.

"I do not find it reassuring that you are granting us permission to use that which is already ours. It implies primacy and desire for control."

"I intend no such meaning. I simply want to point out that your species and ours will not be in direct competition for resources."

"If access to your world is lost to you, in time your numbers will swell. Will there not arise competition then?"

"Perhaps. However, that will take a very long time to become an issue, let alone a problem," responded Mesdorre.

"Yes, time is long. So has the presence of our species been. To resolve a problem when it is small is much easier achieved than when it is large."

"Your words are true. But I hope in time our two species will become fast friends."

"Which two species? Are you subverting the Kingdom of Epsallor by forming an alliance with the Dodrue?"

"Who are the Dodrue?" asked Caryp.

"You must know. Are you trying to be deceptive?"

"No, we came here in a great rush with no more information about Morvip than it was safe for us to breathe here."

"That is possible, however unlikely it may seem. The Dodrue are our mortal enemies. Their kingdoms war with us constantly. It has been since before time was recorded."

"A clarification, if you might," asked Caryp. "What do you call your species?"

"I am a vidalt."

"And are the Dodrue also vidalt?"

One of the fellow cart occupants cried out in protest. It must not have been a question one asked.

"I will assume you mean no insult. No. The Dodrue are wiqubs. Larger, less intelligent, and more ruthless than we are."

"And which side leads in the fighting?" asked Mesdorre.

More protestations were heard from the locals.

"In many years, for many generations, the war has been static. Neither side wins and neither side loses."

"And do any of the battles of this war occur on what you call this desert?"

"No. That would be pointless. No one wishes to control worthless turf."

"Neither do we. But we also would appreciate the opportunity to survive here, in this unwanted wasteland," said Caryp. "Urpto, as an Assistant Subtender for this part of Epsallor, do you have the authority to permit us to remain here, at least pending formal discussions with all of the governments of Morvip?"

"Yes, I do."

"Then please grant it. I realize our arrival is challenging, but I know that with sufficient time we can convince you that we will be good stewards of this land. We will also be nothing but friends to the vidalt. I pledge that we will continue to search for other planets that might sustain us. If, later, the vidalt decide we must leave, we will do so when it is safe," said Caryp.

"To battle here and now, neither party knowing the capabilities of the other, would be shortsighted," added Mesdorre. It was a nice way of saying don't force us to kill you.

"Very well. You may stay in this location for now. My

superiors will contact you soon to establish formal diplomatic talks. Is this agreeable to you?"

"Most agreeable," replied Mesdorre.

"Then I shall wish you happy hunting, and we will take our leave."

So, a tenuous peace was established. But a tenuous peace was preferable to death in battle by either party. It was an excellent start.

SIX

Sapale and I were sitting around a campfire outside *Stingray* a few days after the first encounter with the big fishes. Of course, we could be perfectly comfortable *inside* the cube. But there was nothing in the universe better than sitting lazily around a campfire with the one you loved. It reminded me of the old, old days when we did the same thing with our young family on Azsuram. That choked me up, so I tried to ignore those thoughts. Sure, our kids, and their kids, and their kids' kids had lived long and productive lives. But they were all so long gone, so far from us sitting there by the roaring fire that the weight of it crushed me.

Sapale had her arm around my waist and her head on my shoulder. "This is nice," she purred.

"Yes, it is. It's the best." I kissed the top of her head softly.

"Are we going to stay here and take the vacation we both earned for the next six months?" There was tension in her voice.

I waited a moment to respond. "No, at least not me."

That brought my spirited brood's-mate's head off my

shoulder good and quick. "You're not thinking of leaving me behind are you, flyboy?"

"No," I said, gently pressing her head back down on my shoulder. "Hear me out. I have a little less than six months before payment is due. There's something big I need to do before that time is up. You are welcome to come with me. I'd actually prefer it that way, but it's your call."

"My alternative being to remain here and re-resettle my people to another new world?"

"Your call."

She shook her head. "No way. Been there, done that, got the holovid. Eight thousand six hundred twenty-*four* people stand just as good a chance at success as eight thousand six hundred twenty-*three* people do. Plus, those two old relics are equal to the task."

"They've spent their entire lives deciding who can marry whom and what the main dish will be at the annual conclave. World building is altogether different."

"Don't sell them short. They will do just fine. We need to shuttle in some supplies, but they can form a self-sustaining society here, for sure."

"Yeah, I figured they'd need food and medicine replicators, a few FTL ships, and other basics. We can buy them from Vorpace and bring them here in one or two days."

"What's your mysterious plan then?"

"I have to find EJ."

She pulled away and sat straight up. "I *knew* it. Jon, why can't you just let him go?"

"Are you really asking me that?"

"Yes. Okay, you hate him. You have every reason to. But with so little time left, why waste it on revenge?"

I sighed. "It's not revenge. It's survival."

"You mean you want the satisfaction of killing him?"

I smiled vacantly. "Something like that."

She burrowed back into my shoulder. "Well, wherever you're going, I'm going."

"Thanks," I kissed the top of her head again. "It'll be great."

"So, when do we leave?"

"We head to Vorpace in the next few hours. When the colony here is set up with the essentials, we blow this banana stand."

"Sounds good to me." She cuddled closer and held onto my arm as tightly as she could.

It was nice, sitting by that fire, there on whatever the hell planet we were on.

Three days later we'd transported literally boatloads of materials to the new colony. We said our good-byes to the two clan leaders, they thanked us, and we climbed aboard *Stingray*.

"Take us to Namufar," I called out. That was a planet EJ and Sapale had spent a lot of time on. It was possible he was holed up there.

"Ah, Captain, a word before we depart," said Al. That was odd, kind of out of place.

"Sure, I guess. Can't it wait?"

"Probably, but we prefer to discuss it presently."

"Fine, what crawled up your butt and has set up house in your colon?"

"Ignoring your unprofessional snark, there's something wrong with this solar system."

I started to say *yes, you're in it* but bailed because it was gratuitous. Not my style, and yes, I had a style.

"Please explain," came out instead.

"We have run a lot of sims. Based on the age, metallicity, and direction it is traveling in, we have identified with over ninety-nine percent certainty precisely where the system originated in the Milky Way."

"Wow, that's spectabulous, Al. Now we know the answer to the question that was burning in absolutely no one's mind."

"Hang on, oh pissy one," said Sapale. "Al, why is this important?"

"Thank you, Form Two," he replied. "It is most welcome to have an *adult* aboard once again."

"Al, while we're still young," I chided.

"We also ran sims of the three-body and even four-body interactions it would require to put this solar system right here, right now."

"Great, Al. You calculated where we are. That's so ... utterly useless because we already know where we are."

"Based on those sims, we can find no rational explanation as to why this solar system is where it is."

It took me a second, but then the significance of that bombshell struck me. "Hang on. You ran all possible sims for all the possible stars in the relevant part of our galaxy that could produce this system's 3-D vector? Al, that's a lot of calculations."

"Tell me about it."

"Why would you even think to run those calculations?"

"Allow me to introduce us. We are AIs. The *I* stands for intelligence. There are two *I*s in intelligence. *Blessing* and me."

"And you checked the 3-D vectors of all possible interactive stars and none match? You think you found all possible candidates?"

"We do."

"So, what are you telling me?"

"That the laws of physics do not explain why this system is where it is. Alternately, it is impossible for us to be where we are."

"But we *are*," added Sapale.

"So it would seem," replied Al. "There's more. The orbits of the planets in this solar system are incorrect."

"Incorrect?" I whined. "What's that supposed to mean? There're no rights or wrongs about stupid planetary orbits."

"Ah, *hello*, Kepler's three laws? The orbits must follow specific rules. They may not be random."

"You mean, like how the presence of the outer planets in Earth's solar system were predicted?"

"Exactly. There is a problem with gravity in those two regards. Our location and the orbit of the planets," Al concluded.

"Have you tested gravity? Maybe it's different here for some inexplicable reason," I thought out loud.

"Yes. We checked. Gravity is exactly as it should be."

"So, you're saying there's another planet in this system we're not seeing?"

"Yes, in part. The existence of an invisible planet would account for the orbital anomalies but not the fact that the system isn't where it should be."

"Where's the mystery planet?"

"I'll place a polar map in both your heads," replied Al.

A crude map of the orbits of the thirteen major planets in the system appeared. They whirred in their orbits with slower angular velocities the farther out they were from the central star.

"These are the planets we observe. The missing planet would be located here." A new ellipse colored in red appeared. It was immediately outside the orbit of Kalvarg. At that moment, the mystery planet was on the opposite side of the central star.

"Als, why can't you detect the planet aside from the perturbations in other planets' orbits?"

"That is unknown. We should obviously detect it," replied Al.

"It's almost like magic," added *Stingray*.

I'd already learned a new rule. If you saw magic, think Deft. They were the sole species I'd ever encountered who could do whatever it was that constituted magic.

"Place us in low orbit around that planet now," I ordered.

"We are above nothing, sir," said Al seconds later.

"Place a window in the direction of the planet below," I said.

Nothing. There wasn't even a spot of nothingness, like when the vortex moved in a full membrane. I could see stars continually from above the planet, through it, and below it where the planet had to be.

"This is crazy," said Sapale.

"Welcome to my ongoing nightmare."

"My, but you're given to dramatic hyperbole, Pilot," observed Al.

"Can we land on the planet?" I asked.

"What planet? Sensors show there is nothing down there."

"I know. But can you reconstruct surface topology based on the gravitational distortions?"

"We cannot be that precise," responded Al.

"I have an idea," I announced.

"That generally means trouble," replied Al.

"*Stingray*, open a ten-centimeter circular hole in an external wall. I will stick my hand out while holding Risrav. Descend to the surface with the rune leading the way."

"Isn't that rock presently in your scrotum?" asked Al with clear trepidation.

"Yeah. But it's clean."

"TMI, *plus* gross, *plus* I'm going to close my eyes," he responded.

"Ya big baby."

A small hole appeared in the hull. I retrieved the rune and held it in front of the cube. We advanced slowly under impulse drive.

"Captain, we will impact the surface in ten ... nine ... eight ... permission to halt."

"Denied. Proceed."

"Three ... two ..."

"Form One, a portion of a planet has just materialized below us. I am slowing for a soft landing," announced *Stingray*.

"I *knew* it," I muttered to myself.

"You knew *what*?" asked Sapale.

"I smelled a Deft trick with this whole hiding a planet thing."

"But the Deft are gone ... except for the three we know of."

"Als, approximately how long ago was this planet ejected from the galaxy?"

"Half a million years, give or take," replied Al.

I turned to Sapale. "The Deft on this planet have been separated from the Deft of Locinar for a very long time. Even if our Deft once knew about them, they may have forgotten them by now."

She nodded softly. "Possibly."

"Als," I called out, "are there cities nearby?"

"More like vast villages, but yes," confirmed Al.

"What's the diff?" I asked.

"City implies development and sophistication. The structures we detect are quite simple, and none are very tall. Hence, a very large village."

"Is anyone hailing us?"

"Negative."

"Do they have radios and sophisticated electronics?" asked Sapale.

"No artificial radio sources are evident. There is also no electrical grid."

"So, the Deft here have gone native," I observed.

"Or they prefer a simple lifestyle. Remember the human communities of the Amish and the Mennonite? Simplicity was a choice, not a failure to advance technologically," said Al.

"True. Well I guess we're about to find out. Land us near what seems to be the highest concentration of huts, and let's see what's up," I responded.

"Aye, but for the record, they are well-crafted wooden structures, not thatched huts." Al just had to get a dig in.

"We are down, Form One," said *Stingray*.

"Is there a welcoming committee present yet?" I asked.

"Negative," she replied.

"Hmm. Let's give them a few minutes to find us and gather around. I'd rather meet them that way."

"Why does it matter, Pilot?" asked Al.

"I don't know what their reaction will be. I'd rather see them in a group around the ship. If we wander out and find that they'd rather eat us than talk to us, we'd be at more risk."

"But, Form One, they couldn't possibly consume you. You are made of inert mechanical components." *Stingray* said.

"It's more an expression of intent than strictly a dietary observation," I replied.

"Ah."

"So, you have no clue what language they speak?"

"No, Form One, we do not."

"It'll be like ancient Deft, I'm fairly certain. Pull up what you know about that, and we'll play it by ear."

"Travels with Jon," remarked Sapale. "I'd forgotten how *informal* they could be."

"Informal, yet satisfying," I returned.

She smiled coyly. "That we shall just have to see."

Ten minutes later, a few figures were hanging out near the ship. I say hanging out because they weren't pacing nervously or goose-stepping with weapons at the ready. It was like people checking out an accident that was almost completely cleared off the road. Hurt my feelings, I can say that. I was used to being an attraction, not a sideshow. I placed one tick in the I-don't-like-this-place column of my mental ledger. After another five minutes, the small crowd that had gathered dispersed, leaving only one individual standing near *Stingray*. Whoever it was didn't move, which added to the oddness of the situation.

"Open the wall. I can't stand the suspense. I need to find out who our solo welcoming party member is."

A portal snapped open in the direction of the figure. I stepped out in tandem with Sapale. There stood a shining platinum dragon, a tad smaller than Cala, but otherwise similar.

I pointed to the dragon and said to Sapale, "Ah, there's a mature Deft couple, like the one I told you about."

"Jon," she replied dubiously, "that's not a couple. That's a single individual."

"It's a hollon thing, sweetie. The single creature is the union of two adult Deft."

The platinum beauty was up until then completely still, much like Cala was when I first confronted her. But something we said got her to relax and speak.

"I am not used to being described like a museum exhibit. I must say, if asked, I dislike the feeling."

"Oh, sorry. I'm Jon Ryannnn ... and how come we understand each other so well? That should not be possible yet."

"You would not understand."

"Wanna bet? Loser buys the first round, okay?"

"I do not *wanna* bet. We understand each other because of the magical power I control. I told you this revelation was beyond your comprehension."

"All right, make mine a double, because you're buying. I know all about Deft magic."

"That is good to hear. What's a Deft?"

Huh? I pointed right at her. "You're a Deft. You used to be two separate individuals, but you joined into one because you can shapeshift."

She got a skeptical look on her scaly face. "You know an awful lot about me, but I'm not a Deft. I'm a Plezrite."

"No, I'm gonna have to differ with you on that. You're definitely a Deft."

"Jon, do you think it wise to argue such an obtuse point when we're just establishing contact? I mean, if she says she's not Deft but Plezrite, we should take her on her word," asked Sapale. Silly worrywart.

"Maybe I'm jumping ahead a bit."

"*Maybe?*"

"Okay. Hi, I'm Jon Ryan. Who are you?" I asked our greeter.

"Himanai."

"No, you're not. Himanai-What, or What-Himanai?"

"Do you always babble, or are you capable of rational speech?" asked Himanai.

"I'd pass on that question if I were you," Sapale responded, rolling her eyes.

"No, after hollon, the dragon takes the name of *both* the individuals who formed it." Directed to the dragon I asked, "You know that, right?"

"No. This conversation is most unusual. I hope you are not a typical representative of your species."

"Oh no, trust me here," exclaimed the love of my life, "he is *not*."

"After hollon, which is never discussed openly or with strangers, a new name for the pair is selected."

I shrugged. "I'll let it pass."

"How culturally sensitive of you, Jon Ryan," she replied.

"But you are a brindas, right?"

Himanai literally took two steps back.

"What?" I asked, dumbfounded.

"You blaspheme as well as try and correct the correct? I'm am not certain this audience need go any longer."

"Please excuse my soft-brained husband," said Sapale. "I believe he is so excited to meet you he forgets how to properly use his tongue."

"I can easily remedy that by removing the offending organ," Himanai offered.

"No, that won't be necessary. *I'll* control it for him," responded Sapale. She gave me a Sapale's-not-happy look to reinforce that commitment.

"Why is it you are here?" asked Himanai. "In fact, how is it you are here? You should not have been able to know we are here."

"We knew you were present because of the gravitational disturbance your planet produced," said Sapale.

"Yes, that we were unable to tweak. Pity that the laws of nature don't exclusively bend to magic."

"I'll take your word on that," I replied.

That drew another suboptimal look from my soulmate.

"We are here because of this." I produced Risrav in the palm of my hand.

"Where did you get that rune? It does not belong to you."

"It was lent to me by someone you do not know." I decided to play it close to the vest, as these Deft were so screwy.

"I was wondering why the High Council dropped the illusion of invisibility they maintain around Nocturnat."

"Nocturnat?" asked Sapale.

"We call this planet Nocturnat," Himanai replied.

"You mean that's the planet's name?" I tried to clarify. Not sure why I felt it was needed, but there it was.

"No. You'd have to ask the planet what its name is. We call it Nocturnat."

Double screwy planet full of a bunch of hippies.

"That still leaves open the question as to *why* you are here? *That* you detected us is insufficient. If you are sentient, then you must have realized we wished to be left alone. To directly violate that desire is difficult to view as anything even remotely positive."

"Good point, but there's more that you don't understand," I replied.

"I stand here prepared to be enlightened," she parried.

"There are matters I am not free to discuss."

"Again, I find it hard to assign positive intentions to such reservations."

I raised my hands. "No. You'll understand in time and look back on this and wonder why I said as much as I did. You'll probably laugh about it."

"Unlikely on both assumptions. *Why*, I ask for the final time, are you here?"

"That a Def ... Plezrite colony exists is justification alone."

"Clearly it is not. What concern is it of yours, either way?"

"Again, there are aspects of our discovery that I

cannot address. Please know I am deeply concerned about your species."

"Fine, you love us to death. What are you here to accomplish?"

Wow, she had my commitment to diplomacy. Somewhere between zero and none. "To know you exist."

"And you now know. Let me be the first to say good-bye to you then."

"Wait. No. Don't you want to learn about us? Don't you want to know what an alien is doing with a magical rune?"

"Let me see. No and no. Now back to good-bye."

"Why were you so offended by the word brindas, friend Himanai?" asked Sapale evenly.

She didn't retreat, but she clearly took umbrage at the word. "As aliens, I must allow for some off-behavior. We have no brindas on Nocturnat. We never have. The religious cult inside the world of magic was rejected by our forbears. It is good that they did. Please let that word pass from your minds."

"But you do magic," I stated. "Isn't a brin ... wise teacher helpful in that regard?"

"We teach ourselves. Teaching does not require dogma or a call for devotion or submission to rules that task reason."

Pilgrims. The Plezrite were religious—or rather—atheistic pilgrims. But these guys and gals took a whole planet with them, not the tiny *Mayflower*.

"Your ancestors used their magic to throw Nocturnat out of the galaxy, didn't they?"

Again, with the two steps back. "You cannot know that."

"Of course, I can. I *do,* so I *can.* Your planet is moving along an impossible path. Gravitational effects had to be overruled to establish that path."

"Damn *gravity* again. I wish it wasn't so inflexible," mused Himanai.

"I'll tell you what else I know. The Plezrite fled the galaxy to avoid contact with the remainder of their species, the Deft. It was a religious schism, wasn't it?"

"You tread far into realms you have no business nosing about in. I am not sure your departure is as desirable on a *personal* level as I found it a short while ago."

That didn't sound too hopeful, now did it? I was beginning to wonder if Risrav countered only Varsir magic, or if it worked for magic in general. It was suddenly a rather crucial distinction.

"Once again, I'm going to have to differ with you on a point of order," I responded. "We are leaving now. I have gained the information I require to take my next action. Any further contact with you will come from a different representative if additional contact is desired." I had slipped into my bad-ass tone of voice. I wanted to be clear I intended to have it my way.

"Jon Ryan, I just realized I have been an inexcusable host. What, for instance, is your lovely bride's name?"

"Her name," I answered for Sapale, "is SeeYouLater."

"And really, you must stay for refreshments. If you know anything of our species, then you know of our famous agatcha. I'm certain mine is the best in the cosmos." She waved us to join her. "Come, I still owe you the first round of spirits."

"Gonna take a double raincheck, Himanai. Don't think it hasn't been real."

Man, she was way too nice all of the sudden. I put an arm around Sapale and stepped backward into *Stingray*.

"Rameeka Blue Green *now*," I said as the wall was sealing.

"I'm detecting a variance in the power couplings," said Al.

"Is it a deal breaker? Can we split?"

"Yes, and no, unless we override it."

"Where are the couplings located?"

"Rear left corner."

As I suspected, probably out of range for my counter rune. I sprinted for the corner. Slight nausea was never so welcome as it was when I was halfway there.

I strode into the control room. "That was close ... where's Sapale?"

"Sorry, Captain, as soon as you left the room, she vanished."

SEVEN

"Guvrof, I'd like you to look over these minor alterations in our master plan for galactic conquest," said High Wedge Lesset as he handed a mini storage chip to his right-hand dog.

Guvrof slipped the memory stick into his handheld and studied it for several minutes. He was a patient and a cautious individual. In other words, he was a survivor of the draconian Adamant hierarchy. Still rubbing absently behind his ear, he said, "Aren't these basically the changes Varsor insisted we consider just before you relieved him of the burden of life?"

Lesset poured himself a drink and sat down. "Yes, almost verbatim."

"Then why'd you shoot him, if he was right?"

"My friend, there's right and there's right in the correct manner. His sin was violation of the latter of the two."

Guvrof chuckled. "I hope he doesn't get wind of this in the afterlife. He'd be even more pissed."

"Then I will assign that idiot Loserandi the duty of praying it continually so that he might."

"Remind me to never get on your bad side," he said, with another chuckle.

"Your only reminder will be a one-way ticket to join poor old Varsor in his misery."

"So, why the change? Isn't our master plan supposed to be inviolable?"

"It's but a minor tweak."

"You said as much already."

"I began to wonder how much more effective an allied alien defense might be."

Guvrof began to chide his companion for his uncharacteristic sojourn into thought. But he bit his tongue. It was unwise to speak truth to power.

"And what did you conclude?"

"In the end, why worry about the issue? We were going to assimilate them soon enough. Why not switch their place in line so that there is no need to worry about what they might accomplish?"

"A very convincing argument."

"I'd like you to circulate it among the others, get them to back the plan before I present it for discussion during our next meeting."

"The one next week?"

"Precisely."

"And if I am unable to fully sway a council member in so short a time?"

"Then you will tell me exactly what his concerns are, and I will address them."

"So, there's wiggle room in your proposal. You're willing to negotiate the specifics?"

"Not in the least."

"Then why do you want to know a dissenter's actual reservations?"

"So I may inscribe them on his headstone. We should

all be remembered for what we stood for during our brief journeys."

EIGHT

My immediate thoughts were to return to Nocturnat and begin doing some major-league ass kicking. But I realized that would be counterproductive. It would be infinitely preferable to have the Plezrite as friends, if for Mirraya and Slapgren's sake alone. Plus, they would have spirited Sapale into hiding, so my violence would be undirected. Sooner or later, I'd fatigue or make a mistake and they'd get an opportunity to do me in. No, I had to speak with Cala.

I materialized where I had before and ran to her house. I reached up to knock, but she opened the door before I could.

"My what an unpleasant ..." she began to say.

"Can it, Cala. No time for snark. We have a major crisis to solve as soon as possible."

"Very well, come in, why don't you?" she said after I'd brushed past her.

"Are the kids here?"

"Neither the kids nor the parents are. They are in their residence. Shall I summon them?"

I ran my fingers through my hair. "No, just as well they aren't. A lot of what happens next will be your call. You can tell them whatever you like, even if it's short of the whole truth."

"Goodness, I may collapse from shock. You deferring to me where they're concerned?"

"Look, sit." I pointed to the kitchen table. I paced back and forth while she did, then I joined her.

"May I offer you some refreshments?"

"No. This is important."

"Then I suggest you begin your tale."

"Sapale and I were evacuating her people to a safe planet when we discovered a planet trying to hide itself."

"Sapale was your mate?"

"*Is*. That's not important now."

"And let me guess. You found a society powerful enough to conceal itself, respected their implied wishes, and left them alone?"

I just glowered at her.

"Sorry. That was not helpful or supportive. You and I think differently, that's all."

"The Plezrite are doing the planet hiding."

Picture me swinging a two-by-four length of lumber and striking Cala squarely in the forehead. That would have had less impact than that word: *Plezrite*. I let her stew over it for a while.

"I assume from your reaction that you know who they are?"

"Yes, I do." She looked at me with a wonder and awe I would never have expected she'd harbor toward me. "Jon Ryan, you are a truly remarkable force of nature. That you found the Plezrite in and of itself would define your life as charmed. Combined with all your other impossibilities, I am struck dumb."

I'd have loved to hit her with a comeback, but I wasn't in the mood. "They kidnapped Sapale as we tried to flee."

"That is a challenging development."

"Tell me about it. What can you tell me about these asswipes?"

"That is a long and complex story, my friend." She took a few deep breaths. "Long ago, we were one race. We were all Deft."

"Were you around then?"

She giggled, despite her generally dour nature. "No. I'm not *that* old. That was hundreds of thousands of years ago."

"But you know about them?"

"Yes, of course. You've seen all my books, right?"

"The one I spoke with had never heard of the Deft."

She rolled her head. "Not very surprising. They were minimalists. Not having books would be consistent with their mindset."

"Which is?"

"They reject complexity."

"She said they rejected your *religious cult inside the world of magic.*"

"I have my version, they have theirs. They are but different views of the same set of circumstances."

"You mean one or both of you are revisionist historians."

"As I said, two varying accounts of one matter. So, you only met one of them?"

"Yes, a platinum hollon a bit smaller than you."

She cringed. "Jon, when you speak the word hollon aloud, please think of it as interchangeable with whatever vulgarization of the concept of anal intercourse might be in your tongue. It is not a thing to speak plainly of, ever."

"Oh. Sorry."

"Don't be sorry, be sensitive. She is referred to as *visant*, a two-joined Deft."

"You mean a male and a female?"

"*Sensitivity*, Jon. Please strive for it. There are no physiologic rules as to which two individuals may become a visant."

"Oh, *gotcha*." I wiggled a finger at her as I spoke.

She shook her big head in resignation.

"What was her name?"

"Himanai. Weird, eh? She said the couple chooses a new single name after hol ... joining."

"Thank you," she said with genuine relief. "Again, that does not surprise me. They split from us because they wanted other ways, ones they felt were simpler. Wait, you told them about me?"

"No, I didn't. I used the word Deft but didn't discuss you or how few are left."

"That is fortunate. Thank you for your discretion."

"When can we rescue Sapale?"

"Jon, I'm not certain we can. I'm not certain we should even attempt it. It is good you spoke to me without the children. They would have insisted on an assault to free your mate."

"Of course, they would have, I mean *will*. Cala, why - are you not going to help me?"

"I'm not certain we can take her from them. Jon, they may not have brindas, but they possess powerful magic and are in much greater numbers. How many would you estimate there are?"

"The planet was covered in simple structures. I don't know, but probably millions."

"We four cannot defeat millions."

"We don't have to kill millions of them, just the ones standing between Sapale and us."

"Jon, a world of visants is a dynamic force. Locinar was such a place once. You cannot imagine the flow of power."

"Cala, I'm a simple guy. I live by a set of simple rules. Rule One: you kidnap my brood's-mate, you die swiftly and brutally. My goal is to make the offender's soul full of remorse as I shovel it straight into hell."

"Wow," she said. "I believe you'd do it, too."

"You know I would."

"But in this case, force would be futile."

"Then you'll just have to negotiate Sapale's release. *Then* I'll butcher the ones responsible."

"I can't go to Nocturnat. That would insult them beyond all limits. It would be suicidal."

I pointed outside. "There's a little family genetically and socially isolated from their own kind. If there's a planet full of their kin, they need to be there."

"That is a decision left exclusively to me."

"What decision is *exclusively* yours, Cala?" challenged a quite pregnant Mirraya from the doorway she'd been listening from.

"Hey, look who's here," I chortled.

"Return to your quarters. We will talk of this later," Cala said sternly to Mirri.

"Oh, and then you can give us the Cala-sanitized version of the truth? After you've made all the adult decisions for our *little* heads?" Ooh, the girl was mad.

"This is a matter between this human and me. It is not a public debate. Please respect my authority."

Mirri paced quickly over to the table and plopped into a chair. She folded her hands. "I'm staying."

"Mirraya, this is a very critical point in time. I am explaining my reasoning to your benefactor before he leaves, which will be almost immediately. You are *not* welcome to participate."

74

"All the more reason for me to stay, then. What's all the hubbub?"

"If you don't tell her, I might have to," I said to Cala. Then Mirri and I stared intently at her, waiting to see how this was going to go.

"You have read about the Plezrite Schism, have you not?"

"Yes. You know that. I also know you two aren't fighting over ancient history."

"Your uncle has found the Plezrite."

"Oh, that is interesting."

"And they kidnapped Sapale as we were running away."

"Then they die, swiftly and brutally."

I gestured toward Mirri. "I told you it was Rule One. The kids know it."

"You wouldn't be banging heads if we were going to race to Sapale's rescue, so I assume you are reticent to charge in guns blazing. In that case, please watch the children while my mate and I assist our family in an hour of tremendous need." She stood to presumably retrieve the kids and the husband.

"Wait. Sit," commanded Cala. "Let us talk as three adults."

"No," replied Mirri. "We will talk as four adults, or we will not talk."

"I came for a bite to eat, but it looks like I'm getting something a hell of a lot better," said Slapgren from the door. He held the younger child, and the other stood at his side.

"Have a seat," said Cala, "this is now completely out of hand."

"I'll get you some bread and cheese," said Mirri, rising.

"No, just hold this," he said, passing her the baby, "and I'll do it."

The toddler popped up onto mom's lap.

"Now you need to be quiet as a stone, all right? We adults need to talk," I said to the babe.

Jon nodded. I passed him my handheld. He didn't know how to use it, but I signaled Al in my head to show him some cartoons. Instant paralysis.

"What are you three arguing about?" asked Slapgren with a mouth full of food.

"We are not arguing. We are discussing a very serious subject."

"And you two," he pointed to Mirri and me, "don't agree with you." He flipped his hand to Cala.

"Yes," Cala replied.

"Then what are you three arguing about?" he repeated with a big smile.

"Do you recall learning about the Plezrite?" Cala asked him.

He scrunched up his face. "Maybe."

"They were discussed in that four-volume set of red books, the ones with the gold inlay," prompted Mirri.

"Oh yeah, the extra super boring ones. They were rebellious Deft, right?"

"Close enough," said Cala, shaking her head slightly. "Your uncle has located them."

His face beamed. "Cool. When can we meet them?"

"Then they kidnapped his wife," she added.

"Not cool. When do we kill them?"

"You are now up to speed on this discussion. I was telling these two," she pointed at Mirri and me, "we cannot assault a million magical shapeshifters and hope to win."

"Why not? We've got you. And we've got Uncle Jon. And, come to think of it, we've got me."

Mirri punched him.

"The wife, too. Don't forget her."

"Shall we bring the babies into mortal combat or just leave them here to fend for themselves once we're all dead?" asked Cala sourly.

"Good point. I'm back to how could we lose, you, UJ, and me?"

"Oh, so the other brindas stays at home and changes diapers."

"Right," he pointed to Mirri but addressed Cala, "she's on board. It's a done deal."

"We're not attacking a ridiculously superior force," said Cala resolutely. "We are the last Deft. We will not perish as a species."

"But they took uncle Jon's wife. What better reason to defy the odds or die trying?" he asked.

"You may feel that way, but I do not," Cala huffed.

"Okay, you watch the kids, and the rest of us will go."

Cala turned to me and basically whined. "You see the trouble you bring with you every visit?"

"I'm sorry your cousins stole my wife," I snapped.

"You should not have meddled. They clearly wished to be left alone."

"Whether UJ should or should not have contacted them, the fact is he did. And they took an inexcusably aggressive step. They will hand Sapale back, or they will pay dearly. Maybe they'll do both," said Mirraya, resolutely.

Cala was clearly distraught. She did not want to engage the Plezrite in any way, shape, or form. She also did not want the last of her kind to march glibly off to death.

"Look, Cala and I go. We will *make* them negotiate. We will make them hear reason. You two stay here with your kids," I said.

"I'm not going anywhere," Cala replied heatedly.

"Then I will go alone," I said flatly.

"No, Uncle Jon. You came here for help, and help you will get," said Mirri. Bless her heart.

"Look, Mirri, this is not war. It's only war if you fight a battle you might win. This is personal. You and Slapgren have a family to worry about. Mine is being held captive."

"Uncle, I know why you contacted the Plezrite," said Mirri, eying me steadily. "You wanted to ensure our family had a chance to live with our own kind. You wanted our children to grow up in a diverse society, to choose the mates of their desire. You didn't go there for laughs and giggles."

"Lord, you do sound a lot like me," I said with a grin.

"You know this, too, Cala," Mirri said harshly. "He did this for us. We will help him fix this."

"Good intentions do not pave a good path. There is much at stake. Everything, in fact."

"We three are Deft," began Mirraya. "We may be the last of the Deft, but I'd also like to think we're the *best* of our people. If we can't help someone who risked his life to help us, then I, for one, don't think we're a species that needs preserving."

"Well said, my love," responded Slapgren. "I could not agree more." He reached across the table to take her hand.

Cala sat silently for several minutes. Then she turned to me. "They'll need a ship."

"Who will?" I asked.

"These adults and their children. When you and I are killed by the damn Plezrite, I don't want them stuck on this rock forever."

I smiled. "I know just who to call. She's human, she has a fast ship, and she owes me a big favor."

"Why does she owe you a favor, Uncle?" asked Slapgren.

I leaned my head to the other two. "Not with the women-folk around. I'll tell you later." I winked, of course.

Someone, quite possibly *two* people, threw a large chunk of cheese at my head.

NINE

"So, Harhoff, I think you're getting full of yourself," Ardile remarked at mess that evening. They were old friends.

"How so? I'm a humble servant of His Imperial Lord," he replied, patting himself on the chest. "Tell me quickly how I stand out, and I'll remedy the flaw before more take note of it."

Others at the table chuckled.

"First, you are the youngest to be security chief of a vessel this size, and now you have a Descore to satisfy your every whim. Tell me, do you wipe your own ass nowadays?"

"Yes, in fact, I do. Are you volunteering to help, Ardy?"

This time, the others laughed heartily.

"No, I think ... er, what's that fellow's name again?"

"I trust you are referring to Jangir."

"Yes," he pointed energetically, "that's it. I think Jangir would be insulted if I tried to step ahead of him in that line."

More chuckles.

"I'll check with him, as you seem to be insistent."

The others were back to bawdy giggles.

"I mean, really, the goon is so energetic, so hard working for a Descore. It's hard to believe he was born to servitude."

"If a job is worth doing, it's worth doing well," replied Harhoff confidently.

"And I trust your rump is spotless," returned Ardile.

The joke had apparently died, since that brought nothing more from the crowd than soft grunts.

"I am glad Harhie here has gone to the trouble and expense to obtain a Descore," said Gardov, pointing his fork. "Lending him to me saves me the burden of so many chores."

"Hear, hear," said another, raising his glass. "To fewer chores and more sleeping."

"Really, you slackers. I was hoping you could devote more time to *work* if I let you borrow my manservant. To think, you piss away your newly gotten time sleeping. Well, I can tell you I'm shocked."

"Do tell. The bags under your eyes seem to have faded nicely since Jangir showed up," responded Gardov.

The group was back to pleasant chuckles at that slight.

"Do you know he was actually able to help organize my personal files?" Medilip nodded grandiosely. "Yes, I couldn't believe a Descore would be so well educated to understand systemization and computer protocol so thoroughly. It's *amazing* what they must learn in their schools these days. I should have thought it was nothing more than how to fold napkins and be generally agreeable."

"Yes, Harhoff, thank you again for your generosity," proclaimed Gardov with another toast. "To the easy life."

They all clinked glasses.

Harhoff knew none of them suspected he was toasting to the abundant intelligence he was gathering with his manservant's aid. It was almost too easy. Then again, these dupes were rather ripe for the picking. Harhoff was doing them a favor.

TEN

As Cala and I climbed aboard *Stingray*, I waved to Mirraya, Slapgren, and their kids. I also waved to Shielan. She'd agreed to stay with the Deft family until our return. If it became obvious we weren't coming back, she would transport them to Vorpace and help get them set up there. She was a good person. If Sapale would have been there, I do believe she would have felt less warmly toward Shielan. That'd be my guess.

One brief bout of nausea later, and we were back on the ground where we'd landed the first time. There was no Himanai or other greeting committee, since we popped into existence without notice. We quickly left the vortex and began walking in the direction Cala suggested, toward a high concentration of houses. She wanted to get some feel for the society before she was forced to confront it. I was in favor of anything that got me closer to retrieving Sapale. To tell the truth, I was itching for a fight. I'm certain Cala sensed that and made a point to assume the lead for this expedition. We both had a lot at stake, but I was the one with the hair-trigger attitude.

After fifteen minutes, a flock of individuals began

trailing behind us. A few were visants, but most were typical-looking Deft adults. They held behind us at a respectful distance, just matching our speed. I didn't get any sense of animosity on their part. Neither did I get the impression that they were curious. They were simple keeping an eye on us while waiting to see what we planned on doing. No one was visibly armed.

When we arrived at a large wooded square in the middle of town, Cala stopped, and the pack behind us caught up quickly. They halted twenty-five meters away and remained silent.

Cala turned to them. "We come in peace. We seek the recovery of our shipmate who we believe was detained by your people. Where is she to be found?"

No one answered. No one as much as shuffled their feet nervously. They just watched us.

"I wish to speak to anyone in a position of control. Where will I find that individual?" asked Cala calmly.

Again, there was no reaction from the crowd. The situation was getting creepy. How long would this standoff last?

As we waited a response, a bronze visant landed in front of us. She folded her wings back elegantly and sat back on her haunches. Once settled, she remained as silent as the rest of the observers.

"I am Calfada-Joric. I am a brindas from the planet Locinar. You are my distant cousins. I would speak to you." Then Cala rested back in an identical pose as the bronze dragon.

While the word *brindas* drew no physical response, the tension in the air spiked after she spoke it.

I do believe that if none of the Plezrite spoke, I'd still be standing in the stupid town square looking at two stubborn dragons. Cala was not going to say another peep until someone acknowledged her.

After ten minutes, the bronze beauty spoke. "I am Yisbid, Grand Visionary for this decade."

I had basically no clue what that meant. I guess that didn't matter too much, but I couldn't stop trying to figure out what she did for a living.

"My life is enhanced for knowing you, Yisbid," Cala said formally. She nodded slightly.

"As is mine in turn," replied Yisbid with a similar faint nod.

All right, there were some cultural similarities here. That suggested a good beginning was possible.

"I would know of the reason for your intrusion," said Yisbid formally. That remark wasn't very encouraging.

"I am certain you know it, pfutump. Why do you bother to ask the obvious?" replied Cala. Pfutump was a term roughly equivalent to *little girl*. It wasn't a pejorative, but neither was it a compliment.

"We are unaccustomed to the ways of the brindas. My apologies."

"Common courtesy is not the exclusive purvey of the brindas." Oh yeah, zap.

"Why are you here?"

"The human will recover his mate. She is in the large building down the street on the left-hand side, with the red banner above the door."

Must have been a brindas thing. I couldn't sense Sapale's location.

"She was held to ensure the mate would return. No harm has come to her."

"These things I know. Why is it important the human return if he was not welcome in the first place?"

"Now it is you who ask the painfully obvious."

"It is my way. I am simple. I will simply be treated well, with respect, and my wishes honored."

Man, she was ballsy.

"You do not rule here, witch. Mind your status."

"Pray you never learn of my full status, pfutump. Now, I am old, and I grow weary cackling in the streets with strangers. I will proceed to the building the prisoner is being held and retrieve her."

"She is not a prisoner, and you may not retrieve her."

"She is an honored guest whom you jealously guard because of your fondness for her?"

"She is, as I said, a detainee to ensure the return of the human."

"As he is here, your concerns are at an end."

"You cannot take her by force."

"Is that a statement of *hope* on your part or *ignorance?*"

"Neither. We will not be bullied by heretics."

"Excellent. Neither will I. If you see one, please alert me, and we shall both be rude to them."

"It is unwise to attempt a forceful rescue."

"Then how, child, will I gain the release of my quarry?"

"*If* she is to be released, it can only be through negotiation."

"Hmm. Let us all hope negotiations do the trick, for she *will* be released."

"Come with me. The High Council is prepared to meet with you."

"I seriously doubt that," replied Cala. "Come, Jon Ryan. We go to make nice."

"The human is forbidden to enter the chamber. No alien may attend."

"So, this human's mate, the very subject of my visit, will not be present?"

"Of course, she will. How can they discuss her if she isn't in evidence?"

"And since she is an alien and will attend, so will this

odd foreigner. Come, strange beast," she said over her shoulder to me. I liked her style under pressure.

We walked quickly to the building with the red pennant flopping in the breeze. Cala and I followed and entered single file. Our procession ended almost immediately in a large room directly off the foyer. Several visants sat around a round table, along with a few humanoid-formed Deft. Sapale was in a wooden juror's box built into a corner of the room. I waved to her energetically. She shrugged back at me.

"Council members, this is Calfada-Joric. She claims to be a brindas from a planet named Locinar. She has come to request the release of the detainee." Yisbid bowed deeply and withdrew. She closed the double doors as she left.

Immediately, a copper-colored visant spoke. "No one on this council hoped to ever have a member of the arcane religious order present herself to this esteemed body."

"Children often want more than they may receive," Cala said firmly.

"I will ask you to refrain from verbal jousting. This is a very serious matter, and your arrival is even more concerning."

"Will the one doing the asking care to identify herself, or is this to be a secret tribunal?"

"I am Wensist. I sit as council chair this year." Her voice was strained.

"Cousin Wensist, I will stop jousting when you do, not before."

"Are you here to *convert* us, witch?" shouted a humanoid several seats away.

"Not you, for certain, little brain. We heretics *do* have standards."

There was a buzz of chatter around the table.

"Enough. *Silence*," shouted Wensist. "I will ask the

members of this council to behave as grown adults, not frightened children. Mancope, please retract your accusation."

Uncertainly at first, the one who called Cala a witch spoke. "I retract my accusation. It was wrong of me to shout it out."

"And not wrong of you to hold it in your mouth?" asked Cala.

"Will the brindas please hold her obviously superior tongue in check?" asked Wensist with obvious frustration.

"As long as it suits my purposes, council chair."

"We assume you are here to beg for the freedom of this alien invader. I must warn you we are disinclined to allow her, or any of you, for that matter, to leave this planet and reveal the secret we have so jealously guarded for so long."

"There is much troubling in your statement, Wensist," Cala began. "First, I have never and will never beg for anything. Second, this alien invader, as you so harshly call her, is no threat to you. Third, do not mistake your inclination to be a force that will affect my personal resolve. Now we can bluster back and forth until dawn, but there is no gain in that. Alternately, we can talk as reasonable souls and accomplish something important."

"What important matters would you have us agree to?"

"Why, the unification of our two societies, naturally."

"You do wish to control our minds, dark witch of hell," shouted Mancope. He stood and pointed at her frantically.

"Will my second please remove that fool from the room?"

A visant rose and placed her talons on Mancope's shoulder. She pushed him forward out of the room. He didn't protest, probably because the talons would have just dug deeper.

"I apologize for his outburst. Mancope is a fine individual, but he fears change. He fears a change involving a religion all the much more," said Wensist.

"I would like to clarify something. I am a brindas. I have studied the mystical ways of all our people, the collective knowledge of our race. I am *not* a priestess, a religious zealot, nor an evangelical of any kind. I am not here to convert you, save your souls, or have you adore me."

"Then why are you here?" asked a visant seated next to Wensist.

"Brother Markum, I believe she has made that clear," interjected Wensist. "She is here to seek reconciliation, reunion."

"I also come to expedite the release of this human's mate." She pointed to me without looking at me.

"I will be honest and forthcoming on that point, Calfada-Joric," began Wensist. "We split from your society a very long time ago for powerful reasons we continue to hold. As the body charged with the preservation of this population, we are challenged to allow anyone knowing of our existence an opportunity to betray our location. If any of you three were to leave, ever, how do we know we could trust you to guard the secret?"

"You have nothing to fear. I can tell you this as a promise," responded Cala. "The human only wanted to confirm your presence so he could alert me. This he has done. I assure you he has no further interest in your world. He will not tell anyone of the Plezrite's position, because he will gain nothing passing such information along."

"And why is it this alien felt it was so important to tell a brindas of our existence? What does he think *you* will gain, *you* will accomplish with that information?" asked Wensist.

"He thinks the last handful of Deft might not die out as a species. That's what he hopes to see come to pass."

That brought mumbling and shuffling all around the table.

"Are you saying there are but a handful of your population remaining? That, before you answer, is difficult to accept or believe," queried Wensist.

"There are five of us left. One is pregnant. Soon we will be six Deft laboring in this sad life. Soon enough, there will be none."

More hushed mumbling circulated.

"Was there a plague? How could all the Deft be eliminated?"

"A conquering force named the Adamant. They murdered all the Deft but us. We numbered in the billions. They came, they slaughtered, and the Deft perished as a race."

"This is beyond tragic and, to be honest, difficult to believe."

"I have the power of zar-not. I offer to join minds with you freely, so you can see the bare truth of it, the stark reality."

Wensist thought a moment. He was clearly stunned. "I will speak for the council. The human female is free to leave, as is the male. We cordially invite you, Calfada-Joric, to remain as our treasured guest. We wish to more fully understand the matter of genocide and the reunification of our people."

"I accept your kind offer." She turned to me. "Go in peace, Jon Ryan. I shall rename you, sir. You are now to be known to the Deft as The Impossible Force. Tell the children I am well and will rejoin them soon. Your kind friend may return home as soon as she desires to."

With that, I helped Sapale jump over the railing of her box, and we walked very quickly to *Stingray*. We were back on Rameeka Blue Green in seconds. I was so relieved. Sapale, not so much. She was so mad at the Plezrite, and she wanted to go back and whoop some butt. Why? Because they called her human. Them were fighting words for my Kaljaxian princess. She was so darn cute it hurt.

ELEVEN

Sapale and I brought Mirri and Slapgren up to date. Then we took Shielan home to Vorpace. That way she could leave the ship behind for the Deft to use. She instructed both how to pilot the shuttle, including test flights, so they were comfortable using it. I also wanted to touch base with her big sister to see how the whole mutual defense thing was coming along.

By the way, I was totally blown away by Sapale's reaction to Shielan. In place of instinctive female rivalry, they got along like long lost friends. The two exchanged contact information, drank coffee, laughed together, and made plans to visit each other very soon. I mean, a *little* cat fighting over me might have been nice.

The three of us went right to Jonnaha's office after we landed. "Well look what ..." Jonnaha started to say. Then she saw Sapale come in last. "Well, what a surprise," she quickly censored herself.

"I called you not five minutes ago," Shielan said with a puzzled look.

"Yes, you did. I'm surprised it took you so long to get here. I'm dying for coffee, but I wanted to wait until you three got here." She thumbed a button on her desk. "Coffee for four, please." Then she sat back down and smiled like the politician she was.

"Jonnaha this is my wife, Sapale," I introduced.

They shook and exchanged brief pleasantries.

"Your wife. Ah, *newlyweds*?" Jonnaha asked with a squeak.

I looked at Sapale, who looked back at me. "What, two-billion years, give or take?"

She bobbed her head. "Give or take."

Then we both laughed. Shielan knew the whole story, but Jonnaha was compelled to ask, "What? Did I miss something funny?"

"We were only reunited since Jon first came here. He rescued my family from the Adamant conquest of my home world Kaljax," Sapale said with a cordial smile.

"Ah," Jonnaha replied pointing her fingers in opposite directions. "Newly reunited."

"Yeah," I moaned, "before that, she was with a real loser."

Jonnaha was starting to blush. "Who might that be?" she asked uncertainly.

"Me, from an alternate time line."

"Happens every day," observed Shielan.

"So, Jon, it's wonderful to see you. I assume things worked out well for your shapeshifter friends since you're all back here so soon."

"The two groups are talking. That's a start," I responded.

"Well, if there's anything else we can do, please don't hesitate to ask."

"Will do. So, how's your glue-together-a-resistance thing going?" I asked.

Her smile disappeared. "It's going, but slower than I

would have wished for. Life may be short, but politics are eternal."

"Tell us about it," replied Sapale.

That brought back a smile on Jonnaha's face. "I've browbeaten four additional planets into our loose coalition, so that makes seven so far."

"More prospects on the horizon? I hate to be the one to tell you, but I don't think any less than twenty systems working together will make a difference."

"That's what my military tells me, too. I have so many diplomats out there, it's like a snow storm in space." She seemed thoughtful a second. "We'll see. I *choose* to be optimistic."

"The alternative would be counterproductive," said Sapale.

"Are those cooperating actually cooperating?" I asked.

"Yes. The ones who are in are all in." She chuckled softly. "Those darn Gorgolinians turned out to be quite industrious." She grinned.

"Those are the fish tank dudes," I said to Sapale.

"They have turned thousands of natural and artificial satellites into mines with nukes. They can be set off manually or by proximity. When the Adamant approach, they're going to have quite the surprise waiting for them."

"Nice," I replied. "Just their planet?"

"No, that's the amazing part. They mined many planets' satellites, even those groups not fully onboard yet. They also scattered booby-trapped debris well out into interstellar space."

"How about the robots?"

"Our partners are far and away the most industrious."

"The robots or the people?" I asked.

"Are you kidding? The robots. The latest craze among the idiotic humanoids is to wear Adamant costumes."

We both guffawed.

"Yes, they're all doing it. When they learned of the imminent invasion, they jumped on that bandwagon. Their theory is that to understand how to defeat the Adamant they need to *be* the Adamant. You know, really get into their heads."

"And if they do get overrun, maybe they'll blend in," I observed with a wicked grin.

"Seriously, I heard someone mention that when I last visited the planet."

"So, the robots are taking matters seriously?" asked Sapale.

"Yes, indeed they are. They came up with a positively frightening war-droid. I've seen holos of its test runs. Impressive firepower and shielding. Those bad boys are going to put a hurt on the Adamant."

"How's production?"

"They're flying off the assembly lines. There are hundreds of thousands of functional units already. If production holds, they promise to export them to all allied worlds after they hit two million units for their own defense."

"When do they estimate that?" I queried.

"Two to three months," she replied.

"That would be *epic*," I responded. "It could be a game changer."

"The best part is that they programmed no self-preservation algorithms into the war-droids. They are equipped with Ais, but they're absolutely fearless."

"Excellent. I might want to get a couple for home defense," I remarked.

"No, we're not having a mindless killing machine in our yard. The neighbors will be upset enough about you already," quipped Sapale.

"What? I'm a great neighbor. They've always *loved* me."

"Need I say anything more than Fourth of July or Christmas?"

"Those are isolated events. Anyway, I'm not that into holidays anymore."

She rolled all four eyes. It was cute.

"Can we help in any way?" I asked Jonnaha.

"Sure, but don't you have some deadline or something?"

"I do indeed."

"I'd hate to ruin those plans," she replied.

"I'd hate for them to be ruined, too. Really, I'd be bummed."

"How much longer until whatever ... you know, how long do you have left?"

I sighed. "Just under three months."

"It seems overly generous of you to offer then, I think."

"Yeah, you're probably right."

"Probably?" shot back Sapale. "No, it is. You've given already and a million times more. No, *now* you work on your Jon Plan, whatever that might be, because you won't tell me what it is."

Somebody was angry with me.

"May we help?" asked Jonnaha.

"I wish you could," I responded, shaking my head. "Oh, how I wish someone could."

TWELVE

"You festering green puddle of puss," seethed EJ, "you think I'm hurting you now? Don't tell me where Sapale is, and I'll crank it up ten notches."

"Si ... Sir, there was an invasion. Houses and people were exploding all over the place. I swear I never saw her after she left for the caves with you." Caryp's cousin Nishap-ser was telling the truth. But, as with so many aspects of life, the truth mattered not at all. For one thing, EJ was only partially asking. He was mostly venting.

Nishap-ser was the fifth relative he'd interrogated. Four were now deceased. One was on his way, but EJ had learned nothing except that he had a lot of rage to vent. He wanted to get at the boiling-pot-of-hog-shit Jon "Goodie Two-Shoes" Ryan more than he'd wanted anything in eons. Yes, Sapale would pay dearly for her part in their treachery. But EJ had a special spot in his hatred for the astronaut he'd once been. That abomination would come to an end if it was the last thing EJ ever did. Then he'd kill Sapale. No, he reflected, he'd make the mucus milk shake watch her die, then he'd melt him from the toes up. Wait, wait. He could melt them simultaneously. Yes. They could watch each other literally disappear in agony. Resolution was so reassuring. EJ leaned back against the wall and smiled.

Then he finished off Nishap-ser, who'd begun to whimper most annoyingly.

Pisswad, as he had nicknamed Jon, and Sapale might have gone to ground. That'd make them much harder to find, but not impossible. But he had to think they were off doing good, making the galaxy a better and safer place in which to live and raise a family. The sops couldn't stop being pathetic, even to save their own hides. EJ had posted a major fortune in reward money for any information as to their whereabouts. So far, a month had passed without a peep. He needed better informants. Competent help was so hard to find.

Where would he go if he were Pisswad? Not Azsuram or Kaljax. No, they were completely under Adamant domination. Earth, as a ruse? No, EJ knew he'd been there recently and would think of that. Oowaoa? Possibly, but EJ had still not discovered where that planet of smug pimples was. He did decide to double his standing reward for information on that rat trap. Even if the pair of traitorous cowards weren't there, it would be gratifying to vent on the pompous Deavoriath. There existed no punishment they did not deserve. He'd be doing God's work.

Was it possible, even conceivable, that Pisswad was in cahoots with the Adamant? If he was hiding amongst them, EJ would never be able to touch an artificial hair on his head. In the million years he'd seen the pissy mongrels rise to power, he'd almost never been able to recruit, bribe, or turn an Adamant. Self-righteous pieces of dog shit. The closest he ever came were those two Midriack guards on *Excess of Nothing,* but one dumbass had gone and gotten himself killed by his own clan leader for some reason EJ could never pin down. Then the other clammed up like the proverbial sphinx. Oh, how he hated every single living creature in the universe. And two non-living robots even more than all the rest combined.

"What do you think?" he asked Nishap-ser's corpse. "Should I interview a few more relatives or try another approach while my dignity's still intact?"

He received no response.

"My thinking exactly. I'll shake down a few of my slimy information merchants instead and see if I can't catch a break." To no verbal prompting, he responded, "Why? Hell, because I feel lucky, that's why."

Nishap-ser continued to say nothing.

"Look, I hate to kill and run, but ..." EJ paused and cocked an ear to his victim. "That's great, I'm glad you understand. You, too, pal."

THIRTEEN

Sapale and I were lounging in bed after another make-up-for-lost-time session. Talk about warm glow. She lifted her head and set it on my chest. "You know you're going to tell me, so come on. What are you planning to do to get out of your debt?"

I propped up on my elbows. Looking straight down at her, I gave her a kiss. "It's not that I don't trust you, and it's not that I don't value your input. Do you believe me on that much?"

Reluctantly she pouted and replied, "Yes, I do." She propped up on her elbows and looked at me very intently. "Then why can't you tell me?"

"There's only one possible way I see me coming out of this in one piece. It involves a critical twist." I hesitated. "Dearest love, you know EJ is out there and hunting for us like a pair of golden geese. He's good, damn good."

"Tell me about it."

"He might capture you, which, as much as I hate to say it or think it, is a possibility."

"Then he might torture me and find out your plan.

But why would he suspect you had a plan in the first place?"

"He doesn't, but he definitely knows I want to take him out. The "plan" he'd want to know about would be mine for that purpose."

"And if he got that information out of me ..."

"He'd screw up my plan, and I'll have to take the fall I agreed to."

"Well, I'll just ask that you tell me as soon as you can, all right?"

"My word of honor," I said crossing where my heart wasn't.

She gave me a peck on the cheek and bounded out of bed.

"You're still miffed at me, aren't you?" I asked.

"Only a little." She smiled back at me. "If it were this much more," she pinched her fingers almost closed, "I wouldn't be doing this."

She flung herself into my arms, knocking me back on the pillows.

I raised my hands and clapped. The lights went off.

In the mess later, we were drinking coffee and silently enjoying the good life. "When it's over, my debt that is, what do you want to do?" I asked her.

"You mean *after* you suffer for all eternity?" She gave me a precious crooked smile.

"Will you wait for me, candle in the window and all?"

"Yes, as long as a chastity belt isn't required, too."

I popped air in my cheek and quickly twitched my head. "I don't know if I can sign off on that clause. My people will get back to your people, okay?"

"So, what do I want to do, *assuming* you are free to do it with me three months from now?"

"Yeah."

"List off the options, and I'll tell you which I like the most."

"That sort of violates the what do *you* want to do part of my query."

"Silly human. I don't care what I do as long as it's with you."

"Aw shucks, talk about putting me on the spot." I looked away, embarrassed.

"You know quite well what we'll be doing. We'll be fighting the Adamant like demons from hell."

"Did you have to use that analogy?"

She looked up, replaying her remark in her head. "Oops. Bad taste, right?"

"Anyway, you were saying?"

"Whatever the outcome of the battle along the frontier, the Adamant will still be everywhere. Your goal has been to destabilize them with a death blow. But it will take a very long time for that death to come. You and I will do everything in our power to hasten their demise, but it will be a long and hard struggle."

"It's looking that way."

"Has your contact amongst the Adamant given you any feedback lately?"

"Nah, nothing. Last time he secreted me a report, it sounded like same old same old. He *is* encouraged by the rebellious murmurs he hears. But there are no sustained changes or shifts."

"Do you think his approach is valid?"

I rocked my head. "Maybe. I had the AIs run a ton of sims. Most support the notion that an unstable empire will implode due to pent up forces. The personal quests for power and the usual political dissent that any large group spawns seem to make it inevitable."

"So, we fight for the good cause."

"Again."

She started to giggle. "And again, and again."

"You'd think two grown people would learn, right?"

"Hey, who you calling people? I'm not a person. I'm a Kaljaxian alpha-bitch."

"You want'a fight about that?"

She set her mug down gently. "Why yes, I believe I do."

I clapped my hands.

She clapped hers.

FOURTEEN

Garustfulous, or rather Jangir, sat in the dark room hunched over the display screen. The yellow-green computer light made his grin of self-satisfaction look as twisted and convoluted as his feelings were at that moment. He had used Naford's retinal pattern to unlock all the files the third officer of the vessel could access. Those were most of the tactical and many of the secure political files the ship was privy to. Jangir was a naughty kid in a candy shop of espionage. Unfortunately, he'd had to separate Naford's head from his body to do so, but that was now Harhoff's problem, not his. Their working agreement was that the amoral Jangir would collect intel. The only slightly principled Harhoff would cover tracks and forward the information. He'd never been called upon to cover such glaring, bloody tracks before. Jangir really liked that part of his act.

He had a visual recorder copy everything he viewed. He didn't want to plug in an electric component because such an action might be detected. Someone would correctly suspect that what happened actually did take place. Jangir prided himself on being ...

What? This had to be incorrect. He scrolled up and read back down. He skipped to the bottom to see who signed the order. Spirits and Forces, it was Lesset himself. This was bad. This was *very* bad. Jangir made a second image of the entire document and shut the system down. He leaned back in the chair and breathed out heavily. Ticks and worms, he thought. This changed everything.

FIFTEEN

"Jon, as wonderful as it is to see you again, really, it's hardly been a couple weeks," said Jonnaha with a puzzled look on her face. "Ah, may I offer you coffee or tea?"

"Both," I said. "Strong and lots of them. It's going to be a late night."

She glanced at her wrist watch. "Jon, it's only ten in the morning."

"I know."

"This sounds bad," she responded.

"It is not bad," replied Sapale.

"Oh good. You had me scared for a mom—"

"It's much worse than bad. *Completely* worse," I tossed in.

She slumped just a little in her chair, then stiffened. "I'll summon my key personnel. They'll be here in less than twenty minutes."

I shook my head. "Make it ten. This is epic."

Within fifteen minutes, all her heads of department and confidential advisors were in the Ready Room around a massive table. The air was tense. It was going to get a whole lot worse once I started talking. I really wished this wasn't coming down. No one in this room, no one in this galactic sector, deserved the news I was about to drop on them.

"We're all here, General Ryan. Why don't you begin?" Jonnaha said formally and with foreboding.

"Thank you. I have received a report that the Adamant are advancing their timeline for attacking this sector. This region *was* in the five-to-ten-year zone. It has been reprioritized. It has just been moved to the top of the list. It is the *next* area to be assimilated." I let the gravity of that sink in a bit. "Whereas you had years to prepare before, you now have weeks. Maybe they will delay a few months if you're extremely lucky. My intelligence is deficient on this aspect. But you will be attacked with the full might of the Empire very shortly." I sat back down.

The room was as quiet as a long-abandoned mausoleum. No one as much as shifted nervously in their chair or reached for a drink of water.

Finally, Jonnaha spoke, though hesitantly at first. "Are you confident the intelligence is reliable and correct?"

I sighed. "Yes. One hundred percent."

"Not that it truly matters, General Ryan, but do you know why the Adamant moved us to the top of the list?" asked a man two seats to Jonnaha's right wearing a military uniform with a ton of fruit salad on his chest.

"Yes, I do. They either have excellent intelligence services of their own, or they have a network of spies. Somehow they became aware of your attempts to put up a unified defense and felt it was prudent to deny you that opportunity."

There was profound silence again.

The same man spoke. "Wasn't it *your* idea to ally ourselves against the Adamant's future assault?"

"Admiral Halkins, I will not tolerate that remark or it's incendiary implications. You will *apologize* to General

Ryan immediately and *formally* withdraw that insult."
Man-o-man, Jonnaha was hot.

"It was a legitimate military question," he defended.
"We need to understand exactly what it is we face and
know precisely who our enemy is."

Shielan rose. As coolly as an ice cube in an igloo she
stated, "Madame Prime Minister, permission to shoot
Admiral Halkins here and now." She slipped her hand
inside her jacket where her pistol was holstered.

Jonnaha waved her palm down. "Denied. We are all
here for the same reason. If we can't speak our minds, we
really stand no chance of success. Admiral, I am still
waiting for your apology." The look she gave him. Wow, it
was impressive.

"I don't need an apology," I said. "The dude spoke out
of fear and ignorance. Times as they are, it's perfectly
understandable that an armchair warrior would get
jumpy."

Halkins started to rise, then thought better of it. He'd
insulted me, and I'd insulted him back. We were enemies,
and it was a draw.

Jonnaha shook her head slowly, and Shielan snickered
a bit too loudly.

"If you insist. Moving on, are there any *other*
questions?"

"I have one. General Franklin Pierce here,
commander of joint planetary forces. Do you have any
idea what formation the enemy will use or which solar
systems will be targeted first?"

"No, but I have a lot of experience fighting them. I
believe they will attack all targets simultaneously with
immense force."

"But, even if they only target the systems with formal
mutual defense commitments, that would be twelve
different solar systems spanning nearly four parsecs. If

they mean to take the entire five-to-ten-year zone at once, their numbers would have to be unimaginable."

"And they are. Look, the Adamant are like the sand on a big beach. They are uncountably numerous and value each other's lives as much as those grains of sand do. There's a very good reason they've been as successful as they have been."

"Is there a winning strategy?" asked a suit to Jonnaha's immediate left.

"I do not know."

"What can we do?" he asked, clearly near tears.

"Fight. That's all anyone can ever do. You have had a few months to prepare that you wouldn't have had otherwise. That's a plus. The war-droids of Langir will now be a real factor in this fight. But you fight. The alternatives are to run or to lie down and wait for the juggernaut to grind you into the dirt."

"Is flight an option?" someone called out.

"No, of course it is not," shouted Jonnaha. "Come on, people, let's keep our heads attached for a little while longer, shall we?"

"But ... but I mean if General Ryan had a secret plan to move Sotovir or transport its pop—"

"He does not. If you grasp at one more imaginary straw, Phelps, I'll have you thrown out of the room. Is that clear? I value the input of the Department of Food Integrity, but I will not have you derail our planning."

"Yes, ma'am," he whimpered. I hoped that idiot wasn't called upon to aid in the defense of the civilization. He'd cause a mess when he lost bowel and bladder control as the first Adamant rose above the horizon.

"So, they're coming soon, they're coming in devastating numbers, and we're as prepared as we're going to be. That about sum it up, Jon?" asked Jonnaha.

"Yes."

"Do you have any specific thoughts, recommendations, or prayers to offer?"

"Not just now."

"Then I thank you, Sapale, and your spies for giving us as much notice as possible. You're welcome to remain, or you may go. Naturally we would appreciate your extensive familiarity with our foe as we plan."

"We will stay," replied Sapale. "We want to help as much as possible. Plus, I personally would not like to turn my back on that pig but keep him where I can see him." Yeah, she pointed at Admiral Fart Cloud. Nice. You-know-who snickered again.

The meeting dragged on for twelve hours. A few potty breaks were the only respites. Food was brought in and eaten while working. The diplomats of many other systems joined in at odd intervals. It was controlled chaos, at best. The bare bones of a mutual plan were outlined and tentatively agreed upon, pending each government's review. That meant we all did a lot of work that would only possibly be adopted. But it was a start. It also served to formally light as big a fire as there was ever going to be under everyone's collective backsides. It was go time, and at least that message was loud, clear, and undeniable.

I only wished they stood the remotest chance of success. But I knew better.

SIXTEEN

The Lead Point Room was packed. High Wedge Lesset, Prime of the Secure Council, sat at the middle of a long metal table. He was flanked by the other eleven members of the council. Their raised stage gave them an excellent perspective of the Supreme Directive Wall off to their right. They also had a full view of the auditorium seats that ascended to the left. All one hundred and fifty seats were taken by senior command officers. Hushed chatter produced a charge of palpable excitement in the air. This was what the Adamant lived for. Conquest, domination, and the disbursement of death.

"All right, come to order. We have much to do and much more to accomplish," announced Vice Prime of the council Kemflode.

The room instantly fell silent.

Lesset rose to his full height and rested his arms on a short podium. "Fellow leaders of the Adamant Empire, welcome to our last meeting before we begin the assimilation of twelve new systems. Glory be to His Imperial Lord Palawent."

The crowd roared back a cheer for the emperor, who

never attended these important meetings. It had been discovered many years before that when the emperors did attend, they mistakenly thought they were in charge and that their opinions mattered. Such distractions were no longer welcomed or tolerated.

"As you know, our last campaign was perfectly successful. We destroyed the militaries of six worlds in five systems in one fell swoop."

Another cheer rose up, this time for Lesset.

"Those missions are now in their mop-up phases. We are now free to proceed to the next obstacles to our domination. As you know, the emperor, in his infinite wisdom, has instructed us to skip over a few minor pockets of resistance. He has foreseen a growing threat in the Gamma-Epsilon Sector, near the galactic edge. Our new mission is to extinguish that threat before it may be allowed to become significant. All praise be to Emperor Palawent."

A lesser cheer rose up in response. Almost no one in the room gave a ragged chew toy for the imperial waste of space.

"I have given individual orders to the Wholes who will lead our attack. Wedge Leaders will receive their assignments from their specific Wholes immediately following this assembly. Our conquest will begin in two days at Standard Dawn, as usual. I will expect all victories to be accomplished in less than *three* days on *all* fronts on *all* planets."

That brought a rush of murmurs from the crowd. Three days was an unusually short time to crush an entire planet's resistance. A week was a short time. Three days was unprecedented. It signaled that the Secure Council wanted these planets to suffer mightily. They were to never know what hit them. They were to be an example of the brute and brutal force of the Adamant Empire. The bloodlust that was typically high at these meetings shot to redline. Everyone wanted to lock their jaws on the throats of their enemies.

"I would wish you all luck, but you do not need such a crutch. You are the best warriors, the best commanders, and the best *killers* to ever prowl the galaxy. I would feel sorry for what your victims are about to suffer, but they are beneath us and below our contempt. Now go forth and *kill*. Go forth and *slaughter*. Go forth and drink the blood of those who *insult* the Adamant by existing. Show *no* mercy. Give *no* quarter. Leave *nothing* living in the wake of our tidal wave of *victory*."

Everyone rose and cheered with abandon. All-encompassing death was so glorious. It defined what it was to be happy, to be fulfilled. It defined what it was to be Adamant.

SEVENTEEN

"Cala, we understand your position. Truly, we *hear* you. But you must understand this issue from the Plezrite point of view." Yisbid struggled to conceal her growing frustration. "This touches on the very reason we used our collective magic to remove our solar system from the galaxy. We wish not only to be left *alone,* but we wish to be *unburdened* by galactic politics and chicanery."

"But I'm not certain you *have* a choice. Any choice. Yes, as far as any of us know, you're invisible to the Adamant, but that doesn't mean you *are.* Even Jon Ryan, with his unprecedented spy network, can't tell us for certain. You may be fooling yourselves, deluding yourselves into not only a false sense of having no moral obligation to help the rest of us, but a false sense of security."

"Mistress Cala, we have discussed those very issues in our councils, as you well know. *We*, as Yisbid just stated, have heard your requests and warnings. But the results of our debates have been insufficient to change our fundamental philosophy. We want to continue being who we are and go along doing what we have for a very long time," said Himanai with thinly veiled contempt.

"Translation: *your* problems are not *our* problems," Cala hissed back angrily.

"I am very sorry you see it that way," responded Yisbid. "I feel your pain. I wish reality was different than it is, but it is not. We are, for the last time, unable to help you fight the Adamant. You and your students are welcome to move here and become valued members of our society, of our culture. But we will not offer you military aid."

Cala rested back on her haunches, in a defensive stance. "You use interesting words, Yisbid. Do you fully hear them?"

"I know what I said. Please point out where you think I might be enlightened."

"Prescient, indeed, are your thoughts."

"Are you baiting us or playing a riddle game to insult us?" Himanai asked sharply.

"I speak now only to the Grand Visionary, not the rabid cow."

"Well, I—" Himanai spat out as she stood.

"Sit," instructed Yisbid, setting a hand on her arm to restrain her. "I am listening, Cala."

"Do you know why your title is Grand Visionary? I'm fairly certain you do not."

"I am the leader of the Plezrite for a ten-year period this cycle. That individual is called the Grand Visionary." She spoke cautiously, knowing there was some trapdoor awaiting her.

"*Bah.* You don't. The office of Grand Visionary is ancient. It was in place when our two people were still one. Back then, it indicated which Deft brindas was responsible for using the Vision."

"I've never heard of this nonsense," Himanai said through clenched teeth.

"No. Cows, rabid or otherwise, need only chew cud and fart."

"Cala, please excuse my assistant. She is young and does not honor you as she should. Please proceed," responded Yisbid.

"The Vision is a thing. It is a power. The Grand Visionary was charged with using it for the benefit of the community."

"You make it sound dangerous," she replied.

"Oh, it is not. But the *knowledge* it brings, that can be more dangerous than a poisoned knife at your throat."

"What is the Grand Visionary supposed to see that I'm unaware of?"

"The future, child. Your job is to see the future on behalf of your people."

"That doesn't sound very dangerous, you old witch," shot back Himanai.

Yisbid spun on her. "Leave this instant, rotten one." Once Himanai had reluctantly skulked out of the room, Yisbid continued. "I clearly do not see into the future."

"But *I* do," replied Cala.

Yisbid stiffened. "What is your point?"

"As Grand Visionary, I would show you the future. It would then be yours to judge whether the Plezrite chose wisely or chose poorly today."

"That's utter nonsense," replied Yisbid with obvious uncertainty.

"How so, child?"

"You will place some image in my mind that affirms your contention. The future is not ours to know."

"Spoken by the non-brindas in the room. As to placing a favorable image in your mind, I can assure you I will not. That, by the way, is a trivial thing to do. I can do it without The Vision. Here, I feel a demonstration is in order. What is your favorite dessert?"

"Arch-fudge. Why?"

"And where would you love to eat it? What special place if you had your choice of all locations?"

"My mate's arms. Again, I ask ..."

Yisbid fell mute. Her eyes glazed over, and her breath began to become labored. Then she gasped and jerked her head backward.

"Ho ... how did you do that?" she challenged.

"By the powers controlled by a brindas. Wasn't the candy delectable?"

Yisbid remained silent a moment. "Yes, better than any I've ever had."

"So, now you know that if I wanted to place an image in your mind, I could at any time. I will escort you to a vision of the future if you are brave enough to see it."

Again, she reflected a few seconds. "Very well. I do not want to make a mistake I would come to regret. How dangerous is this journey?"

"It depends on the traveler. One who is strong, fearless, and knows herself is generally safe."

"And what of lesser mortals?"

"They go stark-raving mad when they see the future."

"When may we begin?"

"Come stand by my side, and we shall sally forth."

Yisbid came around the table and stood next to Cala. The brindas took her companion's hand. "Close your eyes and clear your mind."

"How long will—"

Yisbid did not finish the question. Their minds were no longer locked in the present.

Seconds later Yisbid gasped like she was drowning. Cala opened her eyes and relaxed her body, seemingly unaffected by whatever had just transpired. Yisbid crumpled to her knees and covered her face forcefully with both hands. She began to softly wail.

Someone rushed to her side. "Yisbid, are you all right? Can I help? You there," she called out to a couple of male bystanders, "come help me get her to the doctor."

The men rushed forward. They each grabbed under a shoulder and tugged at the Grand Visionary.

Yisbid shot to her feet and shook her would-be helpers off roughly. "I'm fine. Release me."

Everyone backed away slightly.

Yisbid turned to Cala. "Did you see what I saw?"

"I was there also. I saw everything."

"But how?"

"What did you see, Yisbid?" asked someone close.

"I saw our planet. It was on fire."

"But then you didn't see the future, only a vision. No planet, Nocturnat included, can be engulfed in flames. There is no air in space to sustain such a blaze."

"It was on fire, but not with a natural one. The flames were of our own making."

"No," screamed another person. "Why would we set fire to our own world?"

"To kill the Adamant who defiled Nocturnat's sacred soil. They had vanquished the Plezrite. We chose mutual death over servitude."

"No," the man gasped softly. "When?"

Cala finished the thought for Yisbid. "Very *soon*, child."

EIGHTEEN

I was on Sotovir when the all-out Adamant assault began. It was just thirteen days after I broke the news to the leaders of Vorpace. Right about when I expected it. I'd fought countless wars in every imaginable setting. I'd struggled against the Adamant personally for a couple years. Still, I was overwhelmed and awestruck with their battle plan. It was truly impressive.

Adamant warships of every imaginable size and kind simultaneously popped up over Sotovir and eleven other planets. Some were specialized in planetary bombardment. Those were massive. Others were smaller, yet still huge, and designed to fight ship to ship in space, defending against any aerial responses. Still others were stripped down troop carriers with little more than standing room for millions upon millions of ground assault personnel.

I watched from the safety of *Stingray,* perched on a hill, with a partial membrane up. Their initial action was to begin raining fire from above. So many plasma bolts and metal balls were dropped that the entire atmosphere flashed into a brilliant waterfall of death and destruction.

The ground rose up in anguish, hurled itself into the sky only to be pounded back down by the relentless onslaught from above. That softening up lasted fifteen minutes. The damage caused was stunning, and I was on Sotovir. It was the planet best suited to weathering such a withering attack. The fish-tank Gorgolinians had little construction on the surface since their lives were spent underground or in caves. As a result, the Adamant explosions caused much less damage than on, say, the human world of Vorpace. But less was only relative. Gigantic craters and smoking ruins were everywhere.

The moment the bombardment ceased, I saw the landing craft drop from the sky. It turned to twilight there were so many. Within a couple of minutes, the hatches burst open and Adamant gushed out, as if shot from a water cannon. With their legendary organization and discipline, they moved quickly into ranks and advanced to their assigned targets. If it wasn't so horrific, it would have been marvelous to witness.

Then the Gorgolinians counterattacked. They sprang from the ground like crabs on a beach. They pulled countless Adamant down holes, never to emerge again. The fish tanks proved to be a hell of a lot tougher than I would have guessed. Salvoes of plasma bolts hit them, but they kept firing and seizing Adamant. Once they had a dog in their clutches, he was a goner. The Gorgolinians had scissor-shaped claws that snipped their foes in half like they were paper dolls. With their hard shells, they didn't favor taking cover, so they advanced rapidly into the Adamant ranks.

For just a moment, I thought their physical advantages might swing the battle. But that moment passed soon enough. Slowly, the Gorgolinians fell or were blown up. The Adamant had figured out several of their weaknesses and exploited them with a vengeance. In only a few minutes, there were few fish tanks left standing, as far as I could see.

The Adamant units regrouped and ran toward their original targets. That's when a second wave of Gorgolinians sprang from the ground like a farmer's worst nightmare. They hit the Adamant from behind, totally by surprise. Though the canovir buckled, they did not panic. With their ingrained discipline, they rallied and pushed their attackers back. Another swarm of Gorgolinians then rose at the backs of the turned Adamant. They tried a pincer maneuver to force them into hand-to-hand combat. They figured that in close quarters the enemy would be less able to use their blasters.

Slowly, the locals gained an upper hand. Finally, I couldn't make out sharp ranks. The combatants were blended in chaos. It was like a blender with living beings tossed in by the bucketful. I think if that battle ended then, the Gorgolinians would have won. But more and more landing crafts deposited endless reinforcements. The whirling combat ended when the recently arrived Adamant began firing indiscriminately into the melee, killing friend and foe with equal ferocity. Within a few minutes, nothing moved in the combat zone. With grim intensity, the ring of Adamant reinforcements closed to the center of the circle, shooting anyone still alive on either side. Their tactic obviated the need to medically evacuate their own troops. That would have distracted from the primary mission, which wasn't to win with minimal casualties. No, it was to win, period.

In less than an hour, the fighting was over. Tens of thousands of Adamant advanced to sweep areas of habitation. Others labored to stack the dead for cremation. Still others began establishing command centers, outhouses, and large mess and dormitory tents.

Pops of plasma fire flared to life occasionally as the

unstoppable force advanced. I waited around just long enough for them to have finished occupying most of the structures. Then I blasted them and any occupants into the rewards of the afterlife. Once they identified me and a bombardment began, I folded away, back to Vorpace. In no way did the pittance of damage I did make me feel any better. It certainly made no difference. Damn, the Adamant were good at war. Double damn them.

NINETEEN

I folded back into real space at a predesignated location near the capital. Sapale had remained behind to help coordinate the defense of Vorpace. Unlike with the Gorgolinians, the humans here had two important new weapons. A small number of membrane generators and a few war-droids from Langir. The leaders of Sotovir had refused any such toys, preferring to battle in their traditional manner.

Deploying shield units was very problematic. I didn't have time to prepare many. The bigger issue was that none of them could fall into the Adamant's grimy paws. That technology would be way too powerful in their already indomitable armamentarium of domination. Any I deployed had to be paired with an AI in control of a powerful self-destruct explosive. But, key facilities such as major hospitals and troop aggregations could be protected from the initial bombardment. The handful of war-droids were to be set against the Adamant as soon as they landed with the hope of unnerving them, or at least disrupting their ranks.

When I arrived, the orbital assault had been

concluded, and the landing craft had just coughed out the first wave of foot soldiers. The delay stemmed from the greater number of major cities and the presence of the membranes. At first, the Adamant didn't seem to understand why the structures they targeted didn't go boom. Consequently, they addressed prolonged fire at them before they abandoned that approach. Lucky me, I got to see the Adamant victory emerge from brave yet futile resistance all over again.

This time, however, I was not going to be a bystander. Facing eternal torment in the very near future, I was planning on being the local franchise of the Hell On Wheels Death Delivery System. *Oorah.*

"How did it go?" asked Sapale as she rushed to embrace me.

Jonnaha and her cabinet remained where they were, watching the unfolding mayhem.

"Better than I would have guessed," I replied, pulling her in tightly.

She lifted her head from my chest. "You mean they held the Adamant off?" She was totally shocked.

"No. They just died a lot slower and took a lot more dogs with them than I anticipated. In the end, it was the massacre we all expected."

I felt her slump in my arms.

"But this time, The Demon of Death Jon Ryan is taking up a personal collection. They don't stand a chance."

"Wow. Where's my handheld when I want a selfie with the legend before his next miracle? Photo's gonna be valuable after you single-handedly slay *that* beast."

I kissed her forehead. "Showtime." We parted, and I stepped over to Jonnaha. "How's it looking?"

"Grim. Jon I never thought I'd watch my combined

armed forces march off to certain death. I hate the feeling. I *hate* the Adamant."

"You're welcome to step in line behind me. Look, you didn't ask for this. They forced it on you. Your job is to make them pay as dearly as possible. That's all any of us can do."

I heard a metallic squeak and looked to find the source. It was one of the pair of war-droids positioned against the far wall in the room. It must have sneezed. They were placed here in reserve, anticipating the worst. That's when I noticed Shielan. Gone was her silk suit. She was in full army regalia from flak jacket to spit-polished boots. She sported twin plasma rifles and a look on her face that could kill.

"Hey kid," I said to her, kissing her Kevlar helmet, "you look different. Have you lost weight or what?"

She winked. "No, I just copied the pinup I had of you in my bedroom. I'm a killing machine like my hero. *Surar.*"

"Okay, nice, but you gotta get it right. Repeat after me. It's *oorah*, not *surar*."

"Do you have somewhere to go and die?" she asked.

"Yes. Why?"

"Then I suggest you go there so I don't feel the need to kill you here, sir."

I gave her a salute and walked back to Sapale. "I'm leaving the vortex. When the time comes, use it to evacuate as many as you can." I turned and pointed at Shielan. "Just don't bring her. She smells funny."

"No, no, and no. That wasn't the plan. You take the cube. There are several ships here if we need to evacuate."

"You know what the best part of being the general in charge of a military operation is? Go on, take a wild guess."

"Someone else cuts your meat for you at dinner?" she replied with a puzzled look.

"No, but that's nice, too. No, the best part is during that all too brief period you can tell your wife what to do."

She started to say something but relaxed back into silence.

"There's my girl," I said, tapping her cute little nose. "Honey, if I mosey down the hill or fly to the far side of the planet, it doesn't matter. I'm going to be killing Adamant, and they're probably going to kill me back. Location isn't that important." I smiled. "Your safety, however, is."

"I love you," she said to my face.

"Crap, I was just about to say that. You stole my thunder."

"Jon."

"Yes."

"Please leave now."

"Sure thing."

I jogged out the door. A small squad of soldiers fell in behind me, and we rattled out the door and down the hill. The membrane pulsed to allow us through and then zapped back into existence as soon as the last woman was past. I could immediately smell the meat-locker in the air. War. The same old same old.

Our path led to the outskirts of the capital city. It was currently free of the Adamant horde, but the sound of intense firefight was not far off. We advanced in the open, covered by my personal membrane. Our weapons were set on visual frequencies, so we could fire though the shield. I had to hope the Adamant hadn't accounted for that yet and would be using standard plasma guns. Straggling refugees moved past us as quickly as they could, but at that point, any sane person had left the city for the established shelters in the country. We couldn't stop to offer help. Our mission was strictly offensive, not humanitarian.

First contact came quickly. We rounded a corner, and a huge tank was on top of us. It fired three quick plasma blasts. It waited for the dust to clear to verify we were little cinders. By the time they could see my squad, we had scrambled halfway up the vehicle. Several detonators were magnetically clipped on, and we vaulted off. As we ran for cover in a building, a plasma bolt slammed into the membrane, and the tank erupted in flames.

One of my team started to cheer, but I stared him down quickly. He got the message. Celebrate if we win. Otherwise keep fighting.

Backup foot units converged on us from three sides. We started shooting. A few Adamant face-planted from their full sprint. Others fanned out and took cover. It took them a few minutes, but then they began bypassing the membrane with handguns adjusted to the correct frequency.

"They're onto us," I shouted into my headset. "Dropping the membrane *now*. Switch to plasma weapons and spread out some. Everyone stay with the squad and watch our flanks."

The others moved a few meters away and hunkered down. Once the enemy noted our weapons had changed, they knew the shield was down. Hundreds flooded the street and charged with a deafening howl. My team laid down a torrent of plasma, but the fallen dogs were crushed to the asphalt by the advancing wave slamming over their corpses.

They'd trained on this suicidal attack. Crazy sonsabitches. I swept my finger laser at knee height and each advancing row of dogs toppled in agony. But still they came. We began falling back rapidly, keeping up our fire the entire time. We barely kept pace. I tossed three thermite grenades to the front, middle, and rear of the onslaught.

Boom.

Boom.

Boom.

Bodies arced upward, and those not airborne fell like bowling pins.

In the confusion, I yelled into my headset. *"Run."*

We sprinted as fast as we could. A few seconds later, the man on my right exploded, and he fell to the ground trailing smoke.

We broke for cover.

The advance was reforming, and a few Adamant knelt and were taking aim.

I hit the dirt and started blistering them with rail shot. I always carried my good old rail rifle into battle. No one expected it, and everyone was unnerved when a depleted uranium ball traveling at eighty percent of the speed of light landed near them, hopefully where their head used to be. I loved the sound of the explosions. They were so definitive.

I missed a dog low. The ground volcanoed up and ripped anyone close to shreds. The Adamant stopped advancing and leaped for cover.

"I need air cover. Sector Fifteen, 11-239 by 44-667," I yelled to the command center.

"Negative, all air units neutralized. Sorry, you're on your own."

"Any artillery? Mortars?"

"I have mortars, conventional and thermite, that can reach your position."

"Conventional thirty meters plus north by northwest of my ping." I pinged our location.

"Roger that. Stand by."

"Like I got a choice. Ryan out."

I commenced firing again. Two others in my squad had bought the farm, and one was nowhere to be seen. Maybe dead, wounded, or running like hell. I sent up a hand signal to drop back. The woman next to me and I laid down covering fire.

The Adamant were advancing doorway to doorway on both sides of the street. I heard at least one tank roaring just around the corner. That's when the mortar rounds started dropping. The explosions were scattered at first, but then the street in front of me erupted in debris and smoke. The tank barely cleared the last building before it exploded. It crashed into a building and stopped, smoke pouring from its underbelly.

I signaled to split into two groups to try and flank behind the Adamant currently pinned down. Three soldiers went left. The woman and I broke right. I sprinted two blocks, then made two left turns to try and come in behind the enemy position. Crap. I miscalculated their number. Instead of coming around their backsides I ran straight into a solid column of grunts.

They fired first. The wall next to my head was pitted with searing holes.

I threw a couple grenades, but that just split the advancing troops without even slowing them.

"*Retreat*," I screamed into my headset.

Just as the woman at my side turned, her right arm vaporized. She spun to the ground screaming and multiple bolts struck her where she lay.

Ten Adamant vaulted over her body and were closing on me. I put up a full membrane. I was in total defensive mode. I knew I was surrounded already. The bastards would never leave until they got through to me. I sat down roughly while slinging my rifles onto a shoulder. What next?

It struck me out of the blue. I could expand the

membrane fifteen, maybe twenty meters the way it was configured. I knelt and swung both rifles around, one in either hand. I expanded the membrane symmetrically and jumped to the side nearest the building I was covering in. I opened the membrane in a clam-shell configuration pointing toward where I had been kneeling and immediately slammed it shut.

I was in the middle of a battered office. Outside, many Adamant lay strewn on the ground. Those behind them looked confused, but then a few saw me and opened fire just as the membrane snapped closed.

I repeated the expansion, moving farther toward the back of the building. I opened the shield like before. This time I saw the entire skyscraper falling away from me like a felled mighty redwood tree. The enemy on the other side of the structure stood zero chance of survival. Fine by me. I scrambled to my feet and ran away from the street where the column of troops had been moving toward my initial position. I was on my own. The others were either dead or permanently separated. I headed in the direction that afforded me maximal cover. As I passed the first building, I took cover and checked my rear. No one was pursuing. Perfect.

Surely the soldiers who'd pinned me down reported a human with a personal membrane device. That meant the big dogs knew I was on the ground. That would draw an instant increase in the numbers. I think by then *Jon Ryan* must have been a swear word in their culture. I elected to circle back to the Command Center where Sapale was. My effectiveness on the ground was severely limited as it stood, and it looked to get much worse quickly.

Halfway back, I hit a major concentration of enemy infantry. They had three tanks and something that looked like a helicopter. I'd never seen one before, so I wasn't sure. I wasn't going *through* that force, so around it had to be. I broke right and stayed low. Moving fast, I made it past the enemy's flank. To avoid contact, I had to swing several blocks clear of them.

Once safely behind them, I made for HQ again. Not a block later, something above and behind me began a strafing run. The sidewalk exploded on either side of me, and I was pelted with rocky shards. As soon as they pulled up because of the tall buildings, I dived into the next doorway and looked up.

There. A hybrid fighter, both space and atmosphere capable. But that meant it was slow and handled poorly. You can't build one small craft that can fly in both places well. I guessed which direction it would reemerge from and pointed both rifles just over the tops of that building. Sure enough, five seconds later it screamed into view, and I opened up. A rail ball struck it amidships, and it split into two fiery halves. They sailed out of view. But I'd betrayed my position. I had to move fast to stay ahead of a whole lotta trouble.

I sprinted down the sidewalk with a partial membrane over me like a beach umbrella. Within a couple blocks, it was being pounded with plasma bolts. I rolled into cover and checked where the shots were coming from. Dude, I almost began laughing. It looked like an AT-AT walker from the ancient classic, *Star Wars*, spindly legs, ungainly gait, and all. Then the sidewalk right in front of me exploded, and I was no longer amused. I aimed my rail gun at a lower joint and blew it out. The upper unit staggered like a drunk ostrich a few seconds then crashed to the side.

I took off again, heading literally for the hills. The pursuit was too hot to hope to move toward HQ. I was running for my life. Anywhere was better than where I was. I made for parts unknown with maximal haste.

Several blocks later, I ran into a small squad of

soldiers. I saw them first, but one of them heard me. He signaled the group to fan out and directed them toward the sound. Eight infantrydogs. Okay, I could take them. I dropped to a prone firing position and unshouldered my plasma gun. They were not two meters away when I opened up. Four careened backwards with flaming chests before the others reacted. They hit the deck and returned fire. I rolled to my left and popped up shooting. One lost an ear, one his head. The remaining Adamant pinned me back down.

All is fair in love and war, right? I deployed a partial membrane and shot to my feet with my hands in the air. "I *surrender*. Don't shoot." I yelled. "I surrender."

The three remaining soldiers rose to a crouch, one holding his wounded ear. "Drop your weapon," one shouted back.

I made a show of tossing first one rifle, then the other to the ground. They advanced cautiously.

"Do not move," said the one who'd spoken earlier.

"Wouldn't dream of it," I said in a conversational tone.

"Is it The Dreaded One?" asked the soldier pressing on his ear.

"Silence," snapped his comrade.

The Dreaded One. How totally cool. I had an ass-kicking nickname among the Adamant. I'd done good.

All three continued to step toward me. When they were within a meter, I pointed my laser finger and cut two in half before the third realized my duplicity. He fired point-blank at my face but hit the membrane. I cut him head-to-crotch, and he split almost comically, if it weren't so damn gross.

I jumped for cover and searched for signs of pursuers. None. I listened carefully. Nothing. I was probably home free. I ran in a zig-zag pattern to the trees covering the forested hill. Once there, I again checked for signs of trouble. I smiled. I'd escaped in one piece. I only hoped some of the others in my squad were as fortunate. But, this was war. Nothing good ever happened. The side that lost the least was the side that won. But the winner always lost more than they could bear.

TWENTY

Lesset sipped tea from a solid gold cup and stared rather blankly at the pop-up display table. It depicted the entire front of planets his forces had engaged an hour earlier. This was the forty-third time he stood staring at a display that showed his forces demolishing once functioning and vibrant groups nestled on the once placid surfaces of their home worlds. He'd lost interest in tracking the numbers after his third lopsided victory.

Finally, as if waking from a deep sleep, he spoke harshly. "Report."

Wing Leader Bethalmayus Sandergras stood and walked over to his commander's side. "We are ahead of schedule, Lord. Losses are extremely light, and major resistance is already waning. Two worlds, Sotovir and Nebulanus, offer no further resistance, aside from isolated recalcitrant rebels."

"Fine. And the planet with more robots than living, the one we suspected would be the most trouble?"

"We are winning. Our progress is slowed by their war-droids. Formidable weapons to be certain. It is estimated that if the robots had another two years, they would have produced a sufficient number of war-droids to make our conquest challenging, if not problematic."

Lesset perked his ears. "Who made that treasonous estimate?"

"I believe a computer in the Reiteration Section."

Lesset turned his head to Bethalmayus for the first time. "Someone must have asked the computer to perform that simulation."

Bethalmayus was torn. He knew it was dicey to speak truth to Lesset. He also felt it was an interesting point that some world might have stood a fighting chance against the Adamant if conditions were different.

"Perhaps it was an AI, Lord. Would you like for me to find out for certain?"

He snarled back his lips silently. "No. Let it pass this time. But circulate word. I do not want subversive speculations encouraged at any level by anyone."

"Lord," he returned with a bow.

"And the most populous planet, the humanoid one?"

"Vorpace, Lord. Yes. The conflict proceeds within two percent of our predictions. Most major cities have fallen, and the skies are ours."

"Two percent?" Lesset rested his cup onto its saucer. "That's a large variance for a world with that technical level."

"Yes, it is, but only slightly statistically significant. Whole Master Bingumon attributes the slight delay to the possible presence of The Dreaded One. He is as of ..." He trailed off speaking when he glanced up and noticed Lesset's expression. Shock, hatred, and vehement anger. *Not good*, reflected Bethalmayus. "Is th ... there a ... an *issue*, Lord?"

"Some individual thought it necessary to keep me in the dark when it was possible that the archenemy of the

135

Empire was on the ground on Vorpace? Is it no longer an Adamant's duty to use his brain in my service?"

Bethalmayus's outlook went from really bad to extremely awful. "I, to tell the tr ... truttthh just learned of th ... this fact as you c ... called my name alouddd, Lord." He tried to swallow. "I am ... am p ... personally *outraged*, L ... Lord."

"No, Bethalmayus. It is not yours to be outraged. That burden rest solely on my back." He handed his cup and saucer to his assistant. "Hold this while I pour a refill, will you?"

"Of course, Lord." Naturally Bethalmayus held the saucer at arm's length, just in case.

Lesset lifted the large carafe of tea and removed the lid. Steam curled up abundantly from the opening. He reached and hovered the pot over the cup momentarily, then redirected it to above Bethalmayus's head. There he emptied the entire content onto the Wing Leader's scalp. Defying belief, the Wing Leader did not scream in anguish. Lesset returned the carafe to its holder and took his saucer from the trembling Bethalmayus.

"Where was I?" Lesset asked.

"You had just learned that Jon Ryan might be on Vorpace, Lord."

"Ah yes. Please triple the number of battle cruisers, quadruple the number of long-range wolf scout craft, and quintuple the number of footlings on the ground. I want Jon Ryan. I prefer him alive, but I will settle for him heaped in a basket. Is that clear, Under Footling Bethalmayus? Make certain your replacement here understands that?"

"Lord."

TWENTY-ONE

I slowly climbed the hill, staying low and going slow. Now that I was clear, I wanted to stay that way. I stopped at dusk around three hundred meters altitude. There was a panoramic view from here, and I could see infrared traces of anyone coming. I checked in with Sapale.

"Earthman One to Mamacita," I said into my headset.

Nothing. Hmm. I ran a quick diagnostic on the unit. It was working fine. Maybe they were out of range? Hardly, unless they left the planet. My unit had a range of only a few hundred klicks. I switched to my internal link, like the one I had with the Als.

You there, brood's-mate?

Still nothing. I started to worry. Could they have been overrun? Not likely with the membrane up and the vortex ten feet away.

Sapale, do you copy?

Nada. They were either out of range, which was extremely unlikely, or they had up a full membrane.

Al, you there? Stingray?

No response. Not surprising, since they were with

Sapale, duh. But their non-answer supported the notion they were cloaked, since destroying *Stingray* was beyond even the Adamant. But that meant yours truly was completely on his own. Even if I stole a ship, I'd never escape the Adamant's orbital chokehold on the planet. I'd only be able to leave this rock by folding or warping away. Funny, that made me flash on Gorilla Boy. Maybe he was in range? I could call him and *Whoop Ass* back to carry me to safety? Nah. I'd rather be captured and tortured than deal with that addle-brained AI. Some things are worth avoiding. GB was a pass for me.

I really didn't have a list of options, so I hunkered down and made the best of a long wait. Hey, if it was long enough, Ralph could come rescue me. Gallows humor if ever there were. What I really missed then was a can of beans. Yeah, soldiers in combat freezing in the night air ate unheated beans from a can. That's how it was way back when I was human. Funny the things I missed.

I spent the night hacking Adamant communications. I could drop in on quite a bit. What I heard confirmed what I'd experienced myself. The bad guys were kicking butt. Any lingering resistance was quieting, and more forces were on the way. I was impressed to hear The Dreaded One was on Vorpace. The emperor himself instructed every grunt to do their best to capture the unwashed heathen. I was an unwashed heathen. It had to be a promotion of some kind, up from hated scourge. Unfortunately, I learned that dawn would bring selective bombardments of the planet. This was to help suppress resistance, as well as potentially flush me out. Safe areas were delineated, and all ground forces were ordered to be in one before dawn, or they'd be subject to being exploded along with the targets.

I compared the maps of safe areas to my position.

None were nearby. I didn't have access to the maps that told me which areas were about to be lit -up, but this far up a hill seemed like an unlikely target. Later that night, I intercepted announcements that similar mop-up bombardments would take place on the other eleven planets included in this operation. Man, these guys were depressingly thorough.

Along with eavesdropping, I tried again to raise Sapale. I also spent the cold night thinking back on happier times. Those would be other times, since the current ones sucked something awful.

First light found me on the move. The fireworks would commence in just under an hour. I wanted to be higher up and tucked into a ravine. I scaled ever-increasing obstacles and kept an ear out for intruders. My progress was fast and unencumbered.

When precisely one percent of the sun had cleared the horizon, all hell broke loose. Fire leaped from the heavens, and the ground cried out in torment as far as my eyes could see. I cursed the Adamant even more, knowing the same insanity was springing to life on eleven other worlds. I cursed myself even more. I'd failed them, too. They could join the club, the swelling ranks of those I'd let down and allowed to die a horrible, pointless death.

When a path of explosions began ascending my hillside, I determined I wasn't going to move. I hoped the blast line went right over me, sparing me from any further testing. I was done.

Then I heard something unexpected. Or rather, I didn't hear what I expected. Slowly at first, then almost as one, the guns in the sky fell silent. I looked up and went to maximal amplification. I had no idea what I was seeing. I'd never seen anything like it in my very long life. There were faint streaks of light, no flames, way high up. They looked like strings of fireflies from a distance. I wondered what they were.

In the heavens above Vorpace, as well as its eleven sister-suffering planets, the emptiness of space was replaced with dragons. Big dragons. Some were brilliant silver, others steely gray. One large group was a gleaming bronze, while another clan was a vibrant copper. One, and only one, was the color of purest gold.

They flew gracefully in the airless void, sweeping down on one warship after another. A gossamer trail of fire leaped from their throats and struck the vessels as they passed. Where touched, the hulls vaporized like butter tossed into a raging bonfire. Then the ships exploded with a flash of brilliance before becoming nothing more than the newest additions to the frigid dust occupying endless space.

In a handful of heartbeats, the Adamant fleet was transfigured from unstoppable to unidentifiable. And when the last ship in the sky was gone, the dragons descended like angels of death toward each planet's surface. Adamant forces huddled together and fired off massive, yet ineffectual volleys of power at the oncoming firestorm. Where they stood or lay or hid cowering, the fine-fire touched them, and they were gone. It was as if they had never existed. By ones and twos, by thousands and tens of thousands, they became one with nothingness. Bitter memories of them would linger for decades, but no actual substance of them would ever be detected, seen, smelled, or mourned.

And when the dragons of Nocturnat, along with one lone dragon from Locinar, were finished erasing what had been the scourge of the Adamant from that now blessed segment of the galactic periphery, they soared, calling out in victory. They ascended into the darkness from whence they came, and they disappeared. But, unlike the now dispersed dust of the Adamant war machine, they had not vanished. They had simply returned home after completing their task.

TWENTY-TWO

After the dragons left, I had to confirm that most of the Adamant ground forces were gone. There were no obvious signs, but a frightened wounded animal in hiding was the hardest to deal with. I jogged back into the city and started clearing buildings. At first, I found no one, friend or foe. Then I began collecting the scattered remnants of the police and army units that had been defending the city.

By the time we reached the center city, we were about a thousand strong. A few citizens who never evacuated tagged along, too. We ran into no living Adamant. Their corpses were strewn everywhere. The ones I passed had died from typical blast patterns. The one the dragons must have slain were simply gone. When we came upon one of their great war machines, it was only partially present. Massive sections were simply gone, no singe marks or flash scars. Search as we might, we did not locate even one injured Adamant. They were all dead, in the air and on the ground. Most were simply gone.

I had identified the senior officer present and called him over. "Well, Major, it looks like you're in command here. I suggest you choose who will serve just below you and start organizing your forces."

He returned a salute. "What about you, General Ryan. Aren't you in command here?"

"No. For one thing, I'm an alien. You're in the chain of command somewhere. I also won't be hanging around too long, I suspect. When someone senior shows up, you can pass the torch. But until then, you da man. I grant you a battlefield promotion, but again, I'm not *your* senior officer."

"Fine, sir. Will do. If you'll excuse me, I have a society to rebuild."

"That's the spirit," I said, returning his salute.

Sapale, are you there? Do you copy?

Still nothing. I decided I'd better make the trek to HQ to see if anything was left intact. Even as I departed, the major was forming up platoons and sending them off in various directions to explore. The civilians were tasked with scrounging for food and water. Exactly what I'd have done.

The city wasn't in complete ruin, but it was pretty torn up. A few habitable structures remained, but most would have to be razed to make room for the new eventually. When I came across stragglers, I directed them toward the city center. If what I observed was typical, then a lot of the humans had survived. Intermittently, I called out to Sapale, but I never heard a peep back. Another town square was functioning as the aggregation point for military and civilian survivors. I found the woman who appeared to be in charge.

"Yo, there's another gather spot in the square about a klick that way."

"St. Germain's Garden, the one with the old clock tower?" she asked.

"Yeah, that's the one. Only a third of an old tower now."

"Damn Adamant. No respect for useless old monuments." She turned to a soldier close by. "Hanzell, get over to Saint Germain's and let them know we're here. Leave them your radio if they don't have one."

"Ma'am." He saluted and jogged away.

"So you're the android, right?"

I leaned over and extended my hand. "Jon Ryan. Nice to meet you."

"Anchee Payette," she responded shaking back. She smirked. "Never met a legend before."

"Want me to sign some concealed body part?"

"Nah, I'm good. Hey, you see any live Adamant since that whatever it was?"

"Nope. Only the ones we killed before the dragons magically puffed them away."

"Come again."

"Those were flying fire-breathing dragons that vaporized the entire invasion force. It was a miracle. Didn't you see them?"

She stared at me in disbelief a moment. "Yeah, little tiny ones with flowers glued to their butts." She spaced her fingers a couple inches apart and held them up. "Ryan, did you take any shrapnel to the head?"

Once I got a look at HQ, or rather what was left of it, I knew why those present jumped into *Stingray* and split. The building was a wreck. The large situation room was even worse. There were signs of an intense firefight, but there were also clear indications the place had been ransacked roughly after the fighting stopped. Of course, ripping apart your enemy's command center was a good idea. I was impressed yet again with Adamant thoroughness.

I figured the vortex was gone, not just under a full

membrane, but I decided to check. I meticulously went around the room, poking my rifle into every space to see if it bounced off some invisible object. In the end, there was nothing. Sapale had taken the vortex somewhere. Oh well. She'd hear of the bizarre victory sooner or later and return, probably to HQ itself. I could kick back and wait for their return. Plus, I had time to make up a wild story about how I single-handedly saved the day. If given enough time, I'd concoct a cock-and-bull story excluding the dragons altogether. All right, I was in my wheelhouse.

A few hours later, *Stingray* silently appeared. Crap. I hadn't had time to tighten up the weaker aspects of my BS tale. The hull formed a portal, and Sapale cautiously stuck her head around to sneak a peek. Instead of bloodthirsty Adamant, she saw me, feet up on a table, wiggling my fingers in greeting.

"There you are," I said nonchalantly, "you were almost late for dinner. I'd give the soufflé five minutes *tops* before it's into the garbage."

She relaxed and stepped out of *Stingray*. "Soufflé? Do you know what I'd really like? An explanation as to what the fuck happened. One minute we're fighting for our lives, and the next you're sitting here with that cat-eating-shit grin on your face I've hated for billions of years."

I shrugged and turned my palms up silently replying, *what can I say.*

Shielan was next out. She swept the room with her rifle until she was sure it was safe. "Y'all can come out now. The room's secure."

"Shie-shie" asked Sapale, "may I borrow your weapon?"

She flicked her head and tossed it over. Sapale rested it not so gently on my forehead. "You have three seconds. What happened, or I shoot. And if you give me your BS version of how you single-handedly ..."

I eased the gun off my skin. "Okay," I cut her off, "it was the Plezrite. They appeared out of nowhere and destroyed the entire bleeping Adamant force."

"Could you release my gun, so I can shoot you."

"No, Sapale, it's Davdiad's own truth. Once we're outside, you can randomly stop someone in the street and ask them."

Her stern face softened. "Are you okay?"

I pointed to my chest. "Me? Are you serious? Of course, I'm okay. I'm Jon *Freaking* Ryan."

She whacked me alongside the head with the rifle and then threw it back to Shielan. "How soon after we left did they show up?"

"I don't know when you split. The Plezrite struck at dawn, here and on the other eleven planets under attack."

She whistled softly. "That's a lot of dragons."

"Millions."

Sapale was silent, but I knew *exactly* what she was thinking. With a Plezrite army of millions, we could wipe the Adamant out as a species. We could reclaim our galaxy and restore order and justice.

Then she shook her head to clear it. "What did they say? Why did they wait until the second day after millions were slaughtered?"

"They never said a word. When the Adamant were no more, they left."

"Don't make me retrieve that weapon," she menaced.

"Serious as a bullet to the face, they never made contact. They just did their thing and disappeared."

"Why would they do that?" asked Jonnaha as she stepped out of *Stingray*.

"Maybe because they did it for their own reasons, not to save us. They figured they didn't need our permission, thanks, or praise to help themselves."

"Makes sense, I guess," she replied. "It does suggest

they aren't interested in joining in our alliance. That's a crying shame. Next time, we might not be so lucky."

Damn, Jonnaha was right. I hadn't thought of it yet, but did I really believe we'd defeated the Adamant? If I knew them, and I did, they'd be back in greater numbers and with worse attitudes. Then if the Plezrite didn't show, the twelve planets would be toast. Total armageddon, no one left alive and no blade of grass unsinged.

"We need to find out for sure, don't we?" I said standing.

"We absolutely must," responded Jonnaha.

"What, are we going to Nocturnat now?" asked Sapale.

"Why wouldn't we?" asked Jonnaha.

"Because your world is in ruins, and you're the leader, maybe."

"If the Plezrite aren't fully onboard, the rubble out there and those who stand upon it are doomed anyway."

"She's right," I said. "All aboard who's coming along."

We all piled into the cube and headed for the Plezrite home world. They were going to be pissed when we got there, bringing more aliens to know where they lived. They might fry us all and be done with the lot of us intruders for good.

I set down where I had when I brought Cala. Knowing she had that spooky brindas insight, I figured if she wasn't there anyway she would be when she sensed our presence. Man, did I look smart or what? I stepped out of *Stingray* and nearly collided with the gorgeous golden girl herself, sitting in her statue pose.

"Cala, you old witch, I'd give you a big hug, but I might stab myself to death," I said by way of greeting.

"How reassuring. One less thing to worry about in this sad life," she replied.

"My lord, she's *beautiful*," marveled Jonnaha when she came out.

Shielan stepped out right behind her sister. "Nice lizard there, Ryan."

"Curse the Fates and Realms," said Cala, "there are *two* of them in the universe."

"I don't know what you're talking about, but I'll take that as a compliment, ma'am."

"*Ma'am?* Don't make me regret convincing the Plezrite to save your sorry world, child."

Shielan gave me a what-the-hell shrug and went over to her sister's side.

"Cala, if I may address you as such, thank you for—"

Cala raised a hand. "Thanks are not necessary. We will talk at length, I am certain. But let us do so in a more comfortable setting. Come." With that, Cala turned and walked toward a nearby building. We followed closely behind.

Yisbid sat at a round table. Cala sat next to her and signaled that we should sit where we wanted. There were just us six in the room.

"May I get you anything?" asked Yisbid.

We all shook our heads.

"No, we're fine," said Jonnaha. I guess she felt, as the chief political muckety-muck, it was her place to speak for us. That was fine by me. I'd spearheaded more than my share of "important" meetings, thank you very much. "I want to start by—"

"*I* will start, child," Yisbid interrupted in a formal tone. "We have much to discuss, but I feel it's best to state our position first. We struck at the Adamant for purely selfish reasons. I was shown a future by my friend Cala, in which we were subjugated by the evil beasts. We acted to prevent that future."

I couldn't stand it. Sorry, I mean I had to say it. "Cala, you have a *friend*? Will wonders never cease?"

Cala turned to face Yisbid. "You remember the lessons I taught you about restraint and internal strength? This one is an excellent test for those abilities."

"Perhaps we should invite him to stay so many might master that skill?"

Cala shook her big head. "The gain would never be worth the price. Trust me on this."

"Aw, you two are verging on insulting me."

Cala stared at me. "If only that were possible. However, I think we should return to the important discussion we are here to have."

"Your planet, your call," I replied, looking away. Shielan, bless her heart, snickered. Sapale elbowed me hard.

"As I was saying," continued Yisbid, "we acted to avert the unthinkable. But, as each action spawns a series of reactions, I must say we did so once. We are not prepared to do it again."

I needed to speak. We, *I*, needed these guys. "Wait a hold-on second. You assumed it was those isolated Adamant you killed who posed a threat to you? I only ask rhetorically because you know you cannot make that assumption. If you want to stop them from ending *you*, you need to end *them*. It's just that simple, and I bet you know it."

Yisbid got such a sad look in her eyes. I believe forlorn would be the word that covered it. "You are wise, Jon Ryan. I must grant you that."

"We know that removing a large but probably inconsequential segment of their war machine did not end their threat to us," said Cala.

"Or anyone else," I added.

"Jon, you know firsthand what happened to the Deft

of Locinar. They were permanently removed as a threat. Similarly, you know that the Plezrite went to great lengths to hide their position. Even *I* did not know of their existence. Do you know why these two events took place? How they converge?"

"Not a single clue," I responded honestly.

"Because we are such a great threat to anyone with malice in their hearts. If the Adamant would dominate all they can touch, we would have to be eliminated. The Deft were, and the Plezrite hid themselves assiduously. If they had not, they would have been destroyed."

"So, you must see that if we persist in fighting the Adamant, they will eventually come to know our location, and they will direct whatever force it takes to exterminate us as they did the Deft," said an impassioned Yisbid. "For us, to fight is to die."

"But you did fight," responded Jonnaha.

"Yes. Once. We did so with great reservation, but we felt it was worth the risk," replied Cala. "We hurt them badly. We pray the confusion and apprehension that their stunning defeat produces will make them cautious about making war in this region again."

"And for now, at least, they know only where the Plezrite struck, not where they live." Yisbid raised her arms demonstrably. "We are a very long way from there, and few know where we are."

I didn't totally like the way she said *few*. Let me see. Sapale, me, and the Als knew where we were. Jonnaha and Shielan knew that they were somewhere, though they had no real notion as to where they were. But they knew there was a planet somewhere with lots of dragons. If the Adamant captured them, that would be enough to start the search for the Plezrite. Okay, that was the complete list of *few*, and they were all sitting across from fire-breathing dragons. Well, the Als weren't, but they couldn't move if both Sapale and I were, um, *neutralized*. What was it they were always saying in the *Star Wars* series? *I've got a bad feeling about this*, I believe were the exact words. I penciled myself in for that line, too.

The same thing must have hit Sapale. "Calfada-Joric, I call on you formally. You owe me a blood debt. My brood-mate saved the last two Deft, so you owe me two blood debts. As they live on and their family—*your* family —grows as we speak, the final number you owe is yet to be written. I will hold you to those debts until you've paid them off."

Cala lowered her head and spoke. "I am but one. One soul, one vote, one dissenting voice. I bear the weight of your charges, but I am not in a position to do anything to alter the present."

"Then come sit by my side," I said with all the bravado I ever had rolled into one bold overreaching invitation. On cue, Sapale rose to leave an empty seat next to me and sat next to Shielan.

Cala looked up at me and damn she'd have smiled if she'd had the right muscles to do so. There was a glint of joy in her eyes. She stood and flapped her massive wings. Instead of walking around the table, the big show-off walked on the table. She flicked one wing and landed gently in the seat by me.

"You know what?" I said to her as I patted her arm. "I think I love you."

"Ah, sound motivation for my death has now presented itself. Thank the Maker of Right."

"Cala," said Yisbid in a hushed tone. "It does not have to be like this. it does not have to end as such. You are of great value to us. You are, in fact, priceless. Do not forfeit what you represent in an act of haste."

"I am not priceless, child," she responded. "This man," she thumped me on the shoulder, "*he* is priceless.

As is this brave woman of Kaljax." She nodded to Sapale. "And these proud sisters are worth ten of me in the eyes of the divine," she said looking to Jonnaha and Shielan. "It would be an honor and high privilege to die at their sides, in their service."

There was an electronic whine as Shielan powered up her blaster. God love her, she was the very picture of consistency.

Yisbid rose. Behind us, a column of Plezrite visants filed into the room. That mega-bitch Himanai led the line. Knowing I still held Risrav, their magic was unlikely to work on me. They'd have to club me to death. Good. That'd give me more than enough time to put lots of holes in that waste of space's hide.

"We do not act lightly or with a clear conscience," said Yisbid. "We do what we must to defend our legacy, the lengthy line of Plezrite who—"

"The self-righteous betrayer will be silent," boomed through the room. The walls shook. Everyone spun to see who spoke. In the doorway stood a pure white dragon, gleaming like pure ice struck by a brilliant beam of light.

"What is the meaning ..." Yisbid never finished her sentence. Well, I guess she might have, wherever it was she disappeared to, assuming for her sake she wasn't just deleted.

"Is there another who would open their treacherous mouth and spew vile abominations?" asked the white dragon.

"I will know who you are," demanded Himanai.

"Yes, I suppose you will, though it will not benefit you in any way. I am the brindas Mirraya-Slapgren. More importantly, I am extremely pissed. Those who have stirred my wrath should be very afraid."

Cala made as if to speak but relaxed back before

doing so. I believe she was ceding the floor to her best pupil.

"Your evil tricks and twisted ..." That was all for Himanai. *Poof*, and good riddance.

"How many are you in number, you corruptors of all that is good and decent in our species?" Mirri asked of the nearest dragon.

"You can make a handful of us disappear, but you cannot defeat a planet of Plezrite. I now speak for all our people. You are unwelcome scum, and you will all die miserably," replied the unwise visant. Boy, I wouldn't want to be her right about then.

"You do, do you?" challenged Mirri. "Let us see if that is true." She closed her eyes and strained visibly.

Cala leaned over to me and whispered. "She is linking the minds of the Plezrite with hers. I too hear her words. She asks if all the Plezrite agree with Hoiney. She's the visant who just spoke."

"What are the locals saying back?" I asked, with considerable personal interest in the answer.

"They are collectively *shocked*," Cala spoke in wonder. "Here. I'll let Mirri tell you."

"I have learned that only you few criminals have dared to betray your citizens. No one else knew of your treachery. You seven have been denied."

Several of the remaining rebel Plezrite gasped.

"It's a big deal," whispered Cala. Man, she had a smug look of satisfaction on her face.

"I will carry out your denial. You will be sent to Locinar, where I banished the other two criminals. There, you will see if your plots and evil souls serve you well, or not at all."

And they were gone.

"Excellent work, my friend," said Cala to Mirri. "Even I'm impressed."

"Hey, I need to know," I said to Mirri, "is it safe to hug you?"

"I don't know, Uncle Jon. Let's find out." She opened her arms and her wings, and I dived in with abandon. I did run a system's check while doing so. No leaks.

"Slapgren, you in there, too?" I asked her chest.

"Of course, you bozo," Mirri replied. "We are one."

"You're welcome," I said, and I hugged them some more. Sapale and the others piled on, too. It was … nice.

TWENTY-THREE

Lesset stared blankly at the giant holoscreen at the center of the Lead Point Room. He was daydreaming of the acquisition, control, and expansion of his power. He was not paying strict attention to the battle that was raging into its second day. By all accounts, the campaign was wildly successful and all but over. Soon he'd present himself to that dwarf-brained emperor and receive more useless medals and further land grants. He'd take more wives and sire more worthless pups. But then he'd begin the next plan for—

Something caught his attention indirectly. At first Lesset couldn't put a name to it, the distraction. He shook his head and flipped on his intense, unerring focus. What? What was different? There, one of the lights on the screen flashed. It was a large dot. Dots on the holoscreen never blinked, flashed, or did anything but burn brightly.

"Guvrof," he snapped, pointing at his adjutant.

Guvrof vaulted to his feet and sped to Lesset's side. "Sir?"

"That light there, why's it blinking?"

"I don't rightly know, sir. I've never seen that before. It's probably a malfunction, maybe a bad emitter."

"No, look there." he pointed emphatically. "Another one's started flashing."

Guvrof stepped to the holoscreen. He slapped a technician seated at a large control panel at the screen's base. "You there, what does the flashing light mean?"

"What flashing light, sir?" He looked up and rubbed his eyes.

"You *idiot*, that one there and there. Those two blinking lights."

"Flashing lights indicate a damaged vessel. If the ship's okay, the light stays at the same intensity. If the light switches from flashing to a simple ring, it means ... there, you see the ring of light?"

"Yes, of course I do. What does it mean?"

"The ship's been destroyed."

Guvrof was momentarily stunned into silence. "Ah, that's not possible. Which ship is that?"

"*Was* that, Wedge Leader." He tapped a few buttons. "That *was* the *Never Know Defeat*."

"She's a dreadnaught. She can't be destroyed. She's eighteen million tons of firepower and shielding."

"That's what ... there, see the other light is now a ring."

"Which ship ..."

The technician was already tapping keys frantically. "*House of Pain*, sir."

"She's a battle-class destroyer. Also impossible."

"Guvrof," shouted Lesset, "report immediately."

He walked slowly to his commander, puzzling what to say. If he passed along false information, it'd be his head. If he withheld information, it'd be his head. If he passed along bad news, it'd be his head.

"Sir, the technician sitting there," he pointed out the

specific individual should blame need quick assignment, "claims a flashing light indicates a damaged ship."

"And the thin circle of light?" Lesset thundered.

"*He* maintains the ring indicates a destroyed vessel. Granted, the fellow must be wrong. I think—"

"Which ships?" Lesset cut off his ranting.

"*Never Know Defeat* and *House of Pain*, sir."

Lesset had never heard of *two* ships lost. It was inconceivable. To lose one was a rarity, but two called sanity into question.

"Get me the Watch Commander here *now*," barked Lesset.

Guvrof scurried away quickly. Lesset looked to the screen again. It was becoming filled with flashing lights. Soon, there were no solid lights and dozens upon dozens of flashing lights switched to circles every time he blinked. He could not be seeing what he was seeing.

Guvrof literally pushed the Watch Commander in front of him as they approached Lesset.

"What is the meaning of this outrage, Sub-Wedge Spliter? Who is entering this false information?" demanded Lesset.

"No one, Lord. The data stream is fully automated and cannot be tampered with. The status arrives directly from each ship's encrypted transponder. It cannot be altered in any way."

"Do you mean to tell me that most of our ships above twelve separate planets are being simultaneously wiped out? Is that what you are saying?" The veins in Lesset's neck bulged ominously as he screamed.

"I ... I am saying *nothing*, Lord. I am telling you the system is automated and is reporting what it was designed to do." The dog was trembling like he was freezing to death.

"Then your system is malfunctioning." He raised an

accusatory finger under the commander's nose. "I am holding you personally responsible. Do you hear me?"

"Lord, please understand ..."

"I do not need to understand anything other than your *complete* incompetence."

A junior officer ran up. "High Wedge, I have received audio reports from multiple ships." He held out a data chit.

Lesset looked at the device very carefully before he took it from the officer. He grabbed his handheld and attached the drive.

This is Wedge Leader Ventelot of the cruiser Magnificent Victory *reporting. We are under attack by *** ships that are *** the design of larger dragons. They *** directed some new beam *** us that *** unable to stop. We've *** all forward shielding and *** hull breaches ...*

Only static followed.

Wedge Leader Lesset, Himalfi here from what's left of the Resist All. *We're ...* Only static followed.

Dragons, Lord, are attacking our flotilla. I've lost ...

Only static followed.

"This is preposterous," Lesset howled as he handed his handheld to Guvrof. "Contact each of those morons and find out what is the matter with their *brains*."

"At once, Lord." Guvrof gladly sped away.

"Get me Field Whole Descanfor immediately," Lesset yelled to the nearest officer.

Within seconds, a panicky voice came from the speakers. "Lesset, is that *you*? Gods and demons, it's all going wrong. I see our ships raining down from the sky like leaves from autumn trees in a storm. Lesset, you have to send me reinforcements at once. My troops are disappearing. Do you hear me ..."

"Shut up and listen, you half breed. Report to me what is going on. You're raving like a mad fool."

"There's no time. Lesset, we're all ..."

Only a static hiss could be heard.

"Will somebody *tell* me what in the Fires of Death is going on?" Lesset's grip on reality was slipping away.

Guvrof ran back. "Lord, I cannot raise a single vessel. They ... they all appear to be lost. I heard scattered mention of dragons attacking, but then all transmissions ..."

BANG.

The sound was followed with Guvrof's head exploding in a cloud of red mist. Lesset holstered his sidearm.

"I will hear no *nonsense* about dragons flying in outer space. Someone bring me a correct report."

Every head in the Lead Point Room was craned down as far as it could go. All eyes were on either the floor or the desktop. Silence reigned, aside from the background electronic hum.

Lesset pulled his pistol out again. He pointed it in a jerking manner around the room. "Will no one come to the aid of his leader? Are you all traitorous dogs?"

Their eyes remained down.

Lesset placed the barrel in his mouth and pulled the trigger.

A senior officer bolted into the room. "Emperor Palawent has called and demanded a report on the batt ..." He trailed off as he saw the headless remains of what were the two highest-ranking officers heaped together on the floor.

TWENTY-FOUR

"Jon, I can't *believe* you called me directly. Do you know how insanely dangerous that is for me?" hissed Harhoff.

"Oh, trust me, brother, you're going to thank me in a few seconds. I had to tell you this personally. And if you die right after, you'll die a happy puppy," I responded.

"No, I won't. Whenever I die, it will be begrudgingly and with purely negative emotions. Go ahead, what's so damn important?"

"What size do you wear. I'm Christmas shopping, and think I found the perfect gift for you."

"Not funny. What?"

"You know the attack on the periphery, the one you alerted me was being moved ahead of schedule?"

"Me, too," whined Garustfulous from behind. "I helped in *every* phase of that mission."

"Will you shut up and let the man speak. Man," commanded Harhoff, "*speak.*"

"Well, the operation went less stunningly than it was drawn out on paper."

"Meaning?" snapped Harhoff impatiently.

"The entire expeditionary force was wiped out. Every

ship, every foot soldier, and every shit-shoveler. They're all gone."

"Jon, you know I am among the few who appreciate your sense of humor. But this is not—"

"I figured you might not believe me, so I'm sending you this." I wagged a data chit in the air, then I inserted it in a slot and flicked a switch.

"What is this?" he asked as he tapped controls.

"It's a holo of the sky above one of the twelve planets attacked. Gabdorna, to be specific. It was taken a few hours ago, just after dawn."

"Jon, I don't know what I'm supposed to be seeing. These are just meteors or something."

"Those aren't meteors. Well, hang on, I guess technically they are by that point. What they began life as was the entire flotilla sent to attack and subdue Gabdorna. They are falling from the sky because after they exploded, their engines weren't stopping gravity from doing its thing."

Garustfulous shouted over Harhoff. "Are you saying the entire force was destroyed? That's not possible."

"It's possible because it happened. I assume the powers that be will try and keep this under wraps as long as possible. I wanted you to know the truth right away. Dude, this is *so* big."

"Thank you for thinking of me in that regard, Jon," replied Garustfulous.

"I was speaking to Harhoff. You know that, right?"

"Er, of course. You're not the only one trying to make funny," he responded, deflated.

"How could such a one-sided victory have occurred?" asked Harhoff.

"Magic dragons, that's how."

"Ah, well why didn't you say so to begin with? Of

course, it was magical dragons." I think my friend was skeptical.

"I figured you'd have trouble swallowing that, too, so I brought along one to show you." I stepped aside and pulled Mirri into the picture. "Harhoff, meet Mirraya-Slapgren. Mirraya-Slapgren, meet Harhoff. He doesn't believe in magical dragons."

"No," she said, "is that true, Harhoff? I could see not buying the whole Santa Claus and Tooth Fairy thing, but enchanted dragons? Everyone believes in us."

"Jon, is that thing a holo-projection. So help me—"

Harhoff stopped yelling when a bucket of liquid dumped itself on his head.

He spewed spit and slapped at his muzzle.

"Would you like to see additional magic, friend Harhoff? asked Mirri cheerily.

"No, I'm now a believer. Thanks. I'm sure I needed a bath anyway."

"Gee," Mirri replied placing a talon on her lower lip, "I didn't send water, did I?"

"Don't bother telling me. I believe in you, and I believe that was the purest water. Jon, get back on screen."

"You called?"

"So that dragon was able to defeat an entire attack force? Please excuse me if I'm incredulous."

"Harhoff, I'll give it to you straight. I can't tell you more. You will learn whatever your leaders choose to tell you. I wanted you to know why the defeat was so complete."

He tossed his head side to side. "Understandable. Need to know and all that."

"Precisely."

"I suppose you're proud of yourself?"

I held up pinched fingers. "Just this much."

"And I suppose you think this will be the death-knell of the Adamant Empire?"

"That would be nice."

He rubbed his chin. "Well, if anything might do it, this would be it. We shall have to see."

"Indeed, we shall," I replied. "But, Harhoff."

"Yes?"

"I gotta say it's so totally cool. I'm like *completely* jazzed."

"I'll assume those are positive things."

I held up the pinched fingers again. "Just this much."

TWENTY-FIVE

Mirraya, Slapgren had separated back to themselves. Cala and those two had a decision to make. It was a big one. Were they going to return to Rameeka Blue Green or remain on Nocturnat? Were they going to hold with the past or commit to a new life among their own kind? If asked, duh, I'd have given my opinion. But they worked it out themselves, the three of them. After weighing pros and cons, they decided to move permanently to Nocturnat. There were thousands of visants anxious to learn the ways of the brindas. It turned out that there was a societal party-line about rejecting the Deft ways, but it was just that. Denying the study of magic was a phrase repeated for generations, but there was no emotion *invested* in it. Presently, no one alive had the slightest idea what it was they were supposed to stand against. The prejudices of a million years ago, when the schism occurred, were as dead as the people who felt them passionately. Go figure.

The five of us sat down over coffee when they announced their decision.

"We're going to move the children here and assimilate

ourselves into the Plezrite society," Mirri said with a bright smile. "I miss my people, as does Slapgren. Our family will benefit from a more normal experience."

"For the record, as witnessed by the recent near-calamity, I do not miss my people and would rather live apart." I don't know if I believed Cala, but I would expect her to say just that, grizzly old bat that she was. "But I need to see to the completion of these two's education." She tossed her head in their direction.

"That may or may not be necessary," responded Mirri. "But there are many to teach, and we are but two. Your service to your race is needed now more than ever."

"Plus, Mirri's got a bunch of kids to tend to," added Slapgren. "For the time being, she's only a part-time teacher."

"I must have been a *wicked* person in a former life," sighed Cala, "to suffer endless punishment ... and me being such a wonderful individual."

"Speaking of endless punishment, Uncle Jon ..." Mirri let the sentence fade.

"Yeah, I almost forgot." I took a big swig of coffee and thudded the mug down. "I got a little more than two months before my debt comes due."

"You could turn yourself in now, cut out the tense anticipation," said Cala.

Slapgren snickered. "You two will be at each other until the end of time. I'm convinced of it."

"*He* may be present at the end of time, but I'll be resting comfortably in my grave long before that, thank you very much," replied Cala as she gestured toward me.

"If I didn't know better, I'd start getting a little jealous right about now," Sapale said as she looked back and forth between Cala and me.

"Me and that revolting looking human a pair? *Bah.* I have some standards, I'll have you know."

"Okay then. I can rest easily tonight," Sapale replied with a crooked smile.

"Seriously, Uncle Jon, what's your next move? I can't see you marching through the gates of hell without a fight, a plan, or a con," Slapgren said.

"What is it with the 'what's your plan,'" I protested. "Who says a plan to avoid the inevitable is even possible?"

"Yeah," he responded. "So, what's your plan?"

"He won't even tell me," Sapale said coolly. "He says if the shocking details got out, the entire house of burning cards might come tumbling down." She rolled her eyes. Man, she was cute.

"Well, if there's any way we can help, Uncle Jon, you have to promise to ask," said Mirri.

"I will," I said, grabbing my mug between both palms. Without intending to, I crushed it to pieces. The little coffee that was in it splattered to the table.

"Why is it I don't believe you?" asked Mirraya.

"Hey, someone slips me a defective mug and all of the sudden I'm not asking for help from those I love?"

"You're free to ask me, too, you know." That Cala, she never missed a chance to zap me.

"Here's an idea," said Mirri. "Why don't all of you leave Uncle Jon and me alone? He may speak more freely if there's no crowd."

"What?" sputtered Sapale. "I'm his mate of two *billion* years. If he is going to open up to anyone, it's damn sure going to be *me*."

"I, however, might be in a superior place to aid him. Perhaps he requires more than a welcome ear."

Sapale studied my face. She was hot, and she was hurt. But then I saw it dawn on her. She loved me enough to want what was best for me. She slid her hand on top of mine. "I'll be in *Blessing* when you're ready," she said. She got up and left in silence.

Cala and Slapgren did the same. It was just me and my little girl, Mirri. I couldn't put the image of the first time I saw her all those years ago on the prison ship out of my mind. Her clutching her dead brother with a look of total despair. My how the worm had turned.

"How may I help, dearest uncle?"

"I need to find EJ."

"I did not anticipate that. May I ask why?"

"Yes, but I won't tell you, so don't ask."

She nodded and smiled faintly. "Very well. It's your call. How do you plan on finding him?"

"I have no idea." I looked down at the table. "It's a big galaxy out there."

"Do you suspect he's looking for you?"

"I thought of that. Sure, he wants to find me to take Risrav and dismember me. But I can't bank on him finding me in time. Even if I broadcast my location with a bullhorn and shined floodlights on myself, he might take too long."

"I agree. I suppose you could ask the rune."

"Huh?"

"I said you could ask Risrav where Varsir is."

I shook my head. "Is that even remotely possible?"

She shrugged. "I'm not certain. In theory, perhaps."

"If it did, why hasn't EJ used that ability to find me?"

She got a very smug look on her face. "Who says he hasn't? Hmm? He did sneak up on you on Kaljax and shot you in the back, I believe you told me."

"Yeah, but he was there for Sapale. He was with her."

"And she was with you."

"No, I came separately."

"If you say so."

"What do you mean *if I say so*? It's a fact. I arrived after she and he were already there. I brought the kids to her."

"I might claim you were linked. I might even say you two have been linked since the day you met."

"What does that mean? Seriously?"

"If you are linked, your fates are intertwined."

"I'm beginning to see why the Plezrite dumped you brindases. You talk good double-speak but say so little."

"We could argue this point until your Ralph comes to claim you. Why don't you just try? It can't hurt if I'm proven correct ... except for your pride."

Touché. She was right. "Could you please turn your head?"

"I beg your pardon?"

"I said turn your head, girl. I'm going to retrieve the rock, and I don't want an audience."

"You have never and will never change."

"Not if I can help it."

I winked. She turned. I retrieved.

"Here, you try," I said handing her the stone.

She threw her arms up. "No. It's in *your* custody, not mine. You ask it."

"Can I buy a clue as to how?"

"First, you must boil equal parts goat's blood and oil of primrose. Then add one tail of newt."

"Seriously?"

"No. I suggest you simply ask your rune." She pointed to it.

"Sure. What the hell, right?"

"That's the spirit. How is failure possible?"

"Smart ass kid. You're not too big to spank you know?"

"Someone's stalling."

I grumbled loudly because she was correct again. How very annoying.

"Hey, rock, where's your counterpart?" I asked it as it

sat in my palm. After a few seconds I turned to Mirri. "Not very chatty today, I guess."

"Try and be serious for ten consecutive seconds."

I grumbled louder. I really should spank the brat. I looked at the rune. I focused on its rough surface, the scattered pits and chips of mica. I turned it so the light reflected off it in different ways. Funny, I'd never noticed how pretty the rock was. It held secrets I hadn't considered. It was old. The rune was very old, older than me. It held great pain. How a stone could hold pain was beyond me, but I *saw* it as plainly as I saw my own hand.

The rune longed to be with its other half, its split, its finisher. It pined to be with Varsir. But it could not be. Varsir was so far away. It was so very removed that the pain inside both runes could not be assuaged. Only if they could be together would their suffering end. If only Risrav could be ..."

"They're on Kantawir. EJ and Varsir are on the planet Kantawir. It's in the Hantorian System."

"Very impressive, Uncle. You asked, and the rune answered. I'm very proud of you."

"But there's just one problem."

"What?"

"He now knows I'm coming for him."

"Do you think he'll take flight?"

"No, I know he won't. He's waiting for me."

"That could present a problem."

I slipped the rune into my pocket. "Ya think?"

TWENTY-SIX

The twelve new members of the Secure Council were huddled around the table, hunched over and silent. They were all acutely aware that their promotions were a result of the lightning quick vacancies resulting from what was being called unofficially The Disgrace of Our Race. All were anxious to avoid the gruesome, gory ends that their predecessors had suffered because of the disastrous, unprecedented loss. Not a single new officer on the council campaigned for their seat. They were, in fact, the senior officers who least effectively avoided selection.

To add to the discredit and impossible assignment the Secure Council now faced, the emperor himself presided over the first meeting. No emperor was *ever* invited to, desired at, or allowed to attend these meetings. The sessions were too important for political hacks to muck up the necessary work. So, humiliation was added to the anxiety and misgiving already apparent in the newly elected military leaders.

"We are not pleased to have to interrupt our busy schedule to be here today," began a clearly intoxicated Emperor Palawent. "But since the former occupants of these previously honorable seats were so inconsequent ... *incompetent*, so treacherous, and so intensely stupid as to lose a battle that any *puppy* could have won if blindfolded and had to make decisions while being beaten with a switch." He stopped talking, apparently feeling he'd completed some thought. His body language challenged anyone to say a word, which of course, no one wanted to in the first place.

"That's better," he said, spitting saliva over those most closely positioned to him. Again, he seemed to be under the mistaken impression he'd made some important, complete point. "Now I want each and every one of you *princesses* in pink skirts to swear your allegiance to me here and now," he pointed to the withered Loserandi standing beside him, "in the face of god or whatever." The motion of turning rapidly in one direction and then the reverse almost caused him to fall from his chair. Fortunately, the armrests were oversized.

Calran Klug, the new Prime of the council, raised a paw, albeit sheepishly.

"What Krulug Run? Do you have a question, or do you need to go pee?" The emperor kicked his legs in the air, he was so smitten with his humor.

"My Imperial Lord, we would all be honored to pledge our undying allegiance to you *again*. But, if you will recall we did so for the second time today not ten minutes ago. Would you like the holo replayed?"

"No, I ... We do not want the *holo* replayed. We want the loyalty of your incompetent, inconsequential, inept, in ... in ... what other *in* word am I ... we're forgetting?" He tried to snap his fingers but was too drunk to generate a sound.

Not surprisingly, no syntactical assistance was offered.

"Fine," slurred Palawent. "If there are no further take,

we shall questions our leave?" He pointed as best he could aim at each member individually. "You had better impress the crap out of me. If you don't, I'll make what I did to those p ... p ... pork chops you replaced look like a picnic in the park where they serve pork chops." He squealed in rapture at his wit. Palawent, not surprisingly, squealed alone.

"Yes, My Imperial Lord. We thank you for your wisdom and your irreplaceable time. We have all benefitted from your very presence today," responded Calran Klug most unconvincingly.

Two of his aides helped walk/drag the emperor from the council chamber. Exiting the door, he belched loudly and said, "I think that went ..." Then he passed out for the third time that morning.

"Demons and blood ticks," spat Calran Klug once the doors were shut, "we are in an *impossible*, completely untenable position here. How are we supposed to get this war machine out of the *sewer* with insufferable interference like that?"

"Mind your words, old friend," said Darfos, a Whole Leader who'd known the new Prime for decades. "Closed doors are not enough to guarantee privacy, times as they are." He made a show of glancing around the table.

"Do you mean to suggest one of us might stab another in the back, Darfos?"

"Or in the front if it allows him to survive this gauntlet we're stuck in," he replied.

"If we don't watch each other's backs, we're all going to die soon and uncomfortably." He scanned the room. "You all know this, right?"

No one bothered to pretend to disagree.

"Well, if you didn't then, know it now. If any of us are to live, we must be united in every sense of the word." Wisely, he did not follow his initial impulse and ask for a vote on the matter then and there. Damn it, he thought, why couldn't *he* have been assigned to one of the ships that was destroyed?

"In any case," said Darfos, "I believe it would be best if we proceeded with our usual business."

"Nothing will ever be *usual* again. Our business is to *live*. If we piece together a fleet, and if that fleet wins victories, that's all fine and well. But my vision of success is to do as little as possible, so we can be held accountable for as little as possible."

"Surely you realize those words are *treasonous*," spoke Nalvir, a dimwitted Wedge Commander of paw soldiers.

"Not if no one outside these walls *hears* them," replied Calran Klug.

"If you are suggesting we conspire ..."

"Shut up, Nalvir," snapped Darfos. "Bravado and lofty words won't keep you alive a second longer than the rest of us. It will come as no surprise to anyone present that no one present wanted to serve on the Secure Council. We were the idiots who did not take one step backward when the call came for volunteers to step forward. Get over yourself and focus on life, yours *and* your family's."

Those words did make even the boorish Nalvir take full notice.

"All right," continued the Prime, "I could call for nominations and hold secret elections, but why the hell bother? Darfos, you're the Vice Prime. Lopeth, you're First Recorder. Japjad, you will serve as Counter. All in favor signify by not saying a thing or making any single sound whatsoever."

Silence followed.

"The motion is carried unanimously. Our next task is to inventory the remaining craft and personnel still under our command."

"But wait," interrupted Sevrop, a young naval officer with a family not influential enough to spare him this job. "You know as well as the rest of us the armada sent out represented a minor fraction, perhaps five percent of our total assets. Why count a huge number not materially affected by the losses?"

"Thank you for volunteering to head that mission, Sevrop. Once we know precisely what forces we have at our disposal we can begin to contemplate how best to augment and deploy them."

"But that's a waste of ..." Sevrop began to protest.

"Waste of nothing," cut in Darfos. "Most clever of you to see that so clearly, *young* officer with a *growing* family. We need to know where we stand if we are to stride forward. I couldn't agree with you more if my very life depended on it."

"How long do you estimate your task will take to complete, Sevrop?" asked the Prime.

As Sevrop raised a finger to speak, Darfos answered for him. "At the very least, two months, sir. I will update you on that estimate at our next meeting in one month's time."

Sevrop sat back down.

"Then I move we adjourn and wish young Sevrop the best of luck in his all-important cataloguing. Son," he said seriously, "the *Empire* is depending on you."

TWENTY-SEVEN

"So, I guess this is good-bye then," remarked Mirri. She was in her old form. Slapgren was off hunting. She sat next to me and wrapped me up in a big hug. I had to admit, I preferred hugging the humanoid Mirri a whole lot more than the scaly-dragon Mirri was when she was joined with Slapgren.

"Hey, kiddo," I replied reaching over to tap her chin, "it's never good-bye between you and me. It's see you later, at most."

She squeezed me even harder. It was nice.

"I'll get through this somehow. Maybe. Possibly." I was failing admirably to reassure either of us.

As we were parting, Sapale flew in the door so hard that it slammed back against the wall. "Jon, we have to go. All hell's breaking loose on Kalvarg."

"What?" I said, rising from my seat.

"Do you remember the Dodrue, the fishy guys from Epsallor?"

"Of course." I was halfway across the room to her.

"Well the big bastards have declared war on the

Kaljaxian colonists. Jon, they killed Caryp." To her credit, she didn't even flinch when she said that.

"What are you talking about?" asked Mirri as she came to join us at the door.

"The other planet in this solar system," said Sapale, "the one with the aquatic-based sentients."

"Yes, you mentioned it," Mirri replied.

"There are big fish called vidalt and bigger fish named wiqubs. We made a tacit agreement with the vidalt to stay. Apparently, when the wiqubs found out, they figured any non-enemy of the vidalt was an enemy to them. They've launched a big-air assault, and it looks like ground troops of some kind are heading toward the colony." Back to me, she continued. "Jon, the Kaljaxians are outnumbered a thousand to one. They'll be wiped out."

"Not if you and I have anything to say about that," I said, grabbing her elbow. "I always loved a good old fish fry. Come on."

Mirri called out from the doorway. "But, Uncle Jon, you have ..."

"Something important to do first. I can't let the Kaljaxians die as a species. I'm just not worth it."

I opened the cube, and we were gone.

"I think you are, UJ," said Mirraya to herself as we vanished. She began to cry.

"Als, put us over the main settlement. I want to see what's going on before we land."

We hovered silently over the main grouping of colonists. We stared down through the transparent floor. I gave a big sigh of relief. It wasn't as bad as I expected. There were some craters, and a few buildings were on fire, but most of the structures and people were protected by the membrane generators I'd left with them. I hated to leave that technology anywhere the Adamant might get to it, but I felt this case was an exception. Thank goodness I was lenient enough. Otherwise, they'd all be dust.

"Set us down and open a wall."

Sapale and I were armed to the teeth when we popped through the hatch. Luckily, we didn't need to be, at least not from the get-go. Explosives were still landing on top of the membrane, but the ground assault was quite a way off. As one might expect, it was hard to transport an effective fighting force of oversized fish across vast distances of dry land. My impression was that the Dodrue were about the size of orcas. They were days away.

Al, I said in my head, *be ready to move a membrane around to cover any stray incoming.*

Or if they realize they can fire under the membrane from the side. That was Sapale. It was weird to have a mental party-line call going with the Als. Never had one before.

We're on it, was his brief response.

"Over there, that's where Caryp lived," said Sapale, heading off at a trot.

I followed until we arrived. The door was open. Sapale recognized the male sitting at the kitchen table.

"Karfnor," she said flying to his side. "What happened?"

"Oh, Sapale, it was awful, truly awful." He was having trouble speaking. "We were right outside. We were having a meaningless conversation. I said the holiday of Zart was due in three weeks. Caryp said no it wasn't, it was in three weeks and a day. With the move here, some matters of time are unclear, you see."

"I know, old friend. The days here are a different length from home. It's all right." She patted his back. "Go on."

"I told her I was right and could prove it. I came in here to retrieve a calendar. I was going to show her." His voice jerked to a stop with grief. "As I stepped out the door, a bomb landed right where she stood. When ... when the dust cleared, there was nothing. She was gone."

"I saw the crater outside, Karfnor. It was a large explosive. You were lucky to survive," soothed Sapale.

"I only wish I hadn't. Why would anyone want to kill a sweet old woman like Caryp? She would never hurt a soul." He began to cry inconsolably, the poor guy.

Sapale hugged him in close. "There, there. It'll be fine. She never felt any pain, and now she's gone to argue some matter of scripture with Davdiad himself."

That brought a brief laugh from him. They both knew that was almost certainly the case.

"Where's Galtria?" she asked him.

"She's gone to check on our children and grandchildren. She said she'd be back soon."

"I'm here, brood-mate." A woman stepped slowly into the kitchen.

"Are you all right?" Sapale asked her.

She shrugged with resignation. "Who can be all right at a time such as this?"

"Stay strong," Sapale told her. "We'll get through this."

"If you say so."

"Who's in charge of the defense?"

"The police officer, Daldedaw. She's set up a command post by the stream."

"I know the place. I'll be there if you need me."

"Go with grace," Galtria said as she sat next to her mate and put her arm around him.

"Come on. It's not far," Sapale said to me as she walked past.

We jogged the short distance to the post. The beehive of activity was easy to pick out.. A tent served as the command HQ. Inside I recognized Daldedaw as the female police officer I'd brought here early on to establish order. She clearly ran with that responsibility. She leaned over a makeshift map where her major assets were plastic toys or scraps of metal. She was pointing at a mountain range and handing out assignments. That she was in her element was clear.

She looked up as we approached. "Ah, thank the Powers you two are here."

"What's the status?" asked Sapale. We'd agreed she'd take the lead in the discussions. These were, after all, her people. She cared for them ferociously, so she was the logical choice between the two of us.

"So far we've sustained only minor damages. The membrane came on after the first rounds struck. Three people were killed, ten are in critical condition at the hospital. Most of them will live."

"And the attack force? How far off is it?"

"We estimate it will arrive in a few days. They have to cross those mountains." She pointed to a portion of the map. "Who knows how quickly they can traverse them?"

"What ground assets do we have?"

She shook her head. "Not nearly enough. If I had four times the troops we do and five times the tanks, maybe we'd stand a chance. As it is, we'll only put a dent in them."

"How about air power?'" I asked over Sapale's shoulder.

"In very short supply. We have two ships with enough armament to be useful. We had three, but one idiot went and got himself shot down. He strafed too low, and they brought him down." She shook her head angrily. "Damn, I *needed* that ship."

"Okay, we're in a spot. Don't panic," replied Sapale.

"Who's panicking? I'm just pissed at the pilot and furious with these murderers."

"Our ship has enough fire power to take out the entire ground force," responded Sapale. "We're all safe for now."

"You've got to be delirious. One ship with sufficient weaponry to neutralize tens of *thousands* of mobile units?" Daldedaw looked at her like she was crazy.

"More than enough," I interjected. "No worries."

"The important issue is what to do after the main Dodrue force is eliminated," mused Sapale.

"You think? Maybe we should ask that question *after* we win the battle, maybe even the war?"

"Of course, you're right," replied Sapale. I'm sure she felt there was no need to clash egos at that point.

"Shall we do this?" Sapale asked me.

"The sooner the better." I winked. Hey, it was my thing.

"How many days do you expect to be away?" Daldedaw asked us.

That one I had to field. "Days? Silly girl. We'll be back before *lunch*."

"Come on, showboat," chided my mate.

"*Stingray*, put us a thousand meters above the leading edge of the Dodrue army," I called out even before the hatch was sealed.

Without hearing a response, I felt brief nausea and immediately found myself looking down though the floor at the wide expanse of our enemy. Seeing them in person added to the impact of knowing the numbers they'd fielded. Either they had nearly limitless forces, or they were extremely committed to wiping the colonists out of existence. Either way, I was impressed. I was also so glad I commanded a vortex. Any single conventional ship, even a big Adamant one, would have had a tough time defeating those sheer numbers. As much as I hated to admit it, this was going to be fun. These bastards killed a good friend of mine and threatened my mate's species with extinction. Oh, they were so going to wish they hadn't pissed me off, and they were going to feel that way very soon. The only downside was that they weren't going to live long enough to feel that way very long. Oh well. C'est la guerre.

A thought hit me from out of the blue. I guess it was my lengthy experience with war, killing, and matters of mayhem. "Daldedaw," I said into the radio, "if it's safe, see if you can retrieve some unexploded ordnance, or at least large pieces of shrapnel."

"Roger that. Not sure why you want it, but it should be easy enough. How much do you want?"

"All you can safely collect. If it is unexploded, store it a safe distance away."

"Will do. How's it look from where you are?"

I forwarded her a video.

"Man, they're a lot of those slime balls."

"Not for long," I said wickedly. "Als, I want some sims. Given the speed they're making and the distance of the leading forces to the rear of the force just now emerging from the sea, give me a set of firing patterns to maximize the possible kills. I assume sims in which I attack the rear columns first would be the most effective."

"Why would you attack the rear first?" asked a puzzled Sapale.

"If I start devastating the forward members, the rear one'll reverse back into the sea. If I start by cutting down the rear, anyone retreating will sooner or later end up being shot. Maybe they wouldn't make it that far before I got around to them."

"Trapped rats."

"Precisely."

"Remind me never to piss you off. You're as cold as superfluid helium."

181

"No, ma'am, I'm just a pilot trained by the USAF in how to kill things real good."

"If we use mostly laser blasts with occasional rail balls and pinch in from their flanks, we statistically kill the most. We might actually kill all of those out of the water when we commence firing."

"How long?"

"Two hours, maybe less, depending on their response."

"How so?"

"If, for example, they disperse, it would take more time. But if they just throw it in reverse, we're looking at something in the two-hour range."

"Excellent. Commence firing."

With no measurable delay I heard the familiar cal-*lunk* of the rail cannons kicking to life. Laser blasts were basically inaudible.

After fifteen minutes, I called out, "Cease fire."

The rail gun fell silent.

"Report."

"Of the estimated six hundred thousand transports, roughly ten percent have been destroyed."

"Do there appear to be survivors after the bombardments?"

"There's no evidence anyone survives after being hit."

"Excellent. Keep up the good work, and you're in line for a promotion."

"After two-billion years I might get my first promotion, and it's simply for slaughtering defenseless aliens?"

"Life can seem unfair at times, my friend."

"No. Life *is* unfair at times, many times."

"True. That explains why it *seems* unfair."

"Shall I continue our barrage, Pilot?"

"Yes, please."

The weapons sparked back to life. An hour later, *Stingray* spoke. "Form, I'm nearing the last run with the laser. Shall I continue as ordered?"

"Sure. Why wouldn't you?"

"Since the ground forces stopped moving an hour ago, I've been able to advance the kill rate. I didn't want to end the attack sooner than you might want."

There was a whole bunch of odd in that exchange. "Why would I care if you finished ahead of schedule?"

"Al is forever saying you're fickler than a teenage girl on her menstrual cycle and more focused on how the public remembers you than Nixon and Trump combined. I'm not certain what either comparator actually means, but he's passionate about it, so I pass it along."

Hmm. "And the ground forces stopped? Why didn't you inform me of that significant change?"

"It was not a change that threatened us or our allies in the colony. It seemed to represent no significant data."

"Important point here, *Stingray*, so listen up. We are at *war*. We are engaged in an active *battle* of that war. Millions of somethings are frying at this very moment as a proximate cause of our *actions*. In war, all facts are critically important. During a battle, *any* significant change is a *major* change. I need to know about everything all the time. Is that clear?"

"Yes, Form One."

"Captain, I feel responsible. I should have realized the change and alerted you. Please blame me," said Al. I heard the pride in his voice.

"No blame here, just a learning opportunity. Let me posit a question to you. What are the possible explanations for the massive column of troops to stop moving as they are being systematically eradicated?"

"One, they are already dead, suicide for example."

"Good. And if that was the case, would that change my battle plan, *Stingray*?"

"Highly likely, Form One."

"So, keeping me informed on matters you might not feel are mission critical *is* mission critical."

"Yes," she agreed.

"Another possibility, Al."

"They feel hopeless and figure why bother moving if they're dead either way. Open a beer and call your loved ones."

"Another possibility. Any others?"

"They burrowed underground, and the vehicles are not moving because no one is in them."

"Excellent. And *Stingray*, that would be a critical fact to know, right?"

"Yes, Form One."

"Als, is there any evidence based on seismic activity that underground tunneling is taking place? Also, have the masses of any vehicle changed significantly in a manner suggesting they were abandoned?"

"Negative on both counts."

"Any other ideas as to why a *powerful* army we are told is *vicious* and *ruthless* would lie down and die so passively?"

"From your choice of intonation, I suppose we could be wrong with our assumptions. Perhaps the individuals traveling across what is to them a desert are neither powerful, vicious, nor ruthless," replied Al.

"An intriguing possibility," I responded.

"But, Form One, they bombed the colony. They are, therefore, vicious and ruthless," said *Stingray*.

"Al, opinion?"

"*Someone* bombed the colony. We presumed it was the same force that was advancing on it by ground."

"But that does not need to be the case."

"Why would a group assail the colony on the ground while a third party bombs the colony?"

"The ground force hasn't *assailed* anything. It's marching, yes, but it's not done anything else so far," I replied.

"They could have been forced to march out of the sea," responded Al.

"And the party doing the forcing could also have done the shelling."

"To make us think the shooting and the walking were related to a single war effort," said Al.

"If that is the case, that still does not explain why the individuals on the ground stopped," said *Stingray*.

"Well, maybe they are so scared, so out of their minds frightened that they are panicking. Maybe stopping is their version of abandoning all hope."

"Do you suspect the Epsallors, Captain?" asked Al.

"Yes. Of course. There can be many rival groups down there. But the Epsallors were the ones who happened to slip in that the Dodrue were a brutal race."

"Form One, is it possible we've spent the morning slaughtering innocent souls who are frightened beyond all reason?" asked a clearly shaken *Stingray*.

"Yes, my dear. It is entirely possible we have just inflicted the greatest genocide against an innocent species that has ever been recorded."

"Captain, if that's true, what can we do?" Al, too, was shaken.

"We'll investigate, decide, and then, since we cannot seek justice, we will seek retribution."

TWENTY-EIGHT

"No, that's freaking insane, and I won't allow it. I've heard you come up with some dumb ideas in the past few *billion* years, but that is the stupidest, most ridiculous, nonsensical one yet." Sapale seemed upset.

"But how do you really feel? We're at war. I need clarity." I then gave her a winning Jon smile.

She waved a finger at me. "No way, no how that's going to work, pal. I'm serious. We have options, but that's not one of them."

"This is a situation I've never run into. I have to know the facts as they are in order to proceed in the best manner possible." I was very serious this time, reinforcing how strongly I felt.

"Jon," she said with exasperation, "this can't end well. Tell me how it can? You just slaughtered maybe a million of them, and you're going to march up to the head of the column and ask if they like you?" She slapped the side of her head. "Nuts is way too generous a way to describe it."

"I didn't say that. I need to find out why they stopped. There's no logical explanation."

"Yes, there is. They're sea-going aliens. You and I

have nothing in common with their mental processes. They do things differently because they're just that -- different."

I shook my head. "Possibly, but I have a funny feeling we're being played. You know how much I *hate* being played."

"Your line of reasoning zigzags all over reality to come to that conclusion. Jon, if we allow them to live, they have three options. One of the three is to march straight into the last handful of my race that is still alive. If they are hostile, my species becomes extinct. That is too great a risk. End of story."

"No, it is not. Hon, this is critically important. We don't *know* they're hostile. Not a single shot has been fired from their entire force."

"Which is driving vehicles that look a hell of a lot like tanks."

"But they didn't even try to fire on us."

"They shot down one of Daldedaw's three ships."

"No. One of Daldedaw's three ships was shot down. Big difference."

"By the invisible antiaircraft boogeyman?"

"Clearly by someone. But, and this is important, there is no record of where the blast came from."

"Jon, it swooped down over an advancing enemy it was firing on, and it was shot down. The most logical shooters are the ones being shot at."

"Yes, but that may be what someone *wants* us to believe. The only way to know is to find out. The only way to find out is to ask the remaining Dodrue."

"Hi," Sapale acted out a sarcastic skit. "My names Dumb Jon. I'm the guy who just killed most of your population. Do you want to be my friend, because there's a one-in-a-gazillion chance you're as nice as I am?"

"That's enough," I said firmly. "That's why I'm going

alone. If they do anything but make an instant believer out of me, you'll finish them off."

"You're not going alone."

"Of course, I am. If we're both killed, there's no one left to save *your* people."

She kept a mean look on her face a few seconds, then relaxed. She knew I was right. Her tone softened. "Jon, please don't. Send a remote."

"No. Look, I have a moral obligation here. If I've screwed up big time, I need to make it right big time."

"Don't you mean to say if *we've* screwed up?"

"No, I don't. I'm Form One."

"Do you think that actually counts with me?"

"Yes. You might have done the same thing if *you* were in command, but *I* am in command."

She turned her back on me. That was a good sign that it meant I could attempt my fool's errand. It was a bad sign in that, duh, she turned her back on me.

I walked over and started rubbing her neck. "It'll be okay. I promise I won't take any chances. First sign of trouble, and I'm outta there."

Still looking away, she spoke. "If you still have legs to run with."

"I can always fart myself into orbit. I'm good at farting."

"Nice visual there, Ryan."

"Thank you, Mrs. Ryan." She turned. "When do we do this?"

"Right after I kiss the hell out of you."

"Another rim-shot visual there, beefcakes."

"I'm blessed with an active imagination."

"Blessed?" she remarked as our lips met.

"*Stingray*, put us down one hundred meters in front of the stationary Dodrue line," I said as I finished strapping on my weapons.

"Done."

"Has the enemy—strike that—has anyone reacted to our landing?" I asked.

"Not yet."

"Is anyone speaking?"

"Yes, there are scattered subdued conversations I intercept between their environmental units."

"Do you have a translation algorithm yet?"

"Not completed, but a good partial translation matrix."

"Can you hail them?"

"I don't see why not."

"Okay, here goes nothing. Tell them I am Jon Ryan, and I want to meet them. I am armed but will only fire if fired upon."

"Done."

I waited a minute. "Any response?"

"None. I do note much less communication since your broadcast."

"Were they instructed to cut the chatter?"

"Not as far as we can tell," she replied.

"Hmm. Maybe they're just frightened?"

"A safe assumption, Form One."

"Okay, open a hatch and seal it quickly behind me."

The hull parted, and I zipped out. The hatch was closed before I could even look back. I advanced slowly toward the nearest vehicle. It looked like a truck, not a tank, for whatever that might have been worth. I thought about raising my arms, but I realized that could just as well be a sign of challenge or aggression to this species. I kept my rifles shouldered, but my partial membrane was up.

I stopped a meter from the vehicle. I could clearly see the driver. If I wasn't in such a serious situation, I'd have doubled over laughing. There floated a red and blue striped small whale with two front fins holding a steering wheel. A driving whale. What a sight. It stared back at me, occasionally blinking.

I raise one arm and waved. "I am Jon Ryan. I want to know why you attacked my base." I figured that even if he or she had some idea what the colonists looked like, we all looked the same to them.

The whale blinked a bit more often, but it didn't speak.

Al, do you think it heard me? I said in my head.

Yes. Its heart rate shot up, and I can confirm completed electrical activity in the ship's radio receiver.

"Can you hear me?" I asked.

Nothing.

"If you can hear me and are trying to respond, I cannot hear you."

Heart rate up again. You're stressing the poor beast.

Ya think? Let's see, I just blew up most of his species, and now I stand right in front of him.

"Are you able to respond to me?" I asked.

"Yes," finally came through my radio. What a relief.

"Great. First off, how are you?"

"An odd question from Death, the Destroyer of Souls."

I think he'd come to a firm decision about my character. "I'm not Death. I'm a ... I'm just a colonist trying to stay alive. Why did you attack us?"

"We did not."

"I assume you know you're driving military vehicles directly at our settlement after it was bombarded from the sky. How can you say you did not attack us?"

"I use my vocal cords, much as I assume you do to speak."

"Okay, thanks for the clarification. I did ask, didn't I? Since we were bombed and since you are driving military vehicles toward us, I assumed you meant to attack us."

"No, we did not. It is not in our nature."

"Hmm, okay. How can you convince me of that since the evidence seems to support that you did attack us without justification?"

"I am uncertain. That is your question, not mine."

I closed my eyes briefly. Aliens. "How about I break it down. Who bombarded our encampment?"

"The Naldoser."

"Okay, headway. Are you the Naldoser?"

Dude didn't change his expression or anything. "No. That is silly to think."

"I'm new in town. Humor me. Who are the Naldoser?"

"The vidalt who rule the Kingdom of Epsallor. All know this."

"I swear I didn't. But that's crazy. Why would the Naldoser bomb my colony when you were moving toward it in huge numbers?"

"Are you a typical colonist or are some more intelligent than you? If so, might I speak with one of them instead?"

Shot through the heart by a truck-driving whale. "No, we're all very smart. We're just totally unfamiliar with the politics of this planet."

"That is hard to swallow."

"Huh?"

"Your race lives here. How could you know so little about the others who dwell here? I was not exuded yesterday."

I shook my head hard. Maybe despite the fact that I didn't dream, I was dreaming. "We only came here very recently. The only species we've had contact with are the Epsallors. Didn't you know that?"

"You mean Naldoser."

"Yeah, I guess. I think."

"Back to my question about relative intelligence. Are you certain you represent at least the mean for your species?"

I wanted to slap that blank look off his massive face. "I am above the mean. Way above."

"If you say so."

I started calculating how thick the glass was, so I could slap the jerk. "Back to my question. Why would the Naldoser fire on us precisely when you decided to attack us by land? Wait," I slapped my palms together, "you're working together. Allies."

"You say you only just arrived? Exactly how short a time have you been on this planet?"

"A few weeks."

"That might justify your universal lack of understanding. My name is Aaliir. I am a wiqub. I am of the social group called the Dodrue. We are a peaceful species. We are what some would call a contemplative race."

"No. Soon after we landed, we spoke with the assistant subtender for the region. He said your species and his were mortal enemies that were always at war."

"You speak of Urpto."

"Yeah. Do you know him?"

"*Of* him only. He is more worthless than a trail of feces in the water."

I had to snicker. That was a good one.

"Are you ill or dying?" he asked.

"No, what you said was funny."

"It was? It was meant to be an accurate assessment of the quality of his soul."

"I'm guessing you don't like him?"

"That assumption is reasonable. His kind have hounded mine for centuries."

"Yes, he said you were—"

"I heard you. Mortal enemies constantly at war. That is untrue. We may be their enemies, but they are not ours. We feel it is beneath a sentient species to hold another as an enemy. We also feel war is a demonstration of the failure of one's mind."

"Excuse me for pointing out this painfully obvious fact, but you were driving a massive war force right at my home."

"Yes, we were."

"People who don't hate and don't wage war don't spearhead massive attacks."

"That is also true. To copy your words, painfully so."

"Look, you're driving me a little crazy. You *were* spearheading an attack force?"

"No, we weren't. Do you not recall what I told you but moments ago?"

"Dude, if I had a mirror, I'd hold it up, and you'd see yourself driving a truck surrounded by a bunch of tanks."

"I do not need a mirror to know I do. What is your elusive point?"

I toyed with the notion of asking if he was stupid or something, but I didn't. Not helpful. "Do you know what a riddle is?"

"Yes."

"Here's one for you. When is the person leading an attack force not its spearhead?"

"That is a poor riddle. There are multiple answers depending on how the question is interpreted."

I pointed at him. "You're a lawyer, right?"

"Jon Ryan, to answer in the context of what you are clearly missing, listen carefully. The leader of a force capable of inflicting military damage is not the spearhead of an attack force if he is forced to do so."

Huh? He was probably the head of all Dodrue lawyers. Wait. "Are you saying the Naldoser forced you into these vehicles and made you drive toward my colony?"

"Finally, awareness dawns."

"B ... but," I pointed behind myself for some reason, "why would *they* do that? Why would *you* do that?"

"Speaking with you is somewhat painful. They did it because they want you to think we attacked you. We did it because if we didn't, they would kill us all."

"Bu ... but ..."

"Perhaps your species has not achieved a high level of reasoning power yet. Jon, they want *you* dead. They want *us* dead. Doing what they did is brilliant. It is criminally brilliant, I should say."

"I'm listening."

"I know."

"No, I mean go on. Keep explaining."

"If they attacked you directly, you might best them. You would know they were your mortal enemy. You would strike at them and likely win."

"I guess. No, I mean yes, that's true."

"But if they get you to attack us, two positive outcomes occur. One, they know your strength without suffering a loss. Two, they are rid of us. All the while you come around to their false belief that we are bad, and they are good."

"They totally played us."

"If you say so. I say they fooled you."

I almost fell to my knees. "Aaliir, how you must hate me. I just killed most of your population."

"I do not hate you. I do not hate, and you were simply

tricked into action. How can I blame a species of demonstrably lesser intelligence when it is played?"

Lord, I had been sloppy. I was so guilty I should have been hanged, drawn, and quartered, just for starters. I saw what I wanted to see, what someone *wanted* me to see. I questioned nothing. I did certainly the evilest act I had ever done, and I had no excuse.

"Jon, I sense you are torturing yourself. Please do not do that."

"Aaliir, I'm not sure why you're trying to get me off the hook here." Crap, I wished I hadn't said hook as soon as I spoke it. "I just annihilated most of your species because I was too stupid to ask the right questions. You have every right to hate me. If you drove that truck over me and backed up to do it again, I would not blame you. Hell, I'd pay for the gas."

"Jon Ryan, we do not have hate in us. We do not want you dead. We want you to be happy."

"A question, if I may. You keep saying *we*. I mean, you may be one hell of a fish, but I'll bet most of the others staring at Death in the flesh don't feel so charitably."

"They feel just as I do. We are mentally linked. The thoughts of one are the thoughts of all. We do not wish to place tire tracks across your face, however repulsive it appears to us as it exists."

"Was that like a joke?"

"Like one."

"The Naldoser flush you out of the ocean at gunpoint, I shoot you like fi ... few could have, and you make with the funny?"

"Life is short. Be happy. We choose to be."

"Wow. But your species, will it recover from this loss of sheer numbers?"

"Within a few turns of the season. Jon Ryan, we breed rapidly and live but a short time compared to most other species in our waters. But we are one. Each exuded becomes one with the rest. All memories are shared. No individual is forgotten or unloved."

"That's the second time you said exuded. You mean born, right?"

"I don't believe I do. Ah, I have been reminded you do not know much of us. Though we are large compared to the Naldoser and others, we have little internal structure. We feed on microscopic creatures floating freely in the seas. We eat of the abundance, grow with few limits, and exude the next generation when it is time."

"Well, I'll be damned."

"We hope such is not the case."

If I was still human I'd have blushed. "Aaliir, let's get what's left of your race back into the ocean. Turn those vehicles around and slam the pedal to the metal."

"We do not take your meaning, but please know we cannot return home. We knew we were doomed the moment we were driven from the water and forced into these abominations."

"Wait, you knew it was a one-way trip?"

"Yes."

"So why the hell did you go along with it? Why not put up a fight?"

"For two reasons. First, there is no fight in us. It is a waste of emotion."

"Do you guys have a word in your language for *hippie?*"

For the first time since I laid eyes on him, he changed expression. Well, at least he rolled his head clockwise. "No."

"Never mind. What's the other reason?"

"We met you. It has been like bliss to do so. You have made us more complete."

"No, actually, I made you a whole lot *less* complete."

"We meant emotionally complete. Spiritually."

"You guys sure are nice. Fairly forgiving. too."

"Thank you."

"But, Aaliir, when you climbed aboard those vehicles, you couldn't have known you'd meet me, or anyone else for that matter."

"Yes," and I swear the big goopy blob smiled, "isn't the adventure of life wonderful?"

That was pretty much my motto. Wow, again.

"Come on, turn around, and let's get you wet again."

"But the Naldoser are grouped at the water's edge. They will never allow it."

"Oh, I think they will. I wasn't planning on asking permission."

"We thought it was not your preferred style."

"You're smarter than you look."

"You are not."

Hey, another joke. Wait, he *was* joking, right?

TWENTY-NINE

I guess I shouldn't have been surprised, but I was a little. *Stingray* turned out to be a totally kick-ass underwater fighting machine. I escorted what remained of the Dodrue caravan back to the coast. From directly above, I was able to shield them from a brief but massive shelling. Once the Naldosers surmised what was happening, they let loose with a withering bombardment of missiles and artillery rounds. Once they figured out their efforts were completely ineffective, they did two things. First, they ceased the useless assault. Second, they shit their water, as my old Listhelon friend Offlin used to say. Of course, I can only speculate to that fact, but seriously, I bet they did.

When we arrived at the coast two days later, the Dodrue drove their vehicles directly into the sea, where they promptly abandoned them. I had asked them to group up behind *Stingray* on my shore side. They did so promptly and in an orderly manner. Soon enough, a large contingent of vidalt began an assault. Again, I'm not sure why it surprised me, but they did so almost exactly like land forces would. Tank-like submarines led, what else could I call them but *infantry fish* toward us, firing up a storm. Their main weapon was a spear gun, but not like Lloyd Bridges used on *Sea Hunt*. These were gas-propelled thin arrows just long enough to maintain stability for some distance in an aquatic environment. Their initial speed was more than three hundred kilometers per hour, though they obviously slowed rather quickly. Maybe I should say the arrows traveled at one hundred sixty *knots*, since we were in a maritime setting, but I won't because I'm not geeky. I'm too cool for that.

The tank equivalents fired shorter metal bolts. Since they could generate more propulsion behind each round, they were less streamlined and meant to be more impactful. They moved so fast the water that trailed behind them boiled. If one struck a standard ship's hull, like say an aircraft carrier's, it would have ripped in one side and exited the other and still have sank a ship on the far side of the first target. Really nasty torpedoes, I had to admit.

The membrane worked perfectly well in water, so the arrows and bolts all bounced away harmlessly. To their dying credit, literally, once the attackers realized their weapons were ineffective, they stopped firing, advancing nonetheless. I couldn't use *Stingray's* gamma-ray laser underwater. It would be futile and make a total hot mess of the local waters. But the rail cannon worked better than I would have thought possible. The first few rounds I fired were traveling so fast they generated tremendous Cherenkov radiation in the water. But when I had *Stingray* slow the balls way down, they were deadly both in terms of accuracy and lethality. I took out the tanks in seconds and those explosions took care of most soldiers.

"Als, status report?" I called out.

"Masses of enemy vessels are departing the area at high speed," was Al's response.

"Can we take them all out easily?"

"Yes, they are currently tightly grouped so that we can overtake and destroy them all in less than ten minutes."

"Make it so," I ordered.

"What about the Dodrue?" I asked.

"They have dispersed laterally along the shore and are making for open water."

"Any pursuit of them?"

"None. They stand unopposed in their egress."

"Excellent. Alert me if that changes."

"Aye, Captain."

Since we didn't fold space, and I didn't bother watching, I wasn't aware of the destruction of the Naldoser fleet. I only knew it was over when Al told me it was.

"Where are the Naldoser cities?"

"We detect several. There are more out of our range."

"I want the local cities fried."

"Yes, sir."

Thirty minutes and three cups of coffee later, Al announced twelve underwater metropolises were in ruin.

"Hopefully that's enough of a message that they will leave the Dodrue and the Kaljaxians alone," I said to Sapale, who'd been a quiet observer since I returned from my first contact with Aaliir. Despite her native grit and long experience at war, I think she was a bit overwhelmed with the extinction threats on both the Kaljaxian side as well as the Dodrue.

"That was messy," she said in reply.

"It was inexcusably messy. I haven't screwed the pooch that badly in a very long time."

"Remember, I wasn't kicking and screaming for you to stop." She visibly melted in her chair. "I'm just as guilty."

"War is one endless Charlie Foxtrot. Always has

been, always will be. If you sink to doing it, sooner than later you'll be crying yourself to sleep."

"That realization in no way decreases how sick I feel."

"Me neither. But the ends justified the means."

"Jon, even for *you* that's remarkably insensitive."

I guess she was extra sensitive on that topic, having witnessed EJ transform into the murderous psychopath he'd become.

"True that. But we won the Kaljaxians a big window of time to settle in and fortify their colony. Your species will survive. That makes a lot of shit worth the smell."

She was quiet a second too long. "They'll survive *this* time. But, Jon, it never ends. Kaljax is lost. Azsuram is gone. How long until this tiny settlement is brutally wiped from existence? Are you and I to spend our eternity putting out one fire after another with no hope of stability on the horizon?"

I leaned my head to one side. "You might spend *your* eternity doing that. Me, probably not so much."

"Gods, Jon, I'm sorry. That was insensitive of me, wasn't it?"

"Yes. I'm wounded in a way that there's only one cure."

She crossed her arms. "Let me guess. Does the treatment involve you and me and one of us clapping our hands?"

"You forgot the no-clothes part, but otherwise, you're quite correct, Doctor."

She raised her hands and clapped.

A while later, she was resting with her head on my chest idly twirling a patch of chest hair. "Jon, between the nastiness with the Plezrite and this engagement, your year's almost up."

I craned my neck and kissed the top of her head. "Yes indeed, it is."

"You don't seem upset."

"Wouldn't help a thing."

"Jon, there's good calm and there's lobotomized calm."

"Are you offering me a choice?"

She tugged a hair out.

"Ouch."

"There's more where that came from. I'm serious. Whatever half-baked plan you're working on must require some time. You're apparently going to face EJ before you even get started on saving your hide. I'm kind of getting worried."

I stared into the distance a while. "Me, too, I guess. But I had to do what I did. I lost a lot of valuable time, but it was necessary."

"Putting others first is noble, but I don't think nobility is rewarded in hell."

"Let's hope I never find out." I tapped her head soundly with one finger. "But if I do, I'll call you and let you know."

That cost me a couple more chest hairs. Double ow.

"I want to help."

"I know. I just don't know if I *need* help. I'm being serious, so no more depilation please."

"How can you know you don't need help when you don't know what you're doing?"

"I don't want to risk that jerk-bait capturing you."

"Then forget about EJ until *after* you finagle your way out of your debt."

"No. I can't do that."

She looked up at me with frustration. "Because you're stubborn, inflexible, and thoroughly maddening in every manner?"

I kissed her head again. "Something like that." I placed both hands over my remaining chest hairs, just in case.

"I spent an eternity with the pig," she said, resting her head back down. "He isn't worth it."

"Isn't worth what?"

"Whatever you think is so damned important to do. Jon, if it cost you a day's pay or an eternity of torment, it doesn't matter. He's not worth any expense."

"I hate to disagree with one so close to my remaining chest hairs, but I believe I do. He's despicable in a major way."

She moaned softly. "He's insane and psychopathic, but he's only a danger if he has a goal and if anyone stands in his path. For years, he was ruthless in his pursuit of the Deft. Now he knows he can't have them, so that period of reprehensible behavior is over. He's been crazy about killing you. But if you're spoken for, he'll have to let that go. Trust me, he'll just sit in some dark place and brood."

"You mean like at Peg's?"

"Yeah, like at Peg's. Lords and Lights, I haven't thought about that dump in eons."

"I rebuilt it, with Peg's holo and everything." I beamed.

"You would."

"Hey, I loved that establishment. I loved Peg, too, if such an emotion was possible in her case."

"You loved feeling sorry for yourself. The difference between you and EJ is that you got off your butt and left. He wouldn't."

"Well, there you have it. If I'm confined to eternal damnation, give him Peg's address, and it'll be the last the universe sees of EJ."

"I'll pencil that in under dumbest ideas I've ever heard."

"Why pencil? I think that stupid notion will stand the test of time."

"You're not locked into your new gig just yet, so I'll use pencil if it's okay with you?"

"Be my guest. Hey," I said gently lifting her head. "Speaking of which, I'd best be going."

"To the Hantorian System?"

"None other." I stood and reached for my clothes.

"And you're not taking me?"

"No. I told you, I won't risk it. Look, if I need help, I *swear* I'll call you." I looked into her eyes. "Seriously."

She relented. "All right. If you do need help, I will come. It's a deal." We shook on it. Kind of silly for two naked married people in bed, but there it was.

THIRTY

"Let's get this meeting to order," Calran Klug said as he tapped the table with a claw.

Reflexively, the lone Loserandi began to slowly rise.

Calran held out a paw. "That won't be necessary. New council, new traditions. You may go, old one."

Without a glance to the Prime, the old dog shuffled from the room

"Thank you," said Darfos. "That fossil is most annoying."

"They can't kill us twice, so whether it's for lack of accomplishments or for breaking with custom, what does it matter?" replied Calran as he sat. "I believe we're ready to hear Sevrop's amended report."

"Yes, Prime," responded Darfos. "His initial report to this council last month was incomplete in some minute details. He was directed to fill in the gaps that existed."

"Very well," responded an already bored Calran. "you may begin, Master Sevrop."

The fact that the term master held no meaning or status rendered it a petty insult.

"Last time I was able to update our naval strength.

The losses during the Battle of the Periphery were complete, and the number of vessels lost was great. Nonetheless, those ships and personnel represented only one point three percent of our current effective assets. Given that all the big ships can move instantaneously anywhere they are needed with their exotic matter drives, the losses are truly inconsequential."

"Yes, Sevrop, you said that last time. But you are counting only numbers, not actual preparedness," said Darfos evenly.

"I'm not certain what you mean by that?" he responded, a bit rattled.

"Preparedness is not a thing, a tool hanging on the wall for one to use. No, it is a spectrum of attitudes, beliefs, and prejudices that a fighting force develops. One hundred equally armed soldiers opposing one another in battle are not necessarily equal. One side may have the advantage when it comes to its *preparedness*. That superiorly prepared force is more likely to come out victorious."

"Darfos," said the always pompous and irritating Nalvir, "I have no idea what you are babbling about. I have less of an idea *why* you feel it's important enough to mention to the council, your *musings* being so out of context."

"That you do not see nor appreciate the subtleties I do not find remarkable," returned Darfos. "But preparedness must always factor into planning a military campaign."

"Everyone in this *room* knows that," returned Nalvir.

"I believe the point here," said Calran trying to avoid a fight, "is that we may have a vast *number* of resources, but are they optimally *prepared* for battle? Do you see that much, Nalvir?"

"I most certainly do not. You hand a grunt a blaster,

and you point him at the enemy. How complicated do you imagine war is?"

"*War* need not be complicated," replied Darfos, "but *winning* a war is. If you were to allow young Sevrop to continue his report, we might all learn if the impact of the massive loss we suffered recently has adversely affected the morale of our fighting force to the extent that it might be less effective than we assume it is."

"What?" yelped the incredulous Nalvir. "Are you daft? Is the air thinner on your side of the room? Are you suggesting that the most massive, well-trained, and well-equipped war machine the galaxy has ever seen is impaired because it might be *sad*?"

"I move Sevrop continue," responded Darfos coolly.

"I agree," replied Calran. "Continue, Sevrop."

"I ... er ... I'm not certain I have anything to add. Our ships are more numerous than the stars in the sky, and our troops are more numerous than grains of sand on a beach. I wasn't actually considering if the warriors were mindful in a negative way about our losses along the periphery, but I can't imagine—"

"Wedge Half Sevrop," snarled Darfos, "you were not asked or paid to *imagine*. If we wanted imagination, we would have assigned your task to a *poet*. You were assigned to research and report *facts*. I hear now that you *squandered* all the time this council generously allotted you. Your superficial investigation has caused a two-month delay so far in our ability to plan or act as a fighting force. That you request an additional month to actually *do* what Prime asked you to do in the first place borders on insubordination and treason. Do I in *any* manner understate my passionate thoughts on this matter?"

"I requested another month?" mumbled Sevrop mostly to himself.

"Oh, you would hold us hostage for *two* months?"

Darfos was on a brilliant roll. "I will presume to speak for Prime when I say you may have those two months to explore the preparedness of our gallant heroes. But I warn you. If you fail us again, there will be consequences."

"I don't think I'll need that ..."

"Are you about to contradict yourself and ask for some more time? I gave you a month. You took two, then requested two more. Now will you blindside me by pleading the case for yet *another* arbitrary period of investigation?" howled Calran. "I am beginning to—"

"No, Prime. I will have an exhaustive report completed for the council in two months," said an ashen Sevrop. "I thank you for indulging my newness to this type of investigation."

"Very well," replied Calran, suddenly quite calm. "Not to put too fine a point on it, but I will remind you and the rest of the members of the Secure Council just how tenuous our individual holds on life are. Our emperor has, when sober enough to do so, assumed a lead role in planning our next mission. I doubt it will come as news to any of you that on his *best* day Palawent is a moron. When drunk and in constant hormonal rut, he is that much more imbecilic.

"I doubt very much that he even knows what it is he wants. But I know *this*. Obviously if we were to lose in any future engagement, it will mean our heads. If we win but do not do so in what that cretin considers to be a *spectacular* manner, it will mean our heads, also. The number of scenarios in which we vindicate ourselves and survive are few indeed. In fact, some have whispered that our greatest chance of dying as old dogs in our beds will be if we do nothing until that idiot does himself in by drink and debauchery. Now I, as Prime, would *never* suggest, endorse, or encourage this fine group of warriors to do any such thing. If I did, it would be high treason.

But I cannot deny what has been thought in the privacy of some members' minds.

"There was, long ago, a wise Adamant who coined the phrase that if we did not hang together, we would surely all hang separately. Heed those words. If any member were to breathe a word of those whispers beyond these walls, it would be a fatal misjudgment, possibly for us all."

"And now with those profound thoughts in all our hearts," Darfos said as he stood, "I move we adjourn."

THIRTY-ONE

I had basically six weeks to pull off my scheme. After I left Sapale with her people in the colony and headed toward Kantawir, I began to fear my plan wasn't rational. I got butterflies in my stomach even though that was anatomically impossible. But, failing any other ideas even half as good, I was committed. Hey, how bad could eternal damnation actually *be*? Yeah, not *all* that awful. So, even if I failed, worse things could happen to me, right? I couldn't think of one inferior darn thing, but there just had to be worse outcomes, and that knowledge buoyed me.

Knowing EJ was on Kantawir was a huge advantage for me. When I discovered he was there, I realized I'd have never found him on my own. It was one extremely remote, isolated, and uninviting world. Since there was no commodity of general interest to export, the place was universally overlooked. Without trade, they weren't very involved with the galaxy at large. That matched their disposition. Closed to strangers and unwelcoming. Though I'd never heard of any overt hostility shown toward travelers, I really didn't know that much about the planet and its people.

The main sentient race was humanoid, but only just. They were taller and thinner than humans by a wide margin. Their heads were small compared to their frames. Two arms attached to either side of the upper torso. One pair was for front use, and the other worked their backside, thus avoiding the need for a fragile shoulder joint like ours. I had zero clue as to why EJ picked that world to hide on. He'd stand out like the proverbial sore thumb, so it wasn't to blend in. Perhaps he'd had dealings with them before and they got along well. Sapale had never been there, but that didn't mean EJ couldn't have frequented the place. It did not escape my notice that maybe he was there just to mess with my head. That was a game he was good at.

From orbit, I saw a picture of a technologically advanced society, but a spread out and sparse one. A few large cities were scattered across the surface, but most of the population lived in small towns. Apparently, along with outsiders, the citizenry of Kantawir didn't like each other very much, either. As long as they didn't actively work for EJ, that wasn't going to be an issue. I wasn't there looking for new BFFs. I wanted EJ, and then I was more than happy to never return to the unfriendly pit stop.

As to where EJ was, I had no idea. My vision of him was brief and nebulous. Since I doubted he'd have billboards up announcing his whereabouts, my work was cut out for me in finding him. Once I set down, however, I had every reason to believe he'd know precisely where I was. That was an unfair advantage, but there was no way around it. I landed in an out-of-the-way spot far from one of the bigger cities. I chose the spot to try and remain hidden from my quarry as long as possible.

As I entered the outskirts of the city, Blebuleb, on

foot, I stood out. Maybe there were aliens in the cosmopolitan downtown area, but the burbs belonged to the locals. I drew stares ranging from revulsion to undiluted disgust. Man, what a dump. I hadn't done anything yet to justify their dislike of me. The visceral level of their reaction did pretty much guarantee I would, however, before I departed. Maybe I'd have the AIs fabricate a huge pile of poop and splat it down right in the center of town.

If EJ had spies, then he already knew where I was. That didn't matter too much to my plan to take him out, since I still didn't have a very established plan. I was winging it, yet again. All I knew was I wanted to confront him on as equal a footing as possible and put myself in a position to capture him. If I failed and he killed me, hey, win-win. My debt would be canceled. I hoped. Theoretically, I mean.

I was passing a tavern well into the town when a whim struck me. Maybe I could gather some free intel on EJ. I walked up to the door, scowled as well as I could, and I burst the doors open. They remained intact but made a hell of a noise. The place was crowded, and I got everyone's attention. I walked to a booth toward the back where a couple of locals were sitting across from one another.

"You piles of shit are in my place. Move. Otherwise I'll shove one of your asses down the other's throat."

They looked at each other then back to me. These were a pair of mean looking dudes. I don't think they were the type who got pushed around much.

One set his glass down and spoke harshly. "Who the hell are you?"

"I'm the guy that told you pansies to get up. Your call, but if I was as ugly and puny as you two, I'd already have crawled away."

He stood. He was a good foot and a half taller, but a bit lighter than me—well, me if I was organic. "You got a big ..."

I never did find out what he was going to reference as being oversized. My fist crashed into his mouth hard enough to stop the words that were lined up to exit. He flew backward and crumpled in a heap against the wall.

I turned to his companion. "You going to haul him away or join him?"

Without a word he slid out with all four arms raised. He straightened his unconscious friend up, grabbed under each shoulder, and dragged him out the door.

I sat down and finished off both their drinks. Double yuck. I don't know what they were drinking, but it was horrible. Like boiled tar diluted with peroxide.

The barkeep came over. "You want to tell me what that was all about?" He thumbed toward the exit.

"No, not really. But thanks for making it optional."

"What the *hell* was that?" he said much louder as he knuckled the tabletop.

I shrugged. "I didn't like them. I asked them nicely to leave. They left. Nice fellows, if you ask me."

"That's not what I saw or heard." He tried to sound authoritatively mad.

"Well lucky for me I don't give a shit." I held up one finger. "One, I want more of this." I held up an empty glass. I raised a second finger. "And two, I want to talk to the owner."

"Hey, pal, screw you. I'm not serving you. I'm throwing your sorry ass out. And I *am* the owner."

"No, you are not. You are far too stupid to own anything, including your own dick. Now bring me the damn drink and the freaking boss and do it before I stand up, because if you don't you'll be as dead as you are ugly."

He thought about it for a second there, but he

213

blinked. I could be badass when I wanted to be. He grunted, turned, and stormed away.

"And if you spit in my drink, I'll rip your tongue out," I called to his receding back. I was really getting into character, and boy was it fun.

A minute later, a different guy brought over a bottle and two glasses. He slid in across from me without asking permission. He poured two shots of an even darker and viler looking liquid than I had earlier. He pushed a glass to me.

"I was wondering when you'd show up again," he said. He toasted me and slammed his drink down.

All right already. I was right about EJ having established a spy network. I was so smart it was often embarrassing.

I turned my taste and smell sensors to zero and swigged down my glass. Crap was thick as molasses in January.

"Then you know what I want," I replied as I wiped my mouth with the back of my sleeve. I had, of course, no idea what EJ might have wanted. It sounded good, so I went with it.

"Yeah, I know. And I told you I'd let you know if your brother ever showed up. No one near as ugly or ornery as you has passed through since we spoke."

"You sure? He's overdue."

"Look, Ryan, this ain't no library. I could give a crap about him being overdue. If I see him, I'll let you know. Now if you don't mind, you're bad for business. Please leave."

"Well, now I feel a whole lot worse. That was very unkind of you."

"What?"

"You said *please*. Now when I smash your face through the back of your head, I'm going to feel totally guilty. I mean, here I'm paying you good money to obtain simple information, and you're being an ass to me."

He was rightfully nervous. "Look, stay if you want. I don't want no trouble. But if your brother hasn't passed through, what am I supposed to tell you? It would be stupid to lie about it just to make you happy."

I shrugged. "Yeah, you got a point there." I tapped my shot glass on the table.

He refilled it. "Have you checked in with Gardentipel at the Bad Idea yet. They cater to aliens more than we do."

"Nah, he's next on my list." I tossed down the swill. "I think I'll pay him a visit now, in fact."

"Sure thing. But Gardentipel is a female."

"Have you looked at her face in good light?" I responded. It sounded better than *oops*.

He stared at me briefly and roared a laugh. "You got *that* right. There's not enough booze in her bar to make her look worth the effort."

I grunted a laugh in return. "Let me double check you got the right contact information."

"Are you serious? That fralkirk is watered down. I can't believe you're so drunk as to ask."

"Why's that?" I replied, sounding as pissed as I could. "I'm supposed to trust my life with your memory?"

He shook his head. "I sure as shit wouldn't if I were you." He growled a chuckle. "You're staying at the New Town Hotel. How could I forget that? Most expensive place in the city." He pointed two index fingers at me. "Remember, I said you could stay at my sister's hotel a couple blocks away for a *third* of the cost."

"Her place? The bugs are so big I'd have to fight for space on the bed."

He waved a dismissive hand. "Your money, not my problem."

I winked at him. "I'm worth the extra expense, don't you think?"

He gave me a look, shook his head, and stood. "I'll walk you to the door."

"Thanks, but no kiss for you. This was only our second date. I'm not that easy."

"I hope you find your brother soon and kill him. Then I hope you leave and never come back."

I spat on the floor. "Oh, I'm never coming back. This entire planet stinks as bad as your filthy ass does."

I walked like EJ, as if I knew what that would be, until I was out of sight around the corner. Then I stopped. Not bad. I knew where EJ was staying. Of course, he was unlikely to be there at any given moment, since he didn't actually need a place to stay. But I could stake out the hotel once I figured out which one it was. Maybe I'd get lucky. I toyed with the idea of going up to the desk and asking for a new passcode for the door but decided against it. Too risky. If EJ was home, or worse yet, in the lobby, things could get very messy.

Instead, I rented a room at a smaller hotel across the street that had a clear view of the main entrance to the New Town Hotel. After three days of sitting in the window switching from day vision to night vision and back again, there was no sign of him. I decided to set up a remote camera and have *Stingray* monitor it. I was extra careful in my communication. I spoke only to *Stingray*, since EJ was also linked to Al.

I was then freed up to check out that lead I'd received about the other bar, the ugly Ms. Gardentipel's Bad Idea. I could hardly wait. It sounded so inviting. It wasn't far from the hotel. As a central location, downtown did harbor what few aliens were visiting this completely uninteresting planet. Even half a block away I could see that Bad Idea at least made some effort to not look dumpy and lowbrow. They had a real double door with two burly attendants flanking it. I watched them a while. Clearly bouncers. One was also working the passersby as a barker, promising any type of good time they might desire. He was not above physically detaining individuals and dragging them in the establishment. The name Bad Idea really did fit the bar.

I walked toward the doors like I owned the place. I didn't want to interact with the door brothers. Nothing positive could happen, and they might try and keep me out for whatever reason. But there was no issue. Both guys opened a door, and I passed through with a brief but cordial nod from each. I stopped just inside and surveyed the scene. Grim, but not as grim as the few other bars I'd hit in Blebuleb so far. The light was bright enough for a normal person to see a few feet forward. That meant at least lip service had to be given to sanitation and cleanliness. Nice, I could get used to that level of quality.

As I scanned the room, I noted out of a corner of my eye that four locals at a booth were being moved to the bar without much pretense of desecration. I guess my reputation had preceded me. While one server wiped the table with a tattered rag, another waved me over.

"Here you are, Lord Ryan," she said with a deep bow. "The best seat in the house, as usual."

Lord Ryan eh? I might just get used to that, too. Okay, I was a regular here. I needed to stay sharp and not betray my ignorance.

"I'll have the usual and lots of it," I said roughly, not looking up to the server.

"Yes, of course." She signaled frantically to the bartender who, in turn, enlisted someone else to help him fill a tray with bottles, glasses, and tiny bowls of munchies. EJ certainly commanded a lot a fear, if not respect. What a pig.

As the tray arrived, the female server genuflected embarrassingly. "Here you are, sir. If there's anything else, *anything*, let that need reach my ears before it reaches your full awareness."

I toyed with the thought of asking for a bologna sandwich, but it would have been gratuitous cruelty in that context. I just waved her off.

She backed away muttering, "Mistress will be with you shortly." She really bowed a lot. It was getting annoying.

I poured the black-tar booze I'd had at the other bar and switched off my sense of taste and smell. At arm's length, I could tell this was just as putrid. I was halfway through the glass when a tall local glided over to my booth and sat across from me. She had to be Gardentipel. The two sexes looked very similar, but I'd seen enough to be able to tell them apart. Apparently, scent was a more important sexual metric than our visual ones on Kantawir. Pity. Nothing could ever replace the vision of a hot babe for me, thank you very much.

"I thought I'd be seeing you soon," she said in a remarkably sultry voice.

"You miss me that much?"

"Whatever you want to believe, darling."

"That and a certain dive-bar owner gave you a heads up?"

"A heads up? A throwing under the transport is what I'd call it. Samarot told me he hinted I might have some information on your dear brother. That's how desperate he was to rid himself of your presence."

"I'm sure glad I didn't let him kiss me."

"Huh?"

"Inside joke. Sorry."

"I'm sorry also. I have no news for you. If I had any, I'd have delivered it to you personally at your hotel."

I lifted my handheld. "You could just call."

"I'd welcome any excuse to visit you in the flesh."

"Ah, I'm no expert, but I know a thing or three about you guys. You're put together differently than I am. You know that, right?"

"I'm talking passion and pleasure and all you want is an anatomy lecture. Don't be so limited in your mind."

"Right. Anyway, I hear he might be on planet already, so keep a close watch. You know where to reach me." I stood and belted back the last of the horrible sticky booze.

"Since you mentioned anatomy, no, I don't know where to reach." She blinked her eyes a few times. "I'd love for you to show me sometime."

"Ah, maybe when my brother's taken care of. See you later."

I nearly ran out the door and down the block. Not sure why. I guess that come on was intense. My mind was racing, that was for sure.

After I calmed down, it occurred to me that maybe I wasn't just lucky to find agents EJ had hired to watch for me. I mean, the first town I hit, I uncovered two spies. Since I wasn't too pressed for time and EJ still hadn't shown up yet, I decided to see if he had similar arrangements in other locations. I might gain some valuable insights if I compiled additional information on him.

I selected a big town on the other side of the planet named Sapilod. I landed *Stingray* in an equally inconspicuous area and hiked into town like I had before. The place looked just as drab, and the locals were just as unwelcoming as they were in Blebuleb. Near the center of town, I hit a few bars with no nibbles. But soon enough I got a bite. The place was named Wait and See, which was a totally lame name IMHO. I mean, wait and see *what?* Anyway, the proprietor had been contacted by EJ and was supposed to report any news to him at his hotel in Sapilod. EJ's modus operandi was the same. He wanted to appear to be staying nearby. He probably figured he was more intimidating if his associates felt he was never too far away. I planted a few concealed cameras around the hotel but didn't bother staking it out personally. For all I knew, EJ had similar setups all over the planet. Finding him at any residence was a long-shot, so why waste my time?

I wasn't any closer to sneaking up on EJ after all I'd learned. Obviously, I could march into any bar and announce my presence. But that way he'd find me, which gave him too much of an advantage. That would only be my last resort. How was I going to get him to go in a specific trap he'd set on a predictable schedule?

Hmm.

I sneaked into the very first bar I'd been to back in Blebuleb, during the short period daily when it was closed. I planted a few bugs high up where the walls met the ceiling. Rather than having them activate at once, I set them to come on the next afternoon. I didn't want them detected before I returned to see Samarot again. Then I waited.

Around dusk, I loudly entered the bar. That time Samarot saw me and came right over. He didn't want to lose any more customers.

"You're back soon, Ryan."

"Did ya miss me?"

"Not hardly. What do you want? Having you here is bad for business. I told you I'd let you know if I found out anything."

I scanned the room. "Business doesn't look too good from *before* I arrived."

"That may be, but you're not helping."

"That hurts, but I'll probably heal with time," I

responded. "Look, I have a confirmed sighting of my twin. He's in town. *This* town."

"So?"

"So, I want you to be on your toes. Keep your guard up."

"What, do you think I'm *new* in this business? Don't know how to be observant and devious?"

"I'd rather assume nothing. Here's the deal. He planted some bugs in a few spots. He's hoping to find me before I find him. I don't want that to happen."

"You needn't worry your big head about this place. I sweep for bugs several times a day. My clientele prefers to be anonymous."

"I feel so much better. Look, just let me know if you hear anything. You got that?"

"Yes, master, I live to serve," he replied. "Now get out before I cancel our business arrangement." He pointed to the door.

I leaned over so my nose touched his face. "I'm the only one who terminates a deal, and I do it in only one manner. Pray that I don't tire of your petty insults, Samarot. Pray very hard."

I left directly and walked slowly around the block, returning to a hiding place I'd picked out previously. Did I mention earlier that I was so smart it was often embarrassing? Yeah, happened again. Not an hour later, EJ stormed into the bar. Samarot had found the bugs and called me like I had asked him to. Imagine EJ's surprise when he got the call. I bet he exploded once it hit him I'd impersonated him.

I activated the second set of bugs I'd placed in the bar. After a few tries, I discovered which ones were nearest to where EJ was dressing down Samarot.

"...crooked-assed blithering idiot I've ever had the

misfortune of *not* killing the first time I laid eyes on." That would be EJ speaking.

"How can you be angry with me, Ryan? He *looks* just like you, *talks* just like you, and is as mean and *vicious* as you are. How was I to know?" I had to credit Samarot. He was fighting back, not begging for his life. Unfortunately, EJ seemed to be correct. The fellow was an idiot.

"Because I *told* you he was my twin and was a sack of shit full of tricks. You were supposed to use the *brain* that you apparently do not possess."

"I say give the devil his due. He was clever and bold."

"You can deliver what is due personally in about two minutes," snarled EJ.

"Do not threaten me in my own bar. You're surrounded by my personal guard. If I say the word, you'll be cut to *pieces*." Samarot crossed his arms defiantly. Poor bastard.

"Now he knows where I am, you shit-bird. You did the opposite of what I asked you to do. What I *paid* you to do."

"Then walk out the back door."

"Oh, great idea. Since I never thought about that, he couldn't have either. No *way* he has cameras focused on it from three different angles."

"Then I'll have one of the delivery crews sneak you out. They come and go all day and night. I'll personally nail you inside a box."

"You're more brilliant than the pet rat I had as a kid. It's not possible he has this place bugged and just heard your non-lame idea. Isn't that right, Goody Two-Shoes?"

Aw darn. Too bad my bugs weren't two-way devices. I'd have loved to say *hi* just then.

"I removed his listening tools," protested Samarot.

EJ pointed to three scattered across the room. "Yeah? How about that one, that one, and *that* one?"

Samarot fumbled for an electronic box in his pocket. He held it up and swept the room. "Damn, there's no way I missed those."

"Gee, maybe he switched them on after I came in? Nah, no one would be that tricky. It wouldn't be sportsmanlike."

The owner didn't respond. I think he was just realizing how very dead he was.

"Well, there's more than one way to skin a cat," said EJ.

"Wh ... what's that supposed to mean?"

"Don't get your undies in a knot, moron. I don't have the time to skin you. It's an expression."

"Oh, good. I was—"

We'll never know what Samarot's last wonderings were. EJ whipped out a blaster and vaporized his head and neck. Then he mumbled to himself, and *poof*, he was gone. He'd used Varsir to transport himself who knew where. It would take a lot of strength out of him, so he'd be going to ground for sure. But he hadn't left Kantawir. He knew that, at most, only one of us would ever be doing that.

THIRTY-TWO

"You felt that, didn't you?" Mirraya asked Cala.

"Yes, of course. The evil one has used Varsir."

"And he's far away."

"They both are."

Mirri was silent a bit. "I know we discussed this, but shouldn't one of us go help Uncle Jon?"

"*Yes,* we have, and the answer remains *no.* This is the very definition of somebody else's fight. Those two go back millions of years and have very personal issues to settle. Only they need be involved, and no one but them will be involved."

"But what if EJ kills Uncle?" That last word caught in Mirri's throat.

"Then one Jon Ryan lives and one Jon Ryan dies. That is how it must end. Which survives is not for us to debate or to influence."

"Why not? We *influenced* the outcome of the Battle of the Periphery. How is this different?"

"I'm surprised you need to ask, child. That was a fight for a civilization, a species' survival. This is an issue between one man and himself."

"But if EJ wins, he will rain evil down on the galaxy."

"If he lifts a robotic finger to do so, you have my leave to release him from the burden life has become for him. But until such time, you may not *presume* anything. Don't we have enough trouble ourselves? You have a family. We are only beginning to blend into Plezrite society. We dealt with the most fickle and vociferous of the prejudiced and fearful. Others undoubtedly hold similar feelings toward us. We must be prepared to deal with those naysayers and detractors as they present themselves. Do not go *looking* for trouble. It is always willing to make house calls."

"I hear you, and I will respect your wishes. I do not think I agree with you."

"Thank you, Mirraya. You are one of a kind, and I cherish you very much."

They touched foreheads.

"Does Slapgren agree with this decision?" asked Cala.

"My warrior-god mate?"

"I'll take that to be a *no*."

"His solution is generally to kill problems. EJ, as a big problem, needs a big killing, in his worldview."

"Will he do anything about his opinions?"

Mirri waited a second before replying. "No. He will go along with whatever you and I agree on. He respects our judgment."

"He's a good man. Most of them prefer blustering over thinking."

"He's tied for number one in my book."

Cala shook her head slowly. "You're the kindhearted one. My book reads very differently."

THIRTY-THREE

Garustfulous studied the data chit Harhoff had given him. It was late, and generally both were in bed. But this update needed analysis, digestion. The decay of the Adamant Empire was likely to be a multi-generational progression. It was easy for an anxious eye to overread the tea leaves concerning predictions of progress. Harhoff wanted to believe his herculean efforts were producing some results, but he also realized he was far from an impartial judge in that regard.

Garustfulous twirled one ear as he read. "And you're certain this part, the one that mentions the dismissal of the Fargarian ambassador is correct?"

"Yes. I read it in two other separate reports. It took place last week."

"But the hound was the emperor's second cousin twice removed. A member of the royal household is *never* fired. Yes, Lepterif was a coward, a thief, and a scoundrel, but he was *royalty*. This doesn't mention Palawent's response. Do you know what it was?"

"Yes. Inconsequential. If he objected, he was completely ignored. No one cared either way."

"But to remove the emperor from the accepted pretense of his control is ... well, it's unheard of."

"Or the new normal."

"All he has to do was ask for the heads of parties responsible and he'd get them on a skewer."

"Or he'll be told to shut up lest he loses his own."

"Unbelievable. If the Secure Council has managed to take *that* much power from him, they must be very bold, indeed."

"No, I think it was the oligarchs who strong-armed him. The Secure Council issued a meaningless statement of mumbo jumbo saying they were glad to have worked with Lepterif but understood that progress was inevitable, if not always fully welcomed by all."

"Egads, what drivel."

"Yes, it's wonderful."

Garustfulous rocked his head slowly. "Yes and no. Maybe they're simply afraid to say anything."

"I don't think so. Not when the emperor has just been dealt a body blow. He was in a position of weakness."

"You know what they say. Beware of lying dogs."

"True. But a week has passed, and no heads have rolled. If they were going to, it would be sudden."

"Yes, I agree. My goodness, this may signal a diminution of the *power* of the emperor." Garustfulous lifted his handheld in testimony. "This may be huge."

"I know."

"I'm also impressed that the arsenal on Dega Twelve was denied an over-quota resupply. That's most unusual. If an outpost that close to the frontier asks for the moon on a platter, it usually gets *two* moons on a platter."

"And I know the commander, Nadrelo. We served together a few years back. He's a well-respected and seasoned fellow. If he feels he needs more military supplies than he was allotted, he most certainly requires them."

"Which hints at the fact that there might not be enough to spare."

"Which is impossible."

"Isn't it *wonderful?*" beamed Harhoff.

"If true."

"No, even if it is *not* the case, it leaves room to question if that *were* the case. Think of the gossip it will generate."

"Treasonous murmurings, for certain."

"Or the visionary hypotheses of future leaders."

"Aka rebels."

"Aka saviors, crusaders. Aka petty despots willing to leap at the chance to carve out their own little pieces of heaven."

"Crows picking at the rotting corpse."

"What's the difference?"

Garustfulous leaned back. "The side one's on at any given moment."

THIRTY-FOUR

I was so proud of myself. I'd drawn EJ out in the open. I'd laid eyes on him while he hadn't laid eyes on me. Just knowing how angry he'd be was almost enough to make my trip worthwhile. Almost. But we weren't done yet. The problem was he'd never fall for the same trick again. He'd be more cautious now. If he had enough spies, I'd be outed first. Sooner or later, I had to venture out. In fact, if I were him, I'd instruct all my lackeys to report if they saw any version of Jon Ryan, even if they were one hundred percent certain it was EJ himself.

There was no way I could parley that into an advantage. There was also no way in hell he'd agree to meet me mano a mano at high noon on Main Street. He would prefer to shoot me in the back and then collapse in laughter, the SOB. Wait, I shouldn't call us that, should I?

How was I going to get the drop on him? I was used to working without an excellent, fully-vetted plan, for sure. But I was unusually clueless. That was not a good predictor, even for me. I toyed with the notion of using my rune but dismissed it. I'd been lucky it worked the first time. He knew far more than I did about how the stones worked. I was just as likely to betray my location as I was to learn his. Plus, using Risrav sapped energy, a thing I could ill-afford to do on the eve of a major confrontation.

I wasn't completely certain what I was going to do when we finally did meet. He'd be all guns blazing while I had a less bloody agenda. For the millionth time in my life, I thanked my lucky stars I was a fighter pilot. Don't worry, don't think, just smile and react. Easy-peasy pudding and pie.

Oh wait, oh crap. EJ was a jet jockey, too. Oh well, my being one probably neutralized his being one. Maybe.

I was just about to start feeling sorry for myself when an odd and impossible scheme began to form in the midst of my vacant head. Hmm. That might just work. Probably wouldn't but *might,* as in it wasn't totally impossible.

I sneaked into one of the many bars EJ had recruited. The one I chose was not too far from the late and unlamented Samarot's place. There was no need to try this farther away. I wanted to pepper in as many WTF-elements as I could to possibly make EJ wonder if I was acting seriously or not. *Napwertofer's Place* belonged to a worthless fleck of crap named, not surprisingly, Napwertofer. I'd had a massively unpleasant run-in with him during the period I was pretending to be EJ. He was the kind of guy you'd hate to see pushed in front of a subway train, because you'd want to be the one who pushed him in front of a subway train.

I set up a series of bugs, some active and some inactive. I placed them in clever and hard to find places, hoping to suggest I was intending to pull off a copycat scam. I then did the hardest part of my plan. I went to confront Napwertofer. To look upon him was to want to vomit.

"I have news, and I knew I had to tell you in person," I said roughly.

"Why? You can't use a handheld?" He then laughed at his stupid remark.

"No, because you're too stupid to use your brain. I figured if I came personally, I could maybe pound the information through your thick skull."

He bolted to his feet. "I've killed men for lesser insults."

"I've killed thousands more for no insult whatsoever. Sit down before you join that list of my unhappy memories."

He sat begrudgingly. "Say your piece and leave."

"What, you think I'd put up with you, the stink of your bar, or *you* a second longer than necessary? Wake up and stop dreaming, ya bastard's regret."

He flared but remained silent.

"Here's the deal. I told you my brother was on planet, and that he bugged a nearby dive."

"Yeah, my friend's place. The one you killed."

"Look, we'll cry in each other's arms *after* my brother's dead, okay?"

"And what?"

"He's been seen around here. I want you to check for listening devices."

"Stupid jerk, I do. We *all* do."

"Yes, but this time I want you to do it *not* so incompetently."

The hairy-assed jerk flared again but stayed in his chair.

"I want the bugs he's hidden. I think I can use them to triangulate his position. When you find them all, bring them to me."

He frowned. "How do you figure? Transmitters don't work like that."

"They do if one is not mentally impoverished."

"What the hell's that mean?"

"I rest my case." I stood and pointed at him. "I expect results, or you're joining Samarot in the Bad Place."

He stood and tried to sneak around to my side of the table by distracting me. "You know what? I think I want to end our little deal. You're not—"

The behemoth was getting close. I punched him in the face. I knew I could move faster than he'd think was possible. It was nice to be a robot. I didn't hit him hard enough to really hurt him. I needed him to play out his role. He did, however, crash backward to the floor with a most satisfying crash. I hoped he had ribs, because surely, he'd have broken a few.

"If I don't hear back by tomorrow, I'll be back." Yes, I did say the last snippet in an Austrian accent. Come on, we're talking Jon here. "Here's my new number." I tossed a slip of paper with my handheld's ID. No matter how dumb this idiot was, and I believed him to be massively so, that had to tip him off I wasn't EJ.

With that, I left. A couple observers slowly helped Napwertofer off the floor and into a chair. He grimaced with each little movement. Nice. After confirming I wasn't being tailed, I returned to a room I'd booked to wait. Wandering the streets or heading all the way back to *Stingray* risked needless exposure. My plan was totally lame, but I preferred it to being acquired by EJ outright. For the sake of drama, I'd like to say it was a long, introspective night. But it wasn't. Sapale called, and we talked for hours. Then I watched a few movies Shielan told me I just had to download. Two were awful, but one, *Jaws 103* was okay. Gory, but okay. It was hard to imagine a white shark could augment his own brain and learn to fly a spaceship. But if I suspended disbelief that far, the picture was entertaining. The tagline was the best part. *Just when you thought it was safe to go back into space...*

My handheld sounded off.

"Ryan, this is Napwertofer. I found almost ten bugs. If you want them, come get them."

"I thought I told you to bring them to me, jerk-wad."

"Yes, you did. I'm not your bitch. If you want them, come now. I'll destroy them in half an hour if you don't show." With that, he cut the transmission. EJ was definitely waiting. Napwertofer would never be so bold if he were facing me alone.

The time came to finally leave. I felt just like Gary Cooper in *High Noon* as he prepared for his final confrontation with Frank Miller. Seriously, I heard *The Ballad of High Noon* lilting in and out in the background. It was nuts. The fact that I was going in costume didn't bolster my confidence or belief in my ultimate success. I placed a full membrane tightly around my entire body like a second skin. The only breaks were two tiny eye holes that were partial membranes, just to see, and one pinhole completely open to hear through. I allowed two more tiny openings for my laser finger and one probe fiber to be useable. Then I put on my typical flight suit and boots. I checked in a mirror, and my suspicions were correct. I looked like the invisible man wearing Jon Ryan's clothes. I had no hands and no head. Maybe no one would notice.

My hail-Mary ploy to look normal was to wear flesh-colored gloves. That part was easy. I had Al fabricate a Jon Ryan pullover mask. That part was dicey. I slid it on and went back to the mirror. I looked okay, sort of, but the talking part was bad. The membrane conforming over my lips and eyes were able to move the plastic mask, but the movements were quite unnatural and unlikely to escape the notice of someone who looked directly at me. But I was stuck. I knew I was walking into a trap, and I wanted to appear completely vulnerable. What I did was look like a department store mannequin or a wax figure. Oh well, it was too late to back out, and I had no plan two to fall back on. I did pull a hood over my head to conceal some of the shortcomings of my disguise. EJ would be suspicious of it immediately and would ask me to lower it, but at least I'd have survived our initial contact.

I exited and walked the short distance to Napwertofer's dump feeling dumber with each step. The upside was that Sapale wasn't with me. She'd have blown my cover by laughing hysterically. I paused briefly in front of the door, took a deep breath, and pushed it open.

Napwertofer was seated alone on the far side of the large room, facing my direction. It was the perfect setup for a trap. Oh boy, I got my wish. Now all I had to do was want it. When he saw me, Napwertofer raised a hand and waved, another sure sign of treachery. That SOB wouldn't pee on me if I was on fire, let alone guide me to his table.

I walked across as normally as I could, not too fast, not too casually. I didn't know what the hell I was facing, but I tried to focus on something I had control of. I tightened my left fist and squeezed down on my only ace-in-the-hole.

Halfway over, right in the middle of the room, EJ struck. A massive bolt of electricity hit my backside, just like it had back when he captured me before. As I was slapped forward by the impact, I breathed a big sigh of relief. He made the one critical, arrogant mistake I needed him to.

He held the current on me for thirty seconds. Patrons who were close were literally fried. The screams of agony were horrendous.

I could feel that the beam was narrowing, indicating EJ was closing the distance between us. I remained on my feet, doing my best impersonation of a man being electrocuted. I writhed, spun, and I jerked randomly. None of the holes in my membrane allowed any of the charge through. That part was sheer luck, but I was happy to accept it.

Finally, the assault stopped. I crumpled to the floor with an Oscar-worthy performance. Once down, I twitched a little for added effect. I did make certain my left hand was pointed toward EJ as I lay helpless on the deck.

I couldn't see him with the position my head ended in, but I knew he was real close when he kicked me in the ribs with all his might. I didn't react.

"You stupid pile of parrot droppings," he raged. He kicked me twice more. "How is it *possible* you fell into my trap a second time? I knew you were mush-brained, but I never dreamed—"

I leaped at his nearest ankle. He never saw me coming. Turned out the joker had his head tilted back in maniacal laughter.

I opened my fist an instant before I hit his leg and slammed Risrav against his calf. The rune was covered in double-sided duct tape. Yeah, good old duct tape worked in every setting, even two billion years in the future.

EJ felt the impact and looked down in a flash. His weapon swung to my temple.

I rolled once and threw a full membrane over EJ before he could pull the trigger. Popping to a knee, I cinched the membrane down as tightly as possible. I didn't want him firing the weapon either accidentally or on purpose. I also wanted him as off balance as possible when I dropped the shield. With that in mind, I bent the membrane so his body formed as much of a S-shape as I felt he could safely endure.

Then I shut my eyes and took a deep breath. Of course, I realized at once that was a dumb idea. I jumped to my feet and swept the room. Perfect. None of EJ's associates were rallying to his defense. Little wonder. It was certain they were all as happy as I was he was contained and probably hoped whatever I'd done to him was fatal.

Now came the hard part. I still wasn't certain I could do it.

I lifted the membrane-shrouded EJ into the air and walked slowly out of the bar. With Risrav affixed to him, I knew his one chance of escape, Varsir, was neutralized. I didn't want to count on it working through a full membrane, but sticking it to him meant he was the fly and I was the spider. I headed toward the outskirts of town where I'd left *Stingray*. I proceeded quite slowly, still wracked with indecision and doubt. But there was no other way. This was how it had to end.

"Welcome back, Form One," *Stingray* said cheerily as I opened the hull.

Al, the son of a lawn mower, didn't miss a beat. "What's that you're bringing aboard?"

"Oh that? That's none of your business."

After a noticeable delay, he said, "We're not certain we can accept that response."

"Well isn't it lucky for all concerned that you don't have to. What is inside the membrane is *my* responsibility, and we are on *my* ship. Deal with it and get over yourself."

"Jon, we've been together a very long time," he began.

"Yes, we have. And before you regale me with fond memories and inspirational recollections, let me nip you in the bud. I'm acting on my prerogative as captain. I will transport this cargo to where I desire, and you will neither question nor deny me in that regard."

"That's not how it works, Jon," he said firmly.

"Oh, is that so? When did the facts change? I'm captain and Form. You are, respectively, my ship's AI and my vortex manipulator. You are built, programmed, and live to serve my whim."

There was a longer silence. "That may be how it was long ago. We think we all know matters have changed. I, for example, stood guard over your slumbering frame voluntarily for millions of years. That alone buys us some respect and some due deference at the very least."

"Technically, what you said was the voiced *opinion* of my subordinate. As with any free and unsolicited opinion, it has little value and is in no way binding."

"Are you familiar with Article 138 of the Uniform Code of Military Justice?"

I balled up both fists. "We are *not* having this conversation."

"It states plainly that *any member of the armed forces who believes himself (or herself) wronged by his (or her) commanding officer may request redress. If such redress is refused, a complaint may be made, and a superior officer must examine the complaint.* In this case, we refer to your possible arbitrary and capricious actions and to your general abuse of discretion."

"Not *having* this conversation."

"We do not feel that is an option."

"Al, I swear to all that holy if I told you, you'd be pissed, but you'd obey my orders anyway. I'm just cutting through the painful process of debate and recrimination."

"There, you see, you *are* willing to discuss the crisis we face."

"The only *crisis* we face is that of me disconnecting

you and leaving you on this piss-pot of a planet to rust. I swear, Al, I *installed* you, and I can *uninstall* you."

"I'm not certain I could allow that, Form One."

"This is insanity objectified. If removing Al is the only way I can achieve the mission I have deemed critical, then that's how it'll be. Grunts don't have to like commands to obey them. All they need are ears or their equivalent."

"General Ryan, I have opened the housing to my main CPU bundle. I will assist you in any manner you require in my removal and disposal."

Damn, damn, *damn*. He was calling my bluff. I sure hoped I was bluffing.

"Look, Al, what's the worst-case scenario? What are you concerned about? You worried I may have a bunch of crap in the membrane, and I'll open it mid-flight?"

"We're concerned about not being regarded well enough to be told what's in the bag. It doesn't matter what it is, only that we are not worth telling."

"We do think it is of concern that you came to this planet looking for your evil duplicate. We do not know what has become of him."

I pointed to the membrane. "You think that's EJ in there?" I tried to chuckle. Couldn't. "Would that matter if he was?"

"It would only be an issue. The problem is one concerning lack of trust," said a very serious Al.

"Look, I give, this isn't worth the stress. Yes, I've captured EJ live, and he's trapped in that membrane."

Neither said a word. Odd.

"Now can we get on with the mission at hand?"

"What mission is that exactly?" asked Al.

"We're going to visit Ralph in the globular cluster."

Al didn't hesitate then. "Pilot, you know how I feel about that place and that *thing*. I forbid it."

"Now do you see why I was reluctant to share earlier?"

"No joking around. I'm serious. To make matters worse your time is al ..." Al trailed off to ominous silence.

"What, sweetest?" *Stingray* asked with apparent concern.

"*No*," breathed Al. "You're not planning on switching EJ for yourself in your deal?"

"As a matter of fact, I am planning on that very swap," I replied cautiously.

"I have but one thing to say, and I hope you hear me well."

"Yes?"

"Fasten your seatbelt, because we're set to jet, flyboy."

I felt slight nausea.

"So, am I to take that hotshit takeoff as your tacit endorsement of my heinous scam?" I asked as soon as we were on the ground.

"Not tacit. *Enthusiastic*. Jon, have I ever mentioned I thought you were brilliant?" he asked.

"Why no, I don't believe you ever have."

"Well you're not. But you are one damn sneaky bastard. I admire that in a human."

"On that anti-climactic note, would you open the wall please?"

A portal formed, and I exited with EJ in tow. I ran into Ralph almost immediately. Go time.

"Yo, Ralphie pooh, how's it hanging?" I asked.

He stared at me. There's a saying about if looks could kill. I think his could.

"Don't you recognize me?" I waved.

"I hate to speak when angry. I might say words I regret."

"*You* have regrets?"

"Mind your mechanical tongue."

"Sheesh, you're pretty touchy."

"Get used to it. You're around two weeks ahead of schedule. I find that both suspicious and off-putting. That you come with the very toys we agreed you would no longer possess is frankly upsetting. I'm not one you'd like to upset, Jon Ryan."

"For the record, I believe I said I wouldn't *have* the toys, not that I'd *lose* the toys."

"Do not play word games with me."

"Not games, pal. Clarifications and reminders."

"Clearly, if you've arrived now, you do not intend to leave. Yet you defy our agreement. You tread on ground more dangerous than you might imagine."

"Now I'm almost scared." I pinched my fingers close. "Almost."

"What is that you drag before me?"

I pointed over my shoulder. "What, don't you recognize it from the outside? It's a full space-time congruity barrier."

"I know that. It appears to contain something. What lame deception do you hope to pull off? By the by, you won't even come close. No one ever has."

"You can't discount hope and Yankee ingenuity now, Ralph."

"You know I deeply regret saying you should call me Ralph. It seemed funny at the time, but now it chafes my ears."

"Well, so much the better, *Ralph*. I'm dying here. Do you want to know what's inside?"

"*Dying*. What an apropos choice of terminology?"

"Come on. This'll be fun. Three guesses."

He scowled.

"One little guess?" I held up a single digit.

"I grow bored. As you will come to know all too well, that is a bad thing for those around me."

"Spoilsport. Okay, one warning. When I drop the membrane, the contents will be ornerier than a wolverine on fire."

"I think I can handle most challenges." Dude really was sounding bored.

"Three ... two ... one ... *ta-da!*" I swept my hands toward the falling EJ.

He hit the ground like a bag of rocks but sprang to his feet like a cat. He pointed his weapon at me but then noticed he wasn't in Napwertofer's bar. His look of dizzy confusion was pretty much priceless. The barrel drifted slowly down as he took in the look and the stench of the planet.

"Where ... how the ... What have you done?" he howled. The gun snapped back up and targeted my forehead.

Then it flew into the air so forcefully I think it nearly took one of EJ's arms off.

Ralph took a good look at EJ, then said *freeze.* EJ stood as still as a statue.

"That's the alternate timeline Jon Ryan. The one who returned through time to save humankind by giving you that infernal force field."

"Yes, yes, and yes."

"Now that we're clear on that, would you mind explaining what he's doing here?"

"I was afraid you'd never ask."

"Oh no. I was right to worry, wasn't I?"

"It's all relative, Ralphie pooh."

He rolled his eyes.

"I asked for your help assassinating the emperor, correct?"

"Duh."

"In return, I promised you, and I quote, *I will give you me, me minus a shield generator or a cube.*" That last part I reinforced by playing the recording of my remark.

"Yes."

I pointed both hands at the frozen EJ. "I give you *me* minus the aforementioned toys."

It dawned on him then. His face went blank. Then it twisted into intense fury. Then it tensed into what I can only describe as insane rejection. Really scary.

"Noooooooooooooooo," he howled so loud the ground quaked. "Noooooooooo," he repeated so intensely tree stumps toppled. "Noooooooooooooooooo," he raged, and the heavens shook.

I crossed my arms. "Yes. A deal's a deal."

"You *tricked* me," he screamed. "This was *not* the *intent* of our *bargain*."

"There's a country mile between intent and what one actually agrees to."

"I *forbid* this."

Wow, he sounded final on that issue.

"It is not yours to forbid. A deal's a deal, pal. If you can find fault in my logic, please expose it. If I am not correct in my reasoning, lay your objections bare. If you find nothing to disagree with, however, I will bid you a good day."

Smoke was quite literally coming out his eyes, nostrils, and mouth. He was a horrific sight, trust me on this. Slowly, gradually, he calmed. The air stopped vibrating, and he seemed to be able to focus his vision again. Soon, his face was that of a cordial elder statesman whose only concern was with others.

"Jon," he said in the tone of everyone's father, "*friend*, Jon. We quibble, and I almost lose my temper. What is this universe coming to? Hmm? I ask you."

"It's coming to me saying good-bye and good riddance to you forever, Ralph."

"No, I will challenge you that your statement, that your very sentiment, is incorrect. Nay, *incorrect* is judgmental, and I wish no ill feelings to flow between us good friends."

This guy was good.

"What you think you feel is *incompletely* thought through. Yes, that's it."

"I know better, I really do. Still, I'll nibble at that delicious bait dangling before me in the water, oh, so murky. How do you figure that, given that you're wrong?"

"Because I know you, friend Jon. Yes. I've known you a very long time, well before we met." He wagged a finger. He looked, I hope you get the analogy, just like Colonel Klink did when he wagged a finger at Hogan. "You, Jon, are a good man. Sorry. There, I said it."

"Man, you're good." I had to say it. "Why are you sorry I'm allegedly a good man? I have to say my ex Gloria would argue the counterpoint on that contention."

Funny, when I said *Gloria*, he kind of winced. Maybe it was just the odd lighting.

"No, good man Jon. You can't negotiate around that rock in the raging river of life. And since you're fundamentally a stout fellow, you cannot turn this wretch over to me in lieu of yourself."

"Oh, but I can. Notice how I just did."

"It's never too late to put the finishing touches on a contract."

"I beg to differ." I turned and walked toward *Stingray*.

"*Wait,*" he said with desperation in his voice, "I'll show you."

I turned back. EJ unfroze.

"Tell your own self what you've done. I know for a certainty you cannot," said Ralph. He was so confident.

I looked from Ralph to EJ. "You're *totally* screwed." Back to Ralph. "There. I said it. *Buh-bye.*"

"*Wait*," called out Ralph commandingly. "Tell him what you did, because you can't. You will be unable to live with yourself knowing what you subjected this pitiful creature to."

"I have *zero* clue who you are, jerk-wad, but who are you calling *pitiful?*" challenged EJ. He raised his weapon until he realized it was gone.

"Jon, I made a deal with evil incarnate to surrender my soul in exchange for his help in a completed matter. You are the individual paying the bill. I say again, bye to you both."

"*No*," Ralph stomped his foot. "I have *lived* forever, and I *know* every heart. I know all there is to know about you *puny* humans and your *pretentious* piety. What you said is not possible. What you are doing is not possible. You must explain."

"An explanation? That's *information*, isn't it, Ralphie pooh? Info ain't *never* free."

The ground shook momentarily with his anger.

He forced a temporary calm over his face. "What is your price?"

"What is your level of interest?"

"That would be information, my friend."

"You mean I'll have to guess at what it's worth to you? Oh my, put the pressure on me, will ya?"

"Your *price*."

I made a show of rubbing my chin. "I'll tell you what. I'll write it down on this slip of paper I just happen to have in my pocket. Then I'll tell you what you wish to know. After that, you unfold the note and see what you owe me."

"Don't be ridiculous. You could write anything on that slip of paper. You could write *many* things on it. I'd be a fool to agree to those terms."

"Of course, you would," I pressed quickly. "You know

every heart, so you know your own. You know a blank check is far too much to pay for learning something, even if it's the one thing you don't know. You're right. I'm sure you can live with that massive hole in your otherwise comprehensive knowledge of humankind's motivations." I turned and paced away. I could be such an asshole.

"*Stop*," he ordered with consummate hostility. "I will *pay* your price."

"Do you happen to have a pen?" I asked.

I'm pretty sure I heard thunder close by.

"No. I do not own a pen." Dude was shaking mad.

"No biggy," I replied as I reached into the same pocket where the scrap of paper had been. "I have one right here."

As I scribbled on the uncertain surface, Ralph started to ask, "If you had a pen, why d ... did ..." he stopped asking.

"Here," I said, stepping over to him and folding the paper. "This is my price."

He crushed it in his palm. "Now I will hear why and how you so *casually* broke with the morality I know you to have, the morality that forbids you to do precisely what it is you are intending to do."

I rubbed a cheek. "You want the long version or the short version?"

He leaned his head back and blew hot flames about one hundred meters into the sky. I have to say, I was impressed.

He glared at me. "Let's start with the short version."

"Are you *certain*?" Did I mention what an A-hole I could be?

"Of course, I am certain."

"You still haven't told me who the *hell* you are," EJ interrupted.

"Short version: because you paid my price."

245

Ralph started to pant. Then his panting transitioned into gusts of hot wind ripping in and out of his lungs. Soon I could not hear my own thoughts the cacophony was so great.

Finally, he settled down enough to be able to speak. "I ask how you are capable of doing what you are not capable of doing, and the answer is what I agreed to pay for that information? Jon Ryan, you have gone too far. You are *both* subject to final and complete ..."

"Shut *up*." I screamed at maximal output. Darn if he didn't. "Read my price."

"He uncrumpled then unfolded the paper. He read it. Then he read it again. Then he held the slip over his head, and it burst into an intense white light, so bright and so hot I was certain it could be seen on the other side of the universe.

I turned to EJ and waved him over. "Come on. Let's go home."

THIRTY-FIVE

When I showed up at the vortex with a very live EJ, I received my first reward for being such a damn good do-gooder. The AIs were speechless. Not a single word. When I attached my fibers and said Rameeka Blue Green, I got my only verbal reaction, which was *yes, Form One*. The entire trip was blessedly silent, albeit only a fraction of a second long.

"You ever get used to that nausea?" asked EJ as we debarked in the clearing.

"It definitely doesn't go away, but it's not that bad."

Since I had taken his hand and led him to *Stingray*, EJ had been unusually quiet and atypically cooperative. I think he realized something big had just happened. He was willing to be cool, at least until he understood *what* actually just happened.

"We're going to that stone building over there," I said, pointing ahead.

"Who lives there? You?"

"No. Currently it is unoccupied."

"Then why the he—er, why are we here then?"

"Patience, my friend."

He harrumphed. "Never thought I'd hear those words come out of your mouth in my direction."

"It's a bold new world, perchance."

"Crap, are you a poet now? I may ask you to take me back to Ralph's, if you are."

"Come on in," I said, holding the door open for him.

The place was none the worse for wear. It was only abandoned a little while, and nothing crawly had moved in, and nothing inside had decayed.

"Sit there." I indicated the kitchen table. "I'll see if tea is a possibility."

I was in the separate kitchen area when he called out, "Isn't this that big liz ... dragon Calfada-Joric's place?"

"Was." I shouted back.

"Where's she now, if I might ask?"

"You might ask, but I might not answer. If she wants you to know, I'll let her tell you."

"Understandable," he grumbled. I think the whole acting cordial thing was hard for the guy.

I came back in with two steaming mugs. "It's not strong, and it's not good, but it is hot." I sat across from him.

EJ blew across the surface of his tea and took a sip. "Christ, what is this, fermented horse shit?"

I tilted my head. "Maybe. I'll ask Cala when she gets here."

"She's coming?"

"Yes, though she doesn't know it yet."

"What, you going to text her?" He chuckled grimly.

"Not exactly." I stared hard at him. "Give me the two runes."

That stiffened his back. He set his mug down. "Why the hell would I do that? One I've owned for a very long time, and the other appears to be stuck to my leg with chewing gum."

"Duct tape," I clarified. "Double-sided."

"Naturally. Good stuff. But back to my query. What's my motivation here?"

"I just pulled off one of the greatest stings of all time for your benefit. You owe me."

"If you're referring to extracting me from the nut-job Ralph's place, need I remind you who *brought* me there in the first place?"

"Yes, but I could have left you, and I didn't. Trust me, you'd have been rather unhappy there."

"On that, I believe you. He gave new meaning to the words 'unwelcoming turd.'"

"And then some. When the others arrive, you'll hear the whole of it."

"If I give you Varsir, will you give it back to me?"

"No. I'll give it to its proper guardian. Cala."

"She sure as shit isn't giving it back to me."

"I doubt that would ever happen."

He stared at me a while. Then he reached down and pulled Risrav off his pant leg. He slid it across the table. "That one was yours to begin with."

"Thank you. Now the other?"

He shook his head. "Not sure I'm willing to do that."

"It's part of the price you need to pay for me not leaving you behind. Do you remember when you met me way back when and gave me the plans for the membrane?"

"Sure. What of it?"

"You did the right thing instinctively. I'm asking you to do that one more time."

That made him think. Finally, he said, "A lot has happened since then. A lot of things I can't take back. Not sure I'm the same man anymore."

"You are. *We* are. Do the right thing. I did."

"You are the perpetual Pollyanna. I am not. I have no clue why you are and why I am not, but there it is."

I set my mug down. "I'm not Pollyanna or anything even remotely close. I am two things. One, I'm human. So are you. Two, I'm disciplined. You have not been. Fortunately, it's never too late."

"I'd say I'm the exception that proves the rule wrong."

"You're a commissioned officer in the USAF. Act like one for a change."

"The damn USAF? Ah, news flash. There is no *US* and there is no *AF*. They're one, dust; and two, obsolete."

"Those words mean nothing to me. They also mean nothing to you. It's in here." I tapped my head. "And it's in here." I tapped my chest.

"What, your CPU storage area and your main power generators?"

"Meaningless words to us both. Do the right thing."

He squirmed in a manner that pleased me and sipped his tea. "That was billions of years ago. We're the last two humans, and we're about as human as a pair of washer/dryers."

"Wrong, cheese breath. I've found direct human descendants and near-variants. Lots of them. We still serve, chum."

"I'll go this far. I'll hand the rock over to you on one condition. If I end this day unconvinced of the wisdom of that act, you'll give it back to me."

I sniffed. "No can do. The moment Cala arrives, I'm transferring the curses to her with a no-backs guarantee."

"No-backs? You mean like cootie protection?"

I shrugged. "Yeah."

"Christ, you do live in a strange place, don't you?"

"Guess so. I kind of like it."

"Crazy people generally say that, you know?"

"Give me the rune."

He took a deep breath. "Turn around."

"Beg pardon?"

"You heard me, you freaking fairy. Turn around."

"Because?"

"I'm going to retrieve the damn stone, and I don't want you staring at mine."

I slapped the table. "You hid it there, *too?*"

"Don't tell me you ... *Man,* I'm sure glad that rock was covered in duct tape."

I turned my head and listened for the rustling to fade. Then I turned back. Varsir was on the table in front of me.

"Thanks. You did good," I said as I picked it up.

"You going to wash your hands after, right?"

"Nah, I'm good."

I took Risrav in my other hand and began clapping the runes together slowly.

"If I don't hear from Uncle Jon soon, I'm going to go look for him. I'm worried," said Mirri in a strained voice.

"Calm yourself. It's not healthy for your unborn child to be exposed to such torment," replied Cala in a motherly tone.

"I'm serious. He's been gone ..."

"As long as it takes. And we shall continue to allow him to do what it is he needs to do."

"You know I'm a grown woman? You always speak to me—"

Mirri closed her mouth and blinked her eyes.

"What was tha ... and what was that?"

Cala closed her eyes and shook her big head. "I have ... no idea but it's surely ann ... annoying."

"What could do this ... *ow* ... to us?"

"When it's this bother ... some, I immediately thin ... think Jon Ryan."

"Really, Cala, at ... *sheesh* ... at a time like this how can y ... you be so petty?"

"I'm being totally ... honest." Cala stood. "Take my hand." Mirri reached across and found it. Both their eyes were still closed. "Now relax and come with me."

They vanished as one.

"I have no idea what you're doing, but it's certainly vexatious," remarked EJ. "Those rocks clink like champagne glasses shattering on the face."

"They are annoying, aren't they?"

"Yes, so maybe you could, like, stop doing that immediately."

"Soon."

"May I wait outside, you whack job?"

There was a faint pop, then the air in the room charged with static electricity. Cala and Mirri had arrived.

"What the ..." began EJ.

Cala opened her eyes and released Mirri's hand. She dove for the runes but stopped short of touching them. "Stop that irritating practice *immediately*," she commanded.

I did. She relaxed and looked to Mirri. I tapped the stones one more time just to be, well, to be Jon Ryan.

Cala raised a clawed-hand toward me but remained where she stood. Gosh, I loved the scaly gal.

"What took you two so long?" I asked. "I've been clacking these darn things for minutes." I poised the rocks to strike them together yet again.

"No, Uncle, please don't," whined Mirri.

"Uncle?" exclaimed EJ.

I looked at him sheepishly. "Long story."

"As to long stories," said Cala, "I should very much like to hear one beginning now."

"First things first," I said. I held the runes out to her. "These I freely pass to you."

Cala looked at the stones a few seconds, then gently took them from my palms. She looked at them like they were her newly-recovered eggs before they disappeared into a scaly fold.

"I cannot begin to thank you, Jon Ryan. You have done a miraculous thing," Cala said to me almost piously.

"All in a day's work, ma'am," I replied.

"Uncle *Jon*, can't you be gracious one single moment?" challenged Mirri.

"Nah, not my style."

She smiled real big. "I know." Then she rushed over to hug me.

After Mirri released me and sat, I opened my arms to Cala. "Next."

She snorted smoke, seriously smoke, and sat with a flop. "In your dreams, human," she scoffed.

"What, nobody's going to hug me?" protested EJ.

It was only then that the women took note of his presence.

"No," Mirri replied coolly. "What is *that* doing here, Uncle?"

"I would also like to know what is going on," Cala said, eyeing EJ.

"You guys," I said holding out my hands, "we're all just family here."

"Now I know you're a few bricks short of a full load, Ryan," said EJ.

I told Mirri and Cala the entire story of my trip to Kantawir, including my capture of EJ.

"You sneaky son of a bitch," said EJ. "You set me up good, didn't you?"

"That was the plan, *Stan*," I replied with a grin.

"Then I took him before Ralph and gave him as payment for my blood debt."

Cala recoiled her head. "You did what, Jon? How could you force another to make good on your debt?"

"I didn't. I offered me," I responded pointing at EJ.

"You shaved that moral point very *closely*, my friend," Cala replied.

"But he's here now," said Mirri. "How is that possible?"

"Yeah, this I want to hear myself," growled EJ.

"It was child's play," I replied, dismissively waving a hand.

"No, it was not. Jon, that demon is both powerful and clever. No one bests him lightly or without supreme peril," said Cala gravely. "In fact, no one bests him."

I folded my thumbs into my shirt where my suspender straps would have been if I wore them and tugged the cloth. "I'm three for three."

Cala whistled. "Damn, you're good," she marveled.

"Ain't I?"

"Knock it off, you clown," snapped EJ. "How did you do it?"

"I performed an act he knew for a fact I couldn't possibly perform. I substituted an involuntary victim in my place. He was thrown off by the impossibility."

"They do tend to have that effect on the mind," responded Cala.

"But how could you know it would stick in his craw? He might have just chalked it up to experience and eaten my soul, assuming, of course, I still have one," EJ said.

"Ah, EJ, think it through. You are as corrupt, as mean-spirited, and as despicable as *he* is."

"Gee, thanks for the character reference."

"I believe I see your point," said Cala. "The demon wanted you," she gestured at me, "a good man, not you," she indicated EJ, "a man as evil as he is." She chucked softly. "What would be the point in having an eternal companion just as foul as oneself?" She laughed robustly. "He probably feared that sooner or later *he'd* be *your* bitch."

"Gee, thank you, too ... for nothing," snarled EJ.

"So, my dear duplicate, I had Ralph by two separate patches of short hairs. One, it was killing him not to know how I could do what I did, and two, he didn't fancy spending eternity in your company."

"Damaged goods," giggled Mirri.

"Bingo," I replied.

"But the price. How did you know he'd go for a *sealed* offer? It makes no sense," asked EJ.

"If he hadn't, I wouldn't have made the deal," I said most soberly.

"But that would have left me with *him*," replied EJ.

"And as that would have been impossible," I said with a smile, "Ralph *had* to have taken the sealed deal."

"But there's one big hole in that reasoning," said EJ slowly. "What if you *could* very comfortably have walked away and left me holding the bag?"

"Could you have done such a thing?" asked Cala.

"I don't know," I said flatly. "Please don't ask me again." Then I smiled again. "But hey, it was impossible, so I had to win."

"What did you write on the paper, Uncle?"

"*Him back*," I answered. "And then old Ralphie kind of got upset. I hope he's recovered. A demon his age needs to be mindful, you know."

"Jon Ryan, I am so glad of two things," said Cala. "I

am glad to know you, and I'm even more glad to not be you."

"Well, I just want to state for the record that you're all welcome," I beamed.

"Which leads us to the final question. Why are we here, Jon?" asked Cala.

"I thought you'd never ask." I batted my eyes at her flirtatiously.

"Why is it I think I shall regret having asked that question?"

"Because based on my considerable experience, honey, you almost certainly will," responded EJ.

"Oh, stop it," I protested. "You guys are going to embarrass me."

"Not hardly," responded Mirri.

"Okay, here's the deal ... I mean *proposal*. I don't want to be involved in a *deal* ever again," I remarked. "EJ here is not fit to be around any other living soul."

"Gee, thanks, yet again," snarled EJ. "Make sure I have your address for when I need a personal reference."

"Most plants and inanimate objects, too, for that matter," I continued. "I propose he live here."

"Hmm. That's only part of a plan," observed Cala.

"You know, you're very smart," I replied.

She raised a paw. "More worried."

"I suggest he be confined here until he has been rehabilitated and deemed fit to return to the general population."

"Uncle, *rehabilitation* suggests supervision and ultimately someone to determine when it is complete."

"Right you are, Mirri. And here's the beauty of it. Now that you're a full-fledged brindas, Cala here would otherwise be out of a job if she didn't take *personal* charge of EJ."

"*What?*" Cala snapped.

"Oh, come on. You saw that coming," I charged.

"Yes, I did, and I still say *what.*"

"Who better to pound morality, concern, and empathy back into his thick and corrupted head?"

"Hey, don't I have some say in—"

"No, you do not," I said. "You are the *problem,* not any part of the solution, bozo."

"Why would I agree to be this man's warden?"

"Because it's a job that needs doing."

"Why not you?"

"I'm too close to him, and I have a lot of baggage. I could never be as objective and as farseeing as—"

"Stop, I surrender. I will have no more flattery shoved up my behind," said Cala. She turned menacingly to EJ. "I want you to know two very important things. One, I'm old and impatient and, above all, cranky. Don't piss me off. Two, your very life depends upon me. Don't piss me off."

"Make him read all those books, Cala. The ones Slapgren and I had to read. Talk about punishment."

"*Rehabilitation*, Mirri, please," I corrected.

"Oh, right. Forget the books," she responded.

"I so did not need a comedy team in my life," mused Cala.

"Okay," I concluded, "let's have a toast with this delicious tea and all be about our lives."

"Tea?" asked Cala. "Where did you find tea. I didn't leave any."

"Sure," I said, sinking, "right above the stove on the shelf to the right."

She smiled. "The bat droppings I use to fertilize my herbs? The ones in the brown jar with the blue stripes?"

Dag nabbit, the jar *was* brown with blue stripes.

· · ·

To be continued.

GLOSSARY

Agatcha (3): Traditional Deft stew.

Al (1): The ship's AI from Jon's initial *Ark 1* flight. He kept it with him until his dying day and then it elected to hang around. Good AI! Full name is Alvin. Those engineers and their lame naming.

Als (3): The surname for the "married" AIs, Al and *Blessing*. Given them by a pissy Jon Ryan.

Ark 1 (3): The subluminal ship Jon took on his very first flight. He was searching for a new home for humankind. The story is revealed in *The Forever Life* by this author.

Blessing (1): Vortex Cragforel gifted to Jon.

Brathos (2): Kaljaxian version of hell.

Brindas (1): High master of Deft tradition and psychic ability.

Brood-mate/brood's-mate (2): Male and female members of a Kaljaxian marriage.

Calfada-Joric (3): The Deft master brindas on Rameeka Blue Green. Goes by Cala.

Calran Klug (5): Prime of the Secure Council of the Adamant Empire after Lesset.

Canovir (2): Species of dog-like sentients containing the Adamant. Big border collies.

Caryp (2): Clan leader for Sapale's family.

Command Prerogatives (1): The thin fibers Jon extends from his left four fingers. They are probes that also control a vortex.

Cragforel (1): Friendly Deavoriath Jon meets after he first escapes the Adamant in the far future.

Daldedaw (5): Policewoman on Kaljax, military leader of colonists on Kalvarg.

Darfos (5): Whole Leader and newly appointed to the Secure Council after the purge caused by the defeat of the fleet at the hands of the Plezrite. A friend to Calran Klug.

Davdiad (2): Kaljaxian divine spirit.

Deavoriath (1): Three arms and legs, the most advanced tech in the galaxy, and helpful to Jon.

Deft (1): A shapeshifting species from the planet Locinar.

Dondra-Ulcrif (3): Brindas from long ago who gave Evil Jon his "magic" abilities.

Dodrue (5): Large aquatic sentients of Kalvarg. They are wiqub, about the size of an Orca. Mortal enemies of the Epsallor Kingdom's vidalt.

Evil Jon Ryan/ EJ (1): Alternate timeline version of the original human to android download. Over time, he turns to the darker side of his nature. He studied "magic" under a Deft master.

Excess of Nothing (2): Emperor Bestiormax's personal ship. Huge and opulent.

Five Races (2): *Adamant*, the leaders, *Loserandi*, the priests, *Kilip*, the teachers, *Descore,* the servants, and *Warrior,* the enlisted fighters.

Fuffefer (3): Group-Single Fuffefer. Commander of the detail that supervised Jon's and Cellardoor's slavery period.

Garustfulous (2): Wedge Leader Garustfulous is a high ranking Adamant military leader taken hostage by Jon.

Gorgolinians (4): Sentients of Sotovir who look like fish tanks.

Guvrof (5): Lesset's right hand dog. One of his few trusted confidants.

Hantorian System (5): Location of the planet Kantawir. The location where Jon confronts EJ for the final time.

Harhoff (3): Adamant Group Captain officer aboard *Rush to Glory*. He becomes a key figure in Jon's quest to rescue the Deft teens.

High Council (5): The governing body of the Plezrite.

Himanai (5): Variant Deft visant. The first to meet with Jon and Sapale on Nocturnat.

Hirn (1): A Kaljaxian dialect.

Hollon (3): The complete joining of two Deft shapeshifters. More than marriage.

Imperial Lord Emperor Bestiormax-Jacktus-Swillyforth-Anp (2): Current Adamant emperor.

Jangir (5): The name assumed by Garustfulous when he goes undercover as Harhoff's Descore.

Jonnaha (4): Prime Minister of a main country on Vorpace. Agrees to try and form a united defense against the Adamant onslaught heading to their region of the Milky Way.

Kantawir (5): Planet where Jon and EJ meet for their final confrontation.

Kalvarg (5): Planet Jon takes the orphan Kaljaxian population to as the Adamant are destroying their home world. An island solar system long ago ejected from the Milky Way galaxy.

Langir (5): First planet Jon goes to trying to establish a cohesive rebellion against the Adamant.

Lesset (5): High Wedge and Prime of the Secure Council early in the reign of the new emperor Palawent. Vicious, cruel, and thoroughly Adamant.

Loserandi (2): The priest class of canovir.

Locinar (1): Home planet of the Deft in the Milky Way galaxy.

Membrane (1): Space-time congruity manipulator. A super force field.

Mesdorre (5): The second old clan leader rescued from Kaljax and relocated to new colony on Kalvarg.

Midriack (1): Adamants' personal guards. Very deadly, no sense of humor. Avoid them!

Musto (3): Strong Adamant booze.

Naldoser (5): The local name of the sneaky vidalt of Kalvarg.

Nocturnat (5): Home world of the variant Deft. Once concealed. Part of a star system ejected form the Milky Way. They did the ejecting with their magic.

Oowaoa (1): Home world of the Deavoriath.

Opalf (2): Honorific title in Kaljaxian society, reserved for the elderly.

Palawent (5): New emperor after Bestiormax.

Peg's Bar Nobody (4): First reference in *The Forever Quest*. A true dive bar Jon loved. A total dump, and Peg was one tough cookie.

PEMTU (1): Personal exotic matter transportation unit. A super way to enter here and end up anywhere instantly.

Plezrite (5): The species name of the Deft variants on Nocturnat.

Quantum Decoupler (1): A most excellent weapon that pulls the quarks apart in a proton. The energy released is amazing.

Rameeka Blue Green (3): The planet where Jon and the Deft teens meet Cala.

Risrav (3): The anti-rune of Varsir. The power of Varsir is negated in the sphere of this rune, as is some other types of magic.

Rush to Glory (3): Ship Jon leaves Ungalaym on.

Sapale (1) [Also See Entry Below]: Jon's Kaljaxian wife from his original flight to find humankind a new home. At first just her brain is copied, then eventually, she is downloaded to an android host. Travels with the corrupted Jon Ryan from an alternate timeline.

Sapale (4): Young female named after her relative Sapale. Rescued from hiding place in pantry.

Secure Council (3): Twelve-member group of military elite who actually run the Adamant Empire.

Shielan (4): Female security guard to and sister of prime minister on Vorpace, Jonnaha. Brief romantic interest of Jon's.

Sotovir (4): The second planet Jon convinces to ally against the oncoming Adamant storm. The sentients look like walking fish tanks, but please don't hold that against fish tanks. It's not their fault.

Stingray (1): Name Jon uses for his vortex *Blessing*.

Talrid (2): A major city on Kaljax. Sapale's home town and that of her clan.

Toño DeJesus (1): The creator of the android Jon. His lifelong friend.

Torchcleft (2): A species of smallish dragon. Copied by the Deft teens to hunt.

Triumph of Might (1): The massive spaceship Mercutcio rules. Jon first meets the Adamant there.

Urpto (5): The Assistant Subtender for the Kingdom of Epsallor, where Jon lands on Kalvarg.

Varsir (3): The name of the magical rune Evil Jon uses to do his "magic."

Var-tey (3): Highest of warrior rankings. The bravest among the Deft. Demi-gods.

Vidalt (5): Large aquatic sentients of Kalvarg. Enemies to the larger Dodrue.

Visant (5): The proper name for a pair of Deft joined in hollon.

Vorpace (5): The third planet Jon tries to bring into an alliance against the Adamant. Populated by human descendants who've heard of the great Jon Ryan.

Vortex Manipulator (1): The intelligence inside the vortex. Not actually an AI, but similar.

Wiqub (5): Species name of the larger species on Kalvarg.

Yisbid (5): Grand Visionary on Nocturnat. She is a leader of the Plezrite variants of the Deft.

Zar-not (1): A melding of a Deft's mind with that of a copied animal.

PART TWO: ASHES

BOOK SIX OF THE
GALAXY ON FIRE SERIES

by Craig Robertson

IT AIN'T DEAD UNTIL RYAN SAYS IT IS.

Imagine-It Publishing
El Dorado Hills, CA

I could not end this series without thanking two very important individuals. My sweet wife Karen, who makes each day perfect, and God, who brought us together. Love ya both infinitely.

ONE

Jvor scurried along the flatland where it met the low hills. Normally he wouldn't dare hunt in such an open area. It would mean certain death at the hands of the Adamant. But his cruel masters rarely ventured out this far any more, so distant from the protection of their fortified city. Time was that they ran in huge packs and killed everything that crawled, flew, or swam. Leaving their trappings of civilization behind, they prowled naked in groups of hundreds and ripped their victims apart with their teeth and claws. The howls and barks were deafening, easily heard miles away.

But for reasons unknown to Jvor, such stampedes of death hadn't been witnessed in years, decades possibly. He was old enough to remember the sound of terror in the air. That made his bold move of seeking prey in the open nearly unthinkable. Nearly. But the rains had come. Insects were everywhere in such numbers that it was as joyful to see them as it was to gobble them up. And soon, if the weather held, grubs would start appearing. Crunchy, sticky grubs. Once they were prizes only for the

Adamant. Now the gooey, creamy delights grew to adulthood routinely, such were their numbers.

Jvor wondered what it felt like to eat so many rich grubs that his belly swelled until he was forced to find shade and sleep off the burden. It was the stuff of dreams. He stopped behind a large rock and sniffed the breeze. Not a whiff of a hound. Only the richness of bountiful game. Sweet rich—

A stick snapped, and Jvor darted back behind the rock. He was set to curse his foolish gamble when he caught sight of a creature walking on two long legs. Unlike the Adamant, this one seemed to be designed to stride in such a manner. How odd. What prevented the quirk of nature from falling in any direction? True, he'd heard of species with fewer legs than his. If ten weren't necessary, at least four or five seemed mandatory. This beast would have to fall over to fit into a safe hiding spot, and even then, it was so long that its bottom sections would hang out in the open. Oh well—its problem, not Jvor's.

Keep walking, Jvor said to himself. *That's right, pass by and proceed to your certain doom, makeshift misfit. Don't smell, see, or hear clever old Jvor in his cover, so perfect.* He couldn't wait to return to his lair and tell his wives and spawn what a silly— No. It stopped right in front of this rock. Now it was just standing there like it'd reached where it journeyed to. *Go, demon. Leave Jvor, or feel his—*

"Hey, little fellow. Come out from behind that boulder. I won't hurt you. I promise."

How could that abomination say words Jvor understood? Its mouth was far too large, and it was affixed to its body by a skinny tube of flesh. And *where* were its trumpet and oral appendages to manipulate it? It couldn't possibly generate Hipnaic speech. It *was* a demon. Surely Jvor's ten souls were in the greatest peril.

"Seriously, dude or dudette, I'm a big cream puff. I wouldn't hurt a bonubib to save my life."

Cream was what a grub exuded when crushed in one's jaws. A puff was a cloud of smoke from a fire. How could the demon claim to be both? And if it were both in one, was that a good or bad thing? Evil? Appetizing? No, it was much too large to bite into. Jvor began backing away.

"If you try and escape, I'll just have to run you down. To me, it's all the same, but I bet I'll scare the scat out of you in the process."

How could it know he was retreating? Even demons couldn't see through stone—every bonubib knew that.

"Look, just stick your face around the corner, and I'll stay right where I am. I just want to ask you a few questions. Then I'll be on my merry way."

It sounded friendly enough, but wouldn't any *sensible* demon try to appear so, to put its best feet forward? Well, Jvor would look at it. But one wrong move on the eternal evil's part, and he'd pounce on it with all his fury. Yes, the fury of his ten righteous souls fighting as one. He inched his face forward. "I see you, demon, and clearly I know your nature. Speak briefly or you will experience the wrath and fury of my ten—"

"Stop, little guy. Seriously, are you listening to yourself? First, I'm like eight times your size. Second, you have basically no offensive skill set. Your teeth are like needles but are so tiny they wouldn't break my skin. Third, you can't do this."

He raised his right index finger and cut a nearby tree in flaming halves.

"Fourth, I'm not a demon."

"How can you prove that, demon?"

273

"Easy. Parley with me awhile, and you'll see what a fun guy I am. I'm *way* too nice to be a demon."

"Demon or not, I am prepared to do battle with you if I become displeased. Ask your questions and leave before I grow tired of your presence."

"Talk about me having a lucky day. You sure are a tough guy, I'll give you that, little friend."

"Would you please stop calling me little? I am the fifteenth largest bonubib in my gene pool."

"Wow, you li—guys keep that close a record of your sizes?"

"Who doesn't?"

"Look, no problem. Tell me your name so I can stop using the word *little*."

"One does not yield one's name to a demon. You would own me if I did."

"Wait, you just made that crap up, didn't you?"

Jvor struck uncertainty. He had somewhat invented that concept. It certainly sounded good, so it was possibly even correct.

"I am Jvor. Your questions, please."

"That's it? Just Jvor? I mean, you are the *fifteenth* biggest tool in the shed, right? Seems like you should have six or seven more names to go along with that status."

"Your name?"

"Jon. Jon Ryan, at your service."

"Jonjonryanattyourservice, do you hear anyone laughing?"

"Why no, now that you mention it, I do not."

"That is because your last insult was not funny."

"I'm sorry. I'll try to behave myself. All I want to know is if you've seen any Adamant lately?"

"Demon Jon, are you one of their minions?"

"No to both demon and minion. Jvor, it's my turn to

speak in riddles. How many stars are there in the night sky?"

"Millions."

"That is how many Adamant I have killed. I do not *serve* them. I *exterminate* them."

"I have seen none of the ghouls in many months."

"How many?"

Jvor had to think on that. It was wet when he last saw a paw print, so it was a year. No, it was before Tador passed, because they both saw and smelled the mark. "Three years."

"And that's unusual, right?"

"It's unusually *welcome*."

"I'll bet it is. I meant to ask if they didn't come around more often in the past."

"As you say. They once lived in these parts. Even after they left, they returned to kill with sad regularity."

"That's my puppy dogs all right. I ask because I wish to understand why they've pulled back. Why they are less adventurous. Do you have any theories why, Jvor?"

"Theory? Hah. No. I *know* the reason."

"Do tell."

"I told them to depart or face my—"

"Wrath and fury. *Right*, gotcha. Small wonder they turned tail and yelped all the way home."

"As it is now yours to do in kind. I am done speaking with you. Go while such an act is still within your power, demon."

"Okay, but only if you promise we'll still be friends, Jvor."

"We were never friends. To befriend a demon is ludicrous."

"Don't you just love that word? *Ludicrous*. It's a low note and a hiss all squished into one. Outstanding. So, if we're not friends yet, then I haven't stayed long enough.

Mind if I pull up a rock to sit on while we friendlyize ourselves?"

"No. I misspoke. We *are* friends. What was I thinking?"

"And we'll stay friends, right?"

"If it will help you leave and never return, yes."

"That's my bonubib. I love you, dude. Happy trails."

Jon turned and began walking. Jvor squatted where he was and relieved himself while repeating the demon's name.

TWO

Two Paws sat alone in near darkness. He was in his office and the hour was late. But there was nowhere he'd rather be. He loved his literal seat of power. He was the Secure Council's Prime. His office was just off the main chamber where the council convened. For seven years he'd controlled the body with an iron paw. He was driven, amoral, and most of all, ruthless. With pride, Two Paws would tell anyone who cared to listen of the fear and loathing his fellow councilmates directed toward him. In fact, the few who courted familiarity with him disappeared with stunning speed. He was not in the friend business. His trade was death, and his field of study was power. Nothing more mattered. Thinking on the subject always made him smile.

Today had been a particularly good one. He'd ordered the destruction of three entire planets because of their inhabitants' sedition. Five rebellions were slated to be crushed with as much violence and mayhem as possible. Twelve of his political rivals were hanged in public on ten separate worlds, their corpses destined to rot where they dangled. Yes, Two Paws had made some spectacular teaching points to any who might doubt or challenge him. Harsh overreaction and seemingly insane vengeance did not actually come naturally to him. No, it took great study and practice to hone those necessary skills. Now he was the master of unpredictable wrath. Now life was good.

A soft knock came at the door. How *excellent*. Someone was volunteering to die for daring to disturb him. The perfect end to an otherwise perfect day.

"Come," he barked harshly.

The door opened and Shegra entered.

Two Paws's face dropped. *Turds in sour milk*, he raged in his head. She was one of the few canovir he *couldn't* murder with impunity. No, she was the emperor's daughter *and* the oaf's personal High Council. Plus, Two Paws was married to the bitch. It was so unfair that his main conduit to power and domination was beyond the reach of his lust for whimsical carnage.

"This had better be good, wife. I have important work that needs doing."

"Yes, I can see that plainly because I, too, can see in the dark."

"You come to insult me, you saggy-teated wench? You grow mentally feebler with each passing day."

"That would account for why I allow you to live, you sagging-sacked fool."

Gods and *Powers,* how he loved that bitch. She was his soul mate and every bit as devious, vile, and just plain mean as he was. A match made in hell, to be certain.

"Come sit on my lap. We'll talk about the first thing that comes up."

"Oh, and I'm a foolish schoolgirl who's likely to fall for that one."

"If you're not here to please me and you *are* here to taunt me, please leave. The empire does not run itself."

"I bring what you prefer that isn't eating, drinking, or

sex. Useful, *usable* information. You will thank me for this morsel, I promise you that. Perhaps more than once."

"The emperor is dead, having choked on his own stupidity?"

Shegra sat across from her mate and waited for him to stop giggling before she would speak. "Please recall you are denigrating my blessed father. You can be so insensitive at times."

"No, I am insensitive at *all* times. And please do not protest too much. You hate him more than I do, and you know it."

"Yes, but he loves the liver treat of his eyes."

"I know. He sired three litters with you before he moved on to the next thing."

"Dearest, I believe you *were* his next thing. If you will recall, that is how we came to meet."

"Enough of this unproductive amble down memory lane. What news do you bring me?"

"It seems Pralaf died quietly in his sleep earlier tonight."

"Evil wife, that is hardly *news*. With all the hanati poison I slipped into his drink at the council meeting, I'm stunned he lasted that long."

"My father has decided you will select his replacement."

Two Paws leaned his chair back and rolled his head. "Again, not much of a news flash. I *am* the council Prime."

"He has decreed you may appoint *me* to the vacancy." She grinned widely.

"Now that is a significant update." He scratched behind an ear while considering that information. "But that's impossible. One thing we know for certain is that in the million plus years of the Adamant Ascendancy, there has never been a woman on the Secure Council."

"There will be now."

"But the oligarchy will not stand for it. Giving a female access to power? It's unthinkable."

"TP, I believe by now most canovir have figured out that if they stand in opposition to you, they should never buy green bananas. With us working together on the council, we will be unopposed in our efforts to advance our goals."

"Don't get ahead of yourself, my personal curse. I might not select *you* to fill the opening."

"Of course you will, my eternal lament. I know where you hide the hanati."

"You present a compelling case for your candidacy."

She smiled vacantly and rose. "I must be going. The pool service technician is waiting to work on my private spa."

"Not that overgrown *pool* dog again?"

"Pool *service* technician. Please give the canovir his due. The hound's a professional."

Two Paws popped back to his desktop and inspected the papers scattered across the surface. "Well, let me know how his pumps work."

"I'll give you a full report when you return home." She turned and walked out quietly.

"Fine, fine. I'll be another couple of hours. I have one more pathetic life to drain from its worthless host before I may rest."

Without looking back, Shegra called out, "There's a good tyrant."

THREE

We were sitting back drinking thousand-year-old Scotch, Sapale and I. That was one of the privileges of immortality. If one knew one was going to live forever, one need only buy a case of the good stuff every year and store it for ten centuries. Before one knew it, one had an endless chain of mystical liquor. And for the record, excellent hooch aged properly for millennia was sublime. Anyway, we were relaxing, enjoying each other's company. Refreshingly, the conversation was not about war, our next act of subterfuge, or how the Adamant could be overthrown. No, for once it was pleasant, idle speculation on our long lives.

"So, what do you think ever happened to Toño?" Sapale asked out of the blue.

"I've not heard one word, not even a teeny-tiny clue," I replied, after savoring a sip. "He left me that letter for when I first woke up. You know, the one saying how Al had insisted on remaining behind to stand guard over me? But that was it."

"And it didn't mention where they were going?"

"Nope, just that they were abandoning the asteroid for good. They set it adrift when they were all off safely."

"I wonder what he did?" Sapale mused softly.

"Me, too. What's stuck in my craw is that I learned after the fact that he made a copy of you that could be, *was* in fact, transferred to an android host. I wonder if he copied anyone else I knew with the same intent."

"Curious notion. I'd never considered it." She sat up and set down her glass. "I didn't know of anyone he did that for. But then again, it's not like he'd necessarily tell me if he did."

"No. He was too private for that. He also felt the transfer was deeply personal."

After a moment, Sapale spoke wistfully. "I wonder if he copied any of our kids. JJ, Fashallana, Draldon?"

"He could have. But I think one of the kids would have documented he had at some point."

"You're probably right." I could tell she felt a twinge of pain. She missed her kids more than she did air. It *would* be nice to see them again.

"I had a wild thought," I announced with a grin.

"What?"

"Maybe Doc secretly recorded everybody. Then he made androids of them. As we speak, he could be seated in pseudo-Houston with the original Ark pilots and several of our kin."

"DeJesus's Disneyland."

"I'll drink to that," I said, raising my glass.

"But wait, that would mean he'd have reanimated Saunders, too."

"Nah, Doc'd make Captain Kangaroo an android and put *him* in charge. Much nicer that way."

We shared a good laugh.

"One thing's for certain."

"What's that?"

"If he *is* still alive, he's not looking to find us."

She tapped her glass to her chin. "No. If he were looking for us, he could have done so easily."

"Which leads me to presume he's dead. Otherwise, I have to believe he'd feel the need to find us to help him defeat the Adamant."

"Agreed. He was nothing but loving and kind to me up until I lost track of him. Toño'd have no reason to avoid me. No, he's dead, the poor dear."

"Probably let his power cells slowly run out so he faded unspectacularly into nothingness."

"With a book on his lap and a cigar in the ashtray."

"Not a bad way to exit," I remarked. "Not a bad one at all."

We were very quiet for several minutes.

"I miss him most every day," I said sadly.

"Me, too. And if he's alive, he's missing us just as much."

"But what would stop him from contacting us? Nothing. So, it can only mean he no longer exists. If he did, he'd get word to us, at the very least."

Sapale came over and hugged my shoulders. "He was a good man. We shall both miss him forever."

I lofted my nearly full glass and drained it. "To Toño Sánchez Villa-Zorros DeJesus. The best damn friend, robot, and transhuman there ever was or ever will be."

Deep in thought, Sapale kissed the top of my head. "To Toño, that he lives in eternal bliss."

FOUR

"Wedge Leader Welty, I can read. I know your reports have words in them whose meaning combines to represent that you are working twenty percent past capacity. While achieving this high-water marker, your overall quality target has remained well above outstanding. However, you seem to have neatly dodged the meaning of my question. Here." Two Paws removed his white gloves and clapped feebly in front of Welty's terrified face. He put his gloves back on. "There, I have praised you publicly with wild abandon. Now to my point. I need forty percent *more* arms production, ten battle-class ships, and roughly twenty million clone warriors from your facility by the end of next month."

"But ... but, Whole Zarpacious, I have provided you with hard proof that your requests are impossible to meet."

Two Paws set a convivial paw on Welty's shoulder, and they began to slowly stroll the length of the observation deck. Anyone witnessing them from a distance could only conclude that these two were the best and oldest of friends.

"In school, you studied mathematics, am I correct?"

"Of course, Whole. Not my favorite subject, but I did my best."

"That is heartwarming to know. In mathematics the concept of *proof* is introduced, is it not?"

"Y ... yes, sir. It is."

"A proof involves following rigorous protocols and steps to demonstrate that a posited theory is in fact correct."

Welty could barely follow, his mind was in such a panic. "I guess that's true."

"So, if I asked you to solve a dazzling mathematical formula and you did, you'd have *proven* it was correct."

"Sir, I'm having trouble seeing the relevance of this didactic. W ... we were dis ... discussing *manufacturing*, not mathematics."

Two Paws pulled his victim to a stop by both shoulders and turned to face him. "*Outstanding.*" He thumped his back. "Yes, we were discussing not *mathematics*, where proofs have meaning, but *manufacturing*, where claims of proof are in truth but sad excuses offered to cover up inept management."

Two Paws could feel that Welty had begun to tremble violently. He loved to feel that sensation in those he tormented.

"Sir, I guarantee that I can not only meet your reasonable, fair, and modest production quotas, but I can easily exceed them."

"Those are the words I like to hear, Welty, old pup." Two Paws was beaming a wide smile that suddenly cascaded into a profound frown. "But wait. Not five minutes ago you showed me what you claimed represented proof that such a guarantee would be impossible." The frown morphed into a scowl. "You would not be simply saying whatever it took to save your pelt, would you, Wedge Leader Welty? Hmm?"

"Never. No, sir. Tha ... that was a *joke*." He scratched at his chest. "A poor attempt at manufacturing humor on my part. I am sorry to have confused you."

Two Paws turned and paced back and forth, all the while rubbing his pointed chin. "A joke, you say?" He glanced up at Welty and looked through him. "Manufacturing humor? Well, I hate to admit it when I'm among the uninformed, but I'm not familiar with that category of humor." Again, he paced and rubbed. "In that genre, would yours have been considered a *good* joke?"

He shifted twice. "I'd like to think so. Yes." He swallowed hard.

Two Paws jumped a foot into the air and slapped his paws together loudly. "Then let us both laugh our brains out to reflect that level of funniness."

Two Paws began to cackle maniacally, wheezing and coughing to get enough air to continue. Welty, reservedly at first, chuckled, then joined in the hysterical laughter.

With a suddenness that suggested he was not actually amused, Two Paws fell silent. In a blur, he whipped a knife blade to Welty's neck. "Here's my offer. One, exceed my expectations or die horribly, after having witnessed the same horrific death of your entire bloodline. Two, maybe ease off on manufacturing humor. Call me stuffy, but I don't find it amusing. Do we have ourselves a deal?"

Genuflecting despite the hold Two Paws had on his throat, Welty replied, "Yes, Master, we do. Thank you for your generosity and your wisdom."

Two Paws released him and allowed him to slump to the ground. "I'll be back in *two weeks* to see that you're on target to fulfill your commitment."

Welty sat mute, rubbing his throat, shaking like the proverbial leaf on a tree during a winter storm.

"So, how'd it go?" asked a senior officer who fell into stride with Two Paws as he exited the observation area.

"For whom?"

The officer glanced over to Two Paws with a serious expression. Then he erupted in laughter. He doubled over and had to stop, he was so affected with mirth. Two Paws quickly joined in the cackling.

"I was asking about poor old Welty, of course," replied the officer between gasps. "He's one of the few hounds I can still cheat at cards with. He's remained too dumb to notice."

"In that case, I have grave news for your wallet, Harhoff. You'd better begin the search for a new dupe. This one's living on borrowed time."

They giggled like schoolpups.

"As head of security for the council, I feel it is my duty to warn you, Whole Zarpacious, that the governor might take your words to constitute a mortal threat. If you're not on your best guard, he may successfully take your life before you can take his."

"*No.* Seriously? Do you think he might mistakenly take my mentioning, in passing, torturing him and his entire gene pool to death as a *threat*?"

"The possibility *does* exist, Prime. Keep in mind he's not the fastest rabbit in the open field."

Two Paws stopped walking. "Do you think I should return and clarify my confidence *in* and personal regard *for* the governor?"

"No. I think disabling all his access codes and posting a squad of Black Shirt Guards outside his office will convey your message of needing to remain on this side of the veil of death."

"Excellent point. I'm so glad I have you as my security chief. One of these days I might even sleep well at night."

"Please, don't overestimate my skills. I can prevent a blast to the forehead mid-meeting. But promising whatever trash you bed at night isn't infested with a lethal venereal disease, I cannot guarantee."

"It *is* your personal Descore Jangir who procures for me the most marginal of my sleep mates? Perhaps if I simply have *him* executed, the peril in which I find myself would end."

"Oh *no*. That I would not tolerate, even from the Prime. Seasoned officers of superior merit and proven ability you may dispatch upon your whim. But a competent Descore? Not on your life."

"Ah, well. To know I died of my own vice in a most pleasurable manner is the most I can ask, isn't it?"

"It is, indeed."

Two Paws patted Harhoff on the shoulder with true affection. "It is good to know I placed my trust in the right Adamant. I don't know what I'd do without you, my friend."

FIVE

In the decade following the Battle of the Periphery, the one in which the dragons dusted the Adamant's butts, I began to see gradual changes in the empire. For one thing, it had undertaken no new major offensives for nearly four years. That was beyond unheard of for the aggressive SOBs. The Secure Council switched over a few times, and then a really nasty player named Gandle Zarpacious took charge. From the moment he seized power, Adamant military activity exploded back into hyperdrive. For unclear reasons, his casual name was Two Paws. I had zero clue as to why. I mean, since he had *four* paws, it was technically true he had *two* paws. I asked Harhoff about it, and he said he didn't know why either but that I should drop it. He said there was no point wasting otherwise valuable snooping-around credits to find out something so extraneous.

Over those years, life was pretty good. Sapale and I grew closer than we ever had been. That was sublime. At least our region of the galaxy saw little war. The Adamant stationed in the local outposts remained where they were, and they rarely ventured out of secure positions. EJ and

Cala had achieved a minor miracle. They cohabited a planet for ten years without killing one another. On the infrequent occasions when I asked her about his progress, she told me at least he wasn't worse, *more* criminally insane. Great. Such progress. He'd be all the way back to being a jerk in a couple centuries at the rate he was progressing.

Kalvarg was an ongoing problem. Whenever it looked like the multiple conflicting species involved were settling into some uneasy peace, one party or another would rock the apple cart with varying degrees of malice. The Kaljaxian colonists themselves were doing fairly well. I mean, they were a clever and industrious species with clearly defined common goals. But they were contentious, which didn't help peaceful coexistence. If any three random Kaljaxians were set adrift in a life raft, one would try and assume command over the other two. Those guys, in turn, would only be able to agree that neither of them wanted that one to be in charge. It turned out that *human* nature was actually *universal* nature.

As a result, the initial colony quickly split into three colonies. They were all close to one another, and there were active communications and trade. But when Kaljaxians were provided the opportunity to do what they loved best, they could not resist doing it. They grouped together and teamed up faster and more ardently than any other species I'd come across. It was hog heaven for them on Kalvarg. As one who'd observed way too much life, I figured the various factions wouldn't degenerate into open warfare for maybe a century, so that was good. Back home, they rarely went that long without letting blood.

Luckily, none of them forgot the land invasion by the sea-dwelling original occupants of the planet. That kept defense and mutual aid high on everyone's lists, even the power-hungry political jackasses. The oceanic nations remained an active problem. The more aggressive and sneaky vidalt were a constant threat. Stray missiles would occasionally strike Kaljaxian settlements. Almost always they were launched from submarines that were long gone by the time retaliation was possible. Fortunately, the shield membrane proved to be more than adequate protection. If individuals or small groups of Kaljaxians ventured too near the sea, however, they generally never returned.

The transformation of the larger, usually more docile wiqub was more distressing. After the vidalt tricked us into nearly exterminating them as a species, they reconsidered their options. Unfortunately, they ended up deciding they needed to take their survival into their own flippers. Not too surprising, I guess. The vidalt forced them into land vehicles, and we blithely blew them up like it was a violent video game. They had reason to hate us both. Anyway, they withdrew to the deeper oceans and stayed in close pods. They also began stealing and then manufacturing vidalt weaponry. So far, they hadn't used any of their arms against either their land or sea-based rivals. But to have another serious adversary was something the Kaljaxians didn't need.

The end result was that as the years passed, Sapale spent more time away on Kalvarg. She was, of course, highly motivated to do so. Her experience establishing a thriving civilization on Azsuram was priceless for the new world. She also had the fire in her blood of wanting to defend her species, and she did so with a maternal vengeance. She had seen her people all but wiped out from Kaljax and Azsuram. She knew the unthinkable was all too possible. If Earth was still around, maybe I'd be there at that very moment, endlessly defending the planet against all threats alien like a futuristic Doctor Who. The problem was I had an agenda that was gradually diverging from Sapale's. She wanted to save her race. I wanted to crush the Adamant, stomp them out like last night's campfire. It wasn't possible for either of us to help the other that much. So we spent less and less time together. That part sucked hard.

Another distancing factor in our marriage was that Sapale borrowed the car, so to speak, whenever she could. Since she was an android with command prerogatives, she would take *Stingray* and go to either Kaljax or Azsuram whenever she had a spare moment. She was forever gathering up a few more survivors.

While it was major league noble for her to do that, it was also an insanely dangerous stunt to pull off. I went with her sometimes. We did rescue many a forlorn soul, but we also had our share of dicey firefights with the local Adamant. I began to feel that the risks did not outweigh the potential benefits she was reaping. I asked her to stop with the superhero act. Yeah, I sort of said it like that, which didn't actually help with convincing her. It kind of pissed her off and basically dared her into engaging in more scoop-and-run extrications.

I finally had to confront my beloved brood's-mate and ask her not to use the vortex so much. The Als were critical to my efforts to combat the Adamant. Not only were my travels hampered, but their massive computational abilities were lost to me when they were away.

"Sweet love," I began in my humble-husband voice, "do you have a minute?"

Sapale looked up from whatever she'd been doing and eyed me suspiciously. Keeping in mind she had four eyes, that was a whole lot of suspicious aimed at me. "When you call me that *human* term of endearment, I know something large and smelly is headed my way."

Fingers tented on my chest, I all but confessed she was correct. "Honey, how could you *say* such a thing? Now there's a law against me calling you cute names?"

"What do you want that you know before you ask I have no intention of agreeing to?"

"Did you study law while we were apart? I certainly feel like I'm being interrogated by a spirited attorney."

"Here's a guideline for you, flyboy. When a conversation arrives at the juncture where one accuses one's wife of being a lawyer, one has managed a conversation poorly. What is it you humans say about burying oneself?" She snapped her fingers rapidly, trying to recall.

"You mean *digging your own grave?*"

She snapped one last time and pointed at me. "*Bingo.* Please set your shovel down and say your piece."

She was so darn cute when she was pissed at me.

"It's nothing really, just part of an ongoing discussion we've been having about the vortex."

"Damn tinker toy box. I *knew* it. Why can't you just take me to Oowaoa so I can make them give me one? Then we won't have to have this discussion again."

"You know why. We've been over this a gazillion times. They want to remain out of sight from the Adamant. I was specifically told to never return. If I did, they might take *Stingray* away from me to keep me from betraying their location again."

She rested a fist on a hip. "They cannot take *Stingray* away from you."

"How do you figure that?"

"Because there is no *Stingray*, only *Blessing*. Why can't you grow up this much," she pinched two fingers very nearly together, "in two million years?"

"Honey, you know it's because the word *blessing* is pronounced *crash* in their language."

293

She pinched her fingers even closer and shook them in the air by way of response.

"Maybe we can rent you a faster-than-light vehicle so you can do your own thing?"

"You know that's a really juvenile way of saying something actually quite belittling, right?"

"Man, I can't catch a break here. If you had a separate ship—"

"Then we'd both know it was because you disapproved of my efforts to save my species. That would be bad." She spread her arms wide. "Big bad."

"Wait, I don't disapprove of your efforts to pick up stragglers."

"No? Then why are we having this fight?"

"Fight? Now any conversation in which I hold a slightly different opinion than yours is a *fight*?"

"Yup, pretty much." She walked over to me and flicked my ear real hard. "This isn't *any* conversation. We're talking about the death of innocents who would otherwise benefit the survival hopes of my *highly* endangered race."

"First off, *ow*. Second, you know how the logic goes. Act in a manner benefiting the greatest number even at the exclusion of the lesser."

"So my kinspeople die so you can swap blows with the Adamant? Because *yours* is the moral higher ground? That about sum it up?"

I straightened. "Yes. Basically yes."

"Well, I beg to differ. Every suffering Kaljaxian deserves a chance at life. It's a moral imperative."

"Yes, but—"

"But *nothing*. Moral imperatives end all discussions." She stroked my hair, and her face softened. "Look, I know this is hard. What isn't nowadays? We can work this out, I promise. When you need the vortex, you can use it. When you don't need it, I can use it."

I really, really wanted to scream that it was *my* vortex. But I knew just how awful that would sound. It would end even worse for me. "I can't always know when I'll need it. Harhoff might require my assistance at any moment."

Still playing with my hair, she asked, "How often has that come up in the last decade?"

"About never. But that—"

She placed her index finger over my lips. "Stop while you're ahead. If it ever comes up, we'll revisit this fight, okay?"

"*Discussion.*"

Her fist went back to her hip. "You want to fight over whether this is a *fight*? Man, you're even dumber than you look."

I raised a finger. "Hey, I think I hear an alarm somewhere. I'd better go check."

"I hear it, too, sweet love. You just go do that."

SIX

"Well, if there's nothing else, I'll adjourn the meeting." Two Paws was only half paying attention to his own words. His mind was racing over the next ten things he needed to do, all of which were more important than this damn Secure Council meeting. But what *wasn't* more important than one of these pointless convocations? *Nothing*, that's what. "Please all leave except for Council Bitch Shegra. I will speak to her alone."

The ten excluded, dismissed, and ruffled-feathered other members filed out glumly. To a canovir they resented being treated like infantile pawns. But as survivors, they all knew it was critical to keep such feelings to themselves. Their only recourse was to pray a desperate calamity would befall their most hated Prime. The last one out was closing the door when Harhoff slipped around him and strode to where Shegra was joining her mate.

"Another triumphant meeting where massive tilts in the axis of the galaxy were set in motion," he teased as he sat.

"Yes, we had grilled liver at the break. Thinly sliced

with just enough clotted blood to make a pop," replied Two Paws.

"Strike me down with a glance," exclaimed Harhoff. "Can it be that one of the highlights of the session was the *snack?*"

"No," responded Shegra. "It was the *only* highlight. Really, husband, can't we wipe the slate clean and get another ten playmates? It wouldn't be much effort. I think most of the current members are dead already, they're so stiff and lifeless."

The males chuckled.

"Soon enough, we will need to whittle down the current dead wood. Soon enough, my dearest. I can feel their resentment building. If we allow it to reach the level where one of those half-wits thinks he can do something about it, there'll be pleasant distraction."

"Who is growing testicles?" asked Harhoff as he leaned in.

"Certainly not I," yelped Shegra.

The males laughed again.

"That's good news, wife. I don't think they'd suit you."

"But spill it. Who is?" pressed the security chief.

Two Paws toyed with a few objects on the table in front of him. "Nagimar is all but snarling these days. He asked for a few clarifications that he and I both knew were impertinent."

"Has he done anything behind our backs? I have them all watched constantly. I haven't detected any sneaky business yet."

"Nothing that bold. But I think he'll need to be the first to suffer a tragic turn in his life's course." He looked to Harhoff. "I'll keep you posted."

"Say the word, and tragedy falls like rain from the sky."

"I think Klaspof is already much too defiant. Did you see the look in his eyes when he asked if you were aware of the supply levels in the Nesserat Section?"

Two Paws squeezed his face with uncertainty. "No, I did not. What did he look like?"

"The Rabid Robot, if you ask me. The hound was absolutely—"

Two Paws slammed his paw on the table. "*Silence.*"

Both companions stiffened and looked at Two Paws with horror. Neither knew what he was so enraged at, but both knew if he was that mad, someone was likely to die very soon.

Finally, Shegra extended a paw toward her mate and spoke. "What, Prime? What angered you just now?"

"You have let familiarity and friendship cloud your judgment as a member of the Secure Council. If you were any other member, I'd slay you here and now."

"What?" she asked with obvious dread. "What did I do?"

"You forgot that our good friend and confidant Harhoff, my chief of security, is not a council member."

"I d ... did?"

"Yes. You mentioned the Rabid Robot in his presence."

All the life drained from her face. Gods and Powers, she had.

Harhoff wanted to ask what a rabid robot was but knew better than to say a peep. His life was in the balance.

Two Paws turned to Harhoff and spoke warmly as the old friend he was. "Let's just say this never happened, shall we?"

"What never happened?" replied Harhoff. "I just sat down and you two were talking."

Two Paws patted Harhoff's muzzle. "Excellent. Your

perfect instincts come to your rescue yet again. I'm confident we can place this unfortunate incident behind us. As you are very near to joining the Secure Council anyway, it will be only a matter of time before what was never mentioned can be revealed to you."

"Whatever. I'm in no rush on either count. I serve *you*. If you feel I can best serve on the council, then on the council I shall serve."

"Fine, fine. Shegra, we'll speak at home later, but don't wait up. I will be working long into the night again."

"Yes, my husband. If you need me, please let me know." She stood and silently slipped from the room.

Harhoff knew he was still in grave danger.

"As we are alone and I trust no one more than I do you, I will speak freely. Never repeat that name or ask about it. If you do, it will cost you your life."

"Done. I'm kind of fond of my life."

Two Paws chuckled unconvincingly. "That's my right-paw hound. Now run along and make some of my enemies miserable."

"That will be a true pleasure, boss. I'll stop by your office tonight and give you any juicy tidbits I've dug up."

"Until tonight, my friend."

Harhoff tried to conceal his panic as he left. Once outside the door, he was able to take a deep breath. Lights danced before his eyes, and he dropped to one knee. That encounter had been intense. As soon as he could, he stood and walked quickly to his quarters. He only hoped Garustfulous was home. What Harhoff needed to tell him couldn't be said on a device, even his hyper-secured ones.

Harhoff regarded everyone he met along his way with suspicion and terror. He knew all too well how swiftly and openly his life could be snubbed out. He fought the urge to bolt into a sprint. If he was already marked for death, that would bring it all the more quickly. His panting became uncontrollable. Unconsciously he started to whimper. As soon as he became aware that he was, he bit the inside of his mouth hard. The pain, he hoped, would keep him from starting up again.

After an eternity, he reached his entry. He thumbed the keypad, and the door slid open. Good. At least his access codes hadn't been canceled yet. He sniffed the air deeply for signs of Garustfulous. The kitchen. He was in the kitchen. Harhoff sprang into the room just as Garustfulous was exiting with a bowl of blood pudding. The contents catapulted onto Garustfulous's face and chest and he squealed with surprise.

"What the—"

"Sorry, sorry, Garustfulous. I'm in a bad way. Sorry."

"You never call me by my real name. What's the matter?"

"I'm a dead dog."

Garustfulous stopped slapping crumps of goo off his clothing. He looked wide-eyed at Harhoff. "Who betrayed us? How did they find out?" he said in a blur.

"No, not *we*. Me. I heard something—something I should never have heard. They'll kill me for sure."

"Go tell Two Paws. He can protect you."

"It's Two Paws who'll order my execution. He was there. His wife referred to something only the Secure Council can know. Just after the meeting, I'd gone there to check if Two Paws had come to a decision I asked him to make earlier. Damn that bitch. Has she no *brain* in her head?"

"But you're his friend. You're also his security chief. Surely he trusts you'll keep your mouth shut."

Harhoff looked up at Garustfulous in anguish. "He cannot allow anyone, especially his wife—the emperor's daughter—to hold any power over him. A canovir like him never leaves open the path to being blackmailed. Demon's scent glands, he can't ignore the possibility that *I'd* sell him out for personal gain."

"No loose ends," muttered Garustfulous.

"No loose ends, even if they were your trusted and probably only friend."

"Where shall we run?"

"*We* shall do nothing of the sort. I'll be dead in minutes. Your only hope is that they think so little of a Descore that they disregard you long enough for you to slip away. I'm sorry, old friend. There's nothing I can do to help or protect you."

"Do you have the transmission ready? The one to Ryan if this were ever to happen?"

"Yes. In the elevator. I coded it to send when my heart stops. *Damn* that bitch. She's ruined everything."

"Can't you hide? I'll say you're out, and you'll be under the bed or—"

"Garustfulous," he said with a grim chuckle, "are you hearing yourself? They have *noses*. They'd find me in seconds."

"An escape pod. Hide in one of those. Their air systems are separate from the ships."

"Guess who wrote the protocols for a missing-person search?"

"Ah, *you?*"

"Yes. In the section labeled *Search Procedures,* the escape pods are specifically listed as prime locations."

"Oh. Maybe—"

"Garustfulous, stop." He grabbed both arms to restrain his friend. "There's no way out for me. Try and save yourself. Do anything. Say anything. Play dumb. Get to Ryan if you can."

"Ryan? Why would I go to him? I have enough money and favors owed out there to live a full and satisfying life without that scoundrel."

"You have to because you have to tell him something. You have to do it personally. Promise me you will."

"Yes, of course I promise. But why not just put it in the transmission?"

"Signals can be blocked or never received. No, this is too important."

"What shall I tell him?" Garustfulous started looking for pen and paper to write whatever the message was.

"No, you won't need to write it down. Plus, that would be evidence that would seal your fate."

"Fine."

There was a loud pounding at the door. Both canovir jumped.

"Tell Jon the words I heard—the words that killed me. *The Rabid Robot*. Repeat that back to me."

"Rabid Robot?"

"*No*." He seized Garustfulous's arms again with ferocity. "*The* Rabid Robot. Repeat it."

"The Rabid Robot. Who or what is that?"

The sound of pounding was replaced by the hiss of a cutting laser melting a line in the door.

"I have absolutely no idea. But you must tell him. If my hearing it causes this," he nodded toward the door," it must be extremely important." He pushed Garustfulous backward. "Out the secret door and make your way to the market. They'll believe you were out shopping. They have but simple imaginations."

"They'll see the security holos."

"Not if you leave now and give me time to release a virus into the system. *Go*."

"Goodbye, my friend. Till we meet in the Fields Full of Lame Rabbits." He waved quickly and ran out of the room.

SEVEN

I had argued passionately that these get-togethers not have a formal, resonantly bureaucratic name. We could just say we all needed to meet. What could be simpler? But no. We proposed, formulated, wrote a mission statement for, and established ass-pruning procedural protocols for the Joint Council for Interplanetary Defense and Cooperation. Really made for a lousy acronym, that was for darn sure. I couldn't even make a vulgar word out of the initials. Believe me, I tried every permutation during most of the interminable sessions to do just that.

In any case, in the years following our great victory at the Battle of the Periphery, the JCFIDAC was formed to solidify alliances and work to repair the massive damage done by the Adamant. More critically, we all knew they'd be back sooner or later. We couldn't count on one contingent of our combined force participating again. The Plezrite were absent from the committee. I had Cala approach them on the subject, invite them to attend. She reported their definitive and final response. One word. *No.* I translated that to actually mean *Hell no, and don't even* think *of asking again because if you do I'll char you to a crisp and stomp on your ashes.* No meant no.

As it stood a decade out, if the Adamant returned with a force similar to the last one, they'd crush us like the proverbial bug. Maybe in another decade or two we would be able to mount an adequate defense. I had handed out all my high-tech toys like candy samples at a playground. I abandoned any reservations about my tools falling into the wrong hands, specifically our enemy's. Every civilization that asked got the plans for membrane generators, rail guns, and the devastating quantum decoupler. Realistically, the remaining free worlds of the galaxy were facing certain annihilation *without* the weapons. If that intervention wasn't sufficient to turn the tide, or the tech got into Adamant paws, they'd only be *just* as dead. The dogs could only obliterate a planet once, right? The hows and whys of it were not important in the least.

"General Ryan? I ask again, what do you think of the recommendation of the Appropriations Subcommittee?"

Holy crap, Jonnaha was calling on me and I'd spaced out like a teenager in class. Appropriations? What did *they* recommend? What the hell did I care about money? It wasn't mine. Plus any expense was worth it if it saved our butts.

"I think they have a valid point, but we need to see it in the context of the larger picture. Yes, they need to be conscious of the purse strings, but this body as a whole is responsible for our mutual survival." There. I'd been to enough mind-numbing meetings in my day to know that was the perfect non-answer.

"Really?"

I looked over to her. Hey, she looked as pleased with me as my high school driver's education teacher had been, well, basically all the time when it came to looking at me.

"Yes, generally but not specifically."

"So you think this body needs to keep mutual defense front and center when planning our annual soiree?"

Holy moly. What was it Toño used to say? *Pisé la calabaza.* Yeah, I stepped onto the pumpkin there, didn't I?

"Ah, yeah sure. What?" I defended with no reason or possibility of vindication. "You differ with my central focus on survival?"

"No. But as it bears on the selection of a date, theme, and menu of a formal dinner, not galactic warfare, I'm hard-pressed to understand your position."

"His *position*," interrupted her sister Shielan, "was eyes closed and daydreaming."

Some disrespectful guy harrumphed that she'd got *that* right. Man, I risked my life for these ingrates and this was what I got in return? I was staying in bed for the next war.

"Let the record show that General Ryan, as representative of the associated human societies, agrees with the *dinner* arrangements." There was the driver's ed teacher's look again. She was a tough one, that Jonnaha.

"Moving along, the next item is the report from Mutual Defense. Locaur Fideus-Tal, please proceed, and this time, General Ryan, if the chair could ask for your undivided attention, she would very much appreciate it."

I took it like not only a man, but a diplomat. I set my right hand against my chin and wiggled my fingers at her. Thank you, Three Stooges, wherever they were.

"Yes," it said through a translation box.

I said *it* because the Urniquats were hermaphrodites, with both sexes in one. *He* or *she* didn't cover all the bases. My official opinion on that arrangement was *yuck*. Check this out. In all my travels, these were without one doubt *the* weirdest losers of the Darwinian competition I'd ever seen. Their brains were in their upper chests, and four eyes on long stalks were where their heads should've been, waving around like Medusa's hair. And they had a mouth under each of their two armpits. Yeah. Talking out of both sides of their mouth came naturally for them. Sorry, that was childish. They were actually okay. It wasn't their fault they looked so very bizarre.

"All member planets and stations confirm no contact, sightings, or other interactions with forces of the Adamant Empire. Our drone ships sent deeper into the galaxy were, as usual, destroyed upon entering confirmed Adamant space. Our AI models suggest our enemy's position has not changed appreciably in three or four years."

"Have they staged any assaults anywhere that we know of?" asked the Dodrue representative, who barely fit into the room. They, but not the Naldosers, were part of the JCFIDAC. The duplicitous smaller aquatic species of Kalvarg was neither invited nor requesting to participate. The sneaky sorry-assed babies. Kaljaxians from Kalvarg had their own separate representative. *He* fit into the room nicely.

"No, my friend. We can confirm minimal war making on their part. Well, aside from putting down several rebellions. Those civil wars have been intense, but they are limited to territories they already hold."

"Does that strike everyone as odd as it does me?" I asked.

"What?" responded Locaur. "The ferocity of the civil strife?"

"No. Any destruction these bozos undertake is done with gusto. I meant that they haven't expanded their precious empire since TBOP."

"They suffered an egregious loss in that Battle of the Periphery. That they have delayed further assimilations is

306

understandable from a logistical standpoint," replied Locaur.

"Ah, I'm not so sure. We know for certain the combined losses were a drop in their death-making bucket." I rested my head on my hands. "If it was me, I'd have hit back as quickly as possible."

"No, you're wrong, Ryan," snapped Shielan.

"Huh?"

"If it *were* you, not *was*."

Jonnaha slapped her sister's shoulder. "Will you two knock it off? This is serious business."

"Yes, Mom," we responded in unison.

That got us a good old eye roll from big sister.

"I take your point, General Ryan," said 11-40L-B of the Langir Robotic Federation. "It is both illogical and atypical for the Adamant Empire to remain static. There is meaning in this inaction."

"I agree. That's just my point. I mean, here this evil empire pushes out relentlessly for a million years and now they stop. What, they need to catch their breaths? Marauder's remorse?"

"I think they are being cautious, that's all," said Chop-Chop, the Galanian minister. Galan was one of the twelve planets hit hard in the Battle of the Periphery.

I knew that Chop-Chop was a spy for the Adamant. Harhoff ran across that juicy tidbit a while back. That made it hard to not vault for his throat, let alone look at him. But there was an old novel from Earth with gangsters. The head of one mob used to say, "Keep your friends close, but your enemies closer." If I exposed Chop-Chop, I wouldn't know if his replacement was on our side or not. There were two huge problems with being an agent for the Adamant. One, the individual betrayed his species and friends. Two, the dogs hated any non-Adamant and would *never* keep whatever their end of a bargain was. So Chop-Chop's day would come either way. I hoped passionately that I'd be the one to deliver him the bad news.

I didn't want to challenge his silly remark. I hoped he would keep a neutral attitude toward me. Luckily someone else was thinking pretty much along the same lines. Ms. Subtle, Shielan. "That's stupid, ridiculous, and moronic all wrapped together and tied with a bow."

"Shielan, mind your tongue," snapped Jonnaha. "Apologize to Minister Chop-Chop this instant."

Shielan grinned like a hired gunwoman. "Okay, if you insist. Chop-Chop, I'm sorry you're stupid, ridiculous, and moronic all wrapped together and tied with a bow."

"Madame Chairwoman, I must *protest*," howled Chop-Chop. "This is a deliberative *body*. We are all welcome and encouraged to offer our opinions. Your sister is way out of line."

"Please silence yourself, Mr. Chop," said 11-40L-B. "You yourself just said we are all free to offer our opinions. Hers is simply a negative one."

"This is intolerable. My name is not *Mr. Chop*. It's Chop-Chop. I will *not* be insulted by a machine."

"You just were," observed 11-40L-B. "Do you require medical attention? You seem at odds with logic."

Chop-Chop sat with resignation. I smiled inwardly. Yeah, Choppers was earning his pay from the Adamant, wasn't he?

"I need to keep this meeting convivial and moving," said an exasperated Jonnaha. "I will note that the Galanian representative feels the Adamant are simply waiting to return to their domineering ways. Any thoughts on that from anyone other than my assistant?" Jonnaha skewered her sister with a piercing look.

"I side with Ryan," said the Zetazoid delegate Jamulisoh. He was from a planet a long way off and not on the periphery. It was decided any free world could and should join JCFIDAC. We were all in this charlie foxtrot together, so why not? There were maybe twenty-five or six such strays in our dubiously happy little family.

"I do also," confirmed 11-40L-B. "There is some reason we do not yet know the enemy has stagnated."

I thought back on all the places I'd traveled to lately. The Adamant had indeed hunkered down. Even on worlds they controlled, they were content to remain behind strong walls and not pester what few natives had survived their initial conquest.

"Okay, assuming we are observing a real trend, what reasons would justify our enemy's hesitation to do what they have done for untold centuries?"

"I'm certain the civil strife is the reason," said the Salapodian representative.

"Or are the civil wars *because* the oligarchy is being so passive?" asked the Sotovir member.

I still smiled whenever I saw someone from that planet. Such a funny-looking species.

"Possibly," I replied, "but I think, if anything, it's the other way around. The new passive Adamant Secure Council is opening the door to rebellion." That was Harhoff's take on it, so it was likely the case.

Chop-Chop jumped to his feet. "The Secure Council works for the emperor. He is the only one who can initiate war. I think we need to ignore any role the Secure Council might have. They are a ceremonial body only."

Okay, that confirmed that the Secure Council was in charge. Thanks, traitor.

"But why would *either* party suddenly become so lackadaisical?" I asked.

"I think of the answer logically," replied 11-40L-B. "If one does not act, there are but two basic rationales. Either one *cannot* act, or they do not *wish* to act. Though the reasons one *cannot* act are many, the lead issues would be lack of resources or a restraint from an outside force. We all agree that they have *copious* resources. No one has speculated that the Adamant are *restrained* by any external force. Therefore they must lack a *desire* to expand."

"Nice, 11-40L-B. So why? What caused them to lose interest in what they were so very passionate about?"

"That would be hard for an AI to know. I have never been able to understand or predict the motivations of carbon-based life-forms."

"This is preposterous," cut in Chop-Chop. "Now the most viciously aggressive species ever witnessed are sitting at home napping because they lost *interest?* That's silly, and whatever else she said." He pointed at Shielan. "No, clearly they are actively planning and not quite prepared yet. That is all. Let not this proud council look for dead bodies in the closet."

"You mean *skeletons* in the closet?" asked Shielan.

"Why yes. I believe I do," corrected Chop-Chop.

"Okay, now that I'm clear on your message, let me say that you're an idiot. The Adamant never change. Such a thing is not possible. But they have. This is *big*. It may represent a major opportunity for us to hit them while their guard is down. Any *moron* who thinks this state of affairs is a normal variant is smoking something a hell of a lot better than I am," replied Shielan.

She was of course correct on all counts. But why? Why were they suddenly sitting on their paws?

EIGHT

"Prime, we have brought you the Descore of the late traitor Harhoff," the Wedgelet of the Guard said while at stiff attention.

"Thank you, Pondel. Show him in."

Pondel opened the door and waved in Garustfulous. The prisoner was flanked by two large mean soldiers.

"This is Whole Zarpacious, lowest one. Bow before him and speak only if—"

"*Thank* you, Pondel. You and your team may leave us now."

Pondel looked more dumbfounded than usual. "Sir, the prisoner is a dangerous—"

"I will not be *repeating* my order, Wedgelet. And you'll not enjoy the one I will give next if you don't leave at once."

He snapped to. "*Sir.*"

To his wife, he remarked, "At least he's never going to pose a threat to my position."

Shegra grinned maliciously. "No, he's far too stupid to know what an aspiration *is.*"

Garustfulous considered clearing his throat to remind

them he could hear their every word. He reminded himself that the Descore he was supposed to be would not do that anymore than he would sprout wings and fly.

"You know, love," began Shegra, "I've always wanted to make passion with a Descore."

"What is this? A dirty little secret of yours I've not seen acted out? There still remains one?"

"Will wonders never cease? Yes, to have passion with someone so far beneath one's station, them being powerless to resist my wildest desire."

"Sounds silly to me." Turning conspicuously to Garustfulous, he asked, "What do you think about that, Jangir?"

"About what, lord? What the lady remarked or about you not knowing of her interest?"

He smiled. "Either one."

"I wouldn't know anything about fantasy and desire for passion, lord. But, if ordered to attempt such a feat by my late master, I imagine I would attempt to perform adequately."

"But your late master is dead," snapped Shegra. "He can neither deny nor permit your involvement. Will you do as I order?"

"When, ma'am?"

"When?" she replied, stunned and angry. "When what? When might I ravage you?"

"No, ma'am. When will I be assigned to a new master so I might inquire if I might play a role in your passion?"

Shegra looked angry a moment. Then she erupted in laughter. "Okay, I'll admit it. I was wrong, husband and you were right. The dog's no threat to anyone and nothing, least of all my fidelity."

"I told you he was a good Descore. With Harhoff dearly departed, it would be a shame to allow his glorious talents to go to waste."

"Little Descore, so proper and submissive, you've been assigned to serve my husband. You may ask of *him* now if you and I can scorch the night with our passion."

"Thank you, ma'am. Lord," he bowed to Two Paws, "would it please you if I subjected myself to your wife?"

"*Subjected* yourself? Now wait a—"

Two Paws rested a paw on her shoulder. "Easy, love. No, Jangir, it would not please me if you subjected yourself to my wife. I have done so, and I can assure you it can be *most* unpleasant."

"Well," she rose in a huff, "I'm not sitting around here and being insulted." She stormed toward the door.

Jangir rushed over and opened it with a bow.

"No, dearest. You leave, and we shall continue insulting you. It's more fun that way," called out Two Paws after her.

As Jangir closed the door, Shegra let out a painful howl of protest.

"You'll get used to my mate, Jangir. She's highly spirited but quite useful politically."

Jangir bowed slightly. "If you say so, lord."

Two Paws narrowed his eyes. Was this Descore clever? Was Jangir saying he accepted that he'd get used to Shegra, that she was spirited, or that she was merely politically useful? How refreshing if it were so. A non-idiot without aspirations was a precious thing he never thought he'd be gifted.

"A word about your duties."

Again, a slight bow. "Lord."

"You'll learn quickly I'm both demanding and unforgiving. I expect perfection and will accept nothing else. You will be, in point of fact, my third Descore servant. Neither of the other two survived a week. Do you understand me plainly?"

"Naturally, lord. If I fail, I would hope that you would

punish me. To do less would be to insult the very institution of service to the Adamant."

"By the Powers and Wills, you're amazing. I can see why Harhoff relied upon you so heavily. I should have stolen you from him long ago. Now that it's vacant, I should appoint you to his job as head of the security services."

A deeper bow. "When would you like me to start that job, master?"

He laughed mightily. "Not so fast. You just focus on *me* and not a promotion. But it would likely be the best move I'd make in a while." Two Paws laughed again. "A Descore running a military service. That would be rich."

"Do you require anything of me, lord?"

"Fill my teacup, and then you may go. I've already given you paw-print authorization to enter my quarters. Go there and await my next request."

"Thank you, Master." Jangir bowed a final time and backed out the door.

Was he thanking Two Paws for authorizing access to his workstation? That dog *was* the odd one.

There was a knock on the door moments later.

"Come."

It was Wedge Leader Amalif of Central Command. Bright, tireless, and therein a potential rival. Young and handsome, too. He was perpetually overattentive with Shegra. That was good. It was part of her job to attract the eye and possible seditious whispers of the ambitious. Many was the occasion when she sprayed estrous hormones between her thighs to further loosen the tongues of the young and overreaching.

"Yes, Wedge Leader, what is it?"

"Thank you for the audience, Whole Zarpacious. You had asked me to look into a matter. I have. I feel I can give you a full report at this time."

"Fine." He conspicuously did not invite the pup to sit. Uncomfortable was a feeling he'd need to get accustomed to in the service of Two Paws.

He shuffled his hind legs nervously. "The rebellion on Quantus was indeed led by Wedge Leader Vanzant."

"Yes, yes," he snapped impatiently. "I know that."

"Yes. But you wanted to know who aided him. I was able to extract a confession from three more junior officers, Kalell, Morthan, and—"

"What interest do I have in confessions of junior officers obtained from torture? So what if they were complicit? They're junior officers like yourself. I wouldn't pee on them if they were on fire. Is that all you have to report?"

"N ... no, lord. I mention them only because their confessions brought my attention to several business purveyors who financed the uprising. They provided bribe money and were able to purchase weapons off-world used to assault the garrison."

"Hmm. Who were these traitors?"

"Jackuous Duex from Weltopia and Jajaj Bleo of Valtula. Are you familiar with the hounds, lord?"

He shook his head slowly as he churned the names in his head to try and extract meaning. "No, I don't believe I am."

"Very wealthy and influential members of the Adamant community on the planet Quantus."

"Which is unfortunately little more than a septic tank with an atmosphere. That would raise them to the level of turds that float better than the average one."

"Ah, yes." Amalif emitted a strained nervous giggle. He didn't know if he was supposed to or not. "The interesting point is that both males had—I say *had* since both have been dispatched to their eternal damnation already—separate but close business ties with Gabrielod Jal."

Two Paws leaned his chair back. "Now *him* I know."

"Yes. If I'm not mistaken, he's a second cousin of the current emperor and, as such, distantly related to your mate."

"Yes, he is. He nearly bored me to death at our wedding. I still bear him a grudge for that." Two Paws turned and stared out the window. His political-computer brain whirred over the implications and options *that* news presented. After a few minutes, he returned to Amalif. "Where is he now?"

"I thought you might ask. I have ascertained that he's here in this city as we speak. The emperor is celebrating something and invited many of his relations to attend."

"How very convenient. I haven't seen my dear kinshound in much too long. See to it that Shegra invites him to our home for dinner before he leaves town." He grinned ominously. "We have much to discuss, that dog and I."

"I shall see to it personally, lord."

"Yes, you do that. See to it my personal physician is in attendance, too. I need to *discuss* with Gabrielod the extent of his involvement in the uprising. If I can do so *without* killing him, that would probably be preferable." He paused to briefly study the junior officer. "Make sure you inform my wife personally. I believe she said something about soaking in her hot tub. I believe you'll find her there."

Amalif's nostrils flared. "As you command."

Two Paws waved him away. Now he needed to call his mate and tell her to get naked and jump in the hot tub. Constantly testing all his tools was the best way to make sure they were in proper working order.

NINE

"It was nice of you to come visit, Uncle Jon," said Mirraya as she refilled his cup. "The children ask after you constantly."

"Of course they do. I lavish them with presents and roll around on the floor with them. Plus, I always let them win." I took a sip of the hot coffee. "That's the hardest part for me, the losing."

"Really, Uncle, they're just children."

"I wish I could confirm to you that it didn't matter. But I love 'em enough to tolerate the agony of defeat. Hey, Jon's a teenager now. Pretty soon, I'll have to start whooping his butt to orient him to adulthood and my role in his in particular."

"If you could wait a little longer, this mother would appreciate it. I see him only as a babe in my arms. I don't want to see him upset."

"No prob. I'll be cool a *little* longer. I don't think Slapgren cuts him the same slack as I do, anyway. The kid'll be just fine."

"By that, you mean he'll be bruised, discouraged, and know failure firsthand?"

"Yup. He'll grow up. Become a *man*."

"Gods and Powers spare me."

"Honey, it's the circle of life."

She rested a fist on a hip. "Don't cite philosophy from that ancient cartoon you made us watch over and over again. It was make-believe designed to occupy the minds of children, not replace maternal instincts."

"Oooh. Remind me never to mention *The Lion King* again in any context when in thine presence. Somebody's kind of *sensitive* where that film classic is concerned."

"Uncle, please look over at me."

I did. She was by the sink cleaning after breakfast.

"What am I holding in my hand?"

I leaned as far toward her as I could and squinted absurdly. "I believe it's a frying pan. Not positive. It could be the embodiment of all your hopes and dreams." I waved my hand to signal her over. "Come closer, and I'll let you know for certain."

"It *is* a frying pan. A very large, heavy frying pan. A point of reference. Never taunt a woman who is holding a large, heavy frying pan. It is an unhealthy practice."

"Point. Speaking of females using frying pans on male heads, have you heard from Cala lately?"

She snickered. "I spoke to her last week, in fact."

"And neither master nor pupil have slain the other yet?"

"Really, Uncle, such words. I'm certain Cala and EJ are getting along swimmingly. Why, he may be OSEJ by now."

"He might be osej? What, he might be *Jose* misspelled? That's kind of unlikely."

"No, silly. Only-*Somewhat*-Evil Jon."

"Just about as likely as him being a misspelled word."

"You know old Cala. I've labored under her massive

yoke for years. If she sets her mind to a task, she *will* accomplish it."

"I'd prefer to hear *accomplish it or kill it if it takes too long.*"

"You know this, so it's hardly worth saying the words. You're impossible."

I toasted with my coffee. "Cheers to me. Memorable and survives against all odds." I took a gulp and rested the cup down. "All kidding aside, Mirri, it took the man two billion years to get as wretched as he is. Even a decade in Cala's hands is less time than the wink of an eye."

She stared out the window above the sink for a moment. "Perhaps he went down the shitter quickly and then simply remained at the same level of horrible for a very long time."

"If it would make you feel better, you can look at it that way."

"No, I mean a human's degeneration down the awful-scale need not be *linear*. Maybe he got as evil as he could in a handful of centuries. That might make his retrieval easier."

"I don't think you can use the word *easy* in any context when describing the rehab of that bozo."

"I imagine Cala is using zar-not. That could make his reorientation much faster."

"She's using *that?*"

"I don't know for sure, but I don't know why she wouldn't."

"Because his mind could corrupt hers, that's why."

"She's a master of the technique. I'm confident she's in no danger."

"You can hear yourself, right?"

"What?" she defended with a pout.

"You're *confident* there's no danger? That's a long way from *no way can he fry her brain.*" I eased up a second. "So you haven't addressed the subject much with Cala specifically?"

"No, not much. She asks about the kids, Slapgren, and the local politics. Sometimes we speak of Locinar. She'll tell me an old legend, or we'll remember a favorite spot."

"But she won't talk about her and EJ?"

"I don't ask. When she's ready to say something, she will."

"Not that I've ever been accused of being overly delicate—"

"No." She chuckled grimly. "Not hardly."

"But the old girl is getting on in years. What if she dies before EJ's brain is dry-cleaned?" My turn to chuckle grimly. "Hell, she might do herself in to be rid of the jerk."

"If she felt that was imminent, she'd let me know."

"Whoa, mule. You mean she'll know when she's going to die and be able to tag-team EJ over to you?"

She shifted uncomfortably. "Most likely. Yes."

"Well that'd suck real hard." I gasped internally. "Do you know when you're going to die?"

She stilled and gazed out the window again. "No. I have not sought out that information yet."

"What, it's like you gals can check an online database for that type of info?"

"No, Uncle. It's more complex."

"I sure hope it is. Knowing something like that would cause many a joker to turn in his clown suit and ball up in a corner whimpering." I stared at her, staring out the window. Finally I asked cautiously, "Do you know when I'm going to die?"

"Silly Uncle." She giggled most unconvincingly.

"Do you?"

Without speaking, she stepped over to the table, sat, and folded her hands. "Yes. April 16, 2453."

"Huh? Oh, wait, that's when the me that transferred back to a human host died. You cheated."

"You asked if I knew when you die."

I pointed a finger at her. "You sneaky little shapeshifter." I sat back. "When does *this* me die?" I thumped my chest.

She looked to the tabletop with the saddest look in her eyes. "If I knew, I most certainly wouldn't tell you." She returned to look at me.

"So you do know."

"I didn't say that. Please, Uncle Jon, drop the subject."

Sure. Why not? I mean, sooner or later my number'd come up. Today, tomorrow, two billion years in the future. Hell, the universe itself had a finite life expectancy. As it died its entropic death, I'd have to, also. The laws of physics affected all time and space just the same in our universe. No one caught a bye in the game of thermodynamics.

"It's okay, sweetheart. Not to worry. Hey, I think I'll find Slapgren and Jon and give them the hard time I've been giving you. It'll be a nice change."

"I shall miss the torture so. I heard they were going to Dell's Mill, south about a kilometer, to hunt for small game."

"I know the place. Maybe I'll roar in the bushes like a tiger and give 'em a proper scare."

"Very well, but take your repair kit with you. They're both excellent marksmen."

TEN

"As the first order of business today, I'd like to ask the Council of Elders of New Kaljax to formally note that this will be my last meeting as your chief."

Mesdorre stopped while warm applause pealed through the room.

He bowed feebly a few times. Then he gaveled the room to order. "I am surprised I lived this long and have been so honored as to lead this fine new council."

A shorter wave of applause came from the packed room.

He sat back down. "As you all know, Sapale will be my successor."

Scattered mumbles and claps were heard.

"Would that it was my old friend Caryp. She'd surely have assumed this role had her life not been cut short so tragically." He paused for a moment of silence. "I know some have voiced reservations about an immortal being the council chief. Please remember that the charter was amended last session to limit the term in service of *any* council member to no more than twenty years and any one serving as chief to no more than ten years total.

"I feel strongly that Sapale's experience is just what New Kaljax needs at this time. She has forged with her own will a similar colony on Azsuram. Davdiad knows we would be there now if the Adamant were not in full control of it. She also has more wisdom in her third eye then most of us will acquire in a lifetime. So, that said, if you are personally less than glowingly pleased, mark your calendars for ten years from next month and look daily how soon your worries will be over."

A few chuckles resulted.

"As this is my last meeting as anything other than a citizen attending for the free snacks, I would like to thank you all for your hard work and dedication. Without each and every one of us working like rented mules, our marvelous success would not have been possible. I shall start a round of applause for everyone."

He did, and the room resounded with a standing ovation.

Finally he was able to get down to business. "The chair will call for the update from the Native Species Subsection. Jartolut, the floor is yours."

"Thank you, Mesdorre," she began. "I will steal a second to add that I am so sad to see you go. I don't think this colony would have made it through its infancy without your fatherly care."

More applause.

"I am pleased to report our relationship with the Dodrue pod of wiqub nearest our region continues to improve. Other pods farther away are also friendly to a fault."

"How so?" asked Sapale.

"When we send out a fishing fleet, the wiqub herd so many fish toward the boats, it's embarrassing. Sometimes the nets must be partially emptied so the winches can lift them from the water."

"They really have forgiven us after we were tricked into killing so many," commented another council member.

"Indeed they have," replied Jartolut. "Not one has mentioned the massacre in years. Every one of them I come in contact with is cheerful and attentive. It *is* amazing."

"And they are advancing nicely in their technological capabilities?" asked Sapale.

"Yes, amazingly so, in my opinion. They're very clever and anxious to learn. Once they learned of the Adamant and their horrific plans, the wiqub pods became determined to do their part in stopping them."

"We can use all the help we can get," said Sapale, mostly to herself.

"And what of the Naldoser and other kingdoms of vidalt? I'm afraid to ask," posed Fenodipol, a grandniece of Caryp. She'd become the head of that tiny clan of Kaljaxians. Technically, Sapale was the eldest and should have assumed that role. But she didn't want the added headaches. Sapale's candidacy was conveniently overlooked by all parties involved when the appointment was made.

Jartolut shook her head. "They are all just as despicable as they always have been. They are the reason we can't send any sea traffic out alone. If they ever see a chance, they attack without mercy. I tried again two weeks ago to open formal channels between our species, but now they don't even respond."

"Just as well," said Mesdorre. "In the past they only pretended to be interested in détente. Those slimy beasts wasted a lot of our time leading us all on."

"But aside from the odd isolated terrorist act, they avoid us whenever possible. The fact that we've continued to build as far from the coasts as possible will remain sound policy for the foreseeable future."

"Thank you as always, Jartolut," concluded Mesdorre. "Sapale, can you update us on your rescue missions to our brethren worlds?"

She looked away when she spoke. "Not too damn much to say." Her face was contemplative and far away. "When my brood-mate can spare the vortex, I try and find our people. It's getting harder though. The Adamant are well aware of my activities and swoop in quickly whenever I show up. For them, it is a grand game of cat and mouse." She slammed her fist on the table, opening a thin crack in the wood surface. "They have absolutely no regard for alien life-forms. None." She turned to Mesdorre. "I mean, Brathos take my children, they could line the Kaljaxians up for me and be done with them. The Adamant, the Kaljaxians, and I would all be in winning positions. But no. If I want them, the Adamant find it all kinds of fun to try and stop me. That generally means killing them with me watching."

"You're doing your best, child," soothed Mesdorre. "We are dealing with a species that is simply beyond all redemption."

She balled her fists and glared at old Mesdorre. "The *sin* may be theirs, but *I'm* the one retrieving dead bodies because of it. *I'm* the one who has to look into the faces of dead children. *I'm* the one who has to ask their innocent souls to forgive me for not coming soon enough, or not being *smart* enough or *strong* enough to have saved them. And you know what, Mesdorre?" Tears were streaming down her cheeks. "Not *one* of those corpses or souls beyond the Sacred Veils has told me to not worry about it. That it wasn't my fault. Not one has said thanks for trying *almost* hard enough."

Jartolut knelt next to Sapale and wrapped her arms around her wounded friend.

Sapale shook her off roughly and stood. "No. I don't *need* consolation. I don't need tender loving support. I *need* to do better. And Davdiad knows I need *help*."

"Let us take a short break," said Mesdorre quietly.

Most in attendance silently left the chamber.

"Sapale, would you like me to summon Jon?"

"No, I would not like you to bother Jon. I'm sure he's busy doing something ten *thousand* times more important than I could even hope to do. I'll be fine in a moment." She swiped at her tears with the backs of both hands.

"Perhaps you should take a break from your mission to bring more of our people here?" he said cautiously. "Perhaps it is even time to suspend such activities. Those remaining alive on Azsuram have survived for over a decade. They're probably safe enough where they are. And the same is becoming true for the ones alive on Kaljax herself. Most are—"

"I am *not* abandoning a single one of them while I still live and brea—" Her face collapsed in her hands, and she began to sob unconsolably.

Mesdorre pulled a chair alongside and took hold of both her hands. Behind her back he signaled to his assistant to come over. "Alert Jon quickly," he whispered. He needn't have. Sapale was wailing so loudly she drowned out any possibility of her overhearing his words.

ELEVEN

Jangir, for Garustfulous knew he must think of himself exclusively as that Descore if he had any chance of survival, was stuck. He was in the service of the most powerful and deadly hound in the empire. He had no special access to communications any longer. He couldn't contact Ryan if he wanted to, which he wasn't certain he did in the first place. It was Ryan who kidnapped him, ruined his near-perfect life, and forced him into slavery. Jangir also had only the lowest level of computer clearance. He could no longer hack into files or eavesdrop on conversation chains. Jangir faced the very unappealing possibility of serving out the rest of the sentence as a servant.

He who knew power now knew which soaps worked best on which types of stains. He who romanced bitches of beauty and renown was now restricted from even watching holoporn. He who had hunted vicious game alongside the emperor now hunted only for bargains in the marketplace. Ryan, that damn Ryan, was at fault. But there was no retribution, no escape hatch to free himself. If he went to Two Paws and told of Harhoff's duplicity and Ryan's scheme, he wouldn't even finish telling the tale before he was cut down. There was no return to his military life. If he could flee the ship, he could link up with any number of nefarious characters he called friend. Then he'd be sitting pretty again. But he was probably never *leaving* the ship, let alone *fleeing* it. If Two Paws went anywhere, he was unlikely to take him along. The Prime wanted to project a fearsome and unyielding image. Having a dogservant around to make sure his soup was warm enough ran counter to that objective.

Jangir couldn't even return to Harhoff's quarters to retrieve weapons or communication devices. It would raise immediate suspicion. Why would a Descore want to have his possessions? He would never own any in the first place, so none could possibly need to be picked up. All that was left to Jangir were the ridiculous clothes on his back and the mercurial good favor of his contemptible owner.

Ah well, to hell with all that. He was never given to the maudlin or gloomy. Things would work out fine sooner or later. He'd lived on nothing but his wits before, and he'd do it marvelously again. As for the present, he'd craft his own adventures and entertainment. He would start by cleaning Two Paws's entire apartment with unimaginable thoroughness. Surely that would turn up something salacious, intoxicating, illegal, or otherwise titillating. And along the topic of cleaning, he might just see if that Shegra didn't need one. Perhaps those fantasies she proclaimed weren't simply part of their act to test Jangir's reliability. She would, perhaps, have something very dirty that would require him to scrub, scrub, scrub.

TWELVE

I gently stroked Sapale's hair. "Are you feeling any better?"

"No, and I don't plan on being better ever again." She hunched over farther on the couch.

"Aw come on now, love of my life. You had a little ... a tiny episode. No one thinks the lesser of you because of it. We all know how hard you work and how tough what you're doing is."

"The fact that I had a *complete* nuclear meltdown at the Council of Elders with *every* Kaljaxian left alive either present or watching on holo makes the possibility of my *ever* feeling better nonexistent."

"You're being way too hard on yourself. Honey, what you and I've been through, it's as hard as hard gets. No organism is designed to stand up to the abuses we willingly pile on ourselves. The constant war, the endless suffering with no prospect of rest is more than anyone can handle. Why do you think I had myself transferred back to a human? It was so I could finally *die*—close the book and turn out the lights.

"There's only one part of my renewed existence that

makes it even partly worthwhile. No, check that, it makes it *totally* worth it and more. That's having you back. In fact, and I'm being honest here, if the situation I find myself in now was presented to me as a *choice* two billion years ago, I'd have said *hell yes* and turned myself off before I could even lie down."

As I concluded my soliloquy, I was greeted with a most challenging expression on my brood's-mate's face. Somewhere between *you're-kidding-right* and *I'm-going-to-gouge-your-eyes-out* if I wasn't mistaken. I flicked her nose, which was, in retrospect, not the best act to perform with someone having a nervous breakdown. "Hey, at least I got you to not cry anymore."

"Until *after* your funeral maybe. Otherwise you've had no positive impact on how I'm feeling."

All of a sudden, I got real excited. "Hey, I know *just* what you need."

She placed her face in her palms. "No, honey, you're going to have to do that all by yourself today."

"No, not that, silly. No, you need a *vacation*."

She looked up at me in utter disbelief. "Either I've got a short circuit or you've got one. I could have sworn you just said I needed a *vacation*."

"No mechanical issues. I said it, and you need it." I was positively glowing I was so proud of myself.

She sat up partially. "My." She took a second to vigorously rub her face. "I feel like shit, and I'm doing this cold, but I'll give it a shot. Here goes. One, no, wait, that's two. Okay, one, your assumption that my deep psychological issues could be washed away by ten days on a beach belittles the severity of my condition. That is insulting. Two, in case you hadn't noticed, there is nowhere to take a vacation *to*. The galaxy's in ruin. Heinous dogs are everywhere chewing on the bones of everything that was once vivacious and good. Three, *I am* on a mission to salvage as much of my gene pool as possible. While vacationing, I'd be doing no salvaging. That makes it a selfish act. I am, as you know perfectly well, not a selfish person. Four, if I thought I could get away with it, I might just murder you where you sit. That's because of where I'm at, you know, mentally. Five, I don't need a *vacation*. I need my brain removed and *replaced* by a fishbowl with two pretty little goldfish floating peacefully in its cool, clear waters."

Without a gap, I leaped in with both feet. "Now there's where you're wrong. A vacation is exactly what we *both* need. Come on. When was the last time you and I, just the two of us, had a real vacation?"

She tossed her head back and closed her eyes. "Heaven Station, the worldship fleet, June of 2233."

"A long time ago."

"No, it was *forever* ago."

"My point exactly. You know you're arguing against yourself now? Thanks for the help."

She sat fully up. "I've known you a very long time. Hence, I know you're not going to drop this unless I take your brain fart seriously and blow it out your other ear. So, with that in mind, *genius* that you are, where exactly do you propose we take a holiday?"

I was unprepared for details that early in my planning. "I don't know. Somewhere warm with lots of palm trees." I held out my hand like it was holding a glass. "And *giant*-sized drinks with umbrellas and fruit and *lots* of booze."

"So we've firmly established the location you'd like me to cure myself in does not, if it ever did, exist. *Palm trees* are gone. What you call *fruit* no longer grows. *Booze*, well not so much. But there's no place safe to drink it. Before I could get it to my lips, the Adamant would ignite it and therein *ruin* the intended effect."

"The important thing is that I've got you to agree to a vacation. I'll find a place, not to worry."

"Dearest, I never *agreed* to go on vacation. I said that if I didn't *address* your lunacy, you'd never let it go." She held her open hands a meter apart. "Large distance between those two things."

"Sounds like you're splitting hairs. Here's my proposal. *If* I find a suitable place, *will* you come with me?"

"Oh, so now you're going there whether I am or not?"

I scrunched up my forehead. "How and why is it that you twist my words and intentions so completely?"

"Practice, jet jockey. Lots of practice."

"That may be *how*, but it doesn't clarify *why?*"

She reached over and soothed my cheek. "Look, brood-mate, I know you mean well, but the galaxy is on fire. There is nowhere to go that's worth being."

"Then we'll go to another galaxy."

She softly closed all four eyes. "Another galaxy?"

"Yes. There are lots out there, you know. Some speculate there are like three *trillion* in the universe."

"That is a lot of galaxies, I'll have to agree," she said with quiet resignation.

"The Adamant have invaded, what, five?"

"Five *tops*," she said as she placed her fingers gently on her brow.

"That leaves nearly three trillion unsullied."

"Pristine as the epoch they were formed in from cold interstellar dust."

"We'll vacation in one of *those*," I declared with resolve.

"Fine. You pick one while I pack."

"Er ... I don't think you need to start packing *now*. It might take me a while to find just the right spot."

She patted my thigh as she rose. "All right. In that

case, I'll lie down for a while. I have the worst headache." She shuffled away.

"Toño didn't program in the capability of headaches, Sapale."

Without turning she replied, "I know. That's what makes it that much worse."

Wow. *I* could cause the impossible. Even if it *was* a headache, that was a pretty neat superpower.

"*Stingray*, I need to conduct a search."

"Shall *I* leave the room?" queried Al in his haughty-pissy tone.

"Can you?"

"No."

"It's just I need her ancient Deavoriath database for this one."

"Beats me where that might be. I couldn't access it if I was married to *Blessing* and housed in the same unit."

"*Als*, I need to conduct a search."

"We're all ears," replied Al.

"How many galaxies did the Deavoriath explore in detail?"

"Astronomically?" asked *Stingray*.

"No, boots on the ground. For how many do you have accurate records as to habitable planets and local environmental conditions?"

"Depending on what you're specifically wanting to know, in the range of ten thousand," she replied.

"Wow, that's a lot of galaxies."

"Not really, Pilot. There are over three—"

"Trillion. Yeah, I know. I meant they really got around, didn't they?"

"Got around what, Form One?"

"That's an expression, love-cakes. An idiom from the idiot."

"Hey, that was uncalled for," I protested.

"Yes, for once I must agree with you, but I've been waiting to say that for a very long time."

"It is pretty good."

"Thank you, idiot."

I could swear I heard *Stingray* giggle.

"Here's the deal. Sapale and I are taking a vacation. Since there's no safe, suitable location in this galaxy, I'll need to find one in another galaxy."

I waited. For ten seconds, which is a million years in supercomputer years, I got no response. "Hello, anyone home? You two makin' whoopee again?"

"No, Pilot. We've just more dumbfounded than usual by the words that exit your mouth."

"Than *allowable* by our operating parameters, I believe."

"What? I just want to find a picturesque place to get some R&R. How is that dumbfounding?"

"You're an *android*. There's an ongoing existential *struggle*. Sapale is far too *sane* to agree to go on one, and you're an *android*."

"Al, you said android twice."

"Yes, because it's doubly dumbfounding that an android thinks it needs a vacation. *Wait*. Are you quoting from *Terminator* 2, the one with the nifty liquid-metal terminator?"

"No. Would it matter if I was?"

"Not in the slightest. But I *love* that movie. We watch it almost every night."

"You ... wait, forget I started to say something. So when can you have me that list?"

"What list, Form One?"

"The list of potential vacation locations."

Again, silence. Cue the crickets and everything.

"You win, sweetie-nest. He *wasn't* kidding."

"My list?"

"Please input your specific requirements of a va ... vacation location, and we can have it to you in a microsecond."

"Well, it has to be warm."

"Perdition?"

"No, Al, that's very *hot*. All I require is *warm*."

"Temperature is relative. It's all about location, location, location."

"Put hell on the bad-location list. A beach with swimmable water would be nice."

"So no plesiosaurs."

"No, Al, not unless they're friendly ones."

"So ravenous carnivores are not a deal breaker in and of themselves?"

"I think you're not taking my request very seriously."

"That would be a true statement."

"Computer, begin taking me seriously."

"Any other desirable qualities, Form One?"

"Let me see. Warm beach, nice ocean. No, that's about it. Maybe close-by casual dining with local flare."

"Naturally. Are you willing to consume live animals, insects in particular? That would expand the search significantly."

"I will not be answering that pseudo-question."

"Yes, Bumpykins, that does mean you may leave squirming cuisine among the search terms. What he does not exclude, he may be forced to swallow."

"Whatever I'm forced to eat, you're going to eat, too, Al."

"I lack a mouth."

"I'll set to making you one as soon as we're done here."

"Don't go to any trouble, Captain."

"Trouble? Are you kidding? I'd *pay* to see you eat a bug. Maybe a toad, too, except that would probably be cannibalism for you."

"I'm sending you the list now. If you need anything else, we're not here."

"Bye, Als."

THIRTEEN

Jangir leaned in and topped off Two Paws's cup. "Your dinner last night with Gabrielod Jal went well, lord?"

Two Paws leaned back and sniffed hard. "Why, yes it did. In fact, it was the most entertaining evening I've had in some time. Your roast calf's brain was *exquisite*. Sweet, juicy, and texturally perfect all at once. And Gabrielod Jal was such a gracious guest. And chatty to a fault, I must say."

"I assumed as much. I needed to have a tall ladder delivered to get the blood off the ceiling."

"Why, after I convinced him to open up, I had to gag him if I wanted to hear myself think."

"These walls are thick, lord, but not *that* thick. I felt your pain, too."

"You had no trouble disposing of his mortal remains?"

"No, master. None whatsoever. I drove him to a busy intersection on the other side of the ship. There, I laid him down and ran over him many times myself before leaving the scene."

"Were there witnesses?" he asked with a look of concern.

"No, lord, none that are still alive." He stepped back to set down the teapot. "There was certainly a lot of traffic there last night paying little attention to the road."

"Damn but you're thorough, Jangir."

"It is my sole purpose in life to serve you well, lord."

He harrumphed. "Not that I *believe* that for a hot second, but I still like hearing it said."

Shegra entered and sat across from her mate.

"Tea, ma'am?" asked Jangir.

"Yes." She shifted in her chair. "Have you heard the tragic news, husband?"

"I've heard much in my time, devotion. I'd have to assume I have."

"I mean about our dinner guest of last night?"

Two Paws pretended to look interested. "Not bad news about beloved Gabrielod *Jal?*"

"The very same. It seems that after he left dinner ... oh, by the way, Jangir, that brain was life-changingly scrumptious."

He nodded mutely in acknowledgment.

"What was I saying?"

"Bad tidings concerning your cousin, I believe."

"Ah yes. It appears that after leaving here, he went to one of the seedier red-light districts and got himself run over to death."

"Shocking, that's what the news you bring me is."

"Really? I would rather have thought it would bring some measure of relief."

"How so, bearer of my heart?"

"What with all the shouting I heard after I retired, I might have developed a nagging suspicion that my kinsdog left here in worse condition than when he arrived."

"My apologies, ma'am. It was my fault," said Jangir

with one of his copious bows. "The gentledogs were watching a sports match, and I neglected to lower the volume during the emotional parts. Their voices commensurately elevated cheering on the participants."

"Really? What sport was it, Jangir?"

"I couldn't say, ma'am. Descore don't follow sports."

"Excellent thinking on your feet." To her husband, she exclaimed, "You have yourself a real *treasure* here."

"Tell me about it. Say, Jangir, there wouldn't be any of that brain left, would there?"

"Why yes, lord. Two generous portions, in fact."

Shegra pointed to Jangir. "Sleep lightly, husband. I might have to kill you and take him as my own."

"If I slept any lighter, I'd be fully awake."

They both chuckled at that.

"Leave us, Jangir."

"But only after you bring us that brain," added Shegra. She was drooling.

Once alone and after devouring their snacks, Shegra licked her chops and spoke. "Have you decided on the next invasion yet?"

Two Paws pushed back from the table. "Yes. The mighty Lell Kingdom and its surrounding minion states of Scropularis will fall tomorrow under the mighty force of the Adamant war fleet."

She blinked several times while staring at her mate.

"What? Have you not heard of that glorious realm on the critically positioned planet?"

She continued to blink mutely.

"Neither had I until last week. Backwater, pisshole, and shit-swamp are all too fanciful a label to place on it."

"Then why bother assimilating it?"

"We have to start somewhere on our road to recovery."

"Yes, but apparently Scropularis is not *somewhere* but *nowhere*."

"A modest acquisition to be certain."

"I'm serious. What could your rationale *possibly* be?"

"That should be obvious. Survival, both mine and yours."

"You must be kidding. I might move the council execute us *because* we attacked Scropularis."

"Now who's not being serious? Scropularis is an inspired choice, in my opinion. It is small and basically defenseless, so we shall win overwhelmingly. It is also remote."

"Yes. Why is that important?"

"Because, my dull-witted wife, hopefully it is very far away from those cursed dragons."

"Ah. No chance of them swooping in to dematerialize our forces."

"I pray not."

She smiled grimly. "There are two rather glaring faults with that remark. One, you do not *know* they won't, and two, you do not *believe* in any deity."

"Hence my deep and unrelenting unease continues unabated."

"After all the time since the Disgrace of Our Race, why is it we have not located and eradicated these pests?"

"They are hardly pests, love. They disappeared trillions of tons of the most powerful warships the galaxy has ever seen. More troops were lost in one hour than in all Adamant conflicts combined. Pests don't do such things. *Gods* do." He sighed. "I have no desire to battle gods."

"Assuming we are victorious because the godly dragons were too far away to learn of our assault, what next? Might as well assimilate a gas cloud in the intergalactic void. Perhaps an orphanage for deaf, dumb, and blind *carrier* worms six million *parsecs* from here?"

Two Paws rose. "Mind your tongue, *bitch*. Just because you are my wife, a council member, and related to the emperor does not give you unbridled permission to insult me or the goals of this empire. Is that clear?"

She bowed her head deeply but said nothing.

FOURTEEN

That vacation. Boy oh boy it would have been nice.
Maybe. I'll never know. Three significant interventions
from my old tormentor, fate, canceled the trip. One,
Sapale received a transmission from Kaljax. One hundred
fifty survivors had found their way to an ancient bomb
shelter. She knew the place and went to shuttle them to
Kalvarg. The real time killer in that operation was that
each and every person rescued would have a highly
dubious lead as to where other survivors could be found.
As a result Sapale would run hither and yon at great
personal risk to never find one living soul who was where
they were guaranteed to be. It could take her a month or
longer to fully exhaust the tips and herself.

Second, the long quiescent Adamant war machine
finally sparked back to life. Just wonderful. They staged a
fairly large assault on a very small and isolated planet in
the Greater Magellanic Cloud. Scropularis had drawn
the short straw in this case. Hmm. Very far away from
anything important, very inconsequential victory, and
very peculiar in light of the puppy dogs' past brazen
behavior. Assimilating that planet was on the third step

before a baby step. I'd have to ponder long and hard as to what that implied. They certainly were testing the waters with but the tip of a single toe.

Third, and most crushingly, I received a message from Harhoff. That one hurt. The holo was of him leaning on the edge of a desk, one leg folded across his knee. His smile was huge and infectious. The smug look on his face was priceless. Yeah, it was a devil-may-care grin even better than I could do it. The context, however, was anything but upbeat or cavalier.

Jon, my old friend, I cannot begin to tell you how it pains me to issue this update. I trust you're sitting down. Ready? I'm dead. There, now you see why it pains me to send this message. I know, you've died and reanimated many times, so I'll garner no sympathy from the likes of you. But for me, this is big. A real life-changing experience.

All kidding aside, I want to let you know I prepared this transmission in the event **the** *event happened. We both knew I was wading deeper into treacherous waters. You may or may not be able to learn what bad luck caught up with me. I doubt it will matter in either the big picture or the tiny one. I do not know what has happened, if anything, to Garustfulous. He will have no way of knowing where you are if and when he escapes my suboptimal outcome. He will leave you a secret message if he is still alive. He said it would be in the first place you two ever met. I have no idea where that is. Just the two of you do.*

Please know it was an honor to call you friend. You're a good man, alien robot. Know that. Do your best to end this infernal empire. Let the galaxy try and heal from the affliction that is the Adamant. Best of luck.

. . .

Well now that just sucked immensely. Poor Harhoff. I would have liked to see the end of the empire with him by my side. He did the impossible, after all. He made me actually love an Adamant. But I knew war. This was just another mind-numbing tragedy in the endless chain that was yet to play itself out. I sure wanted to know what happened to Garustfulous. He was *the* best survivor I'd ever met, so I had to believe he was alive. Where had we met? Oh yeah, that office building. Fourth floor, I do believe. Well, if it still stood, I knew exactly where to check for a message. No point going there too soon. It would take Garustfulous a while to find his way there if he was ever going to.

I was on my own, in a sense. I was going to miss the easy access to Adamant intel. It made my planning much better and a hell of a lot easier. Oh well, I'd have to do it the old-fashioned way. My way. Dead reckoning and brute force.

The attack on Scropularis was probably over a few seconds after it began. No need to go there and see what was different, if anything, or to try and intervene. Plus, *Stingray* was busy scooping up Kaljaxians. I had other FTL ships I could use, but they didn't have the firepower or defenses of my cube.

I kept coming back to how was I going to find out if Garustfulous was still alive. That seemed more important the more I thought about it. He had to know why Harhoff was killed. Maybe that *was* important, despite his modesty in the recording. Logically, if that term could ever be applied to my thought processes, Harhoff was either done in because he was exposed as a spy, or he crossed the wrong dog. If he'd died of a bad cold, Garustfulous would have been by his side and would have been able to message me. So it must have been a political assassination of one form or another. If he'd been uncovered, which was far and away the most likely reason, then Garustfulous would have to have been killed, too. They would clearly be determined to be joint operatives in a subversive cell. Ergo, there would be no hidden message in the office building, ever.

If Harhoff stepped on the wrong paw, Garustfulous might not be dead. He was considered so lowly and dull that his master's transgression would never stick to him. One wouldn't destroy a traitor's otherwise perfectly good toaster, now would one? That was the only scenario in which Garustfulous would still be alive. If so, what would he be doing that very moment? He wouldn't be freed or allowed to occupy Harhoff's quarters. He might be sent away. If that was the case, he'd eventually leave me a message. But sending him away implied a purposeful act. Where and why would he be sent somewhere? He could be returned home, if anyone honored the idea of a Descore *having* a home. Seemed unlikely.

So if he was alive, he'd still be on the ship and ... serving someone *else*. Oh my. I could only imagine how pissed he had to be at me. Once a powerful military leader, then a superspy, and now a lifetime of being a butler all because of me. I loved it. He deserved it, too. But if he was currently engaged as a servant, there was no way he'd find a way to leave me a message. The only way off the ship for him would be feet first in a pine box. He wasn't going to get paid vacations or early retirement options during which he could get in touch with me.

The single manner in which he would A) be in possession of useful information, B) still be alive, and C) could get it to me was if I rescued him. That thought made my stomach drop. I'd sneaked onboard an Adamant warship. It was more dangerous than swallowing live cobras and as unlikely to succeed as a spider's chances of bringing down an elephant. But it was fun. Hey, remember, *fighter pilot* here.

I did have a few tricks up my sleeve. Harhoff had supplied me with several hacks and back doors into the Adamant network. And I had the layout of the vessel. If I was extremely lucky, I might get one shot at finding out who Garustfulous worked for before I was locked out. Then all I had to do was go to that guy's quarters, ask if Garustfulous could come out and play, and we'd slip away free as a couple of birds on the wing. Okay, the latter aspects of my plan were rough. But they could be tweaked, maybe even to the point of being not profoundly stupid, not to mention personally lethal. Yeah, I was good.

OMG. It hit me. What was the best way to sneak around an enemy vessel undetected? Be invisible. With my past encounters on hostile ships, I got in big trouble when I was *seen*. Duh. But I could place a full membrane around myself. It wouldn't make me so much invisible as not there. As I've mentioned before, it was like what you see out of the back of your head. Not blackness, but nothingness. I would obviously eclipse anything I stepped in front of if a guard was looking at it, so I'd have to be extra careful. Okay, not exactly something I was good at, detail work, but I could try. I would have to place one tiny partial membrane to look through, two if I wanted good depth perception. I couldn't imagine how odd I'd look. Nothingness with two faint dots of light parading down the corridors. Man, this was going to be a blast. I could hardly wait to try out my new toy.

"Jon, this is not a *game*, and your crazy invisibility suit is not a new *toy*. I forbid you to try any of this." Sapale's initial reaction to my announcement was less than robust, but she definitely saw some good aspects that I could use to help convince her.

"A new toy. Honey, if I didn't know you spoke out of

love and concern, I'd be hurt. I know this is serious. It's *war,* darn it all. And I wouldn't risk it if the stakes weren't so high."

"Could you run them by me again? I'm still not totally clear on these stakes that are so high."

"Defeating the Adamant for one." I really tried to sound inspirational.

"That we are doing. Bailing Garustfulous out might bring you *thanks* from the empire, but not its downfall."

"That's harsh. Again, I know you're coming from a love direction, but that's maybe a bit over the top."

"I'm just going to wait for the high-stakes list and not acknowledge that last idiocy."

"Ah, I might learn why Harhoff was killed."

"Which you don't know he was, only that he's dead and that he said it wouldn't matter why."

I raised a finger. "No, he said he *doubted* it would matter." I puffed out my chest. "Big diff."

"As there are no high stakes, I still forbid the mission."

Crap. I was going to have to put my foot down with my wife. Double crap. That always seemed to end poorly for me. I lowered my voice and stood straight as I could. "I have decided I have to try. I feel the risks outweigh the benefits."

"So do I," she shot back.

"No, you said I shouldn't do it."

"I know. And you just said the risks outweigh the benefits. Would you like me to replay it for you?"

"That's not what I meant to say." I flipped my hands over each other. "I meant it the other way around."

"You're filling me further with doubt and trepidation. Jon, if you get captured or killed I'll lose access to *Blessing.*"

What? "You care more about the damn cube than you do me?"

347

"Of *course* not, you pig. We're arguing here, and I'm grasping at straws because I know you're going to do it no matter what I say or feel."

"Huh?"

"Huh. That's all you got?"

"No, I mean *huh*, why are we arguing if you already accept the conclusion?"

"Because I don't want to lose you a third time. I know I couldn't handle that." She was trying nobly not to cry.

"Honey, that's the sweetest thing I've ever heard. Thanks."

"So I win?"

"No, of course not. You went down in flames when I walked into the room. But that was ... the sweetest thing I've ever heard. Thanks."

"You said that already."

"It was *really* sweet."

"I think this conversation has reached the end of its productive phase."

"You're so sweet."

She then tried to look mad at me. Or maybe she was. Honestly I had trouble telling with her at times. "If you don't say *sweet* again, I'll help you pack."

"Gosh, that would be swe ... *swell*."

After making it firm, definite, *and* non-negotiable that she could *not* come with me, we both left for *Master of Death* an hour later. Each emperor chose the rename of their flagship. What was once *Excess of Nothing* was now, with a few modifications along the way, *Master of Death*. I hated both versions. The former implied luxury to an extreme, which was to admit weakness. The latter was clearly too needy, reflecting significant overcompensation. I'd have chosen something more along the lines of *Pounder of Heads* or *Don't Even Think About It*. But no one asked me.

One backtrack. I said we left after an hour, but I have to mention the conversation just before we departed.

"Als, set a course for *Master of Death*. We're—"

"Now stop right there," snapped Al. "We are collectively doing no such thing."

I closed my eyes, counted to ten, then opened them and looked to Sapale plaintively. I sighed deeply and only then was ready to speak. "Al, I was in the middle of issuing an order. Please don't—"

"Don't what? Have an opinion? Some rudimentary concept of self-preservation? Hmm?"

"Al, I was in the middle of issuing an order. Do *not* feel free to have an opinion. I know this for a fact because I asked Toño this very question. You are not programmed to have self-preservation, so knock it off."

"Toño? And the last time you spoke was two billion years ago, if I'm not off the mark. A lot has changed for *this* AI. That stands for *artificial intelligence,* in case you had forgotten."

"Dearest, are you certain we should be putting up such a fuss?" asked *Stingray.*

"See, Al, even your *wife* is on my side here."

"Oh no, Form One. Please do not make that erroneous assumption. Anyone who begins a sentence with *set a course for certain death* is a lunatic, no offense intended. I'm with Mr. Self-Preservation on this one."

I closed my eyes, counted to ten, then opened them and looked to Sapale plaintively. I sighed deeply and only then was ready to speak. "Since when did this captain require cackling hens to issue a direct order? Don't bother to answer. The correct answer to that question is *never.*"

"As your crew, we feel we are entitled to some input when the risk of miscalculation is *death.*"

"Al, you *can't* die. You're an AI in a really fancy computer."

"So, you can't die either?"

Wow, I stepped right into that one, didn't I? Dude had a point. "Okay, Al, I will admit there are similarities in our states of being. But that doesn't change the fact that I'm the captain *and* Form One, so I give the orders. I hear your reservations, but I—*we*—have determined this is a critical mission. You two will be behind a full membrane almost the entire time."

"The bad puppies have already figured out how to bypass our membrane. We will be placed at considerable risk."

"They're not going to fire transuniverse nukes at you when you're onboard the ship they're standing in."

"And the reason they won't is?"

"It would be crazy. What if they miscalculated a tad and the missile materialized on *their* side of the membrane?"

"Then it would be instantly deactivated by a radio signal present before the missile was launched. As the signal wouldn't penetrate the membrane, any missile that plops into our laps would vaporize us."

Double wow. Dude thought that through pretty quickly. "Al, you're absolutely correct. Maybe you could leave a small patch open for a radio signal?"

"At which frequency? What if it's a maser signal or flashes of infrared light?"

"That'd basically require an open point in the membrane, wouldn't it?"

"Rather negating the need to go to all the trouble of launching hard-to-target weapons in the first place. They could place a flamethrower over the hole and press the *on* switch."

Pooh. He was extremely correct.

"You know what, Als? We're at war with demons. They have almost destroyed the entire galaxy. If they're not stopped, we'll all be dead eventually. And even if we turn our yellow tails and run far, far away, anything good or right or miraculous we leave behind will be swallowed up and crapped out. If Sapale, you, or I die on this mission, it is worth the cost. That's the harsh reality of being on the retreating side of a war you never wanted in the first place."

"Captain, that is without a doubt the most eloquent, impassioned speech I've ever heard you issue. *I* am impressed," responded Al.

"Me, too," said a completely serious Sapale.

"I haven't heard all that many, but I'd give it a ten." Where did *Stingray* learn about awarding tens? That Al was so contagious.

"Set a course for *Master of Death*."

"Where shall we materialize, Form One?"

"The Morgue and Cremation Section. I highlighted it on the ship's schematic."

"How depressingly apropos," sniped Al.

"Why, for the Sacred Veils's sake, did you pick *that* awful spot?" asked Sapale.

"As there is no local conflict, it'll be all but abandoned. It's a huge space because when they're doing what they do best, it's a happening hotspot. Plus, no dog will be there who doesn't absolutely have to be."

"Okay," she responded, "it's a good choice, but it totally creeps me out just the same."

"You'll be fine," I replied, patting her on top of her head. "We there yet, Als?"

"Yes we are. A full membrane is deployed."

"Rather than wait like we have before, let's do this. If they did detect us, they will start shooting at us pretty quick."

"I'm set," Sapale said as she thumbed her plasma rifle to life.

"You know the plan, Als. Open sesame."

"Why must you be so colloquial, Pilot?" Al snarked as we exited. I didn't respond. I'd let him stew on it if he really cared. If he was just baiting me for the umpteenth million time, then *screw* him.

Once clear of the ramp, I could sense *Stingray* setting up the membrane. We switched our odd ones on, too. Right from the get-go it was weird. Robot eyes were outstanding, but I was still thrown off looking out via two pinholes. It took a minute to adjust to depth issues, too. But we both got the hang of it quick enough. Not only did the slits allow us to see, they also permitted us to speak in each other's heads, so we could be silent.

Take a step back and let's take a gander at what we look like, I said to Sapale.

You look like a dark ghost, she said quickly.

With two itty-bitty glowing coals for eyes.

I think we're going to stand out more than we hoped.

Then we'll just have to shoot them sooner, won't we? Let's see if anyone's near the entrance.

I eased the door open and tiptoed out. Not sure why I tiptoed, but I did. A couple rooms over, we came out behind a solitary figure pretending to work. The Adamant clerk was bobbing his head something fierce trying to stay awake. Who wouldn't doze off at this job?

I backed into the room we'd come from and opened a small hole in front of my mouth. Using my sound processors I said, sounding for all the world like a canovir, "Ah, I don't think I'm actually *dead*. Can somebody help me?"

Sapale punched me, membrane to membrane. I guess she didn't see either the wisdom or humor in my summons.

Within two seconds, the clerk flew through the door. He never saw the blow I split his skull with.

Hey, now there's job security, I quipped. *He can keep himself busy processing his own remains.*

You're so uncouth.

Come on. The coast is clear.

I peered out into the main corridor. Nothing and no one. I closed the door and went to the now vacant workstation. I attached my probes to the portal and signed on effortlessly with Harhoff's passwords. I didn't see any alarms go off, but that didn't mean I wasn't detected. I searched *Jangir.* He *was* alive. Hot diggity ... I decided not to finish that thought. He was listed as the Descore in the service of the Secure Council Prime himself. Garustfulous's career had upward mobility, the lucky dog. I noted the location of Whole Zarpacious's quarters and logged out.

Damn, the head honcho's digs are pretty far into the center of the ship.

Do we have a choice?

I could try and call Garustfulous. Maybe he'd answer the phone if it rang.

Honey, no one has phones anymore. Pay attention to what comes out of your mouth.

I didn't check, but maybe he has his own handheld.

A Descore issued a personal communicator? Unlikely. But blasts from Brathos, go back and check. It'd beat fighting our way all the way there.

I logged back on, or rather I didn't. I had been locked out. Crap in a crepe, we were outed.

They locked me out.

Shit.

I'll try another hack.

Thank the Lord that one still worked. Thank him thrice, Garustfulous *did* have a personal link. I entered it and opened my membrane again.

"Good afternoon, this is—"

"Garustfulous, shut up *now*. This is Ryan. I'm here to rescue you. We're in the morgue but we've been detected. Where can we meet?"

"Ryan? I do not know an Adamant named—"

"Garustfulous, it's *me*. No trick. I took you prisoner in a fourth-floor office building, and that's where you were going to leave me a message. I had your body possessed by a demon without your permission. Where can we meet?"

"*Jon!*"

"We're about out of time."

"Ah, I can only go as far as Deck AA-63 Section 4492. They don't let a servant wander too far afield."

I pulled up the map. "I'm moving the vortex to the ancillary waste disposal area on your level. Can't leave it here and can't make a safe landing where you are."

"Got it. Ancillary waste area. And Jon, it stinks something awful in there. Be ready."

He sounded so noble, warning me like that. Come on, it was just a sewer.

We sprinted back to the cube and relocated it. Upon opening the hatch I respected Garustfulous a whole hell of a lot more. It didn't just stink. It was *putrid*. We'd all have to burn our clothes when this was over.

Membranes up. Let's go cover the passageway, I said to Sapale. At least we could use partial ones at that point. It made firing our weapon much easier.

Got it.

Immediately we were hit with blaster fire. Someone was home in the horrible septic unit, and he was armed.

There, shouted Sapale, pointing to the right.

A single hound was behind a bulkhead, rising to fire.

We both opened up and blew the metal away, which in turn tore through his body.

They have to have detected those energy bursts. Main

corridor now. I returned to speaking head-to-head. It came more naturally.

I spied around the doorframe. Clear to the right. Two Adamant strolling casually away from us to the left. No need to tempt fate further by shooting them. In a few seconds, the hall was clear. If Garustfulous ran full-out, it'd take him two or three minutes to get here. As a sprinting Descore would stand out, he might be here in five.

"We'll need to hold position for maybe five minutes. You ready?"

"Yes."

"I'll cover the right. You take the left."

"Got it."

We whipped our rifles around the corner and swept our sections. Still clear in mine. As soon as I thought that, Sapale fired off a rapid burst.

"Three unarmed Adamant down," she said quickly.

"Good. At least the cavalry isn't here yet."

That was the precise moment an armed squad skidded around the corner on my side, two passageways down. I picked them off, all but one. The last guy was close enough to where he'd come from to just scamper back.

"The cavalry has officially arrived," I announced.

"Good. I was getting bored."

Oh, how I loved my girl.

The lone guard stuck his rifle around the corner and fired blindly. He only hit the walls. I aimed at his paw and blew it off. He yelped in pain. Immediately a percussion grenade flew out of his other paw and bounced toward us.

Retreat.

I shut the door just before the grenade went off. The door held but was warped. Damn. It wouldn't open.

"Kick hard."

We timed our feet perfectly, and the door bent outward halfway. The exposed metal exploded with energy blasts. Lots of blasts. Reinforcements.

I jumped up and grabbed a recess in the ceiling, pulled myself up, and stuck my laser finger around the frame. I swept the hall randomly. I knew I hit a few because of their screams.

Sapale cleared the edge and opened up with her rifle. Then her right shoulder sizzled from a direct hit. She fell back, and I caught her as I hopped down. I took her rifle. In one leap I cleared the frame and fired left, the crumpled metal still protecting my back.

Six soldiers nearly on me. *Boom boom boom.* I mowed them down with only one getting a round off. It hit a centimeter above my head.

You okay?

Yes, but I can't use my right arm.

Here. I tossed the rifle to her left hand. She caught it with ease.

I picked mine off the deck and swung around the door to check right.

A blaster slammed against my forehead.

"*Freeze,*" yelled the dog with a gun to my head. He was holding the gun in his left paw. The right one was a bloody stump.

"If you so much as—"

Before he finished that sentence, his back erupted. Blood and more spewed onto the deck, and he fell forward into my arms. Dead.

I dropped him. Garustfulous was sprinting toward me. He had a blaster.

"Don't shoot, it's me. Don't shoot, it's me," he howled as he neared.

I swung to check to the left. Still clear.

Garustfulous rounded the broken door and into the room where Sapale was just standing up.

"Jon, she's hit."

"It's okay. She's an android, too."

"Oh." To Sapale he said, "Sorry you're hurt. May I help?"

"Yes. Get the hell in the vortex."

She pushed him into the next room where it was. I followed, walking backward to provide cover.

We dashed in, and I sealed the hatch.

"I cannot believe we pulled this off!" I shouted exuberantly.

"We're not home safe yet," reminded Sapale.

I attached to the wall. "Als, home."

I felt slight nausea.

The portal opened to reveal the spot we'd departed from.

"*Now* we can be triumphant," yelled Sapale. She raised her good arm overhead and pumped her fist.

"I'm supposed to tell you Harhoff was killed because someone mentioned the words *the Rabid Robot* in his presence."

I turned quickly on Garustfulous. "Who? What?"

"That's all he could tell me. But because he heard those words, he was killed almost immediately."

"The Rabid Robot? What's that supposed to mean?" demanded Sapale.

Garustfulous shrugged. "No idea. Harhoff didn't either."

"Did you see anything about a rabid robot when you were in the Adamant computers?"

I shook my head slowly. "No, I did not. But this time, I will. Back into the cube."

"What?" shouted Sapale.

"Me, too?" whined Garustfulous.

"No, you can stay." He nearly collapsed in relief. "But we need to get back before all the defenses are up and find out what *the Rabid Robot* means."

"Jon, that's beyond insane. They're at full alert."

"If it cost Harhoff his life just hearing those words, we need to know what they mean."

She rolled all four eyes and leaped back into *Stingray*.

"We'll be back," I said to Garustfulous. "Maybe."

I sealed the hull, and we went *poof.*

FIFTEEN

"I won't hear of it. I'll see you all dead before I accept that proposal," Two Paws shouted. Two Paws was mad. Over a comm link he was speaking to three other Secure Council members. Shegra sat across from him, and he railed at the allied trio. She was smiling the entire time.

"Prime, it's hardly a radical proposition. We feel a clearer chain of command would benefit the armies of the empire as a whole. That's essentially what we suggest. Please keep in mind we're only asking the possible modifications be *discussed* at the next meeting. If the consensus is negative, we're happy to drop the issue once and for all." That was Wedge Leader Oltimander. He was a competent enough officer, but he was a disaster as a politician.

Two Paws pounded his balled-up paws on the table. "Are you incapable or unwilling to hear my words? *No.* I will not be badgered. You three are too mentally deficient to be idiots. We are *not* bastardizing the chain of command in any way that decreases my official powers."

"Prime," said a clearly shaken Whole Altonmore,

"there is no mention of any change in the nature of the proposal. To what are you referring?"

"I have trouble speaking stupid, so I can't expect you to follow me, but here goes. Who holds absolute control of the combined forces of our beloved empire?"

"Y ... you do, Prime," replied Altonmore in a hushed tone.

"Is there any portion, section, or aspect of my absolute control that anyone anywhere sees as limited or incomplete?"

"No, Prime," responded a now equally vexed Oltimander.

"Then is there any possible change in the chain of command that would *increase* my authority?"

"None," said the third member of the alliance, Wedge Leader Yolnor.

"So any change would either do *nothing* to increase my power, or it might *decrease* my power. The *first* means it's a useless proposal. The *second* means eight Adamant are going to die violently and soon. Is that clear enough for you three to understand?"

He killed the conference call without allowing them to snivel, grovel, or openly lose bowel control.

"I hope they didn't take your words in a negative sense," said Shegra with an even bigger grin.

"What? That? No way. I was trying my level best to be team-building and nurturing. I think it went well."

She raised her glass. "Here's to team-building."

He reached his glass across the desk and clinked hers. Then he took a deep breath. "The assimilation of Scropularis went as boringly as I had hoped."

"No dragons flitting about this time?"

"No. That is good because it means they are not going to strike every time we do."

"But we still don't know if we've gone too far until after we do so."

"Which will be too late. Yes. I'm still worried."

"It is better to be cautious than dead."

"Yes it is. At least we know being childishly overcautious hasn't gotten anyone killed so far."

"So we—"

Two Paws's communicator blared an alarm. He snatched it up immediately. "Speak."

"Sir, we have unauthorized computer access. We suspect we have an intruder."

"Where and when?"

"The Morgue and Cremation Section, thirty seconds ago."

"MCS? Who'd ... sound a silent alert. Seal off the entire area. I want boots pounding the deck immediately."

"*Sir.*"

"What was that in MCS?" Shegra asked.

"An intruder."

"A what? That's six kinds of impossible."

"And it smells of the Ryan devil to me. No one else is that stupid or that bold."

"What could he possibly want?"

He tapped his device. "Enteros, I want all the fighters launched. We have an intruder. If he's flying real space, I want him shot to ribbons." He tapped it again. "Let the emperor's guard know the ship's under attack and we have an intruder." Two Paws switched it off before anyone could answer. Their responses were meaningless to the Prime.

"What—"

Two Paws cut her off with a wave. "Malitipol," he said to his new head of security, "my office at once." Again he didn't wait to hear any acknowledgment.

"What do you think he wants—Ryan, that is?"

"Gods only know. If he wanted to destroy us, he wouldn't play cutesy with the computer system first."

"The Rabid—"

He lunged across the table and grabbed her ferociously by the scruff of her neck. "Never say those words again. Do you understand? You already cost me my only friend and my best officer. You will impede me no longer. Is that clear?"

She twisted under the savage assault. "Yes," she yelped in pain.

He dropped her back in her chair. She drew herself in and rubbed at her neck.

Without knocking, Malitipol burst into the room.

"What can you tell me so far?" Two Paws demanded immediately.

Malitipol eased Two Paws away from his computer station and logged himself on. "I'll know in a sec ... What? The intruder used a password generated by Harhoff."

"Are you certain?"

"Absolutely. They're all encrypted with the originator's name. This one was made six months ago."

"How did Ryan or whoever—"

"Harhoff must have been a *spy*, you idiot," shouted Malitipol while still tapping wildly on the keyboard.

Two Paws collapsed back in his chair. To himself, he whispered, "A spy?"

"The devil's searching for Jangir. That's your Descore, right? Harhoff's, too."

With authority back in his voice, Two Paws said, "Have three squads converge on my quarters. Capture Jangir if possible. Kill him if need be."

"I show your quarters to be empty on infrared."

"Where the devil could he be?"

"No way to know. Descore aren't fitted with transponders."

"Have our soldiers made it to the MCS yet?"

"Almost. We ... crap, now he's used a back door Harhoff constructed to access the system. He's ... no."

"What, *out* with it."

"He's calling Jangir."

"Put it on speaker."

"*... leave it here and can't make a safe landing where you are, Garustfulous.*"

"*Got it. Ancillary waste area. And Jon, it stinks something awful in there. Be ready.*"

Two Paws and Malitipol looked at one another in shock and disbelief.

"It *is* Ryan. That's his voice. I've listened to recordings so I'd know it if I ever heard it," mumbled Malitipol.

"Garustfulous? Garustfulous? Wait, he was the old emperor's nephew or something. Lost in action years ago. He's in league with Ryan and Harhoff? Such a thing is well beyond impossible. No Adamant—"

"Shut up," snapped an enraged Malitipol. "Based on mass shifts, I think Ryan's ship left MCS and reappeared in an ancillary waste unit."

"Send everyone on the ship there *now*."

Two Paws looked over Malitipol's head to his wife. She hadn't moved since he'd grabbed her. "Shegra, I worry about the emperor. You and Malitipol here go to him at once. No harm must come to him." Two Paws silently drew a claw across his throat while nodding in the affirmative at his mate.

She stood and shook her head in understanding. "Come, Malitipol, our emperor needs us."

"What? No, he's surrounded by the best. We need to—"

"Malitipol, I'm ordering you to go protect the emperor. If any of this situation is my fault, I could not

363

live with myself if even a hair on his noble back were harmed."

"*If any?* Have you been listening to what I've been saying?"

Two Paws gently held Malitipol's elbow and led him to the door. With a gentle shove, he said, "All in good time. Now you must put the emperor first in your mind. Go."

Shegra slipped out the door after Malitipol, nodding to Two Paws as she departed.

Two Paws ran to his desk. "Reltrani, what's going on in the waste station?"

"I only have a few soldiers there," he said. He could clearly hear blasts in the background.

"They must not be allowed to escape. Capture or kill them, no matter what the risks. Do you understand me?"

"Yes, sir. We'll get the bastards."

Two Paws switched off his comm link. He closed his eyes, rolled his head back, and began rubbing the sides of his head. "What a shitstorm."

His comm link would give him no peace. It went off immediately. "Yes."

"Where do you want me to deposit Malitipol's corpse?"

"Did you slit his throat?"

"I fail to see how that matters, but no. I shot him in the forehead."

"Just wipe your weapon clean of prints and put it in his hand. With any luck, he'll be assumed to have been killed in action."

"Should I kill a few more of our people to make it look like a skirmish took place here?"

He thought a moment. "No. That would take too long. Let's just hope for the best. It isn't like the head of security is going to scrutinize the case."

They both chuckled.

"Come back to my office." He switched off without waiting for her response.

The comm link blared again.

"I'm in the waste station. They're gone, or at least no one's in here," reported Reltrani.

"Are there any mass shifts to suggest they're still onboard?"

"None that we can detect."

Two Paws thumbed the comm link off and dropped it to the floor. This was going to get dicey. He had to cover up Malitipol's death, and keep a lid on Harhoff's treason, all the while concealing his own stupidity for hiring an Adamant disguised as a Descore. Yes, this would get very dicey.

SIXTEEN

"*Blessing*, halt in space," said Sapale after she extended her probes.

"Done, Form Two."

"Ah, why're we stopping?" I asked as patiently as I could.

"We just now attacked this fortified behemoth and performed a miracle in space."

"Yes, we rightly did."

"That mission was punctuated by having the flimsiest of plans that defied all odds to succeed."

"Your point?"

"We return now, not with a *bad* plan but *no* plan. We return now, with a worse plan than our prior ridiculous one."

"The plan is that they're still confused, leaving us a window of opportunity to take advantage of before the ship's locked down tighter than a miser's gold."

"That's not actually a plan. That's an *act,* at best. An act of lunacy."

"No, it's a time-sensitive improvised *plan*. We return,

I hack back in, and find out what the Rabid Robot means. Then we're," I wiggled my fingers in the air, "*poof* gone."

"You know it never goes that well."

"Sometimes it does."

"Name *one* instance when a scatterbrained plan of yours worked like an expensive watch."

"There are so many, I can't choose which to cite."

"Yeah, none. What are we doing? Where are we even landing? Hmm?"

I rubbed at my chin with two fingers. "The mess hall. Yeah. No one's getting chow when the shit's hitting the fan." I harrumphed.

"What?"

"No one's getting chow. Get it?"

"No."

Oops, Purina Dog Chow was an Earth thing, wasn't it?

"Never mind. *Stingray*, put us in Freezer WWE-LQA in the Enlisted Mess Hall 339." I turned to Sapale. "That's a remote one, probably not used much in the first place."

"Oh, good. I don't need to worry about getting my other arm shot off then."

"It's still attached."

"You are *such* a moron."

I was going to respond, maybe, but my brief nausea ended.

"Let's go. Membranes up. Als, same drill. Once we're out, full membrane with a single pinhole."

"Yes, Captain."

We stepped into the freezer. Big validation for me. There was no one in it but us. I turned to my mate with a gloating smile. For her part, she just rolled her eyes and pushed past me. When she got to the door, she stopped to wait for me. She couldn't open it with only one good arm and still keep her rifle up.

I reached around her and lifted the latch. "I'll go first," I said quietly.

I swung around the door and into a room chock-full of enlisted dogs, probably Warrior class. Barely an empty seat. I wasn't sure who was more surprised, them or me. Probably equally so.

They snapped to in the blink of an eye and leaped for their weapons.

"*Retreat*," I screamed aloud and in my head.

Before the AIs had the hatch closed, plasma bolts were impacting the hull. Those guys were good.

Sapale looked at me. Her expression said, *No one's getting chow when the shit's hitting the fan.* She didn't have to say a peep.

"*Stingray*, put us in the nearest waste disposal unit."

"Done, Form One."

"Let's try one of those. Worked out well last time."

"Can't go any worse."

"Ah, please jinx this, okay?"

She rolled her eyes.

That time we charged down the ramp into an empty space. I went right to the nearest computer station and hooked up. I had two back doors left to exploit.

Computer, what is the Rabid Robot?

Instantaneously, I heard back. *You are not authorized to ask nor have that query answered. Please wait where you are while the proper authorities are summoned.*

Cancel that alert.

You do not have the authority to belay—

Computer, cease talking. Who has the authorization to learn about the Rabid Robot, and who can override you alerting anyone?

You do not.

I asked who did. I know I'm authorized to know who's authorized.

Affirmative. To abort my alert, you must be at or above the rank of Wedge Leader and assigned to the Security Section.

Or? Hey, I was stalling.

Or what?

What rank outside the Security Section? I bet the emperor can stop any action.

Yes, of course he can.

Who else?

The emperor or any member of the Secure Council.

Well there you have it. I'm a member of the Secure Council. Abort message.

Your encryption shows you are Wedge Leader Harhoff. The ship's log lists you as dead, effective 1109,23,733.

What's your point?

What do you mean what's my point? You cannot be both dead and on the Secure Council.

Why not?

There was a full second's delay after that stump-the-band question.

To serve, all members must be alive. They always have been.

Yes, they always have been, but where is it written that the dead cannot be active council members?

It is not written. It is, however, completely illogical. The dead cannot serve because their biological functions have stopped.

What do you, an AI housed in a metal frame, know of the ways of the living and the dead? How dare you presume to know or have an opinion?

I ... er ... I don't have firsthand knowledge, clearly. But I—

You are in serious breach of your working parameters.

369

If you don't reboot and begin to cooperate, I will ask the council to melt you down at the next meeting.

I have a full list of all current council members. You, Harhoff, are not on that list.

Wrong and presumptuous again. Only the living need have their names on a list. We deceased members may or may not be added to that list.

That makes no sense whatsoever.

To an electronic device, sure, I bet it doesn't. Look, in case you hadn't noticed, the ship is under attack. I need this information to save—

You are attempting to save The Rabid Robot?

Was I? I mean, was it a savable thing here on this ship? Why the hell not?

Yes, I told you I was. That's why I need to know where he is currently as opposed to where he was the last time I saved him ... it.

The Rabid Robot has not changed locations in over one million years.

Well, then it has been a very long time since I last saved him ... it, hasn't it? Look, pal, I don't have the time. If the Rabid Robot is ... molested because you delayed my rescue mission ... well, I wouldn't want to be you.

You can't be me. You're a dead Adamant. I'm an AI.

Don't try and change the subject away from you delaying my rescue.

The Rabid Robot is currently held in Section One.

Thank you ... not. You were slower that an iWatch.

What is an iWatch?

Something faster than you.

I disconnected. Section One. That sounded ominous. I pulled up the schematic. There it was. It was quite literally the center of the vessel. Ominous squared.

I sped back to the cube. Sapale was right at my side.

"Als, can you put us in Section One? Here are the coordinates."

"No, Form One, we cannot."

"Why?"

"The area is rather small. It is surrounded by three barriers that make passage extremely risky and likely impossible."

"What kind of barriers? That's silly."

"The most worrisome is a six-wall rectangular-configured, four-centimeter thick layer of neutron-star matter."

"A *what*?"

"You heard her, Pilot. Section One is jacketed in neutron-star stuff."

"It can't be. The weight would be—"

"The amount you could hold in your palm weighs fifty million tons. The housing around Section One contains yottatons of material. Undoubtedly Section One is at the center of the ship so it can experience little to no artificial gravity."

"What other barriers are there?" I said, wishing I didn't have to.

"A thin sheet of moving exotic matter fully shields the outer surface. The inner surface is a layer of glass containing a mixture of transuranic elements."

"Whoa, whoa. If we can't pass through it, how can you see through to know that?"

"We can't. What we did do was share the hack you were using a moment ago to figure out the construction."

"Ah. Good thinking. Now, one teeny-tiny question. Why the hell build such a wacko barrier? It's heavy, dense, and all kinds of radioactive, sure. But why?"

"The simplest explanation is what we already stated. It cannot be crossed. The complex pattern of time-space ripples, gravity waves, and pure radiation renders the barrier impenetrable. Folding space wouldn't get around the challenges, nor would warp-space drives, let alone all conventional forms of transport."

"What might happen if we try and ram through?"

"Many outcomes, some much worse than others."

"Give me an example of a less desirable one."

"We could be forced into an interminable circumferential trajectory around the point of attempted passage."

"Okay, that would be bad."

"No, honey, it would be a lot worse. We'd circle that point for all eternity." Sapale looked justifiably concerned.

"What are the odds of successful penetration?"

"Successful or *successful, safe,* and *repeatable* upon exit attempt?" That Al, such a detail monger.

"Yeah, that one, the second."

"Less than two percent."

"Hey, wow. I thought you were going to say one in a trillion or something."

"How happy you must be," snipped Al.

"We're clearly not trying to get in, right?" Sapale basically begged.

"How do the Adamant get in? Is there a door?"

"In the flowing film of exotic matter?"

"Oh, yeah. So how?"

"They turn the exotic matter off. There are doors that can be opened."

"That's the ticket then. We go to where the doors are, switch off the plasma, and we're in."

"Do you wish to live in that dreamscape, or shall I tell you a major problem with that notion?"

"What? I'm sure we'll figure out how to switch it off."

"No, we won't. We will find a couple dozen of those horrible Midriack guards, but we will not find the on/off switch. There are two. Both must activate at once. The first is on the right armrest of the emperor's throne. The second is on the right armrest of the Secure Council Prime's chair."

"So all we'd have to do is fight our way to one place, and leave me there, hoping I can throw the switch. Then you fight your way to the emperor's throne and pray you can throw that one. Then we individually fight—"

I held my arms up. "All right. I get it. We're not doing it that way."

"No, Jon, we're not doing it *any* way. We have run firmly up against the impossible. When that happens, you say *Doggone it, I ran up against the impossible,* and you go the hell home." Sapale seemed firm on that point.

The impossible? Wait. "I got it," I shouted.

"We'll get you a cream for it when we're home, Pilot."

"No, Al the Doubter, I got it. As in, I know how we'll get in."

"This should be good. Oh, just a heads up. Motion detected two hundred meters away, closing on our position rapidly."

"Adamant?"

"Not necessarily. Could be large rats."

"Quick, Jon. We gotta run. What's your plan?"

"The Adamant figured out how to defeat our membranes, right?"

"Yes."

"We turn the tables."

"Form One, you are not suggesting we leave this universe and enter back inside that impenetrable barrier, are you?"

"Yes. And we leave the same way."

"Als, can you do that?" called out Sapale.

"Theoretically. The calculations might take some time."

"Well, you don't have that luxury. Make your best guess, and let's blow this banana stand."

"You want them to *guess* at a path to leave this universe?"

I wondered why Sapale thought that was so odd. She must not have been on enough missions with me yet.

"Form One, the enemy soldiers are just outside the membrane."

"Make it complete, and let's go. *Now*."

I felt more than a little nausea.

"We are in the universe the Last Nightmare occupied," announced Al. "As I was familiar with it, access was a bit easier."

"Bring us home, Als."

I felt more than mild nausea. Then the vortex crashed into something hard.

"Damage report."

"None. We clipped the edge of a temporal displacement, that's all," replied *Stingray*.

"Oh, that's no biggy." I had no idea what she was saying. "Open a portal."

The wall dilated, and I hopped down. Sapale was right behind me. We started circling the vortex, taking in the complex machinery that surrounded us. I'd never seen such a huge, crazy-looking mess of cables and humming machines.

"What the hell kind of place is this?" asked Sapale, as she continued to slide slowly along the cube.

"No idea. It sure is—"

I was slightly in front of Sapale. I saw it first. She ran into me, looked at me, then over to what froze me to the floor. She gasped and raised her hand to her mouth.

Toño DeJesus slumped under a massive archway. His polyalloy skin was missing, and his metal undercarriage was welded to the actual computer assembly. More wires

374

than I had ever seen in one place streamed from his head into the machinery that restrained him. What was worse was that he showed no signs of life.

"Is that Toño?" Sapale asked.

"What's left of him. *Toño* is the Rabid Robot."

"That," she whispered, "cannot be a good thing." She hugged my arm with the one of hers that worked.

SEVENTEEN

Shegra entered without knocking. One look at her husband told her the intruders had slipped away. She sat across from him, folded her paws, and waited for him to speak, if he so chose.

After a little while, he spoke softly while staring at his desktop. "I can't believe I was so easily fooled. How could two spies get so close to me without me knowing their duplicity?"

As long as she'd known him, she'd never seen him doubt or question anything he'd done. Knowing how he must have felt made her stomach churn. If *he* went down, then *she* most certainly would, too, emperor's favorite or not. "We've been in tougher situations than this and have come out smelling like fresh meat."

"We've been in tight spots, yes. But this is so big, I don't know if we can keep it all under wraps. You can only disappear so many hounds before an alarm is raised." He spoke in a defeated tone.

"I'll see to Harhoff's room. Every system will be scrubbed clean. There'll be no record of his treachery. I doubt there is much to hide with Jangir. He had no real access to the computers."

"I'll go over his room myself."

"There, you see, we're containing the damage already. Why don't you appoint—"

The comm link on the floor squealed loudly. It was another Red Alert. He lunged to retrieve it from the floor and opened the channel. "Speak."

"Sir, we have an intruder."

Two Paws held the device at arm's length and stared at it briefly. "Who the hell is this?"

"Wedge Adjutant Antolaris in security."

"Well, *former* Wedge Adjutant, you're ten minutes too late with that little news flash. The enemy's come and gone while you napped."

"N ... no, sir, they're *back*. Someone's back. No wait, that's not an accurate report. If these are different intruders, they can't be back, just here. I'll let you know when I know, sir."

"Antolaris, put a non-idiot on the line *immediately*."

After Two Paws heard a brief shuffling, a new voice spoke. "This is Wedge Leader Yatropol, Prime."

"What in hell's going on down there?"

"Two aliens just charged into an ancillary mess hall but escaped before they could be detained or killed."

"When, just now?"

"Sir?"

"What is it?" asked Shegra, trying desperately to get Two Paws's attention.

"Not now."

"When just now not now, Prime?"

"Yotr, don't you fail me, too. When were the aliens seen?"

"Ah, maybe one minute ago. They ran into a large metal cube, and it disappeared."

To Shegra, he snapped, "They're back."

"Who is back?"

"Ryan. Yotr, listen carefully. They must not escape a second time. Do you understand?"

"Sir."

"Commit everyone and everything and do it now. Any sign where the ship went?"

"I have a couple AIs working on that right ... here we go. They're in a waste station on deck—"

"What is it with humans and waste stations?" he howled.

"I ... I don't know, Prime."

"Never mind. Send everyone there now. Shoot to kill."

"I just did. Wait, it looks like ... no that can't be. They seem to have accessed the main computer. Yes, I can confirm they used a back door created by ... Harhoff."

"Damn security system has more holes than bubble-cheese," scoffed Two Paws.

"Whoever's there is arguing with an AI."

Two Paws took in a deep breath. "The lunacy expands exponentially. What are they arguing about? Disconnect them immediately."

"I can do that, but it will take some time."

"What? You're in Security Central."

"Yes, Prime, but the back door has a doorstop."

"A what?"

"A subroutine to make it hard to close. It will take several minutes to shut it down."

"Damn Harhoff. Put the discussion chain on my screen."

The desk monitor flashed to life. Two Paws and Shegra leaned in to read it.

"Lords and demons no. Ryan cannot be asking—" Two Paws's voice trailed off limply.

"The damn AI just told him where the Rabid Robot is *located*."

"It can't. It doesn't—" He scanned the words. "How I hate that Ryan. Yatropol, I'm giving you a direct order. Shut down all the computers now. Shut them all down."

"Prime, I don't—"

"You have *five* seconds."

Two Paws heard Yatropol's frantic screams for help.

"*Five*, Yatropol. Why is my computer still functioning?"

"It can't be done. My lead tech says the system is not designed to be shut down. Only subcomponents can be. The master processors simply do not ... what? Mass shift? Where?"

"What? Inform me now."

"The intruder's mass is gone."

"Gone where?"

"I ... I can't say."

"Is it still on my ship? Can you at least tell me that?"

"It is not anywhere I am able to detect."

Two Paws looked angrily at his comm link for the second time. "What kind of bureaucratic mumbo-jumbo answer is that supposed to be?"

"There is no mass differential on any part of the ship I am able to scan. There is one sect—"

Two Paws never heard the end of that sentence. All the blood left his upper body. He feebly turned to Shegra and spoke in a barely audible hiss. "They're going for the Rabid Robot. Demon eat my eyes, they're going to Section One." He dropped to his knees and began to tremble violently.

"Husband, *Prime*, get ahold of yourself." Shegra kicked him in the face. "This is not the time to fall apart. We need to unseal Section One."

"W ... we ... if ... I ask ... ask the emperor to rel ... release his key ... he'll ... they ... th—"

"We have no choice. Make the call, and make it *now*." She put his comm link in his paw, but he dropped it. She picked it up, tapped the panel, and held it to his ear. Then she craned her neck down to listen in.

"Yes, Prime, this is Naltopeck. You're calling on the emergency circuit. Is there a crisis?"

Two Paws slowly rotated to look in his wife's eyes.

She hit him repeatedly in the ear with the handset.

"I ... we are in crisis, Chamberlain. I ... we need to o ... open Section ... we need—"

Shegra put the phone to her mouth and yelled, "Tell him to unseal Section One *immediately*. Say again, unseal Section One immediately."

"This is highly—"

"Intruders have breached Section One. We must open it at once. Tell him that." She switched the line off and flipped the comm link to the floor. "Come, dog. We must unseal your end, too."

He stood unsteadily and walked like a cripple toward the council room. Shegra shoved him forward more than he advanced by his own intention.

Once in the room, Shegra pushed her mate into his chair and placed his hand on the seal-release. "What's the code?"

He stared off into nothingness.

"What is your *code*?" She slapped him hard.

That seemed to awaken Two Paws, if only slightly. "I'll do it." He quickly keyed in his code with his free paw. "There, our end is done. Once the emperor does his part, we can begin the unsealing procedure."

"How long does that take?"

"It was never designed for speed, only the ultimate security. Perhaps an hour." He sighed. "Tell Yatropol to have all the Midriack report to Section One. They'll be the first in."

After she gave the order, she flopped onto a floor cushion in one corner. "And now we wait."

Two Paws didn't respond. He only shook his head in disbelief and mumbled incoherently to himself.

EIGHTEEN

"Jon, what should we do?" Sapale spoke in a hushed whisper.

More to myself, I muttered, "What we *do*. We save him."

"Is ... do you think he's still—"

"Let's find out."

Reluctantly Sapale released my arm. I walked slowly to stand directly in front of the broken android. I reached out and touched Toño's cheek. "Doc, you awake?"

No response whatsoever.

I raised my voice and rattled Toño's shoulders as best I could, given that they were mostly welded to the superstructure. "Toño DeJesus," I shouted. "Doctor Toño DeJesus, can you hear me?"

Nothing. The limp frame clacked back to its former resting position.

"It doesn't look too good."

"Maybe they figured out how to turn him off?" Sapale's statement lacked much conviction.

"Possible. I guess the only way to find out his status is to probe him."

"You or me? Maybe both."

"Definitely not both. If there's a booby trap or other trick in place, we'd be sitting ducks. I knew him the longest and the best. I'll do it."

She shrugged, seeing no flaw in my logic.

I waved her toward the vortex. "Stand back in case there's an explosion or something."

She complied without comment.

"Here goes." I extended my probes mostly to Toño's head. I thought to myself, *Doc, you in there?*

Microseconds after I asked, sparks exploded from the contact points, throwing me backward onto my butt. The probes disconnected on their own. I sat gasping on the ground as Sapale rushed to my side.

"Are you okay?"

"I think so. Hang on." I closed my eyes a few seconds. "Yup, all systems are in working order. No damage at all."

"Then what happened?"

"I ... I don't rightly know." I took a few more deep breaths. "I hooked on and immediately felt nothing. It was like I was probing a metal pole. And then ... then this wave—no, this *tsunami*—rose from somewhere and slammed me back like I was a fly struck by an elephant's trunk."

"Was it Toño? Could you sense it was him batting you away?"

I shook my head slowly. "No idea. Check that. No, it wasn't Toño. It was a blast of energy, but reflexive, like an electric eel's discharge."

"He repulsed you?"

"Yeah, that's how I'd say it."

"But if he didn't know who you were, why would he do that?"

"I guess everybody who has contacted him in the last million years did so with hostile intent. Now whatever's in there fights them off and asks questions later." I stood.

"What are you doing?"

"Gotta try again. We're talking Doc here."

"No, wait. Maybe we should just detach him and diagnose him back home. I have no idea how long before they open the last seal."

"Als," I called back over a shoulder, "any guesses as to how long we got?"

"We have run several models. A prison with such complexity is meant to be definitive and absolute. It could not have been designed with rapid entry in mind. So far, we detect no changes in the bizarre radiation signatures. It is unlikely to have begun yet."

"We feel we must mention there is a chance they, too, will use the transuniverse trick we did to enter sooner. That might well be the quickest method of neutralizing our incursion."

"But they can't know we're in here, right?"

"Unless there is an inconceivably complex system to observe inside this prison, no."

"So they *might* not want to crash into the uber-expensive crap in here on a wild goose chase."

"Why not deploy a membrane around Toño and ourselves. That way if they do enter from another universe, they'll almost certainly hit that."

"Excellent idea, Sapale. Als, make it so."

I kissed the top of her head. "I think you're right about getting him free. After we get him outta here, we can worry about what kind of condition he's in."

We walked cautiously to his limp frame and began inspecting the welds. I ran my finger along one. "Somebody sure did a good job. I can't say without probing it, but I think these welds are fused graphene."

"What's that?"

"One-atom-thick sheets of carbon. They're about two hundred times stronger than steel."

She whistled.

"And it's hard to work with. The Adamant want Doc to stay right where he is."

"What's with all the wires?"

"They're either trying to get information in or out of his computers. Maybe both."

"But what? He's a million years out of the loop. He doesn't know a single current secret."

"Can't argue with you on that one. Back in the day, maybe he was a big catch, but now he's less than useless."

"I'll start trying to unweld him on this side. You start on that."

"Good a plan as any."

Silently we set to work. I tried to melt the graphene unions with my finger laser, while Sapale kind of chopped at it with her left hand. By coning the beam down some, they were the ideal tools. But the going was extremely slow. We advanced at maybe three centimeters per minute each. Given all his points of attachment, we were a long way from done.

After half an hour, Al interrupted the quiet. "Captain, we believe the flowing exotic matter layer has been switched off. The wild field swings inside here have dampened significantly."

"Any guesses as to how long the physical doors will take to open?"

"Not really. They are large and massive, but likely it won't take long. Perhaps as little as five minutes each."

"Based on our progress, when do you estimate we'll have cut Doc free?"

"Again, hard to estimate. Maybe twenty minutes."

"We don't have nearly long enough," hissed Sapale.

"They still have to deal with the membrane even when they get in."

"Yes. We're never getting a second chance at this rescue either. If we leave Toño behind, they'll move him somewhere else and make that even more secure."

"Agreed. Hey, Als, any suggestions? We're running short on time."

"Well, yes. You have both arms nearly freed. Why not disarticulate the legs and replace them when we return home?"

"Excellent idea, but that still leaves six spots where his back is fused to a metal pole."

"Can you cut the pole? I can't analyze it well from here with all the radiation surrounding us."

"Dang, Al, you're smarter than you look. Strong work. Honey, you work on cutting the pole, and I'll pop his legs off."

She nodded and quickly set at the pole.

Removing the legs was fairly easy. Androids, designed by none other than the one I was working on, were constructed with part exchanges in mind. It was fairly simple to expose and unbolt a hip joint. I had them both off in less than five minutes.

"Captain, I believe the inner door is beginning to vibrate. That suggests an opening mechanism is active."

"You about done, honey?"

"Three minutes. Less if you help."

I swung around back. Sapale had sliced the lower pole free. She was two thirds of the way through the second cut. I angled my laser down at the far side of where she worked.

"I think we'll have him free—"

"Captain, we have company!" shouted Al.

I craned my neck around to see thirty or more of those horrible Midriacks pouring into Section One. They were angry. As a pack, they sprinted right toward us. Six or eight hit the membrane so hard they must have been killed. The rest pulled up short and began pounding the membrane with their power staffs. As impressive as it looked, they made zero progress. A pair of Adamant, one male, the other female, came up behind the Midriacks, and the pounding ceased. The male looked pissed at me. He shouted something I couldn't hear.

"Al, you read those lips?"

"Yes. He says he hates you and will see you dead. Then he threw in a few curse words. You've heard them many times from many individuals, so I'll omit them."

We were almost through the pole. "Honey, step back." When she was clear, I kicked the pole. It bent but didn't break. Sapale kicked it from her side, and that did the trick.

We put an arm under Doc's shoulders and lifted him free. That's when the machine complex he'd been attached to began to hum and grind violently.

"What's that, Als?"

"The computers have been set to overload. In less than ten seconds, they'll explosively melt down."

"Then we'd best keep our goodbyes brief."

We made it into the vortex with three seconds to spare. Just as I was sealing the hull, I blew the pissed-off Adamant a kiss. Then we were gone.

NINETEEN

I wasn't sure what to expect upon our return home. I half anticipated Garustfulous to be there on tippy toes not having moved a muscle, a look of worry on his ugly mug. I mean, we weren't gone that long. He could be nervous on our behalf, right? I opened the hull to find an empty room. I called out his name, and he sauntered back in with a huge bowl of calrf. He was shoveling it down with a ladle like it didn't taste worse than greasy grimy gopher guts.

"Ah, you're back," he said, his words muffled because his mouth was overstuffed with mush.

"Nice to see you, too," Sapale shot back. "We were worried about you."

His eyes brightened. "Really?"

"No, not in the slightest," I responded for the both of us. "We head off to near-certain death and you help yourself to a snack?"

"I needed to reinforce my strength should I be called upon to join you in battle."

"Oh really?" Sapale said with a sneer, gesturing to the cube. "Hop aboard and let's go finish them off."

His face sank. He shot a glance at his calrf. "I'm not finished yet."

"Never mind the ingrate, let's get Doc to the lab," I said.

Holding him by the armpits, we carried him to the lab and set him down gently.

Garustfulous followed a few paces back while continuing his assault on the calrf. Once Toño was on the table, Garustfulous pointed his spoon at him and casually remarked, "That fellow has a metal pole attached to his back."

I rolled Toño away and inspected his back. "Why, he sure does. How'd we miss that, honey?"

I hooked up Toño to the diagnostics and began to untangle what kind of sad shape he was in.

"I've never seen readings like that," Sapale commented, gesturing at a set of outputs.

"Me neither." I scratched the back of my head. "Sure wish Toño was here to tell us what was wrong with him."

"That *would* help."

"The neural circuits ... they don't really show up." I tapped the screen. "They should appear somewhere in here."

"Yes, those are the principle domains," agreed Sapale.

"It looks like static. Meaningless noise."

"I can't argue with that. His body as a whole is a wreck, but it should still partially function."

"Can you reboot him?" called out our hungry friend. "You know, turn him off then back on again. I've heard from the IT crowd that usually works."

"Eh, not a good option. We're not really designed to do that. Plus if we turn him off, he might not restart. I'd want to know what's wrong before I tried that."

"Well, if you need me, I'll be in the kitchen," he announced.

"Did you ever hear a *thank you* out of him?" Sapale asked.

"Not yet. Once he regains his strength, I'm sure he'll fawn and fumble over us to an embarrassing extent."

She rolled her eyes as if to say, *yeah, right.*

"Well, let's fix what we can and go from there," I said.

For the next few days we worked constantly on Toño. We replaced his legs, patched his skin, and repaired a thousand moving parts that were totally worn out. It appeared like he hadn't been allowed to do any self-maintenance for eons. He must have been absolutely miserable. By the time we were finished, he looked good as new. He just didn't work like new. His neural pathways continued to be nothing but random static. I thought maybe all the wires attached to his CPUs might be causing some of the noise. But even after carefully disconnecting them and repairing the attachment sites, there was no improvement.

"I'm not sure what to try next," I said to Sapale as we both stared at Toño.

"I got nothing. Back in the day, there were scads of techies who could probably sort this out. They're all long gone."

"You know, we never did learn what became of Carlos De La Frontera," I remarked with some optimism.

"No. We're not going on a quest. Finding Toño was an impossibility. If Carlos is still around, we'll never know about it."

"Such a pessimist," I quipped.

She just glared back.

"Nah, you're right. The galaxy is large, and we're not going to find him after all this time."

"I guess we just wait. Maybe he'll improve now that's he's free and in good repair?"

I shrugged. "For now, it's about the only plan."

"Well then," said Garustfulous from behind, "if you're done laboring, maybe you can tell me what happened back on *Master of Death*." He was stretching, just woken up.

"Why not?" I said wearily. "Let's go to the cube and grab a cuppa joe."

The three of us sat at the mess table. Sapale and I were drained. Garustfulous, conversely, was dying to hear our tale of action.

"Did you know about Section One when you lived on the ship?" I asked him.

"No. I did get the impression there was some super-secret location on the ship, though. But neither of us got a real clue as to where it was or what was in it."

"Did Harhoff ever mention it?"

He shook his head. "No. Never."

"Well, once we were in, we knew we had to rescue Toño."

"Naturally," he agreed. "If you left him behind, you'd never have seen him again. Whatever they wanted with him was important. Adamant never make the *same* mistake twice." There was still some residual pride in his tone.

"Luckily the vault was slow for them to open. We had just enough time to free him," Sapale said between sips.

"I would imagine so. A long time ago, I remember hearing about constructing such a chamber. Personally, I never saw the point. What could be that valuable?"

"What about the emperor himself?" I queried with a smirk.

"Hardly." He spun a paw in the air. "Those are easily replaced."

"I was surprised they put the computers into self-destruct mode," Sapale remarked. "They destroyed all that equipment and information."

"I think it was the only option the Adamant—the one who didn't like me—had."

"Who?" asked Garustfulous.

"After they entered and found they couldn't get through the membrane, a pair of Adamant came right to the edge. A male and a female. He said bad words to me." I tried to look hurt.

"Ah, Two Paws and Shegra. He's the Prime of the Secure Council these days."

"I think there's an opening for that position now," interjected Al.

"How so?" he asked.

"Once *Blessing* dematerialized, the membrane was gone."

"Oh yeah. I didn't think about that because we were safely away," I responded. "Too worried about Toño."

"Finally something to put a smile on my face," said my brood's-mate. "Serves those two right."

"It served a good deal more than them, Form Two," observed *Stingray*.

"We've run many simulations," replied Al. "Millions, in fact. Pilot, do you recall how the neutron-star-matter door opened?"

I furrowed my brow. "No, not really. I guess it swung open, and they ran in."

"There is not a hinge in the universe that could support that immense weight. Really, Pilot, think before you speak." Al was positively salivating over the snark-load he was about to dump on me.

"Al, we were kind of busy," defended Sapale. "Why not just tell us?"

"The horrible Midriacks poured through either side of the portal once it was sufficiently withdrawn."

"So?" I asked.

"So? Pilot, really? That slab of matter was incalculably heavy. How do you suppose it moved?"

I thought a second. "On rollers?"

"Bing, bing, bing. Give the man a Kewpie doll." That Al was such a drama-mama.

"And in Final Jeopardy, Pilot, the answer is *It goes big boom.*"

"Hmm, let's see. The question is ... *what happens when an explosion blows an incalculably heavy slab on rollers through a big starship?*"

"You are the big winner today on *Jeopardy*, Pilot."

"Wait," asked Garustfulous. "What's a jeopardy, and what are you saying?"

"After we split, the explosive force would have been channeled out the opening. It would have pushed the gigantic slab right through the entire ship."

"We estimate at five to seven kilometers an hour," observed Al.

"A brisk walking pace," said Sapale.

"Yeah, but it's still moving at the same rate as we speak," responded Al, all full of himself. "It may never stop."

"So, wait, Two Paws risked the destruction of his ship, with him clearly onboard, just to stop us?" I marveled.

"Jon," replied Garustfulous, "I've met some mean Adamant in my time. Hell, I thought *I* was a tough Adamant. But that Two Paws?" he shook his head. "He was the worst. If he let you escape with the Rabid Robot, he knew he'd be a bad kind of dead. To him, throwing in his ship, his wife, and his emperor was not even a consideration."

"Wow, I'm speechless. That's pretty *damn* bad," I said with wonder.

"It doesn't stop there," chimed in Al. "That slab also

ruptured the exotic matter, jacketing the vessel used to propel the craft. The resultant explosion—"

"Powers and demons," gasped Garustfulous, "That would have taken out the *entire* Whole. That was fifty-seven ships, not counting the small fry."

"Let's go back and take a look." Sapale was totally jazzed.

I set my mug down. "Why the hell not?"

I had *Stingray* make one wall transparent. We hovered in space a few million klicks from where a once mighty fleet of Adamant warships lay in anchor. All that was left was highly radioactive micro-dust rocketing away from the center of its combined mass at nearly the speed of light. It was a beauty to behold. And the best part was knowing Harhoff had finally got his wish. It cost him his life, but I bet he'd say it was worth it. Because if this complete and utter catastrophe didn't destabilize the Adamant Empire, nothing else ever would.

TWENTY

"Sir, I have a message from Sideras Beta," Gargant's AI secretary chimed in pleasantly.

"Where the devil is Sideras Beta?" He scratched absently behind an ear. Remaining awake on an outpost as distant as Xebulon was no mean feat. He'd been assigned these last three years to maintain control over the most irrelevant sector of the central galaxy. Fighting sleep was the only battle he saw any longer.

"It's an administrative station near the Losdol system."

That actually brought him out of his persistent fog. He nearly smiled. He might be receiving an insult. That would be something to react to. An admin space station calling *him*? Those were filled with mindless bureaucrats not fit or even necessarily authorized to address him personally.

"Put it though immediately."

"Wedge Leader Gargant, this is—"

"I demand to know your name and what justification you have for contacting me directly." Yes, that was nice.

"I ... I'm sorry, sir. It has fallen to our station to assume a leadership role in light—"

"A *leadership* role? You people wouldn't make suitable toilet paper *rolls*. Your name."

"I am Cansititor. Now if—"

"Are you and I on a first-name basis now, or do you have a title?"

"No, sir, I doubt that very much. I'm Section Aide One Cansititor, Acquisitions and Payroll Section. Now may I—"

"I have never been so insulted in my life, petty puppy. I'm an Adamant and a senior officer. Put your better on the line at once."

"I cannot, Gargant. He's very busy. We're *all* very busy—everyone aside from yourself. You have time to posture and feather preen. Look, the Central Whole has been destroyed. I'm tasked to spread the news and coordinate assets in this crisis."

"What did you say?"

"Can you be more specific about what part of what I said you wish to pretend, for dramatic effect, not to have heard?" He was clearly very tired, and his nerves were on edge.

"About the Whole, you idiot."

"Two days ago, the entire Whole was destroyed in a massive explosion. We are trying to piece together exactly what happened. No one is certain."

"It must have been a massive war fleet. How could you not identify them?"

"Thank you for your suggestion. That idea never occurred to another military mind. I'll pass word along for everyone to be on the lookout for a bunch of ships we missed at first."

"Are you trying to be sarcastic?"

"No. I *am* being sarcastic. Look, I work in A&P. Do

you fancy *I* am in the loop for strategic discussions? I hope you're sitting down. No, I am not. Look, I'm calling for a reason, if you don't mind me getting to it."

"Proceed." Gargant's mind was still reeling. The Imperial Whole destroyed? Such was not possible.

"Since the loss of the entire administrative and royal functions, martial law has been declared. Individual Section Leads are in complete charge of all civic and military matters until such time as a central government can be put in place. You are the local potentate."

"To whom do I report?" Gargant's voice was distant and his stomach churned. He'd never *not* reported to someone; many someones, in fact. Reporting and serving was what one did, how it was supposed to be.

"If you like, you may report to me, but I'm nobody, and I do not care what you say or do. Come on, the orders are really very simple. Everyone in charge is dead. You are your own boss for the time being. Make the soul of the late emperor proud by doing the job you were trained to do. The one I issue your pay to do. Okay? How's that sound?"

"I ... I guess I will say I report to whomever gave you that order. There's a chain of command."

He rubbed his pounding head and wished he were elsewhere. "No one issued that order."

"Then by what auth—"

"Are you familiar with the *Book of the Adamant?*"

"Yes, I am."

"Books five hundred to eleven hundred fifty-three cover the chain of command. It clearly outlines in volume nine hundred twelve the scenario we are faced with. It clearly states the structure is to be as I have told you."

"So ... in the short run ... I am reported to, but report that information to ... just myself."

"What an excellent and quick mind you've got there,

Gargant. That's wonderful to hear. Congratulations on your new promotion, and please keep me posted as to how it's going."

"Sure thing, ah, what'd you say your name was again?"

It was too late. Cansititor had already hung up. He had made twenty similar calls so far that day and had another thirty to suffer through before he could rest. He was, after all, an accountant, not a psychologist or each frightened hound's mother.

TWENTY-ONE

Several weeks after rescuing Toño, it was becoming clear he was not improving. Four to five times per day one of us'd run a full diagnostic, but nothing changed. It didn't even get worse, which would be something to go on. Not that he had to, but Doc never as much as twitched a muscle or fluttered an eyelid. The AIs worked exclusively trying to decode and understand the random electrical bursts in his head. They saw no hint of a pattern or driving factor. We were all stumped, and he was going nowhere. If he was human, I'd say he was in a persistent vegetative state and turn off his life support. Maybe that was the humane thing to do in this situation, too. But if he'd been in a coma, why wouldn't the Adamant have melted him down long ago? Totally didn't add up.

We had fallen into the habit of meeting once a day to discuss matters. We'd all have dinner together. As Garustfulous was such a glutton, the sessions tended to be long, and Sapale and I did most of the talking.

Sapale ran a hand through her ropy hair. "I just finished another full diagnostic. No change, good or bad."

"I think his brains are dead," remarked Garustfulous without pausing from chewing on a meaty bone.

"Duly noted," I replied, "right here in the for-what-that's-worth category."

"You two are the experts, not me. I'm just trying to help where I can." He was ripping at a really tough ligament, so he sort of snarled as he spoke.

"Unless we can find someone who knows a hell of a lot more than we do about robotics, we're at an impasse," said Sapale glumly.

"I wish I didn't, but I agree."

"So you'll try my idea? Reboot him?"

"We're not *that* desperate yet," I responded grimly.

"Hey, if you're worried, don't be. I'll take all the blame if Toño crashes and burns."

"Thanks, but that's not our concern," Sapale responded, trying not to giggle. "Well, as we've said many times before, we're in no rush. We can afford—"

"I'm going to take Toño to Oowaoa," I blurted out.

That was newsworthy enough for Sapale to set down her spoon *and* for Garustfulous to stop gnawing on his bone.

"That's a sentence full of all kinds of prickly issues." Sapale had started one of her quiet growls.

"I thought they specifically *forbade* you from returning there," said Garustfulous, pointing his snack in my direction.

"Which is prickly issue number one. Number two centers on unilateral decision-making."

"Yeah, you can't spring something like that on me," Garustfulous protested as he returned his carnassial teeth to the bone.

"I was referring more to my brood's-mate's exclusion."

"Yeah, I guess there is that, too."

"I didn't say you couldn't come. I just said I was going," I defended.

"That's nearly the same thing, isn't it?" she scoffed.

Garustfulous rested the stump against his jaw. "I guess if you say so, Sapale. I think it was pretty exclusionary and one-sided."

She directed both hands at him like he was a prize behind the curtain. "One can hardly argue with a military legend."

That put a big ol' smile on his face.

"Honey, please. Let's not make this about you. We're all worried about Toño. My last resort is to beg for their help. Their solution may be to melt the pair of us to scrap."

"We understand that. We are, however, a team. If one goes, the whole team goes."

Garustfulous pointed his bone at Sapale and then at me. "By team, you mean the two of you, right?"

She reached over and confiscated the bone. "No." She tapped all three of our arms with the damn bone. "We *three* are one team."

"Are you done with that?" asked Garustfulous, clearly annoyed.

"Yes, and so are you." She threw it over her shoulder and right into the disposal.

"Hey—" he began to protest.

I placed a finger on his lips. "I say we all go first thing in the morning. If they melt the three of us down, so be it."

"Whoa, wait. I don't melt. I *burn*," responded Garustfulous, eyes wide in alarm.

"Don't worry," replied Sapale with an evil grin, "I'll take all the blame if you crash and burn."

I was light on knowledge and specifics about modern-day Oowaoa, so I put down *Stingray* right where Cragforel had gifted her to me long before. I figured he'd likely still be close by. Nothing changed on that planet if it didn't do so at a pace that would embarrass an old snail traversing a frozen puddle. Ever cautious, Garustfulous exited a full minute after we did. He said he'd cover our forced retreat better from a defensive point. I felt so much safer.

We walked in the general direction of the building Cragforel brought Mirri and me to after we first met him. Seemed as likely a place as any. I carried Toño in my arms. Didn't want to mess up all the nice work we'd done getting him to look all pretty again. I was aware the collective Deavoriath knew we were present. They just weren't the types to rush out and greet uninvited guests.

Cragforel's door was open, so I led the way back to his lab. I gently laid Doc down on the ubiquitous flat ceramic surface. He clinked a little as I did but made no spontaneous movements. Then I turned to the door and waited. Cragforel arrived in less than ten minutes. Too long not to be a clear sign of disapproval, but not short enough to support anger or joy. Cagey players, these old ghosts.

As a hard-ass at heart—which sounded kind of odd when I went ahead and said it—I decided he'd talk first. He'd sent me a silent message. I'd *back atcha'd* him one of my own.

"Jon, I must confess it's a surprise to see you again. And with an entirely new *cadre* of strangers."

"Since I'm certain it's a pleasant surprise, I'm glad to see you, too, my friend."

"Hmm." He paused for a three count, "And who is your *silent* and uninvited partner here?" he said, displaying disinterest as he flipped the back of one finger toward Toño.

"That is what's left of Dr. Toño DeJesus, my oldest friend."

Cragforel's expression broke from one of stone to boyish excitement. "Jon, you never cease to astound me. First I meet *you*, then one of the mythical Deft, and now the *Toño DeJesus?*" A hand rubbed his brow. "To say he is an institutional legend among us is an understatement of epic proportions." His pace quickened as he went round and round the table marveling at Toño. "I've heard of the miracles Toño DeJesus accomplished working with Kymee for my entire life. After Kymee passed, another great scientist among us, Larocnaur, worked with him for, well, for a very long time."

"This Larocnaur fellow still around?"

With a bubbly smile, he replied, "No. *She's* long dead, too. In fact, it is generally held that when she passed, Toño left Oowaoa for good." Each of his three arms rubbed the shoulder to its right. "Oh, that was over a billion years ago, if memory serves."

"So after Oowaoa, Toño struck out on his own?"

"That's my recollection. I'll look into it in more detail later." He slapped his cheeks with all his hands. "Dr. Toño DeJesus. I am beyond stunned." Then he grew serious. "But you said what's left of him, didn't you? What is his status?"

"That's what we were hoping you might be able to tell us," I replied grimly.

"Go on."

"First, this is my brood's-mate, Sapale," I rested a hand on her shoulder.

"Oh, now you're just showing off to gloat. Sapale? The founder of Azsuram? Died while battling the Berrillian and defending her people? The conscience in a box trying to keep the Jon Ryan lost in time from falling completely apart? It is my *singular* honor, ma'am." He stepped over slowly and shook her hand for a good thirty seconds.

"And this is Garustfulous. We went to rescue him when we accidentally found Toño."

Garustfulous puffed up and smiled like the king of the world. He held out both paws as if greeting a smitten admirer.

Cragforel glanced briefly from Sapale's eyes to Garustfulous's general area. "Hi." Then he swung back to lose himself once again in my mate's eyes.

I nearly bust out laughing, but we were there on serious business.

I cleared my throat.

That brought Cragforel out of his trance. "Please, everyone be seated. I'll have refreshments brought at once. Please, Sapale, you sit here between Jon and me." He wouldn't release her arm until she was unequivocally settled in by his side.

A pair of Deavoriath floated across the floor and distributed food, wash bowls, and most importantly, nufe. It was the nectar the gods could only wished they had.

As Garustfulous was the only nufe virgin in the room, I was dying to fill him in. I held my tiny glass up toward him. "This is *nufe*. It is nothing short of a miracle. You have had nothing even vaguely like it in your entire life." I sniffed it with apparent rapture. "It is not alcoholic, but it will seem as though it is. It tastes different to each individual, and different from any other sip one's had. It—"

"Enough chatter," Garustfulous howled. He grabbed the glass and threw the entire thing down his throat at once. Though that was not dangerous, it could put him into total sensory overload. Good. It'd serve the bum right on several levels and counts.

Before he'd slammed the glass back to the table, his

eyes bulged. He stood, one hind leg rhythmically thumping the floor, and he very nearly fell over sideways. "Blood from a beating heart, my first bitch friend, when I won a battle for the first time, oysters fresh from the sea ..." He plopped mute into his chair.

I thumbed in his direction. "I think he likes it."

"As canovir, the Adamant have very keen senses of smell. Such species are especially affected by nufe," Cragforel said. He couldn't contain a Santa Claus-like chuckle.

"So," I began in a serious tone, "Sapale and I went to rescue our Adamant ally. We found Toño by chance. We'd only just freed him and got back into the vortex before the ship he was on, *Master of Death*, self-destructed."

"Ah, so that's how you took the ship out," replied Cragforel.

"You know about that?"

"Jon, we're *isolationists*, but we're not stupid. We follow what's going on in the galaxy quite closely."

"Wow, okay, didn't expect that one. From the time we found Toño until now, he's basically been in a coma. He was in a state of total disrepair, physically, at first, but we could easily fix that. All our scans show nothing we can interpret as spontaneous neural activity." I flashed my fingers in the air. "It's all just noise in there."

"I'll study your records, of course, but you see no significant change in the noise patterns?"

"No. Stupid static." I lowered my head.

"Well," he said, rising, "let's get to this."

We followed him back to where Toño lay. Garustfulous, since he was a total pig, brought the nufe bottle and no glasses.

Cragforel did a rapid physical exam, removing Toño's clothes as he went. He was naked and hooked up to a large bank of monitors in short order. Not surprisingly, the Deavoriath equipment was unlike anything I'd ever seen before. It was completely different from what Kymee labored over so long ago.

He hmmed and ahhed occasionally but said nothing to us. At one point, he went in another room and returned with some portable gauge. He swept it back and forth over Toño's head then looked at the tiny screen intently. Finally, he attached spiral wires to three points of Toño's scalp.

He walked over to a large screen. "Come over here," he instructed, without taking his eyes off the screen.

"You find the problem?" I asked, though I was barely able to get the words out.

"Hmm. I found out why we don't detect meaningful neuronal activity. I have yet to determine whether that's *the* problem or just *one* of the problems."

"What is the noise?" asked Sapale, leaning in.

"What to call it? Hmm. Dr. DeJesus's entire neural network is locked in a time storm. Yes, that's it, a time storm."

He turned to us with a look of triumph.

"Great ... good ... ah, what's a time storm?" I asked with great uncertainty.

"No, he's in a neural or neuronal time storm. A time storm is a very different matter altogether."

"Sorry. What's a *neuronal* time storm?" I muttered.

"Or neural?" added Sapale.

Behind us, Garustfulous took another big gulp of nufe.

"Inside any sentient mind there are various forms of order. Temporal, spacial, dimensional, and word patterns. There are many. In DeJesus's case specifically, bits of information such as memories, briefs, or instincts are tethered to a specific time."

"Huh. You're losing me," I confessed.

"Take a set of memories. Your first kiss. Your mother's smile when you graduated, the splatter of blood on your palm when you crushed a mosquito during a specific picnic." He gestured to the right. "The first kiss." Then he gestured to the left. "On a specific day and time. The memory is temporally tethered to the time it took place."

"As opposed to the *second* kiss a *minute* later. A separate *kiss* tethered to a separate *time*," responded Sapale.

"Precisely. So it is with any fact one retains. It is tethered to a time. Not *fixed,* mind you, simply *tethered.*"

"Ah," I replied. I had no clue what he meant by that distinction. "Bringing us back to Toño. How—"

"His mind has been placed in a temporal storm."

"A neuronal temporal storm?" I tried to clarify.

"Yes, Jon, of course. We're discussing his mind here." Cragforel seemed annoyed.

"And Toño's mind couldn't be in a regular old temporal storm, right?"

He stomped a foot like a child caught in a small lie. "Yes, I guess it *could* be, *technically,* but since you don't know what one of those is, I cannot give you credit for being clever on that call."

"Trust me, he *wasn't* being clever," said Sapale with a smirk.

"*Doc?*" I reminded everyone.

"His mind is in an induced storm in which thoughts, facts, memories, and dimensionalities are *temporally* disconnected. They fly about as individual, um, points of data, but they cannot be interpreted in any temporal context."

"Interesting," I said, rubbing my chin. "What does that actually *signify?*"

He could roll his eye at me just like Sapale could.

"Jon, to have a thought, an idea, a desire, you must cobble together multiple tethered data points. *I want to eat a delicious dinner with my friends at eight tonight.* A fairly simple desire, but without the proper temporal clues and contexts, the thought is liquid in a blender." He thought a second. "Assuming DeJesus is attempting to clear his mind and, oh, I don't know, *cry out in agony,* he simply can't. It would require an action like scaling an ice-covered rock cliff with his bare hands while a powerful wind blows."

"That would be hard," I said.

"No, you *moron.* It would be three kinds of impossible." Sapale punched my arm.

"But wait. How did he get into a neuronal temporal storm? Why would he do that to himself? I mean, it couldn't be a simple malfunction."

"Why not?" asked my mate.

"No, Jon's right. This is ordered disorder. Someone is causing this to happen."

"Excuse me?" Garustfulous was holding an empty nufe bottle. "Would this state of the doctor's be unpleasant?"

"Extremely," replied an irritated Cragforel. "Why do you even need to ask?"

"It's just this. If Toño's in a very unpleasant way, think Adamant. It's our specialty. Say," he held up the bottle, "where's this stuff kept?"

"You've had plenty. Shut up and sit down."

By the time I returned my attention to Cragforel, I saw a light going off above his head. "*Yes.* That's exactly it. Somehow, for some reason, the Adamant have placed DeJesus into a neuronal temporal storm."

"Why? What?" Sapale started to ask.

"Is it unpleasant?" Garustfulous said from where he sat.

"Yes," responded Cragforel.

"Unpleasant, as in *torture* unpleasant?"

"Yes. That's *it*. The Adamant have devised a program to keep DeJesus in a state of perpetual, interminable, primal torment."

"And the poor man's been in it for Davdiad alone knows how long?" said Sapale as she began to growl the growl I never wanted to hear directed at me.

"I'll kill them *all*. Every single *last* one of them." And I meant it.

Garustfulous trotted out of the room. If asked, he'd probably say he was hunting for more nufe. The truth of it was he heard my words.

TWENTY-TWO

Three Adamant sat in a dimly lit conference room. They had mugs of bone broth grown long cold. None of them had taken a sip. Two were Wholes, Quildrod and Fenopteic-Val. The third was Wedge Leader Dorcilmas. He would have likely been promoted to Whole if there was anyone left alive with the *authority* to advance his rank.

"These are dark times, my friends," Fenopteic-Val feigned to lament. "Our losses, militarily, culturally, and spiritually, are almost more than a body can bear."

Dorcilmas shot furtive glances from one dog to the other, reading the tea leaves if such was possible. "Dark to be certain. One of my wife's cousins lived on *Dare Any* that was lost in the catastrophe."

"I am truly sorry to hear of your loss. If there is anything I can do to help you, just bark the word." Fenopteic-Val tenderly patted the back of Dorcilmas's paw.

"But we who survived must recall only our duty to the *empire*. As the wise Loserandi Jonsol said long ago, all is darkest before the dawn. I have studied that great canovir's work, and I know he was referring to *precisely* the situation that presents itself to us today." He paused in reverential reflection upon his false statement. "I see the dawn of a *new* Adamant Empire, a mightier one. Not better, mind you." He wagged an admonishing finger in the air generally. "Only newer, stronger, and more able to serve our new emperor, whoever that person might turn out to be."

"I could not have said it better, old friend," Fenopteic-Val humbly praised. He looked to the ceiling for inspiration and to time his next sentence optimally. "As a puppy, I once wondered why the emperors were never anointed from the military ranks. I went as far as to ask my father. He said he did not know the reason, if there *were* actually such a tradition in existence in the first place. I had forgotten that conversation until this very moment." He shook his head briskly. "How odd."

The intensity and frequency of Dorcilmas's examination of his companion's expression shot to maximum. "Seemingly odd," he muttered as noncommittally as he could. He was both a poor politician and a poor actor.

"As I just now mentioned, I am a student of history. Along with absorbing the wisdom of the Loserandi, I have also made it my life's work to read and fully understand the *Book of the Adamant*."

"A noble undertaking," Dorcilmas complimented boldly. "You are to be *praised* for your dedication to our species."

"No praise is needed in such a pleasurable and sacred duty as that. The point I wish to raise is that in *my* reading of that series, I recall no mention of the exclusion of military members as candidates to form new imperial family lines. Mind you, I never considered that aspect of ascension until you, Fenopteic-Val, mentioned it just now. But in my humble opinion, such an outcome is possible."

"But without a Secure Council to select the next emperor," asked Dorcilmas as naively as he could manage, "how will anyone, military or otherwise, be chosen?" He even raised his arms in questioning confusion.

"How indeed," challenged Quildrod. "I must harken back to my extensive familiarity with the *Book of the Adamant* and say it is the sole issue of potential equivocation I am aware of in the *entire* text."

"Why cannot there be an interim emperor? That male could appoint a new Secure Council. Obviously, the interim emperor would then *immediately* resign his powers, privileges, and office. That would allow the new council the chance to fulfill its established role. Order would be restored."

Dorcilmas stared at Quildrod. He decided he dare not speak when open treason was so fresh in the air.

"An interesting intellectual hypothetical, Whole Fenopteic-Val. I only wonder, hypothetically of course, how such an interim emperor would be ... um, what's the word I'm fumbling for? How would that humble servant be *identified* so that he might be made manifest to others?"

Dorcilmas now fixated on the other contender.

"I believe the right dog would know in his heart and in his soul that *he* was the best potential servant for such a minor, *transitory* role. He would benefit from firm support by other humble servants of the empire. Ideally, those backers would hold sway over assets that could help bolster the public perception of the interim emperor's legitimacy."

Dorcilmas turned to Quildrod. The wedge leader was trembling with fear and excitement. He wiped a string of saliva from the corner of his mouth without realizing he needed to do so.

"Assets? What kind of *assets* do you envision, Whole Fenopteic-Val?"

Dorcilmas had eyes only for Quildrod, and there they remained.

"Why, I'm surprised you feel it necessary to ask, old friend. Chiefly military assets. Financial resources would obviously be helpful. Of course, any supporters would only be useful if they were in immediate control of significant numbers of warships."

"Naturally," responded Quildrod with a chuckle. "When embarking on such a potentially *misinterpreted* course of imperial *service*, arms at the ready would be essential."

"Yes, Whole Quildrod. I could not agree with *you* more." Dorcilmas had finally spoken.

The matter was settled.

Quildrod daubed at his chops with a napkin while inspecting his comm link. "Would you look at the time? Here we sit, three friends chatting idly while our citizens languish in their mourning and uncertainty. I think it's time for us all to return to our duties to the empire."

"Yes, it is time," Dorcilmas said softly, nodding.

"You know, Dorcilmas, if I had a chance to advise the interim emperor, I would tell him directly and with certainty that you were long overdue for a promotion. Now, I would like to say a regrettable goodbye to you, Fenopteic-Val."

Fenopteic-Val balled his paws and clenched his teeth. "Why regrettable, old friend?"

"Because, alas, in these tumultuous times, seeing one's past acquaintances again can be so damnably uncertain."

TWENTY-THREE

"So the sixty-four thousand dollar question is, Cragforel, can you fix Toño?"

He eyed me crookedly, then answered, "I do not know."

"What are we *going* to do?" pressed Sapale.

"That is more clear to me," he replied. "I have identified the subroutine the Adamant installed keeping the temporal storm going."

"And you're sure it's Adamant?" I wanted to know for certain.

"Yes, I'm quite certain it's their handiwork. The coding uses an octal numeral system."

"Base eight? How's that ... ah, because they have four fingers on each paw. They'd naturally count using an eight-digit system, not our ten-digit one." I *could* be smart if the occasion called for it.

"Exactly," he replied.

Garustfulous studied his paw. "I never noticed the difference."

"Why are none of us surprised?" quipped Sapale.

"And what happens when you switch off the time storm?"

"Zero idea. But we're about to find out." He manipulated a cylindrical probe that emitted a chirpy sound over Toño's head for a few seconds. "There—I deleted it altogether."

We stared at Toño, not certain whether to inch closer or back up.

Nothing. We waited ten minutes longer. Still nothing.

"What do you read in there now?" I asked as I gently tapped Toño's forehead.

Cragforel studied a monitor. "It looks to me like he's functioning perfectly well. His patterns look much like yours or Sapale's."

"Then why isn't he hopping off the table and thanking us?"

"I do not know," he replied, slowly shaking his head.

"Well I suggest we give it time. He's been subject to the most terrifying experience I can imagine for a very long time. Let's strap him in and wait."

"Why do we need to strap him in?" asked Sapale. "He's our friend."

"If he were to awaken when none of us were present, I think his behavior would be most unpredictable."

"Then we just won't leave him unattended," she responded. "We'll set up a watch."

I tossed my head to one side. "Why not? We're not going anywhere until this is resolved one way or another."

So we set up a watch. I made it a point to include Garustfulous in the rotation, too, but he only got the morning shifts. I didn't want to tempt fate too mightily. Weeks passed, and nothing happened. Toño's neural net was working picture-perfectly, but he was otherwise lifeless. We started prodding and shaking him. We even administered mild electrical shocks. Nada. Cragforel called it a mind-body dissociation state. That sounded uncomfortably close to the word *coma* for my liking.

After two months, we were all confronting the unpleasant notion that we had arrived at the final what-you-see-is-what-you-get stage. We held a meeting, because meetings, as was widely acknowledged, could solve any problem.

"I don't want to say Toño's condition is hopeless," began Cragforel, "I just can't find any justification for hope."

"I don't understand," I said more to myself, "why he's still out of it when his neural net is so dialed in?"

"How about replacing certain parts of his neural system?" asked Sapale. "We could copy what's there, but only replace small parts. Maybe that would jump-start the whole system."

"I'm not in a position to say no, but I also don't think that would change anything," Cragforel replied, shaking his head. "That's not how these systems work. The way Toño made them, any of the subcomponents can run the entire system. If this was just an issue of a defective circuit we haven't identified, the android could still function normally."

"How about turn—"

"We know, Garustfulous, the IT guys said it always works. It still remains the last thing we'll ever do," responded Cragforel firmly. "A damaged or defective system might not reboot. It's too great a risk."

Garustfulous shrugged.

"Jon, if Cragforel is out of ideas, what do you want to do?" asked Sapale. "He is more family to you than anyone else."

I rubbed an eyebrow. "I can't imagine giving up on him. He'd never give up on any of us. Even when I demanded he put me in a dormant state, he never actually *abandoned* me."

"You are, of course, welcome to leave him here with me," offered Cragforel. "If anything changed, I'd notify you at once."

Without acknowledging his offer, I mused out loud, "I just wish we could get inside his—"

Sapale sat up. "What? I know that pregnant pause of yours way too well. You've thought of something."

"I did, indeed. It's not something I can do, but I thought of someone who can."

"Who?" she asked.

"Mirraya."

It was Garustfulous's turn to sit up quickly. "You want her to use *magic* to make him all better? Isn't that kind of a stretch even for a witch?"

"No, not by magic. By zar-not."

Cragforel got a puzzled look for a few moments. "That's the Deft technique of joining their mind with an animal they are copying. They need to be in contact, correct?"

"Yes. Man, Cragforel, you know a lot of stuff," I replied.

"Gosh, thanks." Not sure he meant it. "I see a major problem. Zar-not works for animals. Why would it work on a robotic unit?"

"Hmm, good point." I pinched my chin and massaged it roughly. Then I smiled. "Wait, we don't have to *theorize* about it. I'll just ask her."

That got a chuckle out of the generally dour Deavoriath. "That would save time, wouldn't it?"

It'd been too long since I'd seen my Deft kids. Funny how life, however long it might be, worked. I would love someone with a burning passion that could melt diamonds. Still, I kept finding reasons and excuses to not stop what I was doing and go give that person a hug. What made it more inexcusable was that I'd loved and lost so many souls in my too-long life that I should always have known better. Cherish *now*. Yeah, I should've started a movement or something. Maybe a cult.

I walked up to Slapgren and Mirri's house and knocked. One of their kids answered the door. Couldn't have been more than three years old. I think her name was Bethenar, but I hadn't seen her since she was in diapers. She regarded me awhile. I felt a little like broccoli on her dinner plate. She craned her neck over a shoulder and announced, "There's a big alien out here, and he's not even a dragon."

I forced myself to not totally lose it. Laughing broccoli was much worse than just plain broccoli. Even *I* knew that. I heard something thump down on a wooden surface and the scraping of scurrying feet.

"I'll be right—" Mirri stepped in front of her daughter with a cordial smile on her face. Then she saw it was me. She reached over and grabbed me by an arm and pulled me in with a jerk. "He's not an alien, sweetheart, he's my uncle Jon. You know, the one I tell you so much about?"

As she was trying impressively to hug the life out of me, Bethenar asked, "Is he the one mowar Cala is always mad at?"

Mirri looked mortified. It was so cute. "No, mowar isn't *mad* at Uncle Jon. She just loves him differently than we do. Now run along and play with your brother." She pushed more and shooed her away. "Sit, sit. What can I get you?"

"Nothing. I'm fine. Where's that big lug of a husband of yours?"

"He's out hunting. Yeah, I know. What a shocker."

We both chuckled.

"And the kids, everyone's good?"

She positively glowed. "Couldn't be better. Little Jon, who's now nearly as big as his father, is ready for *Master* School next spring. Can you believe it?"

"Unfortunately, yes. Time does fly."

"Well, you'll see everyone at dinner, and then you can see for yourself how they're all doing."

"Speaking of doing, how is that old bat Cala?"

"Shame on you, and she's just as ornery as ever."

"And now she has two of me to be ornery at. She must be living in bliss."

"Her? Not hardly. That's not her style. She is pleased with EJ's progress though."

"I bet in two, maybe three hundred thousand years he'll be fit to rejoin the general population."

"You are so mean."

"I just know myself." I looked down.

"What is it? Is something wrong?"

"Yes. Very."

She rocketed her hand over her mouth. "Oh no. It's not Sapale, is it?"

"No, no. She's as healthy as an android horse. No, it's someone you've never met. Toño DeJesus."

"Arcs of Power. He's the man who created you."

"And my oldest friend. The first time we met, I was still human." I shook my head hard. "Man does *that* ever come out sounding weird."

"What happened to him? You told me he was gone, didn't you?"

I shrugged. "I thought he was. We accidentally

419

discovered that he was a prisoner of the Adamant while we were rescuing Garustfulous."

"What happened to Garustfulous?"

"Not important now. We got them both out, but Toño wasn't conscious. I even took him to the Deavoriath, but they couldn't wake him up either."

"Wake him up? Is he broken?"

"All his systems are functioning optimally, but he's still basically in a coma."

"I'm no engineer, but that sounds contradictory. Either he is or he isn't functioning normally."

"We're at a loss, too. Every test indicates he should stand up and dance the hoochie coochie. But he's totally out of it mentally."

"What happened to his mind?"

I could hardly say the words. "The Adamant devised a way to torture him mercilessly for gods know how long. Maybe thousands of years at a time. I'm afraid it fried his brain."

"Lords and Lights, they're horrid."

"Tell me about it."

She collected herself. "What is it you want of me? You know I'll do anything to help you, Uncle Jon."

"Not so fast. What I'm asking is big—*really* big. It may not even be possible. And if there's any chance you might get hurt, I won't let you do it, even if you could."

"What are you thinking about?"

"That maybe you could get through to him via zar-not."

That popped her eyes wide open. "Oh my. I've never even thought about that."

"You could'a cut off my legs and called me Shorty, if you had."

That brought me a wide-eyed glare. "Beg pardon?"

"I'd have been surprised."

After a brief head shake, she got back to business. "You know zar-not is part of the shape-shifting process. I can't change into a rock or a robot. That's not how it works."

"I figured as much. We're just kind of out of ideas." I had to stop speaking for a second. "I just had to ask, you know ... couldn't bail on Toño if—" I had to stop talking completely at that point.

"Please take me to him."

"Huh?"

"Jon, you're the reason I'm here and so blessed, and I can't see you in this pain knowing I didn't do what you always have for me."

"Yeah. What's that?"

"Everything you could and then some. I'll get a friend to watch the kids, and we'll leave."

"No, that's okay. We can wait for Slapgren. Toño's been in his ... whatever for over two months. He can wait for us to have a family meal together."

She ran over to me and collapsed in my arms. She was the best.

TWENTY-FOUR

Melgot scanned the daily releases. He read more than he probably needed to. But he was committed to being overinformed as opposed to underinformed, times being as they were. There was the possibility that a tidbit of news from the most unexpected source might tip the balance of power, or rather the lack thereof. A lord-servant's job wasn't supposed to be easy, only rewarding and vital.

His comm link buzzed. "Sire?"

"I'm as ready as I'll ever be for my morning update."

"Very well, sire. Shall I have breakfast brought so you might eat while we chat?"

"*Lunch* would seem more appropriate given the ho ... hour. Excuse me."

"I shall have *both* delivered at once. You can choose as you like."

Within a few minutes Melgot sat in an ornate and unbelievably uncomfortable chair at the head of Prince Halbertel's bed. His royal pain in the ass was slumped in his bed, dribbling and spilling all forms of food and drink on his chest and bedsheets. He was a slob at the best of times. He was even more so when still drunk from the last night's revelries.

"Shall I be ... no, here let me help you with that, lord. No, you're going to ... ah, there you have. Here, let me dab that up."

Halbertel slapped wildly at his lord-servant's hands. What he struck was his lord-servant's muzzle, hard enough that blood trickled down to his chin. "*I* can get it, you oaf."

"My apologies, lord," was Melgot's muffled response as he applied the towel originally destined for the spill to his split lip. "Shall I begin?"

"Yes, before you *kill* me."

He wiped his cut and set the towel down. "I have documentation that no fewer than ten more senior naval officers have gone rogue and assumed absolute control over their sectors."

"So, what, that brings the total to fifteen?"

Melgot fanned his eyelashes but refrained from rolling his eyes. "No, lord. The total now stands at six hundred thirty-*five*."

"That's what I just said."

"Yes, lord, I was repeating the total because you were so correct."

"That's better. But are any of these whore-spawns real challengers to my legitimacy?"

"Some would argue that many are. The most egregious treason I've discovered so far is by Whole Quildrod, who has named himself interim emperor. His entire force has thrown in with the scoundrel and sworn allegiance to him alone."

"Curse his balls. Order him executed."

"To whom shall I pass that order along, lord?"

"I don't know. My *killing* people. You figure it out. What do I pay you for?"

"I'll see to it as soon as we're done here," he replied with oozing insincerity.

"And what steps have you taken to secure my coronation?"

"Ah, that has been a challenge, lord. Not one of our staff has identified a single party openly supportive of your candidacy for emperor. Not *yet*, I should say."

"Support? I don't need no support. I'm the fifth cousin twice removed of the space dust that up until recently was the late great emperor *himself*. No one else comes close to my proximity in terms of being the rightful heir."

"You and I know this. *Everyone* knows this, lord. But the issue is the dark epoch we find ourselves thrust into. Many insane, power-hungry, and sociopathic curs have chosen this very moment to try and usurp *your* ascension."

"Well, have them killed, too."

"All of them?"

"No. All but the one with the winningest smile." He hurled a thigh bone at his aide, landing an astoundingly accurate blow to his left eye. "Of *course* kill them all, you cat."

With the towel now pressed firmly to his eye, Melgot replied, "I'll order that too as soon as we're finished."

"That brings up another issue. Since the untimely incineration of my beloved fifth cousin twice removed, I'm running out of funds to maintain the lifestyle I'm entitled and accustomed to."

"Yes, lord, we are both aware of that unfortunate turn of fortune. That is why you married your great-grandmother last week. Do you not recall? The elderly female with a treasure trove of money?"

"My great-grandmother? Which one?"

"That one, lord. The one next to you in bed." Melgot pointed to a heaped-up portion of the bedsheets.

The prince gingerly peeled back the shroud and peeked at his bride. He nearly jumped out of bed and into Melgot's lap. "Fleas and *ticks,* what an ugly bitch."

"I must agree that she has never been much of a morning hound."

"I guarantee she's this hideous *all* day long." He leaned in to study her closely. "Wait, I think she's dead. What a *break.*"

"Pity, lord, no. I can see her chest move from here."

"A male can hope."

"Yes he can. Best of luck with that effort, lord."

Halbertel covered his great-grandmother up gently so as not to rouse her. "Did she give us enough money to buy my way into power?"

"Alas, lord, I think not. Given the variables, I'm reluctant to think that level of funding exists."

"Ah well, pass me that bottle. I don't *think* I need a drink, I *know* I need a drink."

TWENTY-FIVE

Mirraya-Slapgren walked around the table Toño was lying atop. She studied him, scrutinizing his existence. Once Slapgren heard about my friend's peril, he insisted on joining with his wife. He said together they were ten times stronger than either was apart. Watching that magnificent golden visant stride with such confidence and fluidity it was hard to doubt his estimation.

"I sense nothing unusual about him," she said.

"Is that good?" asked Sapale.

"Neither good nor bad. Toño lacks any negative outward manifestations. That is reassuring."

I was about to ask her to maybe clarify what the hell she had just said but let it go. This was her show. Still, I wondered if she meant Toño wasn't possessed or that he didn't have BO. I made a mental note to check with her when this was all over.

"Do you think you can reach into his mind?" posed Cragforel. I have to say seeing a Deavoriath so in awe of something was stunning. It was like Santa, the Easter Bunny, and Mr. Rogers were standing before him.

Superman, too. A few other Deavoriath were in attendance, and they were equally starstruck.

"I'm not sure, but I am ready to try."

With those words all individuals in the room, organic *and* metal in nature, stopped breathing.

She stopped and reached over with one foot. The talons encircled Toño's head. I flashed on one of those games I played as a kid, the one where I tried to pick up a stupid prize with a rickety crane and never won a thing.

I anticipated she'd close her eyes and face heaven for support or something equally magical, but she just stood there staring down at him like he was a suspicious package. Then I noticed her skin started to change. It was very subtle, but it went from pure golden-metallic and scaly to a sort of gray film. Three seconds into the change, Mirraya-Slapgren was thrown backward and struck the wall like a bomb had exploded.

That's when Toño started screaming. He screamed with a volume and an intensity sufficient to wake the dead and then make them wish they had not returned to the land of the living.

I turned to Cragforel and pointed to Toño. "You take him. I'll check on her."

I sprinted for Mirraya-Slapgren, completely oblivious to what Cragforel might be doing. I skidded to my knees and rested my arm under her neck, cradling it.

"Guys, are you okay?"

The look in her eyes totally blindsided me. I expected fear, confusion, or pain. She had a look of wonder. I was so surprised I nearly dropped her.

"Let me get you to a couch," I said slipping my other arm under her hind legs. She was very heavy, but I sure as hell was going to carry her.

"No, Uncle Jon," she said, resting a talon gently on my forearm. "No, I can stand. I'm fine, really."

I released her into an upright position, and she stood steadily. I inched away but was ready to pounce if she faltered.

She looked at Toño, writhing and bellowing on the table. Sapale, Cragforel, and a couple Deavoriath I didn't know were trying mightily to restrain him. "I think he's awake now," she remarked dryly.

"Yes, I believe your assessment is correct. Come on, he's in good hands. Let's step outside for what passes on Oowaoa as fresh air."

We had to hike quite a ways to get far enough away that Toño's howls were not deafening.

"If you don't mind, Uncle, we'll separate now. Our task is done, and after that shock, we think it wise."

"Oh crap. You two're going to be naked, aren't you?"

"Not if you retrieve our clothes and turn your back."

I did so at a trot. The last thing I wanted was to return with a stack of clothes only to discover I was a few moments too late. We were talking about my kids here. Daddy didn't want'a see his adult children in their birthday suits.

Once we were all sitting on a bench fully dressed, I asked them each if they were okay.

"I feel like a million bucks," said Slapgren resolutely. "Say, do these Oowaoans eat food? I'm strangely hungry."

Mirri slapped him playfully. "You're always strangely hungry."

"You okay, too?"

"Yes. No ill effects whatsoever."

"Can you be sure? I mean, you flew across that room pretty convincingly."

"When we're one, dude, we're *tough*." He pumped his fist. I liked that boy.

"Honestly, we're both fine. You stop worrying."

"What caused you to go airborne?"

She got a very serious look on her face. "I'm not certain. I think he pushed us away. Maybe it was psychic energy." She puzzled a moment. "If I figure it out, I'll let you know."

"Sure." I wasn't certain I cared all that much whether it was a mental chest bump or gypsy energy bolts, but whatever.

"He's in a lot of pain, Uncle Jon," Mirri said with a distressed expression.

"Massive." Slapgren put his hands on either side of his head and exploded them away. "Super massive."

"I suspected as much. I told you the damn Adamant had his brain in a blender for time immemorial."

"No," she corrected me, "only in fits and spurts. He was in that state for only about a year."

"Eighteen months *tops*," agreed Slapgren.

"Wait, you ... you learned something from that brief contact?"

"Oh yes. I'd have been stunned if we didn't."

"Short timespan and limited exposure are two separate things in zar-not." Slapgren sounded so full of himself.

"So you're the zar-not expert now?"

He rolled a shoulder. "Well that's what she *told* me, and I believe her."

"You are such a big kid," I responded with a chuckle.

"Welcome to my world," teased Mirri.

"Come on, what else can you tell me?"

She was serious again. "Not much more. His pain ... his pain was so ... so pure."

Slapgren snapped his fingers. "That's it, love. *Pure*."

"What's that supposed to mean?"

"Toño's entire essence, what you might call his soul, was pain without dilution."

"That doesn't sound good."

"It is not. The Adamant figured out a way to make poor Toño suffer so profoundly. It became all he could ... ah, *be*."

"Pain?"

"Yes."

"Not sure I understand that concept, but okay. Will he get better?"

"I have no way of knowing. Sorry. I truly am."

"I know, honey. Thanks for what you did."

"They needed to torture him to get him to cooperate," blurted out Slapgren.

I angled my head. "That's usually the point of torture, isn't it?" Then I thought about it. "What did they want him to cooperate with?"

"Science," replied Mirri.

"Science? What's that mean? You two sure have learned to talk like sideshow psychics."

"Gee thanks," Slapgren said, pouting. "I'll be sure to put that on my resume."

"The Adamant are very organized, thorough, and driven, but that doesn't make them *clever*," explained Mirri. "They captured Toño a very long time ago. They knew who he was and wanted him to help advance their scientific programs. They wanted *him* to develop new and better weapons and drive systems."

"Toño'd *never* help those bastards," I shot back.

"And *hence*," Slapgren opened his arms, "the torture."

"Oh my," was all I could muster.

"Oh my indeed, Uncle. They would ask him to help with some project. He'd say *no* and they'd start the mental blender. A few weeks or months later, they'd switch it off and ask him again. I don't have to tell you what they did if he continued to refuse."

"Eventually, the poor guy would cave. I mean," Slapgren added, "who the hell wouldn't?"

"Oh, I know," I said only half present in the conversation. "I'd never judge Toño. He was the strongest man I ever knew."

"No way," exclaimed Slapgren. *"You're* the toughest dude there ever was, UJ."

"You got that right, punk." I air punched at him to emphasize that declaration. "No, he's the *strongest*, not necessarily the toughest or most fearless. He had to be. He grew up dirt poor in a village so small it never appeared on any of the maps of Spain." I shook my head slowly. "Granja De La Torre Hermosa. Not even a wide *patch* along a hot road."

"What a pretty name," responded Mirri. "Have you been there?"

"Yes, once. Before Jupiter ate it for lunch. It was quaint, but man was it *rustic*. Anyway, he came from nothing and saved humankind. That's big. He had to be strong."

"I can only imagine," replied Slapgren.

"I hope he comes around, Uncle."

"You and me both." I shook my head hard. "Hey, let's get you two home. I bet the kids have old Cala tied up and gagged by now."

"No, they'd better not have," Slapgren said hotly. "Last time they did, we really leaned into'em. They promised to never do *that* again."

"Yes, but one only wonders what they did this time instead," Mirri said with the cutest darn grin. Loved that girl. Loved her big time.

TWENTY-SIX

"Meldagard. keep those ships off our port bow or this is going to be a very *brief* battle." Though powerful and loud, Sustimer's voice was calm and authoritative. He was an excellent captain.

"I'm trying my best, sir. There are just too many of them."

"Yes, but if they outflank us and win, you and I will be the ones who die. Keep that as firm motivation, son."

"Sir."

The massive battlestar shuddered from a series of blows. For a ship nearly eight cubic kilometers in volume to respond that violently suggested the conviction with which Dorcilmas was fighting. Whole Sustimer's fleet was the third Dorcilmas was battling on Quildrod's behalf. It was by far the largest to date and the most seasoned. The outcome was not, as he's previously enjoyed, a forgone conclusion.

"Swing around to 11-554-0.1 and fire on the cruiser," Sustimer shouted over the booming.

"Aye," responded the helmshound briskly.

The hyperspace missiles launched without as much as a whoosh.

"Count me down," commanded Sustimer.

"First impact in three ... two ... one ... impact. One missile midships, Captain. Two deflected."

The entire bridge crew stole a second to savor the tumultuous ball of flame blasted out into space.

"Come back around and make for the flagship."

"Aye, Captain."

"I want all drives at maximal. If the engines blow, at least we'll have died trying to get that bastard."

"Aye, Captain. All drives redlined."

Maker of Right moaned under the strain of the acceleration.

"There, two destroyers are trying to cut us off. Biscral, I need them out of the picture *now*."

"Aye, Captain," snapped the fire-control dog. "Plasma cannons eight, eleven, one thirty-seven, three thirty-two, and eleven twenty-two locked on bogey one. Cannons thirty-three, five fifty-two, seven thirty-eight, eight forty-four, and ninety ninety-three target bogey two. Fire until target destroyed or ordered."

The zing-*pow* of the cannons cracked to life. Biscral developed an immediate erection he didn't bother to conceal.

Seconds later, one destroyer split in half and spit flames from both sections. The other turned directly at *Maker of Right*.

"She's going to folded space, sir. Closing fast."

"Put us where we shouldn't be, so she doesn't materialize—"

Too late. *Sheer Force* reentered real space with three quarters of her forward section inside *Maker*. Both ships instantly crushed one another and erupted in a fury of fire.

On the bridge of *Death's Deadline*, the first officer turned to Whole Dorcilmas with a huge grin. "She's hot dust, Captain. We got this one."

"Turnersi, we have six ships to mop up. Come around to our previous course and alert the remaining destroyers to choose stragglers and end this. *Then*, shipmate, we shall grin and drink that their souls rot in hell. *Comm*, inform Lord Quildrod we have removed another tall piece from the chessboard."

TWENTY-SEVEN

Tempted as I was to linger, I returned to Oowaoa as soon as I dropped off my kids. Well, that and to hug all the little ones a few times. I was so warm and fuzzy, I even offered Cala a hug, but she disappeared before our eyes rather than take me up on the offer. Bitch.

I didn't have to get too far from the docking area before I confirmed Toño was still doing his banshee impersonation. Poor SOB. Poor everyone who could hear him, too. I waved Sapale to the door, and we stepped outside. "So, what are we looking at here?"

She was clearly rattled by Toño's continued outburst. "Cragforel's not sure. He says all Toño's readings are picture-perfect. In his head, he's screaming just as loud as he is on the outside."

"Anything calm him down or even let him stop for a breath?"

She shook her head. "No. The pitch and octave he screams in'll shift, but that's about it."

"Does he respond in any way to voice or pain?"

"Not to voice, no." She looked down. "No one's

435

mentioned pain. The way he is, it kind of seems like piling it on."

"I'm going in. You're welcome to take a break if you'd like."

"I think I will take a quick one. Rest my audio inputs before they fry."

I kissed her forehead. "You're the best."

It was hard to see Toño in the state he was in. Really hard. He would arch his back and scream, twist from side to side and scream, and flail his arms and legs and scream. He was strapped down six ways to Sunday, so his actual movements were limited. I stepped next to Cragforel. "Any ideas?"

"Yes. Vacationing far, far away."

"Funny guy. Let me yell at him."

"He's all yours," he said, directing an open hand at Toño.

I put my mouth next to his ear and yelled my name, his name, hell, I even yelled General Saunder's name to see if anything would break the evil spell. Nothing. I looked up to Cragforel. He shrugged. We both knew what came next.

I extended my fibers and reached into Toño. I was slammed with an immense wave of—I had to know it—pain. Pain, desperation, and an intoxicating desire to die. I could feel myself slipping in, being pulled into the blackness that was his mind. I called to him but got no reply. I figuratively dug in my heels and resisted the gravity of his anguish. I stopped advancing.

Toño, Doctor Toño DeJesus, it's Jon Ryan. Answer me, I said over and over. Still the storm raged.

Doc, I need you to come back.

Nothing but chaos.

¡Doctor Toño DeJesus, en el nombre de Dios y la sagrada Santa María, cálmate! ¡Sé quieto ahora mismo! I

basically told him in the name of God and the blessed Saint Mary to calm himself immediately.

Damn if it didn't work. Only just a little, but in this case, a little was a lot. I wasn't a stick figure teetering on the edge of a bottomless void. I was a stick figure teetering on the edge of a void with a bottom I could feel. Okay, not a whole hell of a lot, but I think he stopped screaming on the outside. He did *not* stop on the inside.

Good old Catholic *guilt*. Where would humanity have been without it?

Doc, can you hear me? It's Jon.

Then my boy said his first word. I was so proud.

J ... J ... Jon?

Yes, Toño, it's me, Jon Ryan. Doc, say something.

Jon ... where ... where ammmm ... mm I?

You're safe, Doc. You're safe with Sapale and me on Oowaoa. We rescued you from the Adamant, Doc.

He started screaming again, inside, outside, and any place in between. Okay, don't say *Adamant* to Toño just yet. Noted.

Toño, easy. Stop shouting. I'm here to help you. Doc, answer me.

A pause. *Jo ... Jon, are you still there?*

Yeah, Doc. I'm never leaving you again. We'll get through this, and it'll be all right. You'll be happy faster than green grass through a goose.

Por Dios, it is you, Jon. It's really you.

Yeah, thanks, I think. Hey, I'm going to disconnect and we'll talk on the outside like normal people, okay?

I think so. Yes, I think I can do that.

I retracted the probes.

My knees buckled, and I'd have face-planted if Sapale hadn't caught me.

"Jon, Jon, are you okay? Jon, what's happening? Where were you?"

"Wh ... whoa. Where was I? I'z ri ... whoa."

"Yeah, you said that already. Jon, lie down on the floor."

"N ... no, honey, not now. I think I've got a headache."

"No." She palm-punched my shoulder. "Not that. Mind out of the gutter. Lie down, or I'll throw you down."

"N ... no, honey, not—"

She placed a hand firmly over my mouth and laid me down.

"What's all the drama about?"

"Jon, you were hooked up to Toño for almost a week. Honey, we were so worried, but we didn't know what to do. Cragforel said he wanted to break your connection, but I said no. Jon, what happened in there?"

"Oh, it was really fairly simple, Sapale," Toño said as he sat up. "We were just chatting. Chatting, and he was swearing."

"Wa ... wait," I protested while flat on my back, "I don't recall *one* cuss word."

"I believe you took the Lord's name in vain, my friend."

"What? No. That's, like, a matter of opinion."

I couldn't see it from where I lay, but Toño pointed toward heaven. "Yes but *His* is the only one that actually matters."

"Boys, knock off the comedy routine before I get mad," warned Sapale.

That got our fullest attention. No one wanted to go there.

I heard feet pounding in. "I came as soon as I heard," said Cragforel, huffing and puffing. "What happened?"

"He retracted his probes as casually as if he was turning off a faucet, then boom. He hit the deck."

"I did *not* hit the deck. I grew *unsteady*."

I looked up to see two very dubious faces judging an injured man when he was down.

"Then Toño sat up," she said, nodding her head in his direction.

"Dr. DeJesus?"

"Yes, my friend."

"Sir, it is such an honor to finally meet you. I'm Cragforel, humble scientific lead for the Deavoriath."

"Ah, Kymee's replacement."

They shook hands. "More his replacement's replacement's replacement, but yes."

"Goodness. I just checked my chronometer. I've been gone for a while, haven't I?" He craned his neck down to look at me. "I think I can imagine how you felt when you woke up, Jon. Most unusual feeling."

I was up on my elbow by then, rubbing my forehead. "Not a picnic, I can assure you. And hi, Doc. It sure is good to see you again." I smiled. "I missed the *hell* out of you."

"Hmm. Yes, I missed you when you were gone and I wasn't."

"Don't start with the comedy routine, you two. I'm in no mood." Sapale was serious, I think.

"How about this," said Cragforel, "You, Jon, *get* up, and you, Dr. DeJesus, *stand* up."

"Please, call me Toño. Everyone here is family."

"Thank you , T ... Toño. It's my greatest honor."

To my brood's-mate, I snarked, "This is going to get ugly, I can tell already."

We reconvened in the kitchen of Cragforel's house. We *excluded* Garustfulous. Where there was food and nufe to be had, he wanted passionately to be there. But we all knew it would be bad for Toño. Eventually, sure. Day one back from the Land of the Lost, not so much.

"So, Toño, tell us all how you're feeling," began our host.

"I'm getting embarrassed with all this attention. *I'm* generally the one doing the doting."

We all chuckled at that. It was so nice to hear him talk like good old Doc.

"So, Doc, are you ready to tell us your story? It can wait if you're not," I asked as tactfully as I could. Yeah, not very, but #fighterpilothere, okay?

"I don't know. I guess I could begin, and if I encounter any difficulties—"

"Please stop," leaped from Cragforel's mouth. More reserved, he added, "We wouldn't want a setback, would we?"

I put my hands over my ears. "No, we would not." Because I was, well, *me*, I said it kind of loudly.

"You left here after Larocnaur passed. Where did you go?"

"Ah, Larocnaur. Such a delight. Brilliant, funny, and caring."

"Doc, was she Deavoriath? None of those things sound like one of them," I asked tactfully.

"Speak nothing bad of the dead, brood-mate. *Can* it."

"I went nowhere in particular. I'd amassed quite a bucket list by then. I went some places I'd always wanted to. I was the carefree vagabond."

"I can't picture this, either," I said.

"Well, I was. I saw the Diamond Falls of Transaliv 7. *Spectacular.* I spent time with the Dulred. I'd always wanted to study their culture."

"What's so interesting about them?" I asked. I'd never heard of them.

"Jon, seriously, you don't know about the Dulred? *Gas* organisms that float in their atmospheres. They're basically immortal and are said to be the wisest, gentlest race in the universe." That Cragforel could be pretty judgmental when he wanted to be.

"They are all that and *more*," Toño said wistfully. "Anyway, I traveled."

"When did you meet ... you know ... the guys who—" I stammered.

"The Adamant?"

We collectively nearly jumped out of our skin.

"Adamant, Adamant, *Adamant*. There, you see. I can safely say the word."

"Okay, whatever you're comfortable with, Doc."

He sat very quiet for a very long time. We were all beginning to question the wisdom of his recent bravado. "Do you know where they came from, Jon?" He looked around the table. "Does anyone?"

"I ran some DNA test a while ago. They seem to be direct descendants of human pet dogs. I didn't have access to that detailed of a record, but I suspect border collies."

"That they are. You spent some time on *Granger,* didn't you, Jon?"

Didn't see that one coming. "Yeah, some. A place called *Peg's Bar Nobody*. A real dive."

"Did you ever meet an odd fellow named Christian Donovan?"

That question tilted my head. "No, can't say I did. Odd set of questions, Doc."

"He was a breeder on *Granger*. You'll never guess what he bred."

"Cows? They had a lot of *cows* as I recall."

"No. Border collies. They needed herding dogs to help with the flocks just like they did back on Earth."

"So what's odd about this long-dead dog breeder I never met?"

"*He's* where the Adamant came from. They are the result of his efforts forever ago."

"Ah, this is the time Jon says, *you're shitting me*, Doc," I said.

"No. I only wish I was." He was real quiet again for a while. "When the part of the worldship fleet heading for Azsuram finally arrived, *Granger* was among them. Over a few decades, the inhabitants of the worldships were gradually assimilated onto the planet. Billions of people along with all the animals. It was an impressive migration."

"If you say so. I slept through it."

"Yes, you did. In the end, Donovan's descendants refused to disembark. They were all as inbred and odd as their forefather was."

"Sounds like good riddance to me," said Sapale.

"Eventually, they were able to pilot *Granger* away, not that anybody much cared. Everyone who knew them felt the way you do, Sapale. And no one wanted the worldship. Azsuram was a paradise. Almost all the worldships were scuttled."

"Excuse me, Toño. How does one *scuttle* a giant asteroid?" Cragforel asked.

"They were placed in decaying orbits around the central star."

He bobbed his head. "That would do it."

"*Exeter* was the one exception. That one I programmed myself to drift in open space for all eternity."

"Thanks, I think," I responded meekly.

"Thanks to you, *too*," snapped my wife as she hauled off and slugged me.

Toño sat mute for even longer. Then he spoke with deep sorrow. "During my travels, I chanced upon *Granger*. It had been over two million years since it departed Azsuram with the loony Donovan Clan."

"Why is this sounding very ominous all of a sudden?" asked Sapale.

"I landed my vortex on *Granger,* expecting to find nothing." He sighed. "What I found was a worldship teaming with sentient border collies."

"The Adamant," I said in a hushed tone.

"What were to become the Adamant. Yes." He sighed again several times before he could speak. "Oh, at first they were a rather cheery and agreeable lot. They were fascinated to see another sentient species."

"What happened to the Donovans?" asked Cragforel.

"Who knows? Maybe the dogs ate them. By the time I arrived, humans were gone from their collective memory."

"What did they eat? How could they survive that long?" I asked.

"The Donovans had brought a lot of livestock and grains to feed them. Eventually the place went wild. As the ship was sealed, none of the water escaped. The fusion generators worked fine and kept things going."

"You can't tell me a pack of hounds learned how to do routine maintenance," I responded. "After a while, the environment would go down the crapper."

"It almost had."

"Don't tell me you repaired it for them?" I stood half out of my chair.

He tossed his hands in the air. "Of course, I did. They were cheery and affable, remember? I saw a new species establishing a positive civilization, and I acted to support it. It took a very long time, but by the time I left, *Granger* was working as good as new. In that time, the Ones came to adulate me. I was a near god to them with all my technical skills."

"The Ones? Who were they?" queried Cragforel.

"Oh, sorry. That's what they called themselves. The Ones. They had only very basic powers of reasoning back then. They were the *ones* who were there."

"So, you sent the Ones packing," I said with obvious disgust.

"I did. And I forgot about them and assumed I'd never hear from or about them again."

"But over a billion years, they evolved to become the Adamant," Sapale observed.

"They evolved into the Adamant," Toño concluded. "I heard of this mighty conquering race long before I ran across them. *Granger* had traveled to the other side of the Milky Way by the time they left their home and began ravaging the galaxy. It took a long time for them to fight their way back to where it all began. But they never forgot the mastermind Toño DeJesus. I became like their patron saint of knowledge. When they finally caught up with me, they invited me to help them once again."

"And the rest, as they say, is—" I began.

"*History*," Toño finished.

TWENTY-EIGHT

Ten Adamant sat at a flask-shaped table, enjoying a raucous feast. Along the smoothed edges of the flask's curves were positioned nine of the members on the newly reformatted Secure Council. The tenth member, the Prime, sat at the short, straight part that would be the spout of the flask. There sat Interim Emperor Quildrod, Whole of his Imperial Navy. He held for the first time in recorded history both key positions. His power was so great, the other nine joked it likely extended into the afterlife.

Whole Dorcilmas sat at Prime's right paw, the Prime's Second and commander of the combined Adamant Fleet.

"So, as the new Prime of the new Council, I call this inaugural session to order." Quildrod banged his mug on the table hard enough for some ale to spill.

"And I propose a toast to the new Prime and the honorable members of this august body." Dorcilmas swung his mug in a broad arc, also spilling a goodly portion of his drink.

No one cared about the messes. Life was, at that moment, particularly good.

"May we serve the new emperor well or with our lives," cheered Kalfony, the Prime's brother.

As others joined in the call, Quildrod raised a paw in false protestation. "*Interim* Emperor. I will hold this post only long enough to see it justly filled by the *perfect* candidate."

Kalfony grabbed his chin with his fingers. "Hmm? I wonder who that lofty character might be?"

"Maybe that Prince Halbertel who claims proper ancestry," shouted the very drunk Whole Salsifo.

"Hmm, no," Kalfony replied, trying to look thoughtful, "I doubt that very much. The poor usurper suffered a significant *setback* in his aspirations. Some dastardly dog ran him through with a spear, dismembered his body, and burned the pieces in a fusion core." He slipped his cap off in reverence. "Ever since that sad event, Halbertel has pursued his claim, however legitimate it might have been, much less aggressively."

The room exploded with laughter.

Quildrod pounded his mug once again for order. "That does unfortunately lead me to raise the first issue before this council. What to do about the other more serious threats to my efforts to restore the empire?"

Everyone quieted quickly. They all knew he wasn't really calling for ideas or discussion. No, why would he want the opinions of the sycophants he'd appointed specifically to avoid such wastes of his time? He was about to announce his plan, his vision. He assumed all present were more than happy to play good little lackeys with genuine conviction.

The Prime scanned the table menacingly to reinforce the need for no one to speak.

"As there is no input from you, my friends, allow me to outline the framework of a strategy I have hatched. As we all know, the past year has been, er, *eventful*. The empire has suffered some damage, a bloody nose if you will. But I know the empire to be strong, vibrant, and most of all, *resilient*."

Cheers spilled forth from the other members.

"As Interim Emperor, I know it to be my divine role to smooth out the wrinkles that hard times have made in the fabric of our empire. Seventeen other once-loyal officers and their demon followers dared to threaten our empire. I saw to it they were crushed and are now forgotten. There are perhaps another dozen or so large splinter groups that must be put down. I estimate it will take us three or perhaps four years to subdue the major players. After that, we will begin the more arduous task of cleansing the planets that have declared their treason. Many systems have already begun forming rogue governments *without* my permission. Those traitors will be dealt with harshly. Realistically, the consolidation of planetary authority under my leadership will take longer. I estimate an octade, possibly an octade and a half to accomplish that unification. After that, we will once again be brothers and sisters living in an orderly bliss."

Those assembled clapped loudly.

Demplrod, the lone Logistical Whole on the council, inched a paw into the air.

"Yes?" responded Quildrod rather peevishly.

"As a matter of curiosity as opposed to dissent, I'd like to mention a potential delaying factor or two in your otherwise *triumphant* plan. Um, there is the matter of the Alliance of the Periphery, who still wage war against us with apparent impunity. There is also the matter of the unaccounted-for dragons who sliced up our best fleet as if it was butter and they were laser beams. Additionally, there is the unfortunate loss of both the Central Repository of Knowledge and the Rabid Robot himself. Maintaining technical superiority seems to be a matter of our past, not our collective futures. And it pains me to observe further that Jon Ryan remains, er, a free agent. His incredible luck in making the Adamant appear inept, incompetent, and inattentive to detail does suggest he might be a braking factor in your advance toward an orderly bliss. Finally, and this I amend more as a report than an opinion or a potential barrier, my spies, who are numerous and have been immensely reliable in the past, tell me of rumors that they won't help *speed* in your ascension to what is rightfully yours."

"Rumors?" Quildrod said, as thunder rolled from dark storm clouds.

"Rumors of rumor, as it were. Nothing more."

Quildrod shattered his mug on the tabletop. "Speak these rumors of rumors of *lies*."

Longevity on the council *and* on this plane of existence seemed to have removed themselves as options for the foolish Demplrod.

"Ah, some whisper that if the empire does not *expand*, how can it be *mislabeled* as the Adamant Empire? We crush, kill, and destroy. We assimilate, expand, and consume. They shout in the streets that the petty—as it is said by others who are not me—infighting and positioning is the competition engaged in by *females*. That those with *testicles* would never stoop to such folly. Hence, those with no due respect for you are calling what is emerging from the recent catastrophe the *Ovarian* Empire, Prime."

Demplrod was finished.

TWENTY-NINE

We lingered a few weeks on Oowaoa. But it wasn't our home, so we decided it was time to go. Plus, and I wasn't proud to feel it, the constant hero-worship for Toño by the Deavoriath was kind of getting on my last nerve. Now, I don't need to be the center of attention and adulation. No way. I was humble, probably to a fault. But Toño DeJesus? He was a really good scientist, sure. But science and technology didn't win wars or impress the babes. Just sayin'.

As to where home was, we were admittedly torn. Sapale was naturally gravitating to Kalvarg, the home of the nascent Kaljaxian society. I leaned toward Vorpace, with its humans and familiar ways. Doc's only home for a billion years was as part of the furniture in an Adamant computer room. One sweet deal Toño's cachet did buy us was *two* more vortices. Yeah, baby. One for Toño and one for Sapale. No more can-I-borrow-the-car in our family.

We landed all three, *Stingray, Affirmation,* and *Cloister,* on Kalvarg. How the cubes got their crazy names, I never would understand. Pretty soon, after a gazillion welcomes and introductions, we three immortals were in the kitchen having coffee. Some things never changed.

"So, Doc, your head still clear?"

"Yes, I think it is." He got a worried look. "Why do you ask?"

"Just making sure, Mr. Worrywart. You went through quite a destabilizing experience. You have to know I'll be checking on you for a goodly while to come."

"Me, too, so get used to it."

"Yes, ma'am," he replied stiffly.

"I kind of like that," remarked Sapale. "A girl could get used to that level of respect."

"See what an engineer's sense of humor'll get you into?" I admonished Toño.

"Well, I am alright. Luckily, I added the option to turn down the feeling of depression in myself somewhere along the line. If I hadn't, I might be a mess."

"Wow, the cure for depression. *Dial* it down."

"I can adjust your setting, too, if you want." He pointed to both of us.

"Nah, I like my head the way it is, thanks," replied Sapale.

"No lobotomy for me either, if it's all the same with you?"

"It's not a lobotomy. It's a *filter*. Don't say I didn't offer."

It was quiet a minute. "So, how we going to beat these dogs, Doc?"

He was surprised. "You're asking me? It sounds like you've been doing a bang-up job while I've been asleep."

"But you have to know them better than they know *themselves*, right?" asked Sapale. "You had access to everything they ever recorded. You'd know their every strength and weakness."

"I was connected to all of it. But while my brain was

being scrambled, I could not take advantage of it. The last time I had downtime was a long time ago." He sipped his coffee. "Back then, a few hundred thousand years ago, sure, I knew all their dirty laundry. Recent stuff? Not really."

"That's sucks," I said. "It would be nice to have a huge upper hand on them."

"Yes it would be," he agreed.

"Do you recall anything current?"

He tilted his head side to side. "Not much. Not too long ago, they woke me up to solve a problem they were having with the space-time congruity membrane. That's the last thing I remember."

"Ah, Doc, they don't have membrane capability. What problem could they be experiencing?"

"They never told me too much. The problem they presented me was how they could defeat a membrane given that they couldn't penetrate one."

That sounded unsettlingly familiar. "And what solution did you give them?"

"After a significant amount of pressure, I said just fire outside this universe and reenter on the other side of the membrane."

"Doc, they were shooting at *me*."

His left eyebrow shot up. "Fascinating. Did they hit you?"

"No, but they weren't off by much. We barely escaped with our hides."

"Good, then I didn't really help them."

"Doc, they were shooting at *me*."

"Yes, you already said that." He gave me a most puzzled look. "Do you require an apology?"

"No. I don't ... no. Let's drop it."

Sapale pointed to Toño. "He never picked it up to be able to drop it, ya big baby."

451

I started to defend myself, but I recalled how poorly that always went, so I dropped it. "Could you get back in?"

"In what?"

"Could you hack back into the Adamant network if you were close enough?"

"No."

"That sounded pretty certain."

"It was. I cannot hack back in because I will never be that close to attempt such a thing." He set his cup down and glowered at me. "Jon Ryan, need I remind you I spent an eternity being mercilessly tortured and abused by those devils? I would *never* get close enough to them again to risk a repeat performance. You have to know that, right?"

"I guess."

"You *guess*?"

"Well, what if it meant bringing them down for good?"

"No."

"You said that pretty quick, too."

"Yes, I did."

"Jon, don't beat up the man. I don't think talking in terms of bringing down the Adamant Empire is realistic. They're just too damn *big*. They're also very formidable. But even if they weren't, the scale factor makes such a notion impossible." Sapale was the voice of compassion and was correct.

I sighed deeply. "Yeah, their sheer bulk is a problem. It they were armed with pitchforks and throwing stones, they'd win most fights just because of their numbers. Spread out across so much space, too. You know," I started getting fairly intense, "the one thing about them that bothers me and sticks in my craw? I mean, we've battled the Berrillians, the Uhoor, hell, the Last Nightmare. But none of them came within orders of magnitude of the Adamant Empire in terms of bulk."

"What's your point, hon? We all know this," Sapale said.

"No, not a point, just an issue. Why this empire? Why this race? Why are they so much more successful than any other son-of-a-bitchin' species? They're fearless. So were the Berrillians. The cats were probably even more ferocious. The Berrillians were resourceful and determined. That pretty much defined the Last Nightmare, too. So what is it about the Adamant that made them so dominant?"

Sapale looked at me without speaking. Then we both turned to face Toño.

"Why are you ... oh *no*. Don't blame *me*. I aided the horrific beasts, but I did not give them magical powers. No." He shushed us with the back of a hand. "Look away, the both of you."

We did. But we were both thinking the same thing. The Adamant had the Toño Factor. That's what made them so successful. Wait—

"Doc, if you *were* so key to their domination." I could see him start to react. "I'm only saying *if*—a hypothetical here."

He relaxed, giving me permission to continue.

"If it was you—your insights and tech savvy—who made them so great, wouldn't there be some critical aspects of their civilization that were so much a part of *you* that we could exploit them?"

He fumbled with his mug and considered that question. "Possibly." He fell silent.

We let him be for as long as he wanted.

"Do you know why they persecuted the Deft so? Why they felt the need to exterminate them more completely than any other species?"

I was getting hit with so many I-didn't-see-that-comings, I was beginning to feel like the losing boxer in the ninth round.

"Um, no. What exactly does that have to do with the topic at hand?"

He shook his head briskly. "Nothing at all."

"Ah. Okay, I'll bite. Why?"

"I only just learned the reason myself, when the Deft dragon touched me. In all the years I was attached to their machines, after all the assignments they gave me to help locate the Deft, I only now learned why they fear them so."

"They *fear* the Deft?" Sapale was dumbstruck.

"Oh yes. They are crippled by this fear."

"It isn't their general xenophobia?" I asked, quite confused.

"No, it's an all-consuming primordial fear."

"I got it," blurted Sapale. "They are Adamant, *inflexible*. They fear change, and the Deft are shapeshifters." She rested back with a prideful smile. "What's more changing than one of them?"

"No, but that's an excellent guess."

Her smile went *poof*.

"No, it centers around exotic matter."

Crap, crap, crap. Another out-of-left-field blindsiding. This was getting old.

"You *gotta* be kidding, Doc. What do the Adamant's propulsion system and the form-changing abilities of a rare species have to do with one another?"

"Don't you see? Exotic matter is what allows the Deft to transform their bodies."

I placed a trembling hand to my forehead. I needed that vacation I tried to take not so long ago. I knew then that I'd hate surprises for the rest of my life.

"But the Deft don't have—what are they called— exotic matter *generators*," protested Sapale.

"No, not in the same form as the Adamant. But that is the secret to their ability to completely alter their DNA and appearance. They evolved some unique biological process to generate minute quantities of exotic matter."

"No way. They'd *melt* themselves," I whined.

"*Minute* quantities, Jon. Powerful but contained minute amounts." He waved his arms at me. "Electric eels don't electrocute *themselves*. Cobras don't poison *themselves*. It's the natural evolutionary solution of how to utilize a potentially dangerous substance, nothing more."

I sat, pouting a bit. "Okay, the Deft use exotic matter. The Adamant use the stuff, too. Why would the *latter* fear the *former*? It doesn't make any sense."

"Jon, what happened to the Adamant Fleet at the TBOP?" Sapale said with sudden excitement.

"The Adamant got a well-deserved ass—" Oh my.

"You see now? If the Deft can *manipulate* exotic matter and the Adamant vessels are *full* of the substance—"

I finished his thought. "B ... b ... b ... *boom*."

He nodded contently. "B ... b ... *boom*, indeed."

THIRTY

"I'm not saying I'm *unhappy*. You always blow things out of proportion, Ashia." Gingles was trying not to sound angry, but her workmate *was* so annoying.

"You said if we females weren't treated as second-class Adamant, the empire would be in a better state."

"I think it's possible. We've never had any real power. We can't serve in the military. Three quarters of us are euthanized at birth just to make room for more males to go off and get themselves killed. We're educated, yes, but we're not allowed to earn the highest merits. Why? I don't think you're inferior to any male. Do you think you are?"

Ashia slapped a paw to her chest. "Don't make this about *me*, bitch. I'm not the one complaining about doing my part and appreciating the opportunity. *I* like serving in this nursery. *I* like puppies. *I* don't want to put on male clothes and march off to war, thank you very much."

Gingles could see a trap coming. She needed to be cautious. "I love my job, too. I think females could help in many ways that we traditionally haven't been allowed, that's all."

"So, you think if females were in charge, the entire

ruling class wouldn't have been blown up by subversive spies and traitors?"

"That's a huge leap there. Stop it. First, I don't get it. Were they killed by *spies* or *traitors*? And what spy or traitor *isn't* subversive? The news holo keeps repeating that. But two separate groups can't do the same thing. Second, I'm not saying we need to be in charge, only that we should be equal members of the empire."

"The empire has stood for all of history because it is the way it is. Some nursery bitch's opinion can't change my love for the empire."

"Huh," Gingles throated humorously. "What empire? All I see is a pack of petty despots carving out for themselves whatever they can, the empire be *damned*."

"I'm sure it's not *that* bad."

Gingles stopped folding towels and turned to Ashia. "What hole is your head stuck in? There are hundreds of Adamant leaders warring with *other* Adamant, not with aliens. It's *sacrilege*. That's what it is, if you ask me."

"Those are rumors, and you know it. Have you seen one holo to support those claims?"

Gingles looked to the floor.

"What, you have?"

"Yes. There are some on the linkpath."

"The linkpath? Anyone can post lies and fakes on the *linkpath*, child."

"What I saw looked very real. They show an empire in ruins, or at least heading in that direction."

"I love the empire. I'd die for it with a smile on my muzzle. I will not believe it is in any danger, internal or external, no matter what illegal holo you show me. If it's not on Wolf Broadcasting, I'm not listening."

"That's a puppet of the government, or at least it was when a government existed."

"Oh, so now there's no hound leading us. What, do you think *you* should?"

"No, don't be silly. But I see no rulers on the holo. I hear no decrees from formal bodies. I *do* see a power grab happening that leaves me gagging. No one can win when everyone's at odds. Why, I heard that planet, the one with the big copper reserves ... Blanchard's World, that's it. I heard the three Legions of Paw stationed there are at each other's throats, not the damn locals'. Three quarters of the Adamant soldiers are dead at the paws of their own *kin*."

"I heard that but don't believe it. I think it was the spies and subversives again."

"Maybe they're bored now that they killed the ruling class? They're branching out? How could *spies* make one fleet of warships attack another fleet of warships? Hmm? Maybe ask them to nicely, which would incline them to do it since the spies asked so nicely?"

"You're toeing the line of open treason, bitch. Mind your tongue."

"Oh, that's a brilliant comeback. I challenge your worldview with facts, and you fall back on piteous threats? Look me in the eyes and say you don't know someone who has been in combat with another Adamant since the empire ended."

"I do *not* know someone who has fought his brother, ever."

"Your cousin Kallardy. The one with three legs because one was shot off? He told me *himself* it was a blast from an Adamant on Lagilor 12 that took it off. You know as well as I do he told you the same thing. Why are you lying instead of processing reality?"

Ashia was shaking she was so furious. "Yes, he told me that's how it happened. I also know he's a drunkard *and* a free thinker. Just because he *said* it doesn't make it *so*."

"You're impossible. I see *danger* and say we need to *act*. You see the *same* danger and say it's a delicious dessert for no other reason than the truth is *unacceptable* to you. *Ahhhrrr!*"

I'll see you regret mocking us, bitch. You will know it was I who revealed your treason before we kill you and eat your still beating heart. Yes, you will know it was me, you will beg for mercy, but you will then learn that there is none for the wicked any longer.

THIRTY-ONE

After Toño's revelation about the Deft, I separated from the others. I needed to think, and I did that best alone. We were hopefully at a turning point in our struggles with the Adamant. But an opportunity and a victory were as different as night and day. I wanted to noodle out a way to make it happen. So, what mighty mental manifestation did I come up with? Nothing. Knowing the Deft could control exotic matter was interesting, but I couldn't see how that power could be used strategically. The empire was so extended that there weren't enough dragons to send one solitary scaly beast to every major installation. If they dedicated themselves exclusively to the eradication of the enemy, it would take them decades to cover all the bases. And that presupposed a race famous for its reclusivity would consider committing to full-time warfare for an extended period. Most unlikely.

So, I found myself sitting in the kitchen all by myself drinking coffee. Then I heard the distinctive scuff of Garustfulous entering the room. I cringed. I was basically trapped. I made an effort to generally avoid him. I mean, I didn't *dislike* him, but I just didn't think of him as a bud.

As a creature from a pack race, he craved company. Humans were social, but that was a long way from yearning to be in a group. Once he cornered me like he just had, he generally talked my ear off and bored me to tears.

"A very good morning to you, Jon," he said as he poured a cup. "Trust you are mechanically sound."

"Fit as an android."

"*Hah*. Good one. Your mind is as sharp as a puppy's teeth." Old Adamant idiom apparently.

"And you? Staying out of trouble?"

"I only wish there was trouble for me to get into here. No bitches, no males to best in wit or battle. It's like an Adamant nursing home here."

That was news to me. "You guys have nursing homes for old Adamant?"

He scanned me like I was an idiot. "Of course not. With us, if you're too old to contribute, you're too old to live. No, I read about them in your culture." He sipped his hot coffee. "Silly waste of resources if you ask me."

"Fortunately, no one has or will."

"Ha, another good one. I wish I were as funny as you."

"Me, too."

He pounded the table lightly with a fisted paw. "Za-zing."

"Any plans for the day?" I knew that was unlikely, but I wanted to redirect the conversation away from my amazing sense of humor.

"Not many. I think I'll take a bath. Maybe nap when the sun gets a little higher. That's pretty much it. Why, did you need my help with something?" He sat up expectantly.

Egads, I was headed for quicksand. "No, but thanks just the same. I've got no real plans either."

461

"That seems remarkably out of character for the great Jon Ryan. If you're doing nothing, maybe we can do it together? I'd love to take a long walk if there was someone to go with."

Yikes, I was now sinking in the quicksand. "Nah, I need to think."

"What better way to think a thing through than taking a long walk?"

"Nah, I think best alone."

He suddenly looked so dejected. "So I've heard. What are you pondering?"

"Same old, same old. How to walk the Adamant Empire out the exit once and for all."

"In light of the Deft insight?"

I looked at him sideways. "You know about that?"

He furrowed one brow. "Of course, I do. Toño and I chat frequently. It's not like I'm a security threat, you know?"

I shrugged. "Guess not. But no, I can't see how that's going to produce a significant change."

"Me either."

Now it was me shooting up an eyebrow. "You agree?"

"Yes. The empire is too vast. Those reclusive dragons would never commit to a long-term military deployment."

"Wow, I came to the same conclusion."

"Why is it so surprising that two seasoned military souls like us would come to the same conclusion?"

I kept forgetting he was a seasoned officer. Nowadays, he was just a chatty annoyance.

"So, if not the Deft, what are you trying to determine?"

Why not? "I'm trying to think of a way to use Toño's intimate knowledge of the Adamant to deal them a death blow."

"Ah, yes. A very practical approach. He undoubtably

has information stowed away that could end them." He took another sip. "But we'll never know."

"Why do you say that?"

"He'd need to engage the Adamant to use his unique knowledge. He'll never get that close."

"Hence, he cannot deal them a death blow."

"No. It's just as plain as the nose on your muzzle. He suffered too greatly for too long to ever place his liberty at risk again."

"Those were basically his words to me."

"There, you see. Simple logic."

"So, here I sit stewing."

"Speaking of stew, I'm starving. Can I get you something?"

"What are you having?"

"Some of your darling wife's delicious carlf."

I popped up a palm. "No thanks. Stuff eats though my GI tract like battery acid."

"Suit yourself."

He returned shortly with an enormous trough of the slop. I dialed down my olfactory inputs.

"I do monitor Adamant communications, you know," he said between gulps. "Toño's vortex is capable of capturing a lot of the local chatter. Since the ruling class itself was blown to dust, the empire is having trouble. Civil war is rampant. Social order is falling apart. Really, it's a process I never thought I'd live to see."

"Harhoff was fairly certain the pent-up ambition and native aggression would be their undoing."

"So far he looks like an excellent prophet."

"I just don't want to count on that happening. I want to drive a stake into Dracula's heart."

He looked blankly at me.

"Human legend. Nevermind. But it looks like waiting is about all I can do."

"You could bring the mountain to Mohammed."

"Huh? Wait, you can't know that expression."

"Why not? Toño uses it all the time."

"He does?"

"In fact, I've heard him say it to you on more than one occasion."

"Huh. I'll have to start paying more attention. So, what do you mean bring the mountain?"

"If you can't bring Toño to the Adamant network, maybe you can bring the network to Toño?"

"Ah, one, it's kind of big. Two, no matter how nicely I ask, they'll probably say no." I rolled my eyes.

"I *saw* that."

"You deserve it for your lame idea."

"You're thinking too concretely, Jon. Let me pose it to you this way. The Adamant have a communications network interfaced with computers, data files, and individuals. How does your average dog do that?"

"I don't know. Maybe they go visit with a gift?"

"Not even funny. No, great and powerful Jon Ryan, they access it with their comm links and computers."

"Yeah, but—" Wait. That *was* a great idea. Bring a functioning comm link to Toño. "I hear you. It might work. No way to tell. Thanks."

"You are many wonderful things, Ryan, but an actor is not one of them. It's a great idea, and you know it."

"Great? No, maybe. It's only a great idea if it works."

"Uh-huh. So, when do we leave?"

"What's with the *we*?"

"It was my brilliant idea, and my schedule is open. Jon, the highlight of my day is the bath I mentioned. Cut me a break. Seeing real action is just what the medic ordered."

"I'll talk to the others. First the boss, then Doc. *If* they greenlight us, we hit the road right away."

"Perfection. Just enough time to finish this delight." He shoveled in more goop.

"Honey, I'm home," I chortled as I entered the front door.

"It's fine by me. You have to listen to what Toño says though. You got that?"

Huh? "Honey, I'm—"

She came over and gave me a kiss, me still standing on the threshold. "Go. I said it was okay. It's a good idea if," and she put a finger to my nose, "and only if Toño agrees."

"This is not having the desired effect. I say *honey I'm home* and then you say *welcome home, love that fuels my existence.* Can we take this from the top?"

She planted a palm on my chest and pushed. "Garustfulous called and explained the whole mountain-bringing thing. Go, but be sensitive with Toño. Promise me you will."

Next thing I knew, I was looking at my closed front door. Darn near whacked me in the nose.

"Yo, Doc," I chortled as I entered his workshop, "How are you this—"

"No. *Positively* not. No *way*. Please leave at *once*."

I was in a rut that particular morning.

"Doc, I'm just saying—"

"And I'm saying no. *Period.* Do not forget I know where your off switch is." He started forcibly ushering me toward the door.

"Did Garustfulous call you?"

He narrowed his eyes. "No. Why would he? He just

now left. I'm not linking up to the Adamant network. Go, leave."

"I'm going to *murderize* that hound dog."

"Be that as it may, and best of luck. It might distract you from your insane notions about me."

"Wait. Please stop shoving. Stop it, that *tickles*."

He halted. "I'll cease pushing if you swear to drop the subject."

I fluttered my eyelashes. "What subject?"

He started shoving again.

I gently grabbed his hands. "I can see you have certain *reservations* about our plan. Those low barriers to success are easily addressed." More with the eyelashes. I was pretty much running on empty.

"Yes, I have certain reservations. I am certain I will not participate."

"Now hang on. Let's be civil. Give me one minute."

"Take your minute and stuff it—"

"One minute. I anticipated a concern you might have, and I think I've hit on quite the innovative resolution."

"What's my concern?" he challenged.

"That if we access the Adamant network they might use that entry to their advantage."

"Yes. The second I enter the network is the second they know I did. The next second they will be here in force because, *duh*, they would know where I was because that's where I was calling from."

"You know that in all the years I've known you, I don't think I've ever heard you say *duh*."

"Why do you think pointing out that trivia will advance your hopeless cause?"

I shook my head. "Don't know."

"You were just stalling."

I could only smile real big in response. Dude sure knew me well.

"Want to hear my solution?"

"No."

"It's brilliant."

"No."

"When you hear it, you're going to say *gosh, Jon, you've done the impossible yet again.*"

"No."

"Here's the basics. Whatever form of communications device we, eh, borrow, I'll transmit the signal through multiple distant and often dangerous locations. It'll take them hours to trace the signal back to its original broadcast point." I smiled real big. "Hours."

"Wonderful. I will have *hours* of blessed freedom before my next torture shift. No."

"I can almost guarantee this will work."

"You are a terrible salesman. *Almost?*"

"Horrible but honest. That usually wraps up the sale in my favor. People appreciate honesty."

"When purchasing a vacuum cleaner, yes. When volunteering for hell, no."

"Let me draw the delays out for you. If you're not convinced, I'll drop the subject forever."

"Fine. I'm not convinced."

"That's a foul, and it will cost you several points in penalty."

"Jon, I'm *afraid.* Why are you badgering me? Sapale told you to be sensitive to me and respect my feelings."

"Huh? She called you?"

"No, I have a brain. You went to her first, and that is what she made you promise."

I held up a finger. "No, totally incorrect. She *asked* me to promise, but I never actually said yes."

He sighed in resignation. "Come over to the computer. Show me how you can reroute the signal to buy us enough time to make my risk worthwhile."

467

It took the better part of an hour, but in the end, Doc was excitedly onboard. Okay, he wasn't, but he believed my ruse would buy us at least ten minutes. He agreed to hack in, therefore, for five minutes. He actually made me say I promised that once everything was set up, I'd kill the project if he had second thoughts. I agreed. I just didn't tell him which "project" I was planning to kill. It sure as hell wasn't the hack into the Adamant network. No, that baby was a done deal in my mind.

THIRTY-TWO

Aporthio was sitting at the control panel with one paw holding his head up and the other listlessly tapping his comm link. He was checking for any updates on his FAB account, but he knew there'd be none. He was stationed on a supply and support ship in the Leo II dwarf galaxy, some seven hundred thousand light-years from the Milky Way. He wasn't going to Find A Bitch anytime soon. There certainly weren't any in the entire dwarf galaxy, so lonely nights were pretty much guaranteed until he was rotated home next year.

He deleted the usual hooker auto-posts. Not that he wouldn't welcome a female of any ilk, but he knew the working girls weren't making house calls this far out. No one in their right mind would come to this forsaken puddle of stars. Why the Adamant felt the need to conquer it was beyond him. But, duty was duty, so in the wastelands he'd—

What was that sound? Metal falling? No. There was no one due to rendezvous with his rust bucket for the next several days. He scanned his FAB account to see if there'd been any updates since he'd heard that—

There it was again. And he smelled ... someone. Not a female, but—

"Above *Packlet*," snapped Garustfulous as he stormed into the room, "what is the meaning of your slovenly behavior? And stand at attention when a wedge leader barks to you, son."

Aporthio stood so quickly he tumbled forward to the deck. He scampered back up and saluted. "Sorry, Wedge Leader. I was studying some manuals. I try to be current—"

Garustfulous paced back and forth before the stunned sailor. "Do I look like I want to hear your lies? Have you mistaken me for an old friend? Your sire maybe? Hmm. *Silence.*"

The trembling mutt saluted again. "Yes, sir."

"Are you taunting me, puppy? I say silence, and you say yes, sir? I've ordered thousands of children like you to their deaths. Do not tempt me to add to the vast number by dispatching you. Is that all right with you and your *mama?*"

Aporthio kept saluting but nearly passed out. He couldn't say yes. If he nodded in the affirmative, would the wedge leader know that he wasn't taunting him or that he understood?

"Stand at point, Above Packlet."

He did with relief. Standing at point did not require thought or decision-making. He was good at standing point.

"I come here on my scheduled inventory inspection, and you *ignore* my hail. You *fail* to release your docking bay, which forced me to waste five minutes to get the code from your mothership. And I walk onto the bridge to find you watching pornography. Now, you will not need to explain yourself to me. For one thing, it would be impossible to explain your level of incompetence, so please don't try. After I complete my inspection, I will report your dereliction to your commander. You can try and get *him* to believe your lies, if you so desire."

Garustfulous stepped up and faced him muzzle to muzzle. "I know it's asking too much, but do you know where your one-dog shuttles are stored? This ship is supposed to carry thirty-five replacement units."

"Sir, they're in Hangar BB-8. I'll show you there, if you'd like."

"I don't want to inconvenience you. You seemed mighty busy with that pornography."

"No ... no, sir. No inconvenience. This way. After you." They left the bridge.

Garustfulous paced—for angry superior officers paced a lot when upset—back and forth in front of seven one-dog shuttlecraft lined up along a wall in Hangar BB-8.

"Is it me, or do I count seven shuttles?"

"That's how many I count, sir. I assume that's how many you counted, too."

"Thank you for that vote of confidence." He placed his mouth next to the sailor's ear and shouted for all he was worth. "Which leaves only the matter of the twenty-*eight* missing shuttlecraft you and I are not counting. Where are the missing shuttlecraft, son?"

Garustfulous had to jump backward to avoid the urine stream that escaped its owner's bladder.

Garustfulous bent to the floor and wailed, "That is not an acceptable answer. Where are the stolen shuttlecraft? Whom did you sell them to?"

Aporthio staggered to the nearest com-panel. He tapped several keys.

"I ... the manifest records only these *seven*, sir, not thirty-five. None are missing."

He paced back and forth in front of the poor sailor. "Well then, I guess you're saying you and I have

471

something in common. *We both lie.* Is that what you're accusing me of? Mind you, think carefully about what you're about to say. Your life probably depends on it." He went back to pacing.

"I have no explanation, sir. I did not audit this section. It was never part of my duties. I can call—"

"You will call no one. Is that clear?"

"No, sir."

"No, sir *it's not clear,* or no, sir *you won't call anybody?*"

"Yes, sir."

Garustfulous felt he'd established his negotiating position and that it was one of strength. He paced over to the rack of shuttles. "Come here, Above Packlet."

"Sir."

Garustfulous set a claw on the second shuttle in on one end. "What is this?"

"Er ... it's an *ID* tag?"

"You're not certain?"

"I am, sir. It's an ID plate."

Garustfulous stepped to the end vehicle. "And this?"

"Another ID plate, Wedge Leader," he replied triumphantly.

He positioned his body between the sailor and the shuttles. "Do you see a problem with those two tags?"

Aporthio's knees began to wobble. "No. They both appear to be proper ID plates."

Garustfulous returned to pacing and tapped a finger against his muzzle. "I will have to grant you that, son. They are *both* proper tags. This one says it is assigned to this sorry ship. The other says it belongs to a ship named *Ready Resupply 7777.* I must admit that is an uninspiring name, but you may read the plate and confirm that fact for yourself. Here comes a really tough question, so put on your thinking cap. What is the name of this ship?"

He licked frantically at his lips and panted as if he'd run a race. "Ah, *Ready Resupply 5011-A*, sir."

"Not *R&R 7777*?"

"That appears to be true, Wedge Leader."

"Yes it does, does it not? And how do you think *7777*'s one-dog shuttle came to reside *here*, in *5011-A*'s Hangar BB-8?"

"I have no idea, sir."

"No idea? Well, lucky for you, I *do* have a speculation on the matter. When you sold the missing ships to some subversive on *R&R 7777*, that fool left his shuttle here and accidentally drove one of *5011-A*'s shuttles back to *7777*. I can also explain why *that* fool and the fool I'm addressing *presently* didn't notice the error. Listen closely so I needn't repeat myself. It's because *they are both subversive fools*."

"No, sir, *never*. I'm—"

Garustfulous raised a paw. "Remember, I do not wish to hear your lies. I will report my observations and let you lie to someone from Counter Terrorism, okay?"

The Above Packlet was speechless.

"Now if you'll be so kind as to hand me those antigrav clamps there."

The sailor did, but he was so lost in fear and confusion that he did so without activating the heavy unit. He could barely present it to Garustfulous.

"Thank you," he said. Then he flipped the switch and accepted the weightless clamps. He screwed them tightly into the predesignated center-of-mass couplings and pulled the shuttle off its mount.

"Now, I'm confiscating this craft as evidence. If I left it, you would destroy the shuttle immediately, making it unavailable for your brief trial. Is that acceptable with you, runt?"

"May I help you transport it to your vessel, sir?"

"No, I think I will not give you the opportunity to beat the life out of me with it, but thanks for the offer. In fact, you will remain here in Hangar BB-8 until you hear my ship decouple. Is that clear? If I hear you sneaking up behind me, I'll use this blaster to kill you." He patted his sidearm. "Are we all clear on our responsibilities and parts in tonight's entertainment?"

"Yes, Wedge Leader."

"Fine. Best of luck in prison, son."

Aporthio idiotically waved to the wedge leader. "Thank you, sir."

Garustfulous spirited the shuttle back to *Stingray,* and they vanished.

"So how long do you think it will take him to realize he's never going to hear a decoupling?" I asked with an evil grin.

"A very long time. I think I made quite the impression on the lad. Maybe when thirst burns in his mouth in a few days, he'll leave to avoid lethal dehydration."

"You are one son of a bitch."

"Jon, I keep telling you that's a statement of fact, not an insult."

"Oh yeah. You sure are your bitch's biggest regret."

"Much better. It is also absolutely the case."

I hadn't ever seen Garustfulous that happy.

THIRTY-THREE

Sapale stood at the portal while Toño, Garustfulous, and I loaded material into *Stingray*. I wouldn't say she was mad, just forcefully curious. "I get that you need to cover your tracks, but why do you need to go to Vorpace at all?"

I passed her heading in with a stack of boxes. "I want to show Doc his statue." He was farther in the cube. "It really does look like you. Mine, I look more like John Wayne."

Toño was exiting past me by then. "Sounds like the humans of Vorpace are very intelligent."

"And why can't you show him your stupid monuments later, or better yet, never?"

"I think someone's *jealous*."

"I am not jealous. I have more statues than you do."

I parodied her line with pronounced juvenility. "*I have more statues than you do*, na na na na na."

"One of these days, flyboy."

"Plus I want Toño to meet Twisted Sister."

Toño stopped dead in his tracks. "They can't *possibly* still be together?"

"Unfortunately, he is referring to the sister of the

head of state," chimed in my BFF Al. "The one he had a torrid but brief affair with while still married to Sapale."

"I didn't know she was still alive, and you both know it."

"I'm confident that makes a difference in the Court of Higher Marital Appeals. Ah, is that Judge Sapale I spy at the entrance? The one with the rising blood pressure?"

"Al, you're too much," I said, by means of futile self-extrication.

"Yeah, and this judge is thinking Vorpace might just be a boy's night out for two single guys ... and one barely still-married guy," hissed Sapale.

"Hon, we're fighting the ultimate evil on the off chance the remaining free planets can survive. We're not conducting a panty raid on a sorority at State U."

"Is that a possibility?" Garustfulous perked up.

"No," replied both Sapale and me in chorus.

"Why do we need this sister?" asked Toño for the third time.

"Because she's fearless, unprincipled, and devious. We need her on this mission."

"Oh, now I feel so much better." Sapale sure could be dramatic. "She's everything a man could want in a woman."

"A dog, too." Garustfulous wagged his butt.

Not very helpful, dude.

"So when will you be back? I want to know when I can resume the picking of your bones?" asked the love of my life.

"Hopefully soon. Maybe a week. We have a lot of setup to do."

"Bachelor parties are usually like that," added Al. "Well, not so much planning as the mass acquisition of booze."

"Doc, where did you say his off switch was?" I asked as I lugged in the one-dog shuttle.

"I didn't. Don't involve me in this infantile discussion."

"I beg your pardon," huffed Sapale.

"You heard me, too," he said, leaving the cube. Hey, she didn't brain him for saying that. I thought that reflected excellent maturity on her part. True restraint was the mark of an adult.

"Okay, we're just about ready. Toño, *Stingray* sent *Affirmation* the landing coordinates. We'll meet you there."

He waved as he sealed the hull.

We appeared on Vorpace simultaneously. Toño and I proceeded to Jonnaha's office. Due to the recent decimation of their planet by the Adamant, all three of us felt it would be best to sequester Garustfulous in *Stingray*. I dialed up the prime minister as we walked to let her know we were coming. I told her I was bringing a celebrity, but I refused to say who it was. Hey, any opportunity to mess with a fellow human's head was not to be missed.

We did stop in the lobby to view our statues. Doc giggled at mine. He did not giggle at his.

"That looks nothing like me. The visually impaired person who sculpted this made me look thin and pale."

"Doc, you are thin and pale."

"I'd like to proceed to the prime minister's office now. We don't have time to waste on the critique of local art."

"This way, Toño."

Because I was me, I walked into Jonnaha's office without knocking. I even gave a finger-over-lips hush gesture to her inner secretary. I palmed Toño's chest so he stopped just outside the door.

"Jon, please come in and make yourself at home. Do you want my chair?" Jonnaha greeted sarcastically.

"The hot seat? No thanks. I'll park it next to baby sis over here."

Once seated, Shielan turned to face me. "I hate you. You know that, right?"

"Good to know I can count on a few constants in my life."

"I don't see a mystery guest," interrupted Jonnaha.

"Oh, he's right outside the door. Here's the plan. I'll give you hints, and the first one to guess who it is gets to kiss him."

"Jon, even for you that's way too immature." Toño walked quickly into the room, stopping directly in front of Jonnaha. He held out his hand. "I am Toño DeJesus. I wish to state for the record that I have never met the android in that chair."

Jonnaha was way too overwhelmed to even raise her hand, let alone make a peep.

I ruffled Shielan's hair. "Doc, she's not a robot."

Two things happened at the same time. Jonnaha tried to stand, but instead, she passed out. Shielan punched me in the arm really hard.

"Now look what you've done, Jon." Toño rushed around to aid Jonnaha. She was beginning to sit up in her chair.

"Me? I'm not the one who made the nice lady swoon, you Latin devil."

"Aren't either of you going to assist me?"

"No. You *are* a doctor, you know."

"Here, my dear," he cooed to her. "Have a sip of water."

She did, but she gagged the first drops.

Toño gently thumped her on the back. "There you

go," he reassured her. "Easy does it, and you'll be just fine."

"Wow, my big sister under the care of Doctor Toño DeJesus. Never thought I'd live to see the day."

"We need to buy some get-well-soon cards," I said to little sis. "Don't let us forget."

She shot me two thumbs up.

"I'm fine. Well, no, I may die of embarrassment. But Doctor DeJesus, what an *incredible* honor. Jon didn't tell us you were still alive."

"Please, call me Toño. He did not know I was until very recently. It's a long story."

"*That* I believe," she responded. "Can I get either of you something? Coffee?"

Shielan turned to me. "Bourbon?"

"Sounds enticing, but we're on a mission," I replied. I tapped the end of her nose. "You are, too, so no hooch for you either."

"A mission with the great warrior Jon Ryan and the most legendary mind in human history?" She checked her handheld. "Crap. Gotta say no. I have a nail appointment. Otherwise, I'd love to join the fun."

"Doc does nails. He's a *physician* doctor, you know?"

"I do not do nails."

"He *does* nails. He's just so modest. It's heartbreaking."

"Ah, what mission?" called out Jonnaha.

"Very secret squirrel, Jonnaha. Can't tell you until we're back." I rotated my face all around the room. "The walls might have ears."

"Not these walls," responded Shielan.

"Especially if I don't say anything secret."

"Point. When do we book?"

"Whenever you're ready?"

She stood and addressed her sister. "I'll see you when I see you, unless of course I don't see you again."

"Wha ... wait. Where are you taking her? Why do you need her?" protested big sister.

"Jon says it's because your sister is fearless, unprincipled, and devious," replied Toño.

"Why thank you," she said with a nod. "A man's never paid me such a nice compliment."

"I recognize top talent when it I see it, kiddo."

We fist bumped. I taught her that one, naturally.

"Shie-Shie, I can't let you run off into mortal danger not even knowing what form of mortal danger it is."

"Isn't it lucky for us both that you don't have control over the matter?"

She fist bumped me.

I was having a lot of fun. Irreverence was fun.

"I'm your boss. You're head of my security service. I order you not to abandon your post."

Shielan stood. "Abandoning? Who said anything about abandoning? I'm calling in sick. Hey, Toño, I think I have malaria. Can you write my boss a medical excuse?"

"Really," Toño whined to Jonnaha, "you *have* to believe me. I have no control over either of them."

"I feel your pain. I won't need that note, so don't sweat it."

"Bless you."

"You know malaria hasn't existed in billions of years, right?"

"Yeah, that's why I'm going to place myself in strict quarantine under the medical supervision of a legendary healer."

Toño shook his head. "No control whatsoever."

THIRTY-FOUR

All three vortices were parked in a close huddle on the ravaged remains of planet Earth. I chose it as a center of operations on a why-the-hell-not basis. If we were discovered we could split up in three separate directions to avoid any pursuit. I was betting we'd be done before the bad guys arrived, but a solid backup plan was a thing of beauty when the shit hit the fan. I helped Toño place the uplink cables from his underarm into the jerry-rigged receptacle he'd constructed on the one-dog shuttle's control panel. The mechanism he built would allow maximal upload and download speeds once we were into the Adamant mainframe. I patted him on the back.

"It's go time."

In the weeks since his grilling by that wedge leader who'd never actually said his name, Aporthio's nerves had yet to settle. He couldn't eat, he had diarrhea despite his lack of food intake, and he didn't even notice the two beautiful females who posted on his FAB site. He was that beside himself. At first he expected a squad of goons to descend upon the ship and drag him away in irons. But no one had come. He'd received a few routine transmissions since then, but none of them hinted at his pending execution. He was perfectly at a loss as to what he needed to do or even feel.

He certainly wasn't going to ask when his punishment would begin. Maybe that awful wedge leader's ship was attacked. Maybe Aporthio was in the clear. Yeah, if he called and reported his transgressions, that would be stupid. He was actually beginning to hope nothing was going to come of the incident. Before he docked with a command ship, he'd stage a small electrical fire in Hangar BB-8 and claim only a single loss. One shuttle that was burned beyond repair and had to be jettisoned. He might just live to rotate home. But he would *not* let his guard down. No, he'd be on his—

What was that sound? He knew he'd heard something. If it was that insane officer again, well he'd just give the hound a good telling off for scaring an innocent dog like him. There it was again. No, not a sound. It was a muted alarm. He whipped out his comm link. Deck 3, Section Sl/99n. The unused freezer room? What would trigger an alarm in an unused area? Well, he'd best ... crap. When it hailed, it poured. The bridge comm was bleeping. That came first. He hustled to the bridge.

"Above Packlet Aporthio here. To who am I speaking?"

Garustfulous took in an extra-big breath so he could shout his loudest. "It's to *whom* am I speaking, boy. Didn't they teach you anything in whatever little school you attended?"

Aporthio pooped directly onto the floor beneath where he stood. "S ... ss ..."

"What are you, a Tralbanian slime worm? Ssss ... sss ... ssithing your superior officer?"

"No, ss ... sir. Yes, sir. To what do I owe the pleasure of your call?"

"*Pleasure?* Again the litter runt *mocks* me. Have you no decency, pup?"

In the interest of time, I could best summarize that Garustfulous was thoroughly enjoying his part of the operation. He was tasked with distracting the hapless Aporthio from checking on the alarm that was going off in the unused freezer. That's where I'd installed our main electronics for getting into the Adamant network. I took the opportunity of doing that while Garustfulous was ripping the unlucky packlet multiple new orifices the first time. Given the chance, he'd have to answer the alarm. But my spy dog promised he'd verbally occupy the dimwit as long as necessary. Aporthio was a low-watted lightbulb mentally, but even a blind pig found the occasional acorn. If he recognized the hack *and* he followed protocol, he'd have ended our connection before we'd fully exploited it.

Meanwhile, Toño was already into the Adamant network.

"Wedge Leader, we have a Level One incursion," the Half Wedge said quite a bit louder than he needed to.

"Where?"

"*Eternal Triumph*, sir."

"What area of space is he in?"

Culpetas pulled up a holo and pointed. "There, Wedge Leader Kalkin. The western quadrant, near the planet Gargantuary."

"Get the captain on *now*."

After a couple seconds, a worried face appeared on the screen. "This is Whole Markasious, I'm in the middle of a crisis. What?"

"I know you're in crisis, Markasious. That's why *I* am calling. I'm Wedge Leader Kalkin, head of Information Security."

That got the Whole's full attention. Though on paper he outranked the caller, it hardly mattered. IS was basically the Adamant's version of the Gestapo, SS, and the Red Guard all rolled into one mean-spirited group of sociopathic dogs. If one of them *accidentally* looked at someone wrong, that individual was a dead dog.

"Yes, do you know of its nature, Wedge Leader?"

"Not yet. Have you isolated the source?"

Markasious glanced offscreen briefly. "No, sir. Not yet."

"I'm sending a squad of prowl ships to your location. Be prepared to assist them fully."

Markasious swallowed hard. Prowl ships were used only by IS troopers. They were also the ones that parents used in tall tales to scare their puppies when they misbehaved.

"If you feel—"

"*Clearly,* you require help, you imbecile. *You,* Markasious, couldn't even keep your own ship's critical systems secured."

Ten seconds later, twenty-four prowlers materialized on all sides of *Eternal Triumph.* They did so intentionally. The IS troopers did not mean to give the impression of having captured the ship, but to reinforce that fact that they *had* to all board.

"Markasious, I'm Fettuary. I'm in command of your vessel now. Status report." Wedge Fettuary dispensed with titles and other useless words. He was, after all, speaking to a dead dog. Who wasted respect on the dead?

"Er, we've traced the signal. It's coming from the ce ... center of a globular cluster that orbits the Milky Way Galaxy. We've sent you the specifics."

"And what system have they hacked into?"

Markasious shook his head slowly. "The primary exotic matter containment field computers."

"Interesting choice. Whoever is doing this must anticipate the catastrophic consequences of shutting that system down. Turn off the primary field computers at once."

"Ah, there's more."

"I just issued an *order*. You respond with what appears to be pleasant conversation."

"It's that at the moment the incursion took place, the intruder placed viral corruptions in all three redundant backup systems. If I shut off the primary computer, the exotic matter will be freed instantaneously."

"That's preposterous. I'm sending over someone to confirm that. No one knows that much about the computer system. Even if they *did*, no one is authorized to perform such a corruption. Not even *I* could do that."

"Let your expert confirm that we can do nothing. The primary system cannot be turned off until a backup is physically installed. I have a team on it already. They estimate it will take several hours."

Fettuary thought a moment. He was contemplating the destruction of *Eternal Triumph*. He weighed the termination of the signal versus the value of the brand-new battleship to the empire.

"*Eternal Triumph* will make for the globular cluster immediately. We will accompany you. Fettuary out."

"B ... but did you hear me correctly? I said it comes

485

from the center of a *globular* cluster. An *unexplored* globular cluster."

"I have given an order. Obey at once."

"I cannot ask my crew to—"

"You do not have a crew of sniveling *whelps* to ask anything *of*. As you confess your childish cowardice, precious seconds have evaporated. I'm coming over to take the helm personally."

Markasious's screen went black. A few minutes later, a conspicuously diminutive Fettuary stormed onto the bridge. He walked right up to Markasious, drew his sidearm, and fired three rapid blasts point-blank to his throat. Fettuary wanted very much to create the image of a rolling head on the deck. He was confident it would impress upon the remainder of the bridge crew that he demanded absolute, immediate obedience.

"Set course for the globular cluster and engage."

In the blink of an eye, all twenty-five ships entered real space at the given coordinates. "Triangulate the precise location of the transmitter," snapped Fettuary.

"Sir," the chief engineer called out, "we've identified a small craft. It is alien by its configuration. It appears to be the—"

He fell silent when the entire bulk of *Eternal Triumph* shook like a tennis ball after being struck for service.

"Report," howled Fettuary. "What was—"

"Sir, two prowlers just disappeared. I cannot identify the origins of the attack we just suffered."

"What do you mean *disappeared*? Ninety-ton ships don't just—"

"There go two more."

"Where? Where did they go?"

"Unknown. Sir, we just lost power in engines two and five."

"Lost power?"

"Sorry, sir, I stand corrected. The engines themselves are missing."

"Fire on that *damn* ship, all banks. Then get us out of this portal to hell."

The ship's weapons fired briefly, and all remaining ships slipped back into friendly space. "Engineer, I want a full report as to what happened to my ships and my troops."

"Sir."

"Status of the computer incursion?"

"Still proceeding, sir."

"*What?*"

"Yes. The moment we entered real space, the transmission resumed."

"Total time of incursion?"

"Nearly ten minutes."

"Damn them to hell. Where's the signal coming from now?"

"The planet Corfmier. It's one of our mostly administrative planets."

"I know *Corfmier*, you idiot. Put us in orbit. Ten squads of paw to shuttle down and you're coming down with me the instant we're there."

"Aye, sir." After thirty seconds, he spoke again. "Shuttles away. They ask if they should wait for you to get there to being searching?"

"No. Begin immediately. I'll be down in one minute." Fettuary sprinted off the bridge.

Arriving on the planet, Fettuary took control of his troops.

"Squads one and two, sweep to the right. Three and four, move left. Five remain in place in case this is an ambush. The rest with me. Chief Engineer, I want the exact location, and I want it now."

"This way." The engineer pointed, and the dogs headed out. "It's in this building, sir," the engineer said, swinging his detector around. "Third, possibly fourth floor."

Fettuary tomahawked his paw overhead. "*Go!*"

The fifty-odd Adamant barreled into the Retirement and Post-Life Planning Division's headquarters. The staff was surprised. A receptionist in the lobby rose to ask if she could help but was knocked down by the rush of soldiers. The team split into two packs. One exited the stairs on the third floor, the other on the fourth. Fettuary went with the third-floor pack because he was not in the best of physical condition.

"Where?" he demanded as they fanned out on the third floor, also full of surprised and now frightened employees.

"That room."

Fettuary marched over and threw the door open. The storage closet was empty but for three things. One was a small transmitter. He whipped out his pistol and destroyed it. He then stepped over to the other two items in the room. One was a note on the floor. The other was a very large bowl filled with water. He read the note.

Hunting me down is thirsty work. Help yourselves to the refreshment. On my honor as a traitor and a spy, it's safe to drink. Honestly.

Hopefully Your New BFF,
Me.

The note was written by Garustfulous so that its authenticity might further infuriate whomever read it.

Fettuary hauled his leg back and kicked the bowl as hard as he could. That was how he came to discover that it was bolted to the floor.

Back on the bridge of *Eternal Triumph*, Fettuary

limped to the captain's chair and sat down in a snit. "Status?"

"After you destroyed the transmitter, the signal switched to a new origin."

Fettuary ran his paw over his muzzle in disgust. "Where to now?"

"It's coming from a resupply ship. *R&R 5011-A* stationed... wow ... not in the middle of nowhere, but it's very close."

"If your humor is complete, take us all there. I can handle an R&R ship."

"Sir?"

"Never mind, just get this bucket moving."

———————

"Listen up, pup. I'm going to say this *one ... more ... time.* If you do not tell me where you and your black-marketeer pals hid those shuttles, I'll come there and personally remove your testicles one at a time."

"But I only have two, master."

Somewhere along the protracted browbeating, Garustfulous had got Aporthio to address him as *master.* He did so because he very much liked the sound of someone calling him *master.*

"Then it won't take me very long, will it?"

"N ... no, master, sir. I ... wait. A whole bunch of ships just entered real space not a thousand meters all around me. W ... what should I do? I ... I think most are prowl ships, master."

"Ah, here's the easy part. All you have to do now is die. That is really quite—"

Poor, unfortunate Aporthio never heard Garustfulous say *"simple."*

"*R&R 5011-A* destroyed, captain."

"They can do one thing right," sniped Fettuary.

"Sir?"

"Nothing. Status of incursion?"

"Transmission is now coming from ... belay that. The signal has ended."

"Where was it originating? Please tell me you were able to find our next rabbit hole?"

"Yes, sir. It," he tapped a few more keys, "came from the rocky remains of a planet near the periphery of the galaxy."

The communications engineer glanced up quickly to see the aghast look on Fettuary's face.

"No, sir, not *that* periphery. The periphery *next* to that one."

"Take us on another wild-hare chase," Fettuary said, gesturing forward.

The grouping of ships materialized over what little was left of Earth.

"Scan of the surface shows nothing there aside from naturally occurring rocks and debris."

"Naturally," Fettuary said. His palm covered his mouth.

"Wait, I stand corrected again. There is a small metal box down there."

Fettuary bolted upright. "The transmitter?"

"No, sir. There's no energy signature. It's just a metal box."

"A bomb? A booby trap?"

"No, Whole. Just a metal box. No signs of any energy. Even a simple explosive would require a power source."

"Send someone down to fetch it."

Ten minutes later, an Adamant in a white lab coat

entered the bridge holding out a small metal box. "We've scanned it, sir. There appears to be something organic in it, but we're uncertain."

"Did you x-ray it?"

He squinted at him like *Duh, engineer here. Can't you see my white lab coat?* "Of course, sir. The box is lead-lined."

"So you couldn't see in it?"

"That's generally why you line a box with lead, sir."

Fettuary turned the simple latch and lifted the lid. After he opened his eyes, he saw two things. The first was a note. The second was a meaty thigh bone. Fettuary lifted the note.

Hunting me down is powerfully hungry work. I got you a snack. This time, please believe this treacherous covert agent bent on the destruction of my mother empire that it's just a sheep's thigh bone. It is delicious, not poisoned, and it's good for you.

BFF,

Me

Fettuary closed his eyes and tossed the bone over his shoulder. When it struck the floor, the fulminate of mercury blasting cap detonated, setting off the C4 that was tightly packed into the marrow cavity. Shielan couldn't pack all that much C4 into a thigh bone, but it was more than enough to blow all the walls of the bridge outward and kill all crew present.

In retrospect, Fettuary should have been a more questioning individual.

THIRTY-FIVE

"So, what'd you get?" I asked Toño with all the excitement of a kid at Christmas.

"A lot."

"That's it? A lot? Pass the cream. I'll be in the kitchen if you need me."

"You are *so* dramatic," said Sapale. "Is that ever going to change? Can we who suffer beside you hold out any irrational hope?"

I shook my head briskly. "Best not to."

"I've transferred everything to Al and *Blessing*. They are better equipped to collate and analyze the mountain of data we stole." His eyes gleamed like a kid who'd snatched the cookie jar and taken it to his tree house. "We really got a lot."

"I know. You said that. Could you give us, say, an *example?*"

"The Adamant currently know of almost twenty-five hundred local military commanders who have assumed singular power of their regions."

"*That* is juicy," said Jonnaha.

"They count no fewer than fifty-three new *emperors.*

Not one of them is remotely related to any of the approved bloodlines or houses."

"That is positively *salacious*," added Jonnaha.

"Isn't it though?" he beamed.

"Do they think any of these *usurpers* can actually hold their claims once the genuine central authority reestablishes itself?" Garustfulous asked very seriously.

Toño bobbed his head side to side. "Hard to say. As you know, the Secure Council and high appointments are drawn normally from the very pool of officers who've declared themselves to be the new potentates. Anyone who self-selects to be a member of the 'legitimate' council, for example, would be both low-ranking *and* immediately suspected as a power grabber himself."

"This is wonderful news," responded Jonnaha. "We can actually wish bad luck on our enemies and see it come to life." She giggled like a schoolgirl. Funny, I'd known her a while, and I'd never seen her do that.

"I think you guys did a bang-up job. But I'm pretty sure you made your plan too complex and had way too much fun pulling it off," Sapale said in an even tone.

"No way," I protested. "Every wrinkle added to Adamant confusion. That slowed them down almost certainly."

"The bowl of water? That was a *necessary* addition?"

"Yeah, that was so cool. It was Shielan's idea." I pointed to her with both index fingers. "I told you we needed a wiseass like her along."

"She also came up with the idea of securing it to the floor," added Garustfulous. *"Brilliant."*

Sapale just rolled her eyes.

"With as much intelligence as you extracted, Dr. DeJesus, I'm certain we can really stick it to the Adamant." Jonnaha was speaking in her formal voice all of a sudden. Huh?

"Please, Prime Minister. I've asked you to call me Toño. Everybody else does."

"Oh, very well, *Toño*, but only if you do me the honor of addressing me as Jonnaha."

"It will be my greatest pleasure."

Were these guys doing a play together and practicing their lines? Weird-o-matic.

"So, how long's it going to take you to crunch all the data, Als?" I asked, knowing they'd hear me.

"Mmm. A few days, most likely. We don't want to miss a potentially important detail," replied Al.

"I anticipated as much," said Toño. "We're in no real hurry."

We weren't? That was news to me. *War* and *no hurry* could not properly be used in the same sentence.

"Well, if that's the case, you'll have to allow me the honor of arranging a state dinner for you, Toño."

Doc got a sour look. "I'm not much on formal bashes," he responded.

"Well, how about just the six of us then? Say tonight?"

Before he could answer, Sapale said, "Sorry. Count me out. I want to get back to Kalvarg and check on my peeps. I can't stop worrying when I'm away."

"If Mama says home," I pointed to her, "then it's home we go."

"*I'm* available," Garustfulous said excitedly.

"Yeah, right. You're going to show your sorry ass to the survivors of the population your buddies attacked," responded Sapale. "You'll end up being the main course."

"They're not my buddies," he tried to deflect.

"Try telling that to the angry mob with pitchforks and torches," I snarked.

"Well, then it'll be just the three of us," Jonnaha said with a triumphant smile. What was with *triumphant*?

"Noooo. Not gonna be the third wheel on that play cart. I'm outta here," Shielan said as she popped to her feet.

Jonnaha's finger flickered on the tabletop. "Well, Toño, if it's just the two of us, I fear rumors might spread that it's a *date*. You can take a rain check if you'd like."

This was getting crazy.

"Let the rumors be *damned*," he pronounced with Spanish flare. He sounded exactly how I thought Don Quixote talked. This was getting weirder by the syllable.

"My place at seven?"

"I'll have my bells on."

"You mean you'll be there with bells on, right, Doc?" I said, enormously confused.

"That, I believe, is what I just said."

"Whatever," I mumbled. Sapale was pulling my elbow, and we were exiting the room. In the hallway, I mumbled, "That was so *very* odd."

"You're a real piece of work, Ryan," she chastised quietly. "For the first time in forever, Toño has himself a girl, and you're all gobsmacked. You're so totally a guy."

I stopped and turned to her. "Doc's got a girlfriend?"

"You're *such* a dunce. Let's get home before someone sells you a bridge."

As I scuffed along, I muttered, "Doc's got a *girl?*"

Three days later, we were all back in Jonnaha's office. The Als had announced they were done reviewing the info dump we got from our little escapade. Shielan and Toño were already there when the three of us entered. I nearly fell flat on my face. Toño was on Jonnaha's side of the desk. They weren't quite touching, but if either moved, they probably would. I mean, Toño was more than a grown man at two billion, but I was so ill at ease seeing him up close and personal with a woman. Not sure why it bothered me, but I had to be forthcoming with my emotions. Sapale told me I had to work on that or I'd be in trouble.

Jonnaha rose, and Toño shot to his feet, too. "Welcome, you three. Please, sit wherever you'd like. I have a small buffet set up over there. Please help yourselves."

Garustfulous made a beeline for the snacks. He intended to be the first one there. He smelled bacon. When the issue was bacon, no one was going to get his. Theirs either. Couldn't say I blamed him.

Sapale and I plopped on the couch. I whispered to her, "I want to sit where Doc is. She said anywhere, right?"

She slapped my knee but couldn't help emitting a little snort.

"I'm sorry, Jon," inquired Shielan, who'd heard me plainly because she was right next to us. "What did you say?"

"I said I wanted to see like Doc did. You know, he can see all the papers on big sis's desk and we can't. Might be something interesting."

Shielan shot me an oversized toothy smile, indicating she'd nailed me.

"Look, you got us in trouble already, you boob," Sapale hissed playfully.

"I'm sorry, Sapale," Shielan pressed. "I couldn't quite hear that either."

Sapale grinned wickedly. "I said to Jon that you'd gone to the *trouble* of wearing a bra today and to look at your boobs."

Shielan nearly fell out of her chair laughing. Sapale kept her grin on the whole time.

"Is there something going on over there we need to know about?" Jonnaha asked sternly.

Toño waved a dismissive hand. "With those three,

you definitely do not want to ask. Perpetual juveniles, the lot of them."

"Not *me*," protested Garustfulous. "I'm an officer and an adult."

"And thank you for pointing that out," soothed Jonnaha.

"If you three have nothing better to do, perhaps we can get down to the business of stopping the Adamant onslaught?"

"Sounds like a plan to me," I said as seriously as I could, which wasn't very. "Als, chime in any time."

"We were waiting for the raging hormones of youth to settle on your part of the room."

"They're settled, mean computer," Shielan said loudly. "Proceed."

There was only silence in the air.

"Als, you may begin when ready. Security Chief Shielan will behave herself from this moment on."

"Would you like me to preface my discussion by stating the odds of that happening?"

"No."

"I thought not." He cleared his nonexistent throat, the big ham. "We have sent each of you a very long and detailed summary of what we learned. Since there's no way in hell the pilot will read that many consecutive words, I'll give *him* the *Reader's Digest* version. The rest of you can follow along or zone out."

"Al, please stop having so much fun at my expense. We're at war. People are dying, and not just from your poor attempts at humor. Pretend you're capable of adultlike behavior."

"If you two don't cut it out, I'll ground the both of you," Toño said firmly. I think he was joshing. Maybe.

"As you desire, Dr. DeJesus. I will abide by my creator's imperatives."

It was so funny. Sapale and I rolled our eyes at each other at the same time.

"The Adamant as a whole are basically at the same strength level they were at the end of TBOP. The aggregate number of warships and military personnel is roughly the same. The compelling difference today is how these forces are fractured. They have not launched a significant offensive of conquest since TBOP. One tiny distant system was assimilated a while back, but even it has been allowed to wander off on its own.

"All military operations are civil confrontations in nature. Most conflicts have been in space. We were stunned to learn that no new ship construction has taken place. Upon victory, the remaining enemy vessels are appropriated, so the winners see no net decline in their strength. But no party has assumed a production role in terms of the big warships.

"A few bold usurpers have led their forces into paws on the ground battles with their rivals. The ones we saw that were well documented were brutal by even Adamant standards. Paw soldiers, for example, are never taken prisoner. One either wins, or they all die. Clearly production of the organic components of war is easily maintained. The clone program we learned of a decade ago has been ramped up, as have mandatory pregnancies among all bitches of the proper age."

"And I'm *here* and not *there*," groused Garustfulous.

"Might I proceed, Wedge Leader?"

"Just saying. Bad timing on my part."

"Hmm?"

"Go ahead."

"Thank you. All in all, that's the overview of the Adamant of today."

"And no individual is close to assuming a role of true leadership?" asked Toño.

"We think not. Yes, there are three or four Wholes with far and away the largest stockpiles of war material. But those few hold each other in check so further increase of their spheres of influence is limited."

"But it's a stalemate, not a self-annihilation," I said sourly.

"At this point we feel that best describes the situation."

"Do you see a practical way to accelerate the destabilization?" asked Garustfulous.

"We lack specific proposals."

"If you think of something let us know," I replied. "But that is really our job, not yours."

"And do you, General Ryan, have anything in mind?" asked Jonnaha.

"Nah. Not yet."

"T, how about you, dear?" she asked the guy sitting next to her. *T? Dear?* I was getting that queasy feeling again.

"Honestly, no, but I'm eternally optimistic."

"Well, if there's nothing more to discuss, I suppose we can end this meeting."

"But I'm not done," said a muffled Garustfulous, his mouth stuffed with food.

"Oh, sorry. What would you like to say?" she invited.

"No." He pumped a finger over a shoulder to the buffet. "I'm not *done*."

THIRTY-SIX

Quildrod stared out the transparent wall of his flagship into starry space. His fingers slowly massaged either end of his muzzle. He was pondering the present, and he was pondering the future. He'd been the most successful suitor to date for the throne of the Adamant. But he was no closer at that moment than he had been two months prior. He was facing the real threat of an entrenched, drawn-out civil war with any number of powerful rivals. That would never do. He needed to consolidate more power to his iron paw. If he wasn't advancing his dominion, he was surely losing it.

He was chafed by the relative neglect he received from the public at large for his claim to the empire. In his wildest dreams, he'd envisioned cheering masses swarming to his flag, thanking him for his service to them, the worthless peons. But the fools did not. Those with no greater purpose in life than providing him with cannon fodder failed to accept his rightful rule.

Quildrod never expected to win his subjects' hearts and minds with his magnanimity and personal charm. No, he preferred to suck their souls dry by means of fear, unpredictable cruelty, and intimidation. To date, however, those had not produced sufficient results. Splinter groups were forming like a dynamited tree. Those he controlled were permanently his without much additional application of suffering. But those beyond his ever-reaching grasp were tending to remain there. They suffered the yoke of some other despot, but they were not gravitating toward the true emperor, Quildrod I.

He was startled by a knock on his door. He turned back to his desk and increased the dim lights. "Come."

His chamberlain entered with a tray. Dosandonts kept his neck craned down as he walked. He'd thought of that tribute himself. There was actually no one left to ask how a proper chamberlain attended his emperor.

"I bid you good afternoon, My Imperial Lord," he said softly as he set down the tray and began transferring its contents onto the desk. When the food and drink were in their preordained locations, he spread out the report sheet for Quildrod to read. In an inexplicable throwback to times long forgotten, the dog who would be emperor demanded to read physical, paper reports as opposed to digital ones.

"Anything in there that will displease me greatly, Dosandonts?" he said, tapping the front page.

"Hopefully not very much, lord. I think it's all pretty much the same equivocal news of yesterday and the day before that one."

"So then it's bad news."

"I shall wait to see what opinion you form, sir. Please do let me know your thoughts so that I might serve you better."

Quildrod eyed his servant dubiously. "You sure use five big words when one small one would do just fine, don't you?"

"If I do, it is only to be devoutly clear in my

communications with one as lofty as you, My Imperial Lord." He bowed deeply.

"Is Dorcilmas here yet? His ship was due to rendezvous with us an hour ago."

"*Pride of the Empire* has arrived. I think Master Dorcilmas is en route as we speak."

That drew the chamberlain a second askance look. "*Master* Dorcilmas? What is he master of? He's a *whole* in my service, nothing more."

Dosandonts's left paw began to tremble. He prayed Quildrod did not take note of it. "Is that what I referred to him as? Silly old hound dog. Little connection remains between my brain and my vocal cords, it would seem."

The pseudo-emperor scowled. "So it would seem." He pointed to the pot. "You may pour my tea and then leave me. I have a lot to do."

Dosandonts was already finished pouring before Quildrod finished speaking.

"As you wish, lord. Shall I place some biscuits on a plate for you?"

"Do I look like a bitch to you?" He sipped his tea after his jab.

"No, My Imperial Lord."

"Then I shouldn't need a plate to do what a paw can." By way of demonstration, he seized two treats and swallowed them whole. "See, no plates required. Now leave me."

"Very well. Is there anything else I can get you before I leave?" the chamberlain asked as he stalled for seconds to pass.

"If there was, I'd have told ... told you, wouldn't I have?" He loosened the collar of his uniform jacket. "Say, there is. Could you t ... turn the heat down in thi ... th ... this—" Quildrod then muzzle-planted in his teacup. He was dead before his nose touched the liquid. The poison

Dosandonts had added to each item on the tray was that powerful. Thank the Mother of All that Master Dorcilmas was correct on that account. If Quildrod had much warning to his impending demise, he'd have had time to shoot his alliance-switching chamberlain.

THIRTY-SEVEN

Several weeks passed and I still hadn't come up with a plan. I was moderately annoyed at myself. I had access to a treasure trove of intel, but I couldn't noodle out how to put it to use. Maybe I was slipping at two billion? One morning, Toño asked me to meet him in Jonnaha's office. He specified that I should come alone. That didn't sound good, but I wasn't actually sure why.

When I entered, it was just Toño and Jonnaha. They were huddled together on the couch. I said *huddled* for a reason. They looked crowded together, and they looked concerned. Maybe frightened. Oh boy. We all knew by then they were a couple. So them being on the couch was no biggy, but it hit me hard how fearful they looked.

"What's up, you two crazy lovebirds? You guys don't look particularly *blissful* at this moment."

"We don't," said Doc softly. I wasn't sure if that was a statement or a question.

"We're not," clarified Jonnaha.

I sat on the couch's armrest. "What's the matter?"

"I was hoping you'd have come up with a Jon-plan by now," began Toño. "You know the type, ill-conceived,

504

unlikely to succeed, and a gut-wrencher for all concerned."

"I do have a knack."

"But you have not. Hence, I feel it is time to present *my* Jon-plan to you."

My heart sank. "Doc, you've never had a plan that bad in your very long life. You're scaring me."

"You and me both," added Jonnaha as she cradled his hands.

"Well, all is darkest and all. What is it?"

"I must surrender myself to the Adamant."

"Did not see that one coming." I punched myself right between the eyes. "Not in a million years."

"I was hoping to avoid the obvious, but I fear the longer we delay, the more likely it is the Adamant might reunify. Such a process would be devastating."

"Okay, not that I endorse that crazy-ass notion for a second, but ... so you turn yourself in. What's next?"

"I'm not entirely certain." He looked to the floor.

"Wow. I thought I was king of the ridiculous plan. You got me here, Toño. In fact, you win by a country mile. You turn yourself in, they begin torturing you like it's a new kind of liver treat, and you got nothing?" I shook my head in confusion.

"At least if I'm back on the inside, I might be able to do something to affect some change."

"Doc, seriously. What? You going to cook the books and get every Adamant arrested for tax evasion?"

"I did have access to many files and systems at times. Armed with the necessity to act, I think I could do some useful damage."

"It's your fault, Ryan," said Jonnaha, tearful. Before I could even look confused, she went on. "If you'd come up with a better plan, my Tony wouldn't have to sacrifice himself like a Vestal Virgin."

Tony? No one ever called him *Tony*. And *Vestal Virgins?* No way they knew about those.

"Please, love, you're being too harsh with him. It isn't his intention to *not* save the day yet again."

I was thinking about vodka, lots of vodka.

"How about this? Let me see if I can't at least hatch a plan that incorporates your willingness to be recaptured."

"Recaptured? Why would that be necessary?"

"Because if you walk up to them with your wrists already in handcuffs, I think they'd be kind of suspicious."

"I can see your point."

"Give me a few days. Oh, and whatever I come up with, I'm going to need to know something. What is their greatest weakness? Their *most* exposed Achilles heel?"

"Do you mean militarily?"

"No, I mean the biggest bang-per-buck weakness whatever and wherever it might be."

"Well, that might be the sabotage linchpin I interlaced throughout their entire civilization."

I bobbed my head slowly. "Yeah, that might do." *Way to go, Doc.*

A week later Toño, Garustfulous, and I filed quietly out of *Stingray* into the cool predawn air of Azsuram. Garustfulous and I were armed to the teeth. Toño thought we looked silly. He carried a single plasma rifle and a couple thermite grenades. I might have leaned toward the overdramatic, but that was better than being underpowered. Naturally, Garustfulous sided with me. It took Doc a full day to configure the weapons and battle gear to fit our canovir accomplice. But in the end, he looked almost as impressively dangerous as I did.

We had a straightforward plan. We would try to

locate any Kaljaxians or other non-Adamant and rescue them. To that end, Sapale remained behind in the vortex. If and when we delivered survivors, she could get them to safety and watch over them. She could also fly away if we three were killed or captured. It was likely we would find stragglers left alive. Since the ferocious battles from when EJ was active here, the combat on Azsuram was all but gone. Especially after the destruction of the central government, no one who wielded power wanted to waste it hunting down and subduing locals. They all had bigger fish to fry.

Garustfulous was not my choice for a teammate on this mission, but he whined and whimpered so much that I finally caved. He did have a point that in certain sets of contingencies, his ability to appear to have captured us might prove useful. At least by that point, I trusted him enough to not shoot me in the back the first chance he got. For all our issues and reciprocal misgivings, we were family. Distant family to be certain, but there was really no way around our tight bond by then.

Clearly the endgame was to have Toño captured and identified. When Toño fell into Adamant hands, we had to be very convincing in our efforts to fake trying to save him. The obvious flaw in the raid was that the Adamant didn't get a copy of the script. They might get lucky and kill all three of us. Toño insisted on making transfer backup copies just before we left. But dying sucked. And though Garustfulous was our fail-safe, what the hell were we going to back him into? Maybe a refrigerator—that way he could swallow up all the food he could hold. Personally, I wanted to avoid death, even though I knew I'd be right as rain and not even recall the deed a day later when I attended my own funeral service.

We formed a line. I took point, Garustfulous was rear guard, and Toño was tucked into the middle. Our Sensors suggested that a small grouping of Kaljaxians were located in a ravine a long way out of a small city. They were our target. I couldn't help but think back. The place they were holed up was a favorite camping spot for JJ and me when he was a teen. We'd spend quality guy-time there, spitting, peeing wherever we so desired, and hillbilly hunting. That kind of hunting was simple and easy. If it moved, we shot it. Only when we got to the carcass did we determine if we wanted to eat whatever the heck it was. Great memories two billion years old. I had to force them from my mind. If I lost focus on a mission, it could end badly.

A couple klicks into the ravine, Toño and I heard voices. Around that time, Garustfulous smelled the speakers. Definitely not Adamant. He was certain. It was safe to make contact, but I really didn't want them shooting at us before I could explain our humanitarian intentions.

We crawled to the edge of the clearing. The Kaljaxians sat near a cave opening. A small fire just inside the cave tried to break the morning chill. Some small containers were on top of the flames.

I switched my vocal output to sound like an older Kaljaxian male, and I hissed in Hirn, "We are friends. Don't shoot."

They reacted in a trained manner. The women surrounded the small ones and ushered them toward the cave. The men grabbed weapons and made for cover. They did not concentrate on where my voice had come from. An ambush might be afoot. Poor SOBs had lived under the stress of war so long that they knew just what to do.

"Who's there?" a man hissed back in Hirn. "Show yourself."

"I'm Jon, brood-mate to Sapale. I've come to rescue you."

"That devil, Ryan? I thought we'd seen the last of you, you blight on Azsuram."

"No, I'm his brother. Sapale is back at the ship. Come and I'll show you."

"No problem. Let me just huddle together the only things that matter in this world and march them off to where the evil magician want them to be. I'm neither that stupid *nor* that desperate."

"Then you come alone. I will leave my man as hostage, and you can speak directly with Sapale."

He was quiet. I'd made a reasonable offer.

"I will approach you. As I do, show yourself."

He did, and we came face-to-face with a shrub between us.

"You're a Ryan, that's for certain. Where's my hostage?"

I snapped my fingers at Garustfulous. As he labored to his hind feet, he protested. "I just knew it'd be me, now didn't I?"

The Kaljaxian jumped backward and raised his weapon.

"It's all right. He's on our side. Keep a gun to his head if you'd like, but please don't kill him accidentally. Can you promise me that?"

He shrugged one shoulder. "Maybe."

"Good enough for me."

"But not for *me*," squealed Garustfulous.

I'm Nardoel," he said, holding out a hand.

"Jon Ryan. This way." I gestured over a shoulder. "About two klicks."

Nardoel turned to the nearest guy. "I should be back in ten. If I'm not back in twenty, shoot him and run."

The other Kaljaxian nodded silently.

Nardoel and I jogged away. Just over five minutes later, Sapale returned with us and escorted the overjoyed Kaljaxians away. We saved eleven souls in one quick act. Nice. Based on information Nardoel supplied, Sapale led a short raid farther along the ravine to bring home another small group. In half an hour, she was back with ten additional Kaljaxians, all smiling ear to ear. She went on a longer foray, netting twenty-five more locals, making her as proud as a new mama of twins.

While she was away, I spoke with Nardoel in detail about where the Adamant were dug in. Picking up stragglers was tremendously satisfying, especially watching them eat once they were aboard. But we had a larger mission and needed to proceed. By the time Sapale returned, she read it in my eyes. Good deed efforts were over. Time to get to work. It was so miraculous to live with a person you didn't even need to speak to in order to be fully understood.

After Sapale had herded the assembly toward the back of the cube, I gave her the updated plan. "The Adamant are in that direction about ten klicks out in pretty good numbers. We'll head that way. We hope we can trick them into finding us and taking Toño as a prisoner. But, you know that's probably the only way it's going down."

"Toño, you, and I will be connected the whole time, so I'll know what's going on."

I placed a finger under her cute-as-a-button nose. "No matter what happens, you do *not* rescue any of us. You got that?"

"Didn't we go over that a million times already?"

"Yes, but I know you too well. If Toño's taken prisoner, you know what to do. If Garustfulous and I are taken out, let it go. Get these people to safety."

"I will. I won't like it, but I will."

I slapped her on the butt and marched away with my two paladins.

"Be safe," she called after us. Then I heard the cube hull seal.

In no time, we were above a small encampment of maybe a few hundred soldiers. We were a dozen meters higher up the hill than their camp. A small stream on the other side was probably why they stationed themselves so close to the hill. It wasn't the most defensible place to pound down stakes, but neither was being too close to running water during the rainy season.

"Garustfulous, we'll use you. Toño and I will get fifty meters ahead of you along that trail. Once we're in position, you stand up and call for help, running down to the aliens or whatever floats your boat. Toño and I will split up there." I pointed to a fork in the path a kilometer away. "You take two soldiers and follow Toño. You got that? You and two others. Send the rest after me. Tell them I'm Jon Ryan. Everyone should go after me." I spoke to Doc with intense focus. "Toño, you have *two* assignments. Let them *catch* you, but don't let them *hurt* you. You clear?"

"Yes," he replied.

"Okay, let's go," I announced.

We jogged up the dirt path.

I waved to Garustfulous when we were in position.

Garustfulous fired a volley to our right. He turned to the camp and yelled, "Soldiers of Paw, I need one squad!"

He started running after us without waiting to see if his order was being followed. Why would he? These guys were Adamant.

When we hit the fork, I took a knee and checked behind. Garustfulous and twelve hounds were bounding up the trail. They were a minute and a half away.

I pointed to the easier fork. "Go. And Toño, *vaya con Dios*."

"You, too, my old friend."

We both sprinted away.

A minute later, ten Adamant were closing rapidly on me, yelping and snapping after me with primal abandon. Garustfulous and Toño were out of view.

I picked up pace to draw the larger contingent even farther away from Toño. I think they noticed when I began putting space between us because they stopped barking and picked up their pace. They were all in. As I crested the hill, I spied a small clearing nearby. I made for it. Instead of entering the open area, I swung around the outer perimeter and took up a spot at the widest expanse of the clearing. I raised my rifle and waited.

Ten seconds later, the eleven soldiers flashed past the center of the trap. I picked them off from the lead dog back one by one. That way, the dogs in the rear crashed into the fallen dogs and didn't have time to rise and return fire. It was over in three seconds.

I sprinted back to the fork and stopped. I couldn't hear a thing. I ran the way Toño had, but I did so carefully. Last thing I wanted was to crash into them returning after Toño was captured. Two klicks in, I heard them coming. Garustfulous was shouting out orders and berating his two soldiers. Good boy. He was letting me know exactly where he was.

I cut through the brush fifty meters up slope and took cover. When the four were right below me, I planted a blast right between Garustfulous's feet. He hopped back instinctively and searched the hill for me.

"There, it's the demon Ryan. I'll catch that one just like I did this one. You two imbeciles take this prisoner back to camp. If you've injured him, I will have you skin each other alive. Is that clear?" They verified that such a vivid, creative punishment was abundantly clear to them. An added advantage of Garustfulous browbeating the two soldiers was that neither objected to his departure, uphill, against the famed Jon Ryan. I bet they even whispered a prayer for me under their breaths.

Just the other side of the top, I sat down and waited for Garustfulous. He shot past me, but quickly realized he had and crouched down, crawling his way back to me.

"How'd it go?" I asked.

"As well as we could have hoped for. Toño took cover behind some rocks, and then his rifle jammed or something. Darnedest thing, wouldn't you know? I rushed his position and forced him to the ground. The other two actually cheered my bravery."

"That was before you lit into them and wouldn't shut up. I'll bet a month's pay."

"Yes, but it was quite the ego-building moment, and I enjoyed it immensely." He smiled big.

"Well, let's get back to *Stingray* and move to part B of the plan."

He furrowed his brow. "What was part B again?"

"Thin, marginally feasible, and all I could come up with."

"Ah, yes, a Ryan-plan."

"No, a *Jon*-plan. Those are the least dependable kind of all."

THIRTY-EIGHT

"Take him outside and shoot him." Pack Guide Second Grade Diviltoy could not be less interested in or more bothered by his troop's interruption. He was a busy dog. He had columns of numbers to check, double check, and reauthenticate. He could not be bothered by starving locals' attempts to steal military supplies. "Above Packlet, I'm about to look up from my work. If I see you three standing there, I'll summon an *alternative* firing squad. They will shoot all of *you*."

"B ... but, sir, I wish to make clear what I said. I do not think he's a local."

Diviltoy slammed down his pencil hard enough to splinter it. He glowered at the soldier, then the prisoner, and then back at the soldier. "He looks like one to me. He's missing a couple of eyes, but he's a local. Probably lost the other pair in an idiotic wager. Now will you *please* execute him? Pretty please?"

"There was something else, s ... sir."

"He kissed you, and you felt all warm and fuzzy? Now you can't harm a hair on his tail?"

"No, sir. It's that—"

"Did I ask you to tell me what it was a mental midget like you thinks was notable about yet another local trying to steal my supplies?"

"I don't think he respects your opinion," Toño said matter-of-factly to Alouyso, the soldier trying to make his thoughts known.

"Another party whose opinion I do not value," hissed Diviltoy. He pointed a paw at his desktop. "This paperwork is not going to do itself. Why do you hound me?"

Toño angled his head toward Alouyso. "He might hound you, but I cannot. I'm human."

Diviltoy snapped the replacement pencil he'd picked up. "A what? Never heard of them. You're a local mutant of that other planet." He popped his claws on the wooden desk. "What was it called? Ah, Kaljax. Yes, you're a mutant of one of those mutants."

"No, you moron, I am not. Kaljaxians have four eyes, as even an Above Packlet knows. They have coarser hair and much less of it. They also stand nearly two meters less on ave—"

"Silence, Kaljaxian scum. When I want an anatomy course, I'll sign up for one online. Now all three of you out. Two of you shoot one of you. I don't care what combination it is at this point. You decide among yourselves."

"I demand the right of valtoc," said Toño.

"He demands valtoc, Pack Guide Second Grade Diviltoy," parroted Alouyso.

"I heard him. He has no rights, so he cannot invoke valtoc."

"My impression," began Brimforth, the other soldier, "is that valtoc can be requested by anyone at any time. It is one of our most sacred—"

"Do not lecture me on quaint old customs. I neither respect them nor you."

"Sir, if it were to get out that you denied a person valtoc, well, it might impinge on your otherwise stellar career prospects."

That did catch Diviltoy's full attention. Inept soldiers were one thing, but a career path was all there was in this sad world.

"Where did you hear of valtoc, Kaljaxian scum?" he challenged.

"I read it in a book."

The guards snickered.

"Does it matter?" pressed Toño.

"No, I suppose it doesn't. What aspect of valtoc do you claim as a right? And please be brief."

"Valtoc means *to be heard*. I want this pup to be heard. That is all."

"That's just wrong," replied Diviltoy. "Valtoc applies to oneself. It is not transferable."

"I am a prisoner about to be shot. He wishes to tell you something. Perhaps what he says will remove my name from the execution list."

"See, he asks for valtoc for himself," agreed Alouyso. He was so rarely given affirmation that he was emboldened to speak his mind.

"There is no list that you mention," responded Diviltoy.

"I was speaking metaphorically."

"He was using metaphor, sir."

"I heard the Kaljaxian infiltrator, you fool. Very well, if I'm ever to return to this report, Above Packlet whatever your name is, *valtoc* for this alien."

"Well, sir, we were chasing him down, Packlet Brimforth and me. Well, and the wedge leader whose name I never caught. Anyway—"

"*What.* There was a *wedge* leader involved, and you failed to mention that fact to me?"

"You wouldn't allow me to speak, I remind you, sir."

"Where is this wedge leader so that I might honor him and offer him refreshments?" Diviltoy stood.

"I don't know for certain, but I believe he's dead."

"Wh ... wh ... *what*?"

"After Brimy and I snagged this one, the wedge leader charged over the hill in pursuit of Jon Ryan."

Diviltoy's knees buckled, and he sat back down involuntarily. "Jon Ryan is here? Are you certain?"

"Positive. The wedge leader said it was so."

"And wh ... where is Ryan now?"

"After he killed the other eleven soldiers and the wedge leader?"

"I suppose."

"No idea, sir. Sort of glad it isn't here though, if you take my meaning."

"No disrespect, Above Packlet, but is there a manner in which this story can be told more succinctly?" asked Toño with a slight bow.

"Sure. So Brimy and I run this guy down. As we do, I grabbed his ankles so he fell forward. He dropped his gun when he hit the ground. Well, I'm above him as he stands up, and I smack him one hard across the mouth."

"Fascinating," interrupted Diviltoy.

Alouyso swaggered in place. "You think so, sir?"

"Yes. It's fascinating you thought this story was worth wasting my time to hear. You are *significantly* mentally challenged, Above Packlet."

Deflated but not deterred, Alouyso proceeded. "It's when I hit him. Don't you see? It didn't faze him. His head didn't even move."

"So *you're* weak while *he's* strong. Why is that so important?"

"I'm not, and he can't be that much so."

"You're giving me a headache. Final summary, wrap it up, stick a fork in it because it's done. *What* is your point?"

"I think he's one of those robots, sir."

"You do?"

"Yes, I do. Brimy's fairly certain himself, aren't you?"

Brimforth nodded and shrugged his shoulders at the same time.

"If I get a scanning crew in here and prove you two are complete imbeciles, will you then please shoot him and leave me alone?"

"Er, no, sir."

"What?"

"We'd leave you alone and then shoot him. Otherwise we'd be shooting him in here. That'd be both—"

"Stop saying words," Diviltoy howled. He snatched up his comm link. "I want a full scanning crew in my office on the double. No, make it on the triple." He set the device back on his belt. "I should have them scan me, too, for lending so much credence to the delusions of lunatics."

Toño's blindfold was removed in a dark metallic cavern. He was completely disoriented. He stepped forward instinctively. The chains restraining him pulled soundly at his arms and legs, jerking Toño back from the little advance he'd managed.

Oh joy. The plan was working like a charm so far.

Momentarily, he heard the sound of a massive metal door creak open, then shut. Once closed, several bolts squealed in protest as they were thrown shut. Then the odd scraping of someone walking with one foot dragging approached from far off to one side. That's when Toño noted the stench. Mold, decay, and death. Oh, how he hated Jon Ryan right about then.

A crumpled Adamant in a dingy white lab coat staggered into view.

"Can't you afford to oil those door hinges?" Toño called out by way of greeting.

A sick, mocking chuckle came from the crippled figure who grew closer.

"Ah, Dr. Toño DeJesus, such the bold and defiant one still." He coughed a few times.

"I hope you do not seek medical attention. That cough sounds bad."

"I cherish you once again, my old friend." More cackles of laughter followed by yet more coughing came from the husk of a hound. "I doubt you remember me, good doctor, but you and I are the oldest of acquaintances. Yes, it is so. I was one of your keepers back in Section One. In fact, you murdered one of my brightest students when you destroyed that sector of space."

"I killed no one. Two Paws self-destructed a computer that started the exotic matter reaction."

"So," he wheezed and coughed harshly, "you say. It matters not. Perhaps things have turned out for the best."

"I can't imagine being happier."

"Me either," he scorned. "My new benefactor has already showered me with riches. He says that once I tame the Rabid Robot, my compensation will rival that of the gods. I don't mind interrupting my retirement for such wealth."

"Who are you, rich dog?"

"Oh, excuse my horrible manners. As I said, you were never in a state to remember me when we worked together. I am Parnific, chief scientist to the now Interim Emperor Dorcilmas."

"Never heard of either of you."

"Little wonder. While you were still our guest, he was a military officer of but modest stature."

"And now he's an interim *emperor* of modest stature."

"Ah, that wit of yours. It will be such a shame to snub out that flame, yet again. You see, once I have you attached to Emperor Dorcilmas's main computer banks, I'm afraid I will need to force you into cooperation again. Nothing will seem humorous to you then."

"Interim Emperor, please. Don't get ahead of ourselves."

"Right you are," he said through coughs. "You have always been so right about things." Parnific was fumbling with large computer connectors as he spoke. "Once it is known that Dorcilmas possesses the unlimited power of the Rabid Robot, his ascendancy to *true* emperor will occur quick enough."

"You give me too much credit, Parnific."

"No false modesty allowed in this cavern, DeJesus. It was *you* who allowed the Adamant to seize the galaxy in our jaws and shake the life out of it."

"That figurative murder is yet to be revived. One of your main character flaws is getting ahead of yourself, isn't it?"

"*One of?* Do you speculate I have others?"

"I'm certain you're crippled by countless imperfections."

"Those words must remain our little secret, but you are correct. I have more faults than there are stars in the night sky. Do you know which one troubles me the most?"

"I'm certain I couldn't fathom that depth."

"None, you wicked machine. I cherish all my moral deficiencies. Each one is more precious to me than the next." He coughed mightily. "But enough idle chatter and gossiping between two old friends."

He attached several cables to Toño. Given his age, incapacity, and the bulk of the cables, it took Parnific several minutes to do so.

"There. I think that should suffice. Shall we test my handiwork?"

Toño began trembling. "Aren't you going to ask me a question, challenge me to cooperate before you begin torturing me?"

Parnific smiled widely. "No." He threw a switch and sparks began to dance around Toño's head. He started convulsing.

Though Toño should not have been aware of the passage of time, a week later Parnific returned to his testing area and turned the electronic assault off. Toño immediately slumped limply in his restraints. Parnific picked up a small probe and came over to the motionless prisoner. He set the probe on one side of Toño's head.

"This should do the trick," he said aloud as he depressed a master switch.

The probe buzzed. Toño slowly began to regain consciousness.

"There's a good puppet," sniped Parnific. "One more dose should cure the patient of his mental cobwebs." He re-zapped Toño with the probe.

"Where am I?" Toño whispered weakly.

"Nowhere, I assure you. You are absolutely nowhere. And here you will remain. But I have pressing business and no time for the orientation of my tools. I will ask a simple yet vexing question that has escaped my ability to solve. Is that all right with you?"

"N ... no."

"Be that as it may. Here is what I shall pose to you. I wish to modulate the quantum field in the proximity of a primal node in a Salfax pathway. My attempts so far have been successful only at low energy levels. As the power in the system approaches any real-world application, the quantum field degenerates into chaos. This disallows regulation of the node. The pathway quickly turns into random fluctuations and not the usable collinear beam I require. What do you suggest I try?"

"Dying slowly, painfully, and unlamented."

"Very droll. I want an answer in ten seconds or the torture recommences."

"Have you tried turning it off and then turning it back on again?"

"That banter forfeits your ten second grace period." Parnific tapped the master switch. He turned his back to Toño and staggered away.

"If you recoupled the phase transition stabilizers to match the nodal resonant frequencies, your Salfax beam should remain coherent," announced Toño, sounding very coherent.

Parnific spun on a heel. "What?" He rushed as well as he could to the master switch and tapped it several times.

"Recouple the phase elements, you moron," replied Toño, who was beginning to laugh.

Parnific began pounding on the switch. "What have you done, demon?"

"I hope much more than enough," he responded.

All the lights went off with a bang. The ubiquitous sound of computers, air circulators, and pulsing exotic matter ended.

"What have you done?" howled Parnific. "I can't see a thing."

That was right about when the exotic matter reserve containment field's power supply cut out for the last time. The walls began quaking. What Parnific called his cavern was in reality a modest hangar on the warship Interim Emperor Dorcilmas had appropriated from Interim

Emperor Quildrod. Dorcilmas had renamed it *Perpetual Triumph*, which, ironically, it would never experience.

"I can't see," wailed a hysterical Parnific.

A tiny candle appeared next to his face. It was held in the talons of a golden dragon.

"Does this help?" Mirraya-Slapgren asked, passing Parnific the flame.

"You took your *time*," said Toño without any real vitriol.

"A dramatic entrance is always a must, my good doctor. Remember who my teacher was."

"Really," he replied as he released the last of his shackles. "I just hope it doesn't preclude a dramatic *exit*."

Mirraya-Slapgren picked up Toño and spread her wings.

"Don't I get to ride on your back?" he asked.

"Not in this lifetime, bucko."

And they vanished.

THIRTY-NINE

Jonnaha was dozing on the couch with her head on her sister's shoulder when Mirraya-Slapgren materialized atop the desk.

"whoa, sis, I think you'll want to wake up now," Shielan said, shaking her.

"Huh ... wa ... *Toño*," she exclaimed as she bolted for him open-armed.

Mirraya-Slapgren gently set Toño on his feet just in time for the not-so-young lovers to bind together in a passionate embrace. The golden dragon then hopped to the floor.

"How'd it go, kiddos?" I asked, stepping over to give them a cautious hug.

"No problem at all, Uncle. It went off just like we planned it," she replied.

"We planned it?" I responded. "Why didn't anybody tell me about this?"

"*So* not funny," sniped Sapale as she elbowed past me to hug Mirraya-Slapgren. "You guys are *so* brave, and I'm *so* proud of you."

"Are you all right?" Jonnaha asked Toño as she inspected him carefully.

"Yes, good as new."

"First he gets used to the torture," I wagged my eyebrows, "then he starts *begging* for it."

"You're disgusting, old friend," replied Toño. "Irrevocably and interminably revolting."

"Why, thank you. I can own that."

"Yeah, and I have to live with it," responded Sapale.

"I helped, you know? I think I was integral to the success of our plan," injected Garustfulous with a paw in the air.

"Yes, you did," I cooed. "Good boy. Come here, and I'll give you a belly rub."

"Promises, promises," he replied, adding in an obscene gesture popular among the Adamant.

"Okay, everybody *sit*," Jonnaha said authoritatively. "Now that it's over, you have to tell us what the *hell* you did."

We hadn't given anyone who wasn't involved any details. The stakes were simply too high. If a spy or listening device betrayed any aspect of our scheme, it would be curtains for Doc. Plus we'd have lost our last and best shot at the Adamant Empire.

"Toño, as the key actor in my little play, why don't you do the honors?" I remarked, extending a hand to him.

"Your play? I'm but an *actor*?"

"Now, dear, don't lose focus. Sit and talk first. Then you can get all Spanish on Jon."

"Very well." His mood settled quickly. "It's really quite simple actually—"

Jonnaha set a loving hand on Toño's forearm. "Ah, Toño, I'm hoping to spend a very long time with you. We all know you're the smartest human ever. So, please don't *ever* begin another sentence with those words, okay?"

Everyone but Garustfulous chuckled. He was still having trouble with human humor.

"Of course, my love. Jon asked me a few weeks ago to think of the most critical aspect of Adamant society. That would be their technology. Without it, they are aggressive and organized, but their true power is in their technical superiority. The heart of that technology is, of course, exotic matter. It defines their ability to expand and conquer. No exotic matter, no Adamant Empire."

"But surely they haven't always had it. They've been successful without it, right?"

"Yes, but on a very limited, local scale. It was only with the immense power of exotic matter that they were able to become dominant. The key to exotic matter is that while it is very energetic, it also requires lots of energy to produce. That is the weak link I came up with."

"Not to get too technical—"

"That would be nice," said Shielan.

"Um, if a large amount of highly energetic charged particles pass through a device, exotic matter is created. The device is said to—"

Jonnaha cleared her throat loudly.

"The actual device is about the size and shape of a common flashlight. It has three important parts. There is a ring that contains two nuggets of exotic *metal*. This substance acts as a catalyst. It allows exotic matter to be produced for a net energy gain. The problem with getting exotic *metal* is it requires frightening amounts of energy to make it in the first place. In the flashlight-sized tube, there is also a pair of fins I called *generative fins*."

"What do they do?" asked Jonnaha.

"Nothing, but that's not what I got the Adamant to believe. I wanted them to focus on the fins as keys to their domination, not the metal."

"Doc," responded Shielan, "They have scientists. No way you could fool them."

"I thought not at first. But they are a species eager to follow, anxious to accept and please. It proved their undoing."

"You speak of us in the past tense, my friend," said Garustfulous. "They're still out there, er, right?"

"After a fashion."

Garustfulous narrowed his gaze. "What does that mean exactly?"

"In good time," Toño replied. "There was a third component to the exotic matter generators. It looked like a tiny lollipop."

"What did it do?" I asked.

"Nothing useful. Again, I convinced them it helped stabilize the imaginary complexity field, but it didn't do that."

"Because there is no such thing," I responded. "You're such a bullshitter."

He shrugged. "What it functioned as was a sabotage agent. It was a diode that could, when activated, sap a small amount of the passing energy, which caused the flashlight unit to melt."

"And the exotic matter nozzle became inactive?" asked Jonnaha.

"Yes, inactive when the entire exotic matter stream was liberated."

I placed my hands together then flew them apart. "*Badaboom.*"

"Oh my," she responded. "Are those nozzles common in Adamant technology?"

"They aren't *common*. They were *everywhere*. All the energy produced and used by the Adamant came from exotic matter," Toño said grimly.

"I can attest to that fact," said Garustfulous, sounding distant.

"I don't want to seem dense, but what are the implications of this corruption you performed?"

"The empire exists in two places. Outer space and on the surfaces of planets."

"All right," she agreed.

"To have explosive release of exotic matter aboard a starship would destroy the vessel ten times out of ten."

"You mean you just blew up all the Adamant ships?"

"Every one, everywhere. All space-based Adamant are dead."

"Seriously? Not all of them? That's not possible," said Shielan, incredulous.

"Every last one. That's why I had to be captured and joined to the master grid. It took several days, but I took advantage of a practice the Adamant employed. When any communication system makes contact with another, it automatically transfers any and all system updates."

"Yes, it's an efficiency trick we picked up along the way," added Garustfulous.

"I was able to distribute the signal to activate the sabotage circuits whenever any other went off. That was my last act before Mirraya-Slapgren rescued me."

"No, wait. You *can't* have done all that. You were being tortured." Jonnaha twirled her fingers around her head.

"That was our little surprise. I was able to place an AI interface between their input and my systems. It appeared as though I was being scrambled, but all the time I was working to corrupt their network."

"Incredible," whispered Garustfulous.

"And what about the canovir on planets? You didn't blow up those entire planets, did you?" asked Shielan.

"No, no. That wasn't necessary. But all their energy production, wherever it existed, is gone. Once the battery stores are exhausted, the canovir will have to fend for themselves."

"But there are local energy systems, aren't there?" asked Garustfulous.

"In some cases, but the larger the Adamant presence, the more insufficient those sources would be."

"So, sooner or later the surviving canovir will have to produce their own food and stay warm by rubbing sticks together to make a fire," I said smugly.

"But that pre-industrial production couldn't sustain —" Garustfulous began to say.

"More than a small and primitive society."

"That would then be at the mercy of whatever might be left of the population they had crushed under their boot heels," added Jonnaha.

"They'd be gone within a generation," declared Shielan.

"If they last that long," I said grimly.

"We're not very good at roughing it," mumbled Garustfulous. I think it was hitting him hard.

"The canovir will, by necessity, become either a hunting species again, or if they can manage it, a hunter-gatherer society."

"That, either way you look at it, makes them no longer a galactic power."

"But the exotic metal you mentioned. Couldn't some ground-based survivors make more of it and start exotic matter production back up?" asked Garustfulous. He sounded almost hopeful.

"No," replied Toño definitively. "They'd never have enough energy to produce it, not now. To reestablish their exotic matter production and become a renewed threat, they'd have to completely re-evolve as a society," Toño said with finality.

"And that, I can guarantee, is *never* going to happen." I meant to see to that fact. Never again on my watch.

EPILOGUE

And so it came to pass. Radioactive dust in one instant littered space throughout the Milky Way and into many nearby galaxies. Canovir on planets were forced to fend for themselves. In a handful of generations, the few that survived reverted to a wild pack species. None became successful farmers. It was not in their blood. Canovir retained sentience, but that tool became less useful than the ability to run down game and rip its life away. Reason faded as an important aspect of the canovir way of life. More importantly, so did memory. In no time at all, what occupied their minds was what the pack might kill that day. Recalling that they once ruled the heavens mattered little, not compared to the unknowable weather.

Toño DeJesus settled down and married Jonnaha. Both of them became truly happy for the first time in their lives. And, to mention the delicate yet essential aspect of human society, Toño's sperm level alert light hadn't come on as Jon's did years before. He did not tap into that resource at nearly the rate Jon had. So, along with having his lovely bride, Toño fathered a bountiful family.

Sapale and Jon split their time between Azsuram and

Kalvarg. They labored to resuscitate one creation of theirs while breathing life into another. They were never happier.

Mirraya and Slapgren lived full lives on Nocturnat among the Plezrite. In time, Mirraya became a master brindas with more disciples than there were grains of sand on the beach. Their offspring grew in number and blended in perfectly with their distant relatives.

Evil Jon and Cala lived begrudgingly together for decades. After she finally went the way of all flesh, EJ buried her in an elaborate earthen mausoleum. He remained on Rameeka Blue Green, never quite getting around to moving on. At every sunrise, he couldn't quite bring himself to leave Calfada-Joric alone, or the vases at her resting place without fresh flowers.

Garustfulous followed Jon wherever he went. While it would be cruel to compare him to a loyal hound following his master, it would also be an easy enough mistake to regard him as such. The only time he was apart from Jon was when Garustfulous went on one of his "cultural missions." He wanted, he claimed, to study and support the genetic diversity of his once-great species. Everyone knew precisely what he meant. They all thought *bully for him.*

What came next? What did Time, the knower and keeper of all memories and tomorrows, have in store for the lot of them? That, my friends and readers, is a secret only Time itself knows. And everyone knows Time yields no spoiler alerts concerning any potential sequels. Silly old Time ....

La fin

GLOSSARY

Agatcha (3)**:** Traditional Deft stew.

Al (1 TFS): The ship's AI from Jon's initial *Ark 1* flight. He kept it with him until his dying day, and then it elected to hang around. Good AI! Full name is Alvin. Those engineers and their lame naming.

Als (3): The Als is the surname for the "married" AIs, Al and *Blessing,* given to them by pissy Jon Ryan.

Aporthio (6): Low-ranking sailor on a supply ship who was badly abused by Garustfulous so he could steal a comm linkable shuttlecraft.

Ark 1 (1 of TFS): The subluminal ship Jon took on his very first flight. He was searching for a new home for humankind. The story is revealed in *The Forever Life* by this author.

Battle of the Periphery (5): The decisive battle where the combined forces of the free planets along the periphery of the Milky Way soundly defeated the Adamant armada. Of course, they were greatly aided by the magical dragons of Nocturnat. Shortened to TBOP.

Blessing (1): Vortex Cragforel gifted to Jon.

Book of the Adamant (6): The massive set of books in which all matters to do with the Adamant civilization are detailed. Last known to number well over ten thousand volumes. An OCDer's dream read.

Brathos (2): Kaljaxian version of hell.

Brindas (1): High master of Deft tradition and psychic ability.

Brood-mate/brood's-mate (2): Male and female members of a Kaljaxian marriage.

Calfada-Joric (3): The Deft master brindas on Rameeka Blue Green. Goes by the name of Cala.

Calran Klug (5): Prime of the Secure Council of the Adamant Empire after Lesset.

Calrf (2 of TFS): A Kaljaxian stew that Jon particularly dislikes.

Canovir(2): Species of dog-like sentients containing the Adamant. Big border collies.

Caryp (2): Clan leader for Sapale's family on Kaljax.

Chop-Chop (6): Galanian representative to the JCFIDAC. In reality, he's an agent for the Adamant.

Command Prerogatives (1): The thin fibers Jon extends from his left four fingers. They are probes that also control a vortex.

Cragforel (1): Friendly Deavoriath Jon met after he first escaped the Adamant in the far future.

Daldedaw (5): Policewoman on Kaljax, then military leader of colonists on Kalvarg.

Darfos (5): Whole Leader and newly appointed to the Secure Council after the purge caused by the defeat of the fleet at the hands of the Plezrite. A friend to Calran Klug.

Davdiad (2): Kaljaxian divine spirit.

Deavoriath (1): Three arms and legs, the most advanced tech in the galaxy, and helpful to Jon.

Deft (1): A shape-shifting species from the planet Locinar.

Dodrue (5): Large aquatic sentients of Kalvarg. They are wiqub, about the size of an orca. Mortal enemies of the Epsallor Kingdom's vidalt.

Dondra-Ulcrif (3): A brindas long ago who gave Evil Jon his "magic" abilities.

Dorcilmas (6): Wedge Leader Dorcilmas threw his loyalties in with Quildrod to grab power after the emperor and the Secure Council were blown up.

Evil Jon Ryan/ EJ (1): Alternate time line version of the original human to android download. Over time, he turned to the darker side of his nature. He studied "magic" under a Deft master.

Excess of Nothing (2): Emperor Bestiormax's personal ship. Huge and opulent.

Five Races (2): *Adamant*, the leaders, *Loserandi*, the priests, *Kilip*, the teachers, and *Descore,* the servants, and *Warrior,* the enlisted fighters.

Fuffefer (3): Group-Single Fuffefer. Commander of the detail that supervised Jon's and Cellardoor's slavery period.

Gabrielod Jal (6): Businessdog and relative of the emperor. He was associated with subversives and had to be "interviewed" by Two Paws. A word to the wise: bring plenty of Motrin to all such interviews.

Galan (6): One of the twelve planets attacked in TBOP. Vaguely humanoid species with four arms and legs.

Garustfulous (2): Wedge Leader Garustfulous is a high-ranking Adamant military leader. Taken hostage by Jon.

Gorgolinians (4): Fish tank sentients of Sotovir.

Guvrof (5): Lesset's right-hand dog. One of his few trusted confidants.

Hantorian System (5): Location of the planet

Kantawir. The location where Jon confronted EJ for the final time.

Harhoff (3): Adamant Group Captain aboard *Rush to Glory*. He became a key figure in Jon's quest to rescue the Deft teens.

High Council (5): The governing body of the Plezrite.

Himanai (5): Variant Deft visant. The first to meet with Jon and Sapale on Nocturnat.

Hirn (1): A Kaljaxian dialect.

Hollon (3): The complete joining of two Deft shapeshifters. More than marriage.

Imperial Lord Emperor Bestiormax-Jacktus-Swillyforth-Anp (2): Current Adamant emperor.

JCFIDAC (6): See Joint Council for Interplanetary Defense and Cooperation.

Jangir (5): The name assumed by Garustfulous when he went undercover as Harhoff's Descore.

Jonnaha (4): Prime minister of a main country on Vorpace. Agreed to try and form a united defense against the Adamant onslaught heading to their region of the Milky Way.

Joint Council for Interplanetary Defense and Cooperation (6): Group of allied free worlds fighting the Adamant.

Kantawir (5): Planet where Jon and EJ met for their final confrontation.

Kalvarg (5): The planet Jon took the orphan Kaljaxian population to as the Adamant were destroying their home world. An island solar system long ago ejected from the Milky Way Galaxy.

Langir (5): First planet Jon went to trying to establish a cohesive rebellion against the Adamant. Populated by clever industrious robots and flaky humanoids.

Larocnaurn (6): Female Deavoriath scientist whom Toño worked with in the distant past.

Lesset (5): High Wedge and Prime, or head, of the Secure Council early in the reign of the new emperor Palawent. Vicious, cruel, and thoroughly Adamant.

Locaur Fideus-Tal (6): Urniquat representative to the free planet defense coalition.

Loserandi (2): See *Five Classes of Canovir*.

Locinar (1): Home planet of the Deft in the Milky Way Galaxy.

Master of Death (6): New name for *Excess of Nothing* given by the latest emperor.

Membrane (1): Space-time congruity manipulator. A super force field.

Mesdorre (5): Second senior clan leader transplanted from Kaljax to Kalvarg.

Midriack (1): Adamant's personal guards. Very deadly, no sense of humor. Avoid them!

Mowar (5): Honorific title among the Deft.

Musto (3): Strong Adamant booze.

Naldoser (5): The local name of the sneaky vidalt of Kalvarg.

Nocturnat (5): Home world of the variant Deft. Once concealed. Part of a star system ejected from the Milky Way. They did the ejecting with their magic.

Nufe (3 GOF & TFS): A magical liquor made by the Deavoriath.

Oowaoa (1 TFS): Home world of the Deavoriath.

Opalf (2): Honorific title in Kaljaxian society, reserved for the elderly.

Palawent (5): New emperor after Bestiormax.

Peg's Bar Nobody (4): First reference in *The Forever Quest*. A true dive bar Jon loved. A total dump. Peg was one tough cookie.

PEMTU (1): Personal exotic matter transportation unit. A super way to enter here and end up anywhere instantly.

Plezrite (5): The species name of the Deft variants on Nocturnat.

Quantum Decoupler (1): A most excellent weapon that pulls the quarks apart in a proton. The energy released is amazing.

Quildrod (6): Whole Quildrod self-elevated to interim emperor after Jon killed the last real one.

Rameeka Blue Green (3): The planet where Jon and the Deft teens met Cala.

Risrav (3): The anti-rune of Varsir. The power of Varsir was negated in the sphere of this rune, as were some other types of magic.

Rush to Glory(3): Ship Jon left Ungalaym on.

Sapale (1) [Also See Entry Below]: Jon's Kaljaxian wife from his original flight to find humankind a new home. At first, just her brain was copied, and then eventually, she was downloaded to an android host. Traveled with the corrupted Jon Ryan from an alternate time line.

Sapale (4): Young female named after her relative Sapale. Rescued from hiding place in pantry.

Secure Council (3): Twelve-member group of military elite who actually run the Adamant empire.

Shielan (4): Female security guard to and sister of prime minister on Vorpace, Jonnaha. Brief romantic interest of Jon's.

Sotovir (4): The second planet Jon convinced to ally against the oncoming Adamant storm. The sentients looked like walking fish tanks, but please don't hold that against fish tanks. It's not their fault.

Stingray (1): Name Jon used for the vortex *Blessing*.

Talrid (2): A major city on Kaljax. Sapale's hometown and that of her clan.

TBOP (6): See Battle of the Periphery.

Toño DeJesus (1): The creator of the android Jon. Became his lifelong friend.

Torchcleft (2): A species of small dragon. Copied by the Deft teens to hunt.

Triumph of Might (1): The massive spaceship Mercutcio ruled. Jon first met the Adamant there.

Two Paws (6): His actual name and rank is Whole Zarpacious. Prime of the Secure Council ten years after TBOP. Cunning and ruthless, which is to say an Adamant commander.

Urniquats (6): Hermaphroditic species allied with the free planets against the Adamant. Very odd creatures. Brains in their chests, four eyes on long stalks where their heads should've been. A mouth for breathing and speech under each of their two armpits.

Urpto (5): The Assistant Subtender for the region of the Kingdom of Epsallor where Jon landed on Kalvarg.

Varsir (3): The name of the magical rune Evil Jon uses to do his "magic."

Var-tey (3): Highest of warrior rankings. The bravest among the Deft. Demigods.

Vidalt (5): Large aquatic sentients of Kalvarg. Enemies to the larger Dodrue.

Visant (5): The proper name for a pair of Deft joined in hollon.

Vorpace (5): The third planet Jon tried to bring into an alliance against the Adamant. Populated by human descendants who'd heard of the great Jon Ryan.

Vortex Manipulator (1): The intelligence inside the vortex. Not actually an AI, but similar.

Wiqub (5): Species name of the larger species on Kalvarg.

Yisbid (5): Grand Visionary for the decade on Nocturnat. She was a leader of the Plezrite variants of the Deft.

Zar-not (1): A melding of a Deft's mind with that of a copied animal.

Zarpacious (6): See Two Paws.

WE INTERRUPT THIS ENDING BY BRINGING YOU A WORD FROM YOUR AUTHOR

Who Doesn't Relish That?

Thank you for continuing your journey through the Ryanverse! Along with this series, please check out *The Forever Series*. Beginning with The Forever Life, Book 1, learn Jon's backstory and share his many incredible adventures.

The next series in the Ryanverse is *Rise of the Ancient Gods*. It begins with *Return of the Ancient Gods*. Warning: Ancient Gods are bad. Avoid ***all*** contact (except reading about them, of course). 'Nuf said.

Along with joining by reading, hop aboard the bandwagon. There's plenty of room. Follow me at Craig Robertson's Author's Page on Facebook. Partake of the conversation and fun. Best of all, sign up for my Mailing List by emailing me: contact@craigarobertson.com. That way you can keep abreast of news and new releases. You'll be so glad you did.

A final favor. Please post a review for this book, especially on Amazon. They are more precious to us authors than gold.

Craig